THE GRANDMOTHER TREES

A Story of the Salzburger Exile
and
Emigration to Georgia

By

Rose Shearouse Thomason

Foreword by George Fenwick Jones

Copyright © 2002 by Rose Shearouse Thomason

ISBN 0-7414-1017-6

Published by:

PUBLISHING.COM

519 West Lancaster Avenue
Haverford, PA 19041-1413
Info@buybooksontheweb.com
www.buybooksontheweb.com
Toll-free (877) BUY BOOK
Local Phone (610) 520-2500
Fax (610) 519-0261

Printed in the United States of America

Printed on Recycled Paper

Published February, 2002

Dedication

For Herbert Samuel Shearouse

and his descendants

This life therefore is not righteousness,
but growth in righteousness.
Not health, but healing.
Not being, but becoming.
Not rest, but exercise.
We are not yet what we shall be,
but we are growing toward it.
The process is not finished,
but is going on.
This is not the end,
but it is the road.

Martin Luther

Then Samuel took a stone and set it up between
Mizpah and Jeshanah, and called its name
Ebenezer, for he said, "Hitherto the Lord has
helped us."

I Samuel 7:12

Foreword

By George Fenwick Jones

This narrative begins on the *Purysburg*, a little vessel bringing Protestant exiles from Salzburg to the Colony of Georgia in the year 1734. The story is interrupted numerous times by flashbacks depicting Archbishop Firmian's expulsion two years earlier. He had not realized that 20,000 of his valuable subjects would prefer to give up their ancestral Alpine homes rather than their Lutheran faith, which they had practiced for centuries.

The author tells the sad stories of those peasant and miner families who were expelled and found their way to the Main and Rhine, then to Rotterdam and Dover, and finally to the new colony of Georgia. There, after suffering disease and many deaths in an ill chosen spot, they removed to the Red Bluff and found a lasting sanctuary.

Thus, this story is an epic, one relating the hardships of a brave people who finally found a city. But the reader will hardly notice this, being gripped by the suspenseful action. Except for several fictional characters, the tale is true and concurs with historical documents. Despite the large cast, the author has made her characters very much alive, and their actions and words are most convincing. The tale will be enjoyed by all, not just by the Georgia Salzburgers' many descendants.

Preface

A soft summer breeze can barely sustain the tonal clamor of bells from forty Catholic Church towers, banging from mountain to mountain, drowning out the remembered cries of tortured Protestants once heard in the Hohensalzburg, the fortress on Monks Mountain, high above the city of Salzburg, Austria. The almost visible sound waves herald the approach of Pope John Paul II, as his caravan winds through the narrow streets of the ancient city, on its way to the Capuchin Abbey, perched on the mountain opposite the fortress.

It is June 1988, and this is an historic visit, for the Pope will speak, for the first time since all Protestants were exiled from Salzburg in 1731, in a Protestant church now attended by the spiritual descendants of the exiles. He will fall short of apologizing for the actions of Archbishop Leopold Anton Eleutherius von Firmian, Prince of the Salzburg Province, two hundred and fifty-seven years ago, but a step will be made to heal the lingering wounds of an old religious persecution.

Suddenly, the bells stop, and guns are fired from the fortress, reminiscent of the brute power wielded by Prince Archbishop Firmian over the peasants of the Salzburg Province in 1731. Following the Treaty of Westphalia in 1648, ending the Thirty Years' War, each Prince in the Holy Roman Empire was empowered to determine the religion of his subjects but was required to give dissenters three years to relocate. *Cuius regio, euis religio.*

Firmian forced the practice of the Roman Catholic faith on his subjects, though most of the Alpine peasants, descendants of ancient Celtic tribes, Roman conquerors, and Germanic tribes, had been Protestants for over a hundred years. They resisted his stern orders. Thus, in the name of the same Christian God, opposing winds of religious fervor swept through the valleys of the Salzach and Salaach rivers, creating a cyclonic upheaval that blew twenty-one thousand people into exile, most with only eight days notice at the start of winter.

They dispersed north across Europe, where comfortable Protestants opened their hearts and homes to them. Their forced trek as martyrs of the faith inspired a religious revival. King Wilhelm welcomed nineteen thousand into Prussia.

This storm of fanatic Catholicism swept one small group of equally pious Lutherans to the shores of Georgia in the New World. They sought land and the freedom to worship God without persecution, placing their hopes in an offer from England, where the German Protestant King, George II, felt compassion for their plight. The church people of England, through their contributions to the Society for Promoting Christian Knowledge, made it possible for several groups of Salzburgers, as they became known, to become settlers in the new Colony of Georgia in North America.

This new colony had been conceived as a benevolent enterprise to give fresh opportunities to hard-working, devout, but poor Londoners. A young Member of Parliament and trustee of the Colony of Georgia, James Oglethorpe, had already sailed with the first boatload of English settlers, whom he had selected from many applicants.

In the fall of 1733, the first group of Salzburg Protestants formed a transport at St. Anne's Church in Augsburg, under the leadership of Pastor Samuel Urlsperger. In January of 1734, they boarded the *Purysburg* in Dover, England. The wind filled the sails and carried them across the ocean, where they joined other religious exiles, people seeking fortunes and adventure, and those trapped in servitude, to build a new reality in a wilderness inhabited by Yamacraw and Uchee Indians.

The 260th anniversary of their landing in Savannah was remembered by a monument given in 1994 to the city of Savannah by the city of Salzburg and placed in Yamacraw Square. This is the story of that first transport of Salzburgers to Georgia.

Acknowledgments

My primary source for information about the Salzburgers in Georgia has been the eighteen volumes of *Detailed Reports on the Salzburger Emigrants Who Settled in America*, written by Martin Boltzius, edited by Samuel Urlsperger, and translated by Dr. George Fenwick Jones. I also relied heavily on Dr. Jones' translation of *Henry Newman's Salzburger Letterbooks* and his *The Salzburger Saga: Religious Exiles and Other Germans Along the Savannah*. He kindly read my original manuscript and made valuable suggestions, attesting, as well, to its historical accuracy.

I am indebted to Dr. Gerhard Florey at the University of Salzburg for his many writings on the expulsion of the Salzburgers, but particularly for *Geschichte der Salzburger Protestanten und ihrer Emigration*.

Die Salzburger Emigration in Bildern, Angelika Marsch's book of pictures of the emigration, has been useful beyond measure in providing a visual image of the Salzburgers.

I owe great appreciation to Dr. George Crossman, who translated many chapters, articles, letters, and the sermons of Hans Mosegger. He also carefully proofread my original manuscript and offered helpful suggestions.

Members of the Georgia Salzburger Society have offered encouragement and research assistance, particularly the late Amy LeBey, the late Sid Waldhour, Monk Joudon, and Steve Shearouse. Ms. LeBey and Mr. Waldhour spent hours showing me the church and museum at New Ebenezer. Monk Joudon walked me over his land, which is likely the site of the first Ebenezer settlement, and Steve Shearouse spent a lovely spring afternoon taking me on a boat ride down Ebenezer Creek.

The help of the late Dr. Jürgen Schweighofer in Wagrain, Austria, was invaluable. He took me to the farm his ancestors lost in the expulsion, and to the farm of Hans Mosegger, the famous Protestant preacher. He also directed me to Schwarzach, where the salt oath was made, and to the Entrische Kirke in Gastein, the cave where Protestants worshipped secretly for two hundred years.

I am grateful to Rosa and Tony Burgsteiner from Salzburg, who guided me to the Saalfelden area of Austria, where we visited the probable farms of Barbara Rohrmoser and Johann Mosshamer.

I owe a debt of thanks to my writing group in Alexandria, Virginia--Debbie Griffin, Jacquelin McDonald, Karen Master, and Julie Heidemenas--who patiently listened to this book, chapter by chapter, for several years. I incorporated many of their suggestions and might never have completed the book without their encouragement.

I am grateful to my father, the late Dr. H. Samuel Shearouse, who inspired me to write about the Salzburgers. He told me the tales of our Salzburger ancestors from my birth. He also shared his library of resources and provided financial assistance.

I owe a huge debt of gratitude to my husband Robert, who traveled with me tracing the journey of the exiled Salzburgers, assisted in the research, corrected the manuscript, and sustained me during the writing with patient care and love.

Most importantly, I am grateful for the brave, stalwart Salzburgers and their two pastors, who risked their lives in order to be faithful to their God.

Rose Shearouse Thomason

Addendum

Rose died on April 8, 2001, before this book could be published. She completed the manuscript in the summer of 1995 and was seeking a commercial publisher. After retiring from her primary career as a reading resource teacher in the public schools of Alexandria, Virginia, in June 1997, we moved to Palm Coast, Florida, where she devoted herself to writing, forming another writing group. With them, and with an ongoing class on writing memoirs, taught by Linda Short, she shared her work, as was her style, revising and re-creating in response to their critique.

Like most authors, she was always working on revisions of whatever she had not published, including this manuscript. When she died, my first task was to identify the latest version of her work. I would never have accomplished this without the assistance of Lorraine Ruhl, one of the members of her Palm Coast writing group. Lorraine has been my co-editor as we have sought to discover Rose's latest version and to perfect the final manuscript. It has been a joyful labor of love for us both. I have rediscovered the richness of the Salzburger story, and Lorraine has experienced much of it for the first time.

To Lorraine and the other Palm Coast writing group members, Linda Short and Barbara Lynch, my thanks for your support of Rose in her writing and your helpful suggestions to her as she sought to make her book better.

Thanks are also offered to Alma Nemrava, friend and neighbor, who read the manuscript and offered helpful suggestions.

Special thanks are offered to Dr. George Fenwick Jones--skillful translator, eminent historian, and faithful chronicler of the Salzburger story, who kindly wrote the Foreword.

Thank you, too, to Joe Sermarini, neighbor and friend, who designed the cover and title page, and helped to solve whatever computer problems I encountered in preparing the publication. And thank you to Ann Williams, dear friend, who with her husband Elwyn took dozens of pictures of "grandmother trees," one of which graces the cover.

Mostly, though, I am grateful for Rose, my soul mate, partner, and friend for forty-two years, for entrusting me with this expression of her innermost being.

Robert T. Thomason

Table of Contents

Part II: Ebenezer 304

Illustrations

- **Cover**: Joe Sermarini created the design, and Ann Williams made the photograph of the "grandmother trees."
- **Title Page**: Joe Sermarini created the drawing.
- **Dedication**: The photograph of H. Sam Shearouse in front of the Salzburger monument in Savannah was made in 1994 by Robert Thomason.
- **Page 2**: The painting of *Die Vertreibung* (The Expulsion) was done by Professor Friedrich Martersteig in about 1867, and hangs in Evangelische Christuskirke, the Protestant Church in Salzburg.
- **Page 304**: Robert Thomason made the photograph of Ebenezer Creek.
- **Page 491**: Robert Thomason made the photograph of Rose Shearouse Thomason.

Prologue

New Ebenezer, Georgia, 1741

Spanish moss gracing the whispering live oak trees surrounding the tiny, wooden church resembled the hair of gray-headed grandmothers, flung forward over their faces to dry, Gertrude thought. She paused briefly, clarifying her heart in the imagined presence of the elders. Secretly, she believed the old, twisted trees housed the spirits of the many Salzburgers who had died in this Georgia wilderness. She searched the sprawling branches for a glimpse of her mother floating in the early morning breeze, and for Mamma Anna's newly released soul.

Her sister Catherine's footsteps crunching fallen leaves aroused her, and she grabbed her apron to polish again the silver chalice coated with the mist that rose each night from the Savannah River. Catherine arrived with a neatly ironed, embroidered linen altar cloth. Behind her, Maria, their half-sister, emerged from the shrouded air holding a loaf of freshly baked communion bread and a decanter of muscadine wine.

Solemnly, the three young women entered the church and arranged the simple wooden table with the elements of their Lutheran faith.

When the task was finished, they stood back to observe the table, their arms around each other, tears silently sliding down their cheeks, while they repeated ritually, "Hitherto hath Thou brought us thus far." The words from the First Book of Samuel were like a signpost, encompassing the journey they had traveled and pointing towards the future.

PART I

THE EXPULSION

1

On Board the *Purysburg*, 1734

Golden hair flashing like lightning behind Gertrude mimicked the approaching storm her arms were extended to embrace. The pious Pastor Boltzius stared in rare fascination, forgetting momentarily his orders to warn the Salzburgers to get below. The ship tossed skittishly, causing Barbara to hold both her daughters around their waists. Gertrude, her fifteen-year-old, leaned back in ecstasy, exclaiming, "Look at that glorious light shining around the edges of the dark clouds."

Her older daughter, Catherine, gripped the rail tightly, fear of the rolling sea outlined in her stiff neck. "Those are storm clouds, you silly goose," she said tensely.

Maria, Barbara's stepdaughter, joined the women. "Pastor Boltzius says that Captain Fry has ordered everyone below. A tempest is forming to the southwest." As she made this announcement, darkness covered the light as the clouds obliterated the last rays of sunlight.

"I'm not going down into that stinking hold," announced Mamma Anna from her perch on top of a storage barrel. "I'd rather take my chances with God's clean rain than die from the smell of piss and puke." The ship began rolling with the swells, and Mamma Anna toppled from the barrel, grabbing the railing with both hands. The barrel banged into a group of Englishmen, causing them to fall into a screaming jumble of arms and legs.

Pastor Gronau dashed over to the women with a coil of rope in his hands. "If you're staying on deck, tie yourself to the mast to keep from being washed overboard," he shouted over the wind. Catherine eagerly joined the young pastor, followed by Gertrude and Maria. Barbara reluctantly followed the girls, along with other passengers who chose to ride out the storm lashed on deck. Mamma Anna decided to wait before tying herself down with that crowd of Salzburgers. She stood alone, gazing at the dark sky reflected in the black sea while sailors hurriedly closed the hatches and struggled to lower the sails.

Without warning, a fragment of ripped mainsail wrapped around Mamma Anna as her white-knuckled fingers clung to the railing, blinding her to the suddenly ferocious storm. Leaning forward, she braced her ample belly against the bar and frantically pulled at the suffocating, wet canvas. The *Purysburg* suddenly tilted the other way and sent her sprawling on her back across the slippery deck like a sausage in a greased frying pan.

She screamed as she caromed off a mast, unable to grab hold as the ship swooped sideways down a massive, black wave, almost capsizing. She could not stop her slide toward the railing, which had been crushed by careening barrels. She reached out desperately, trying not to be swept overboard. Cold, swirling water filled her mouth and nose as the deck dipped into the sea. Flailing, she felt something snatch her arm, and in her panic she fought to free it. Howling air hit her face as the ship rose high into the air.

"I've gotcha. Hold on to me."

Her conscious mind began to reemerge as she reached toward the barely audible voice and realized someone was holding her arm, halting her plunge into the watery caldron. She wrapped her arms around the neck of her rescuer, climbed astride his lap with her face smashed into his, and coughed up seawater mixed with stomach bile.

"Hey! You're strangling me, woman," he yelled in her left ear over the roar of the storm. "Grab me around the waist."

She tried to make her arms move, but they no longer seemed to be controlled by her mind.

The little sailing vessel righted itself momentarily, which calmed her enough to be able to shift her arms to his waist. They clung together as if in a lover's embrace.

"Oh, God, I thought my time was up," she sobbed into his right ear.

"It ain't over yet. This is a bad'un. You should've lashed yourself to something if you was going to be on deck during this bluster."

The boat tossed wildly, and Mamma Anna could not anticipate which direction the deck would slant next. Her hand felt the rope that held the man to the mast, and she hung on.

Mamma Anna spit out the water that had filled up her mouth when she'd opened it. "Are you a sailor?"

"Ja."

As the convulsive ocean pushed the front of the ship up into the air, more barrels tore loose and rolled toward them, causing a thunderous vibration. As the aft reared, the rolling barrels reversed their direction, as if they had changed their minds. Ribbons of screams were heard when the barrels slammed into the Salzburgers tied to the foremast. Luckily for Mamma Anna and her sailor, the next slant slid the splintered barrel pieces over the side through the hole she had just vacated. The deck leveled out again for a few minutes, giving a sense of normalcy to the frightened passengers.

"Hold on to me!" the sailor shouted over the howling wind, and he slid them both around the mast toward a wooden compartment built on the deck. The door of the compartment was flapping rapidly, and some of the contents of the small storage area had already skidded across the deck. Coils of rope were stacked two feet deep. With one hand he pushed some of the rope out and it slid away.

"Get in here," he yelled into the ear of the woman who had a death grip around his waist.

Mamma Anna could not see where he meant and was in such a state of terror that she was unable to respond. The sailor scuttled along, carrying her on his lap as he backed into the opening.

After considerable scrambling and bumping against the low top, they managed to squeeze themselves into the small amount of space. The storage box leaked freely, but they were somewhat insulated from the horizontal pounding of the wind and rain and the thirty-foot waves that were washing over the deck. The wind slammed the door shut, and the swollen wood stuck, sealing them in and lowering the volume of the roar.

"Are you all right?" the sailor asked.

"I think so," Mamma Anna gasped.

The rolling ship rocked the two in every direction, knocking them against the sides and top of the storage bin. After a considerable time of sloshing about like pickles loosely packed in a jar, Mamma Anna became aware that she was mashed up against a man's body, and she had no idea who he was.

"Who are you?" she asked.

"My English mates call me Deutsch. It ain't my real name, but if they knew that, I'd be in the brig or worse. There's all kinds of us sailing this ship. And who be you?"

"Anna Burgsteiner from Saalfelden. Just call me Mamma Anna. I'm an exiled Salzburger, bound for Georgia."

"One of the saints, huh?" he chuckled, giving her soft body a squeeze, for she was still in his lap, facing him in the darkness.

"Well, I doubt Pastor Boltzius would think I qualify for that title, but at least I'm not a papist." Seawater poured into the cracks between the boards, and they both gasped.

"How long do these storms last?"

"Depends on what kind they are. This one feels strong as a hurricane, but them's usually in summer, not February. You can't never tell for sure."

"You've made this crossing before?"

"Several times and lived to tell the tale."

The ship continued to roll like a toy in the vast Atlantic. The darkness was so complete that not even an outline was distinguishable. Mamma Anna became aware of the difference between the wetness of the rain and the salty water of the sea as both streamed over her water-sogged, heavy woolen clothes. She shivered as the ship calmed itself enough for her to begin to feel again. Her freezing back made her aware of the warmth her breasts were absorbing from the man who held her. She couldn't see him but felt his long, hard arms and a stiff beard scratching against her face.

"I haven't been wet this many ways since I was a baby in my mother's womb," Mamma Anna said. "I'm a midwife, you see, and have spent a lot of my life bringing babies into this world. In fact, I birthed a good many of the people on this boat. God willing and with your rescuing hand, I may live to welcome a few more. You ever see a baby born?"

"No. Seen a good many leave this world, but never saw one enter."

"Well, I'll tell you," she said, talking rather frantically in order to keep in touch with being alive in this unnatural tossing. She felt like she was riding a bucking horse. "I helped pull Barbara Rohrmoser out of the womb feet first, and then I've seen her have six babies of her own. She brought two of them out of Salzburg with her--the two oldest girls, Catherine and Gertrude, and her stepdaughter, Maria; but she had to leave the others behind with her husband Peter, who wouldn't accept the Protestant faith, at least not enough to give up his farm."

Their clasped bodies rolled to the right and then jerked back to the left. Mamma Anna and Deutsch tried to brace themselves, but their awkward position made that impossible, and their bodies just absorbed the blows.

"Unh," they both groaned. As Deutsch refastened his hold, Mamma Anna felt faint and put her head down on the sailor's shoulder.

"You're not passing out on me, are you? Just hold on. We'll make it." He tried to think of a way to keep her conscious, knowing her limp weight on him would be even worse. He encouraged her to keep talking. That way, at least, he'd know if she fainted.

"You were talking about a Barbara. Which one is Barbara? Did you say Rohrmoser?"

"Well, her first husband was a Kroehr and the father of Gertrude, Catherine, and Maria. But her second husband, the one she left behind with the younger children, was a

Rohrmoser and a Catholic. She's the one with the star-shaped birthmark on her forehead. First thing I noticed when she was born. Turned out right pretty, actually."

"I think I've seen her telling Bible stories to the children. She don't seem like the type to up and leave her husband and little ones that way. Why on earth would she do a thing like that?"

"Well, she's powerful religious. Her father was kind of the leader of the Protestants in our Saalach River Valley where Saalfelden is the largest town. Then, when he died, her brother Hans took his place and...well, it's a long story. You probably don't want to hear the babbling of an old woman who's talking just to know she's still alive."

"Got nothing else to do, and it helps keep my mind off the storm. It's going to be a long night, and we're stuck here together. I've been wondering about why you folks from Salzburg would leave the Alps to settle in the Georgia wilderness. But let's see if we can shift a bit. My legs have got plumb numb, although you've done a good job of keeping me warm."

"Humph. Well, I ought to take offense at that, but I'm long past bashful, and I guess I owe you something since you just saved my life." Very carefully, Mamma Anna shifted her weight to one side and wiggled her leg around. After much twisting and turning, they were nestled together like two spoons. There wasn't room to sit up, and they could not stretch out their legs.

"That's better. Now tell me more about Barbara and her family."

"Well, I especially remember that July day in 1731 when Peter Rohrmoser came riding up to my cottage, screaming for me to hurry. You see, Barbara was expecting a baby, and I knew that she had babies fast. She didn't mess around. She's always been one to do what needed to be done and get it over with. Had three sons myself and saw them all die along with their father, one after the other, the same cruel winter. It like to broke my heart that I couldn't save even one of them. That left me to fend for myself, and I did it by midwifing.

"Anyway, I jumped up behind Peter Rohrmoser on that horse of his with my birthing basket, holding on to him for dear life. He made that poor horse gallop all the way to their farm. You're the first man I've held on to since that day."

2

Saalfelden, July 1731

Barbara gazed at the Leogangertal Mountains through the red geraniums growing in the box on the balcony outside the bedroom window of the hundred-year-old brown log and white mortar house she had lived in since marrying Peter. The chalky white peaks cut a jagged line across the blue sky.

"I will lift up mine eyes unto the hills from whence cometh my help. My help cometh from the Lord, who made heaven and earth."

Her father's Lutheran Bible was open on the bed beside her, but she did not need to read those words, having said them every day, all her life, it seemed. She laid her head back on the pillow as another labor pain grabbed her. It was strange being in bed in the middle of the morning.

"Another one?" asked Maria. Maria was Barbara's twenty-six-year-old stepdaughter, who was more like a friend or sister than a daughter.

"Uh, huh," Barbara groaned. She relaxed as the pains eased. "You should be having this baby instead of me. I'm getting too old at thirty-five to be having more children to raise."

"Do you think Hans and I will ever be able to marry?" Maria asked wistfully. She had been betrothed to Barbara's younger brother Hans for five years.

"I don't know, Maria. I wish this farm was larger and there was room for you and Hans to raise a family, but you know how crowded we already are, and then this new baby. This farm is barely large enough to support us. If we didn't have to give half of the harvest to the Capuchins, it would help."

"I know your husband is doing all he can. I, unfortunately, fell in love with a poor, landless peasant, but the handsomest peasant in the whole valley."

"Hans wouldn't have been without a farm if the Capuchins

hadn't stolen my father's land, but Father always said it was God's will that he preach the Lutheran gospel, and whatever happened to him was God's will, also."

"That's what Hans says, too."

"You've had other offers. Perhaps you should have married one of them, although it breaks my heart to think about it."

"No. As long as Hans loves me, how could I think about marrying someone else? I do hate the life of a servant in someone else's home, however. Sometimes I get so frightened for Hans, Barbara. He could be arrested or killed for some of the things he's doing. He takes such chances."

"You must trust in God, Maria.

"Ooh!" Barbara clinched her fists around the coverlet while she waited out another contraction. "They're coming regularly now," she said breathlessly. "I hope Peter gets back with Mamma Anna soon. Otherwise, you may have to help me."

"Oh, he'll be coming along. Don't worry. I can just see them now, with Mamma Anna bobbing along on the back of that horse, her arms around Peter. He'll hate for that smelly old woman to be hugging him so."

Barbara and Maria both laughed at the thought of the spectacle. Mamma Anna was the best midwife around, but she was fat, dressed in old clothes, and carried a big basket filled with her healing things. She always brought along an empty sack to carry back whatever payment people gave her. They seldom gave her clothes that were not old. Barbara had always admired her independence, living on her own as she did.

"Shame on you, Maria. Don't make fun of Mamma Anna. Besides, it hurts when I laugh."

Barbara was not overly worried, but she had lost one baby at birth, and she certainly did not want to go through that again. It was the one after Gertrude, who was twelve now, so it must have been eleven years ago. Mamma Anna had called it her "come see" baby. Those are the babies that come to see how they like it, and then decide to go back to Heaven where they came from, she had said.

Catherine, Barbara's eighteen-year-old daughter, opened the door. "I've got the water boiling. How's everything going?"

"I'm doing fine. Keep a close watch on little Hans. He still gets upset when he can't see me and know I'm all right. Send him around to the window, and I'll wave to him. Also, tell Gertrude to check on that sow. She mustn't get into the front garden. Do you need Maria to help with the strudel?"

"No. I know how to do it," Catherine replied, withdrawing to the kitchen.

Barbara remarked, "Catherine's turned into an accomplished girl, hasn't she? She can spin and weave better than I can, and her embroidery is beautiful. She'd make some man a good wife, but none of the young men can afford one, and most of the old men have wives."

Barbara paused as another wave of pain swept over her. When it eased, she continued. "If the church didn't demand so much in taxes and indulgences from everyone, men might be able to put aside enough to buy a piece of land."

"That's, of course, if the church would sell it," Maria added. "The Capuchins own most of the land around here. Why should they sell their land when they've got us to work it for them, and give them most of the harvest?"

"Yes, I guess you're right. Oh, quick, come help me up here. My water broke."

Maria leaned over and eased Barbara off the bed and onto the wooden chair with a hole in the seat and a chamber pot underneath.

"I told Catherine to bring little Hans around to the window. It'll scare the poor child to death if he hears me groaning. Is he out there?"

Maria walked to the window. "No, he's with Gertrude, out weeding the garden. Relax and groan all you want to." She began mopping up the wet bed with old cloths.

Barbara remembered, when Catherine was born, how embarrassed she had been to let someone else see her in such personal ways. She was less worried about that sort of thing now. Being a mother taught you not to fret about foolish pride.

Catherine opened the door with hands covered with flour. "Are you all right? I heard you groaning."

"Yes, Catherine, go on back and get that strudel made. I expect we'll have several visitors when they see Peter and Mamma Anna riding by." She spoke more sharply than she really intended and instantly regretted it.

"Holler when you see them coming so I can get back in the bed and look presentable." For some reason, Barbara was more comfortable with Maria than with her own girls when experiencing the indignities of childbirth. She sensed that Catherine resented being relegated to the kitchen. Catherine was often hard to understand. She was dutiful but easily offended.

Catherine had no sooner closed the door than she called, "They're here, Mother, and someone is with them. It looks like Aunt Eva. How could she know the baby was coming today?"

"Eva always knows when women go into labor. Sometimes she gets confused on which woman it is, but she always knows. You ask her how she knows. I'd be interested in what she says."

Barbara got up and eased herself back into the bed. She pushed her father's Lutheran Bible up under the pillow so that Peter would not see it. Being a Catholic, he did not approve of the German Bible, but she could not bear to part with it. Usually, she kept it hidden in a space above the ceiling in the front room. She needed it today, though, while this baby was being born. The Bible really belonged to her brother Hans, who could not keep it because the priests suspected him of organizing Protestant meetings, and he was subject to regular searches. No one would think to look in Peter Rohrmoser's house, though, for he was a good Catholic.

Hans had become the leader of the Protestants in the Saalfelden area after their father's death. He relied on her to keep the Bible and take it to their secret meetings in her basket. Now, with a new baby, she could hide it in the cradle.

The door to the bedroom suddenly opened and was filled with Mamma Anna and Peter, both trying to get through at the same time. Barbara stifled her laughter at seeing the disgust on Peter's tanned face when he got stuck with Mamma Anna in the doorway. Finally, he remembered his manners and backed out to let her enter first. Then, the room filled with people, as her sister Eva, Catherine, with flour all over her face, five-year-old Hans, and twelve-year-old Gertrude all squeezed into the small room. It was as if no one wanted to be left out of the excitement.

Mamma Anna began bustling about in a calm but purposeful way. "How often are your pains? Has your water broken?"

Barbara nodded her head at the last question, but could not speak as pain grabbed her body again. Peter walked over to the bed and took her hand, and she gripped with bone-crushing intensity. His face turned pale when he saw her grimace with the pain. He had lost one wife in childbirth. He remembered that terrible loss and felt again the pangs of guilt for inflicting this on his present wife.

"Catherine, is there water ready?" Mamma Anna asked.

"Yes, should I get it?"

"Not yet. It'll probably be some time yet."

When the pain subsided, Barbara looked around the room at the gaping faces. "Eva, how did you know to come today?"

"Oh, you know me. I just know these things. Don't ask me how."

"Well, do you know if this one will be a boy or a girl?"

Eva laughed. "No, I don't have that kind of insight. I just feel the twinge of labor pains."

"I'm glad you're here. Have you seen Hans?"

"No, I expect he'll show up today sometime. Half of Saalfelden saw us parading out here with Mamma Anna. The other half know your baby's coming by now."

Everyone laughed at the way news traveled through the valley.

Barbara suddenly screamed as a strong contraction took over her body. At that moment, the baby decided it wanted to join the crowd and began pushing its head out. Barbara screamed again, and the baby's shoulders popped out like a cork from a bottle, and the baby landed on the bed to the astonishment of all.

Mamma Anna was the first to recover her senses and reached under the cover for the baby, shouting orders over her shoulder. "Everybody get out of here. Maria, you stay. Catherine, get that boiled water up here."

Maria shoved everyone out of the room, and Barbara lay back on the bed, laughing and crying with pain and embarrassment.

The cord was cut and tied, and the little baby girl let out a loud cry. Barbara took the baby and laid her at her breast, as Mamma Anna kneaded her stomach for the afterbirth to pass. Barbara moaned as Maria proceeded to clean up the mess, then wiped the blood and birth fluids off Barbara and the baby with the water Catherine had brought.

"Well, you certainly made a grand entrance, little one. You didn't want to get left out of this family gathering, did you, Pumpkin?" Maria cooed at the baby as she bathed and wrapped her in a clean blanket, then laid her in the crook of Barbara's arm.

Barbara lightly caressed the tiny head and touched her hand until she clung to her finger.

"It's a good thing you were in the bed, or you'd a dropped that one right on the floor," Mamma Anna chuckled. "You didn't need me much this time, dearie, but I wouldn't have missed this birthing for anything."

"Thank you anyway, Mamma Anna. That was the quickest delivery I've ever had, or ever want to have."

Barbara looked down at the red-faced infant with wisps of

wet blond fuzz. "What a marvel," she said. "I already love this baby so much it doesn't seem possible, and I'm just seeing her for the first time."

"Peter, you can come in now," Barbara called weakly. He walked in awkwardly, and Barbara motioned the two women out of the room.

"Here's your daughter, Peter. What shall you call her?" They had decided in advance that he would name this child.

"Her name is Barbara, after her mother," he said, rather formally, and leaned over and kissed Barbara on the birthmark on her forehead. "I think she's going to look like you with that round face and blond hair. What color are her eyes?" At that moment, the baby opened her lapis-blue eyes and gazed up at her father. He smiled at his wife. What passed between them in that look made Barbara feel contented and happy. She closed her eyes and fell into an exhausted sleep.

As Barbara and the baby slept, Mamma Anna watched over them, while the other women prepared food. Relatives and neighbors began visiting as news of the new baby spread. There was much laughter as Peter told and retold how the baby had been born in the midst of a room full of people.

By the time supper was laid out on the table in the kitchen, there were fifteen people in the house or standing around outside. As Peter passed around homemade beer to the men, making the party merrier, he saw Maria staring down the road.

"Who do you keep looking for, Maria?" Peter asked, winking at the others.

Maria blushed, but she was not intimidated by her stepfather's rough humor. Turning with a saucy flaunt, she smiled over her shoulder, flashing the dimples in her cheeks, walked out the door, and climbed up on a large stone outcropping in the front yard. She shaded her eyes in an exaggerated way and gazed off into the distance.

The men all laughed at her spirit. She riveted their attention, for she was uncommonly beautiful. Her thick, brown hair had partially come loose from its usual braiding, and some long, wavy strands blew in the summer breeze, making a pretty contrast to the white blouse that outlined her full breasts. Her tiny waist was cinched with a black vest that laced up the front. Her red dirndl skirt and green apron came just to the calves of her legs, which were covered with hand-knitted, blue woolen stockings.

The meal was almost over before Hans' jaunty walk was seen coming down the road from Saalfelden. His nearly-white blond hair shone like a light as it reflected the slanting rays of the sun. When he entered the house, his sky blue eyes sought out Maria's as he greeted everyone.

Maria wanted to sing for joy and throw herself into his muscled arms, but instead she went into the kitchen to get another plate. Peter told the birthing story again, and Hans laughed his deep, uninhibited laugh.

Going up to visit Barbara and the baby, he entered the room quietly. He walked over to the cradle and looked at little Barbara, sleeping on her stomach. He smiled as the baby made tiny, sucking noises. Sadness came over his face as his longing for a child of his own overwhelmed him.

"She's beautiful," he said with a smile, but a catch in his voice betrayed emotion, and his eyes glassed with tears.

"And how are you?" he asked softly, as he took Barbara's hand.

"Everything's fine. How are things with you?" she asked. It was more than a polite question, for she knew he was deeply involved in organizing the Protestants to resist Prince Archbishop Firmian's latest dictums.

"Very interesting," he replied with a wink.

"Now tell me. What's happening with the oath-taking plans?" Barbara asked, ignoring the fact that nosy Mamma Anna was pretending to sleep in the chair in the corner of the room.

Hans, more conscious of the need for secrecy, bent over and whispered in her ear, "Next week in Schwarzach in the

Pongau."

"Be careful, Hans."

"Don't worry, big sister. It's safer with more people involved. They can't arrest everyone."

Later, as Maria served Hans supper, she laughed and
joked with whomever she could, realizing that his presence
made her tingle inside as if lightning were running through
her body. She thought she would die from loving him.

Friends and family began scattering, some to go home,
others to help with the evening chores on the farm. Maria
and Catherine washed the dishes and put away the food
while Eva went up to sit with Barbara. After a while, Catherine said, "I'll finish here. You can go now."

Maria gave her a grateful smile and walked outside,
where Hans was leaning against a tree. He smiled conspiratorially.

"Let's go for a walk," he said, without asking.

He took her hand as they walked up the mountain through
the swaying hayfields. When they reached the tree line, they
broke into a run until they were deep into the fir forest. Hans
pulled her to him, somewhat roughly, and hugged her
fiercely. Maria stifled a gasp and clung tightly to him. It
had been so long since they had been alone together. She
lifted her head and held his face in her hands.

Flushed from the desire that was coursing through his
body, he kissed her with a hunger that seemed insatiable.
Maria felt her body responding in powerful surges, making
her feel that she might explode. Wildly, she caressed his
back and chest with her hands. He pulled her down onto the
forest floor, cushioned with pine needles. He lay on top of
her, and, suddenly, she was frightened.

"We can't do this. We're not married." Her mind raced
madly as Hans rubbed her body with his. She could feel his
hardness against her abdomen, and her own body longed for
the natural completion of lovemaking, but her caution won
out.

"No, Hans, no," she gasped.

"Maria, we can't wait forever. We may never be able to marry." He put one hand inside her blouse and caressed her breasts. His other hand rubbed between her legs.

Maria's body suddenly exploded and jerked in an ecstasy she had never known before. She lay back limply, tears running down her face. Then Hans entered her, pushing until pain cut through her.

She looked up at the dark green hemlocks arched over their heads, filtering the late evening sun into golden shafts. Her mind swirled in a million circles as she lay back, feeling the full weight of Hans' body on hers.

Oh, God, what have we done? We've sinned against you, she prayed silently. She only partly regretted that Hans had entered her, and for that feeling of gladness, she felt the edge of guilt. She tried to force the possible consequences of their lovemaking from her mind, savoring the delicious feeling. She loved him, and she knew he loved her. How could love be a sin? Yet, a lifetime of fear of losing her chastity before marriage crowded against the joy of sexual fulfillment.

Hans straightened his clothes and looked at her as she relaced her bodice. He smiled. She was the loveliest woman he had ever seen, and the most desirable. Her disheveled brown hair framed her face with its flawless skin. His eyes followed the line of her neck downward to her breasts, too large to fit comfortably in her blouse, and to her small waist and curved hips.

"Are you all right? Do you forgive me?" he asked.

She looked him firmly in the eyes. "Yes, Hans, I love you, and I forgive you, but does God forgive us?"

"God made me a man and you a woman. Is it a sin to act like a man and a woman? Life is to be lived abundantly, not hidden under a bushel. Jesus came to bring us life, not a half-life." Hans spoke with a defiance that betrayed his frustration with her question.

"But what if...." Maria did not finish her sentence since she saw impatience contort his face. She knew he must feel some guilt, as she did, or he would not have been so defensive. One of the things that she admired about him was his courage and brashness, but it was also the thing that most frightened her. The questions did not evaporate from her mind, however, just because she did not say them aloud. What if I get pregnant? What if you get arrested? What will happen to us? she thought.

"Let's go watch the sunset from the rock."

With their arms around each other, they strolled further up the mountain until they came to the end of the trees, and the light opened up. From their special stone ledge they could see across the valley to the mountains beyond. The sky was turning pink as the sun descended.

"When will I see you again?" Maria asked.

"You know that I've been trying to organize the people of Saalfelden to resist the new requirements of Prince Archbishop Firmian. I've met with men from the Pongau area. We all agree that the only way we can ever have religious freedom and get out from under the intolerable taxes, indulgences, and fines is to stand together."

"You'll be arrested, Hans, if the priests or soldiers find out what you're doing."

"I live with that possibility, Maria, but I refuse to submit to being only a laborer, with no home of my own and no hope for one. The only way things are going to change is for people to resist. The church is certainly not going to give the people land and let them be Protestants," he said, his voice filled with fervor. "And I refuse to bow down to a corrupt religion that robs the poor to feed the greed of the wealthy. That's not what our Lord Jesus Christ died for, but the people must be able to read the Bible in their own language to know that. The priests keep the Scripture secret with their Latin Bible, and then tell the people what they want them to hear. I will not submit to that heresy. I cannot."

They sat in silence as the sky streaked brilliant pinks and reds, constantly shifting combinations of hues, each mixture more beautiful than the last.

"Oh, how I long for the freedom to worship God openly

as a Protestant," he continued. "I've heard about cities like Augsburg in Bavaria, where Protestants and Catholics live and worship together in peace. That's what I want for us in Salzburg. If it can happen in Augsburg, why not here?"

Maria looked at a tiny, blue vein pulsing in his intense face as he stared at the horizon. "I'll pray for you constantly," she said, "and may God watch over you. I'm not sure I could bear it if something happened to you. Particularly not now that...."

"Pray especially for me next week. I'm going to Schwarzach to a meeting of Protestants from the Pongau and Pinzgau areas. Johann Mosshamer and I will be representing Saalfelden. We'll prepare a statement and swear to follow it, pledging solidarity and unity among the Protestants of the Lutheran confession in Salzburg."

"Can I come with you?"

"No, it's too dangerous. You're my wife now, Maria, even if we're not married." He held her hand in both of his and brought it to his lips. "I'm involved in this because I love you and I love God. I also hate the way it feels to submit to a lie. I must stand up for what I believe, even if it's dangerous. Do you want that kind of husband, Maria?"

"I want you for my husband, regardless of what you do or don't do." They held each other and kissed until Maria pulled back. "Say a prayer with me, Hans."

The young couple knelt in their customary way, facing, their hands on each other's shoulders, their heads bowed, their eyes shut.

"O God, creator of this beautiful world, may we be faithful to your will for us on this earth. Give us the courage to lead your people in the true faith that Jesus taught us in the Holy Scripture. Forgive us our sins, which are many. We know this life is a trial for the life to come. May we stand that trial, faithful to your will. Guide us every minute of every day. In Jesus' name we pray. Amen."

3

On Board the *Purysburg*, 1734

Mamma Anna sighed wearily. "I saw those two sweet-hearts run off into the forest from Barbara's bedroom window, and then come sneaking back in after dark. Maria looked different that evening. I knew something had happened between them and that Hans was taking risks, but I couldn't have foreseen where it was all going to lead. Here we are, more than two years later, on this miserable ship trying to survive a.... What kind of storm did you say this was?"

"I said it felt like a hurricane, though they usually hit in the summer. But I think it might be, because we seem to be reaching a lull," Deutsch observed.

They noticed that, although the ship was still rocking in rough sea, the sky had cleared enough for eerie, pale green light to ooze through the clouds, and the force of the wind had diminished.

"Don't be fooled by this calm. Afterwhile, it'll come back the other way, just as fierce. We'd better stay put 'cause you can't tell how long the calm will last."

"That's about the way life is sometimes. Just when you've learned to manage the last batch of trouble, something else terrible happens."

Mamma Anna shifted her aching limbs as much as she could and tried to make out the face of this person she was hanging on to life with, but her weak eyes needed more light to see the features of a face. The screams and wails of some of the passengers could be heard as the winds quieted, mixed with the strains of a hymn. She recognized the voices of some of the Salzburgers, singing their praises to God. It comforted her, knowing that she was not the only one who was surviving this latest storm. They had been through so many storms together, and this near-death experience made them seem even dearer to her. She found herself spilling over with tears, as if she weren't wet enough already.

"What's the matter?" Deutsch asked, feeling her body shaking with sobs.

"Oh, don't pay any attention to me." She sniffed and rubbed her nose on his shoulder since her hands were wedged in tight. She was surprised at herself for caring so much about the others. There had been many times when she had been thoroughly fed up with them and their pious, judging ways. "I just turned to tears when I heard the Salzburgers singing."

"Singing hymns is a funny thing to do during a storm."

"Well, you know, it may seem strange, but hymn singing can build up your strength and help you keep going when you feel like giving up. I've seen it work many a time with these Salzburgers. It gets your mind off your problems. I tend to talk, myself, but singing's good, too. Maybe God does hear them. Something has protected us tonight. 'Course their prayers and songs wouldn't have helped me much if you hadn't grabbed me at the right time, but maybe God had a hand in that, too."

"Now don't go making me any instrument of God. I'm one of the damned of the earth, and that's all right with me."

"You've been mighty kind to protect me this night. You can't be too bad of a fellow."

"I may throw you overboard yet, if you start trying to make a saint out of me. Besides, this storm ain't over, and if we survive that, the ship may be too damaged to make it to America. So if it's the hymn singing that will save us, they'd better have a lot of them to get us safely to shore again."

"Oh, the pastors have a heap of them, whole books full. I can't read, myself, but they're all written down, and someone will read the words and teach the others. I don't sing these new ones, though. I prefer the ones I learned back home."

One strong baritone voice soared over the other singers as they launched into the *Song of the Exile*, written by Schaitberger, himself an exile.

"Now that one I know. We learned it on the march out of

Salzburg. That's Peter Gruber you can hear above the others. He's one of the Gastein miners who joined up with us in Augsburg to come to Georgia. They told me about the men singing in the choir at the church in Gastein and changing the words of the Catholic hymns into their own. That would have been Peter and Hans Gruber, Tobias Lackner, Lorentz Huber, and Thomas Gschwandl. The priest didn't catch on for the longest time, until some Judas told him. Firmian didn't want the miners to leave Salzburg because he needed the gold and coal and salt they were mining, and they knew it. Finally, their subversive actions got to be too much, and some of them were expelled, too.

"I'd already met a few of the folks from Gastein before we gathered in Augsburg to come to Georgia. Delivered Margaretta Gschwandl's baby back in Memmingen, where the Kroehr girls, Barbara, and I spent some time before we went to Augsburg. She had a hard time, being a narrow-hipped young woman, and she was living in a barn at the time, which didn't help. I managed to save her and the baby both, and during those long hours of sitting with her, she told me about how she and her husband, Thomas, and her sister, Anna Hofer, had come to be in Memmingen, living in a barn."

4

Gastein, July 1731

Melted snow seeps out of the mountain, streaming down an ancient path through the Gastein Valley, then joins the Salzach River and flows past Schwarzach, Werfen, Hallein, and other Alpine villages before it reaches Salzburg and continues its journey north to the Inn River. Clear, light air surrounds Margaretta, who kneels beside the mountain stream, cupping the icy water in her hand and drinking in its purity. The liquid surface reflects the bank's purple and white star-shaped flowers, creating a contrast of light and dark. Thomas's face appears in the stream and, next to it, the reflection of a smaller version of the same face, belonging to his ten-year-old bastard son.

Margaretta sees Thomas's reflected eyes glance nervously downstream, but she sees only Anna Hofer, her sister, who has stopped on the trail to pick some of the purple flowers. She watches as Anna stands and threads the stems through the black laces of her bodice. Thomas rises, offers a hand to Margaretta, and lifts her to her feet.

The family party looks innocent enough, on a picnic on a warm summer day, but they move with a slight furtiveness, relaxing their breathing somewhat when a stand of trees conceals them as they climb.

The twenty-year-old Margaretta had been hesitant about marrying Thomas a few months before because he had always seemed dull to her. Now, she knows his quietness runs deep. As she watches him climb the mountain ahead of her, she breathes deeply of the delicate mountain air and realizes, for the first time, that she is beginning to love him. He has been so good to her and to her sister, Anna. Their life would have been very difficult after her father's death if Thomas had not married her and let Anna live with them. She and Anna would have had no choice but to become servants in someone else's house.

The Gschwandl family will hike forty minutes before reaching their destination. It is imperative that no priests, or soldiers, or even loyal Catholics follow them or suspect that this peasant family is doing anything but having a picnic.

They stop to rest on a ledge and wait for their breathing to return to normal. Thomas opens the basket he has been carrying, and Margaretta gives everyone a piece of fresh bread and cheese.

"Bless this bread to the nourishment of our bodies, and our bodies to thy service. Amen."

These are the only words spoken, as each person silently gazes at the layers of mountains shading from green to blue to gray, tier after tier stretching across the horizon. Streaks of snow still clinging to the peaks shine against the blue sky. Margaretta and Thomas smile at each other, feeling the beauty of the Alps but needing no words to describe that feeling.

The four peasants continue up the mountain until they reach the arched stone entrance to a cave. Margaretta approaches with both fear and joy. She fears the darkness and the bats within the cave, and she fears the possibility that the Prince Archbishop's priests or soldiers will discover them holding an illegal Lutheran service. But the joy she feels at being able to worship God the Protestant way, to hear the words of the Bible read in German, and to sing the hymns of Martin Luther, overshadows her fear. Surely, God will protect them.

The Gschwandl family is soaked with sweat, but they walk as casually as possible to the cool opening and duck inside. They hesitate for a minute to let their eyes adjust to the darkness. Noises are heard from within, and Tobias Lackner's lantern emerges out of the darkness. Thomas takes his own lantern out of his basket and fires the wick. Tobias, a foreman in the Gastein coalmines, is at home inside the mountains and leads the way.

Nothing is said as they walk back into the cave. Margaretta treads carefully, for the rocks are slippery with dampness. When they come to a hole five feet up the slippery rock, Simon Reiter is at the top with a rope ladder to help them. For twenty minutes they walk into the mountain before coming to the large, black chamber where Protestant services have been held for a hundred years, since the time of Martin Lodinger. Margaretta wonders how the men can work inside the mountains every day, all of their lives. She gags on the stale, earthy air.

Pale, flickering light from scattered lanterns illumines about fifteen upturned faces already assembled in the chamber. Luther's Bible and a hand-carved, wooden cross are displayed on the natural stone altar. The noise of the people singing, "A mighty fortress is our God, a bulwark never failing," led by Peter Gruber's strong baritone voice, reverberates off the walls, creating such vibrations in her soul that tears run down her cheeks. Thomas takes her hand in the dark, and they join the other worshipers. Margaretta tries to avoid brushing against the wet, slimy walls.

Soon, others appear in the passage, their faces a creamy glow from Tobias's lantern, as he leads group after group into the chamber. Margaretta looks around at the barely visible faces of friends and neighbors she has known all her life. Balthasar Fleiss, another miner, takes the lantern from Tobias and goes back for the next party of Protestants.

Quietness envelops the worshipers when the song ends. Hans Gruber reads from Luther's German Bible, and several men pray aloud, including Thomas. With no minister, the people share the responsibilities of the services. Everyone stands and recites the Augsburg Confession. Young Thomas, Margaretta's new stepson, is proud that he can say most of it from memory now.

When Hans Gruber raises his lantern, light falls on the face of a stranger. The people shift uneasily, realizing that someone they do not know is in the cave, and knowing that an outsider could be a Catholic spy who might betray their secret meeting place to the authorities. The squeaking and fluttering of bats can be heard in the silence that shivers through the people.

"Neighbors and friends, you can trust this man. This is Rupert Stulebner, a smith from Huttau. He's a devout Evangelical Lutheran and a great preacher who's been organizing the Protestants throughout the Pongau area. Tonight, he has an important message for us. We need to be in touch with the other Protestants during this time of persecution. Trust him, and hear what he has to say."

"Friends, I've heard about your cave church for years, and I am privileged to worship here with you today. It is truly an Entrische Kirche, a gloomy church, but one filled with the joy of the Holy Spirit."

The collective fear of the people begins to dissipate, and they lean forward to listen to this man who has dared visit them.

"My friends, it is time for us to stand up for our faith and practice it openly. The Archbishop's latest taxes and persecutions are too outrageous to be borne. We cannot feed our families and pay for the excesses of the Catholics in Salzburg any longer. People are being arrested, and men have been torn from their families and sent into exile. Prince Archbishop Firmian's new Chancellor, Christian von Rall, has, in effect, declared war on the Protestants. Priests who have been tolerant of our religious preference are being chastised. Everyone will be required to attend mass, wear the church's hated scapular, and openly say the rosary."

These persecutions are well known to the people present, for they have experienced them also. Only the miners have escaped the worst of the harshness, since Firmian relies on the mining industry to keep his coffers filled.

"The time has come for us to act like people of faith. We need to show our strength together so that Firmian will know that most of the people in the province stand against the Catholic Church and its policies, which favor the rich and rob the poor. He needs to know that we have been Protestants for more than a hundred years, and we will never bow to his Catholic heresy. We will never be free to worship openly and have the protection of our ruler unless we stand firmly together. We need to convince our Prince that we do not defy him; we only ask for his protection.

"Therefore, representatives from Protestant groups are organizing a meeting in Schwarzach on July 13, to prepare a covenant to stand together and remain faithful to the Augsburg Confession and the teachings of Luther. I am here today to invite you to join us in this undertaking. We are inviting representatives from all the Protestant communities in the Salzburg Province. Together, we can work for the establishment of religious freedom in Salzburg or, individually, we will continue to suffer persecution. Are any of you willing to come? I should also tell you that the great preacher Hans Mosegger from Hollereck will be there and has promised to speak to us. Again I ask, are any of you willing to come?"

Margaretta is startled when she hears Thomas say, "I'll go," in his quiet but firm voice.

Tobias Lackner calls out, "If Thomas will, I will."

Peter Gruber's deep baritone voice booms around the chamber, "Count me in."

Others call out their willingness to participate.

"Thank you, and God bless you," Stulebner says. "I knew we could count on the people of Gastein. You stand in the tradition of the great Martin Lodinger from Hofgastein, whose sacrifice for the Protestant faith inspires us all. Remember, we have support from the Corpus Evangelicorum in Regensburg, which includes representatives from all of the Protestant domains in the Holy Roman Empire. We do not stand alone. What we need is to ask our Prince Archbishop to protect our practice of religion, and we will be loyal citizens in all other matters. But we must stand firmly together, or we will all lose."

He adds more quietly, "You realize, of course, that we must be prepared to suffer persecution or exile, like Joseph Schaitberger. The Prince could not afford to exile us all if we stand together."

The meeting breaks into lively discussion, with the unique sound of each voice being the main means of identifying who is speaking in the dark chamber. The light from the lanterns does not pierce very far into the blackness surrounding them.

Hans Gruber calls out above the noise, "Let's all join in the Lord's Supper. Herr Stulebner, will you lead us?"

A hush falls over the group as Stulebner repeats the familiar words and serves the bread and wine to the people.

Margaretta feels the significance of this "last supper" more than ever before. It might be the last supper for Thomas and the others, just as it was for Jesus and the disciples. A chill of fear runs through her body, and she wonders what sacrifices she might be called to make. She involuntarily chokes on a sob when she realizes she might have to sacrifice her husband.

5

On Board the *Purysburg*, 1734

Mamma Anna gasped as she tried to continue talking. The vibrations of the wind jiggled the sounds back into her mouth, making them unintelligible.

"Here it comes again. Didn't I tell you?" Deutsch warned."

The renewed buffeting of the wind and rain, along with the tossing ship, seemed unbearable to Mamma Anna. She buried her face in Deutsch's shoulder and prayed, not knowing whether it was aloud or not.

"Help us, O Grandmother, help us. Jesus, be merciful on this old woman. I've not been much of a Christian, and I'm not a pietist, but Jesus, I have loved people and taken good care of them. That ought to be worth something in Heaven. Jesus, you said to love your neighbor, and I've done that, most of them, anyway. It's been right hard for me to love Archbishop Firmian and the Jesuits, but I do have a soft spot in my heart for Father Jacob, if that helps any. O Jesus, I'm sorry for all the bad things I've done, but, aside from hating that bastard Firmian, I can't think of any right now to confess. I promise I'll try to love even Firmian if you'll let me live a little longer, although I know I've lived longer than most already. If you're ready for me to die, though, I'm willing. This is awful."

Mamma Anna's mind drifted away from her prayers, as she began thinking about the snatches of information she had collected about Archbishop Firmian. Being a born snoop and traveling from house to house as she did, since even Catholic women needed her services, she had learned a great deal about this man who had caused them all so much trouble.

In one rich Catholic man's home, while attending the lady of the house through a long labor, she had overheard the master telling his friends about meeting the Archbishop.

"He's a tall man with a noble profile, dominated by a prominent nose and a wide, handsome face. At the reception at Mirabell Palace, he wore a white wig parted in the middle, with immaculate curls cascading down. He was dressed in a red cassock over his fine silk shirt, cuffed with exquisite lace. A sheer collar tied with gold tassels was tucked high under his double chin, and a jeweled cross hung on a heavy gold chain around his neck. He's fairly young for a prince, but he certainly looks like one. Looks more like a prince than an archbishop, in my opinion. Of course, I didn't see him during a mass. He had an arrogant, standoffish way about him."

She had listened intently, standing in the dimly lit hall near the open door to the library, where the gentlemen were drinking wine after dinner. She tried to learn as much as she could, because she had already heard that the Catholics were spying on the Protestants, searching for Protestant literature. Possessing it could condemn a man to prison. They were also checking to see if everyone kept the fast days and wore the scapular. It had gotten so you did not know whom to trust. Priests were even questioning children to get information about their parents. Someone needed to find out about the other side. Usually, no one paid much attention to her in the great houses, just ignored her presence, except when she was needed.

She could not see the gentlemen and dared not look into the room, but their voices grew louder as they drank more wine, while the master continued.

"He's said to be a pious man. I've heard he prays alone most mornings before mass in the Cathedral.

"As a matter of fact, the night before the hunt he told an interesting story about that at the dinner he hosted at Hellbrun. Just that morning, he said, he had experienced God speaking to him in a dramatic way while he was kneeling in prayer at the altar railing in the gray light of that huge sanctuary. You know how dark that cavernous place can be. Well, he was asking God to help him solve the problem of the contrary peasants who had embarrassed him by sending a petition to Regensburg to the Corpus Evangelicorum. They'd even asked him to appoint Evangelical Lutheran pastors in the villages."

"No. They didn't ask for such nonsense."

"That's what he said, and so did Christian von Rall, his new chancellor."

"How many signed the petition?"

"The rumor was that nineteen thousand peasants' names were on the petition. I don't believe it. Not that many even know how to write their names." This remark was followed by laughter.

"We're interrupting you. What happened to the Archbishop in the Cathedral?"

"So he was praying about this problem, and the solution had just come to him when this huge bolt of lightning struck, causing him to fall back, and as he did, he looked up at the altar painting of Christ ascending into Heaven, and the picture was lit up. He asked those of us present if we thought it was a sign from God that he had found the solution to the problem. We naturally said, 'Yes.' Who's going to contradict the Archbishop on a religious opinion?"

"What was the solution he had devised?"

"He said he had just reviewed in his mind the situation that Philip II of Spain had experienced when Spain had become filled with heretics. King Philip had systematically purified the Catholic faith by rooting out all who were not good Christians, so that they would not contaminate the others. He said such action in the Salzburg Province would be for the good of the peasants, whose souls were in danger of Hell because a few troublemakers were leading them astray."

"How does he plan to do this?"

"This is the best part. He's going to bring in a hundred Jesuit priests, ten at a time in order not to upset the Capuchins, and assign them to investigate every house in every village and identify the leaders of this movement. They'll make every person sign a statement of loyalty to the Catholic beliefs. Those that won't sign will be exiled."

"He'll have to give them three years to leave, according to the Treaty of Westphalia."

"Well, I don't know about that. It wasn't discussed."

"Enough of politics. What about his horses? Does he really have an Arabian stallion?"

"He has a stable full of the finest horses in Europe."

"I hear that's not all he has in his stable. I hear he has a cuckold." Drunken laughter followed. "Did you see the wife of the groomsman? Was she at the hunt?"

"You'll have to seek elsewhere for that kind of information. I'll not risk my friendship with the Archbishop by gossiping, but I will tell you this much. I did see a beautiful woman whom everyone was talking about behind their hands. It was whispered that he made few decisions without consulting her. Sometimes, they say, he even travels to Klessheim Palace, where she lives, to get her advice."

"Who is she?"

"Well, I think she's...."

At that moment, Mamma Anna had been interrupted by a servant, who chastised her for prowling around and who threatened her with dismissal.

So she had not learned any more that night. She particularly hated missing the gossip about the Archbishop and the mysterious woman. She had hardly been able to wait to finish the job so she could let Barbara Rohrmoser know what she had learned. She knew that Barbara would rush to let Hans know about the Archbishop's plans before he went to that oath-taking she had heard them talking about. Hans might not trust her, but Barbara did.

6

On Board the *Purysburg*, 1734

Mamma Anna's mind was as numb as her freezing limbs. She opened her eyes and looked up into one of the ugliest faces she had ever seen, and instinctively recoiled. The left eye was sewn shut, and a thick, red scar connected the side of the head where the right ear should be, with a corner of the mouth, which was pulled out of shape and showing a few brown stubs of teeth. Pox scars dotted the rest of the gruesome image. Her first thought was that she was in Hell, face to face with the Devil.

Deutsch, accustomed to people's reaction to his frightening countenance, automatically began to withdraw into his shell of hardness that the protective darkness had earlier relaxed.

Mamma Anna looked around her, trying to get her bearings. The sight of the broken railing and people sprawled on the deck in the early gray dawn brought her back to her senses.

Half-drowned, exhausted sailors, English settlers, Salzburgers, and other passengers were untying themselves and rubbing their bodies where ropes had cut into them during the storm. She saw Catherine Kroehr lying on the deck, with Pastor Gronau kneeling beside her, holding her limp hand.

"We made it," the face above her said. "You all right?"

Mamma Anna realized that she was lying with her head in the sailor's lap. She did not know how long she had been there. She must have fainted or fallen asleep, and when she tried to sit up, she fell back, unable to lift her body. He must have dragged her out of the storage box.

Captain Fry yelled orders from the bow, and Deutsch gently laid her on the deck. He was covered with bruises and abrasions from banging against the box all night. He stood up slowly and stiffly to take his post.

"Wait. You're Deutsch." Mamma Anna was beginning to

connect her mind to what was happening. "You saved my life. How can I repay you?"

"Anybody would've done it."

"I'll make you a poultice for those cuts."

"That ain't nothing. They've had enough sea water to cure it." As he stood all the way up, he suddenly groaned and doubled over again. "Must've cracked a rib."

He ducked his disfigured face and walked unsteadily away to join his mates in the clean-up operation already getting underway.

Mamma Anna tried to stand up, but her strength was spent, and her body was shaking and aching from having been tossed around all night like a seed in a baby's rattle. She carefully tried to straighten her legs.

People will be hurt. I need to get my basket, her mind said, but her body did not seem to hear; instead, her eyes fluttered closed. In a mist of confusion, she could hear voices around her, first Barbara yelling for help, then Maria placing an ear on her chest.

"Her heart's still beating. Where's Mr. Zwiffler? Barbara, you take care of Catherine. I'll look after Mamma Anna."

Maria pressed her finger to Mamma Anna's neck and felt the weak beat of her heart. Mamma Anna had taught her to do that.

"Johann, over here. It's Mamma Anna." Johann Mosshamer made his way across the crowded, slippery deck. Almost every passenger on the ship was on the deck, searching for family and friends and looking over the damage.

"We need to get her below and out of these wet clothes. She has a high fever. She'll die up here in this cold wind."

"I'll get Thomas. We'll carry her down. I don't think I can lift her alone."

Pastor Boltzius knelt to look at Mamma Anna as he made his rounds, checking on all the Salzburgers. He had just come from Catherine.

"How is Catherine?" Maria asked. She was holding Mamma Anna, trying to keep her warm with her own body heat.

"She's already revived, thanks be to God. She must have fainted. God has brought us through this dreadful storm without destroying the ship. We'll have a service of prayer and thanksgiving as soon as we can. How is Mrs. Burgsteiner?"

"I'm afraid not too good. Her body is badly bruised, and she's not conscious. Her fever's high, and she's shaking all over. Johann has gone to find Thomas, so we can move her below deck and get her out of these wet clothes."

"Don't forget to change your own clothes while you're taking care of others."

"Say a prayer for her, Pastor. We all love her so much. I can't bear the thought of losing her."

"Her life has been hard. We should only hope that she is ready in her heart to meet her Lord for all eternity." Boltzius was none too sure that Mamma Anna had properly prepared herself to face that heavenly trial. She had not appeared to be serious about her faith; she did not regularly attend the daily prayer services and had made no attempt to study the Scripture or learn the hymns, as most of the Salzburgers had done.

"Heavenly Father, look with mercy on this woman. May your love be wide enough to take her home to Heaven if it be thy holy will. If now is not her time, guide her heart to be a more willing servant of thy will. In Jesus' name we pray."

"Don't worry, my child. We're all in God's loving hands," he reassured Maria.

Johann returned with Thomas Gschwandl. Thomas held Mamma Anna under her arms, and Johann took her feet. She was short, but she was stout, although her size had diminished since they had been on the *Purysburg* with only one meal a day. The salty diet and lack of fresh foods had caused the characteristic swelling associated with scurvy.

Mamma Anna's mind roused itself as the two men struggled to carry her down the ladder to the tiny compartment below, partitioned off by canvas, which she shared with Barbara, Catherine, and Gertrude. The stench below deck caused them all to gag.

"Be careful; the floor's slippery with vomit," Thomas warned.

Mamma Anna moaned as they laid her in the filthy bunk. "Is that you, Johann, and Thomas?"

"Yes, Mamma Anna. Thomas and I brought you down. Now Maria's going to take care of you."

"Maria, is Hans back yet?"

Johann and Maria looked at each other, realizing that Mamma Anna must be delirious. "Let me undress her. You go see about the others," Maria said, closing the canvas curtain between them.

7

Saalfelden, 1731

Mamma Anna's feverish mind revisited those tense days in the summer of 1731 that had decided their fate. She had rushed back to the Rohrmoser farm to report what she had heard about the Archbishop's plan for the Protestants, who were mostly peasants. She had found Barbara working in her fenced front garden.

"Good afternoon, Mamma Anna. What brings you here today?"

"I just wanted to give you some herbs to plant in your garden," Mamma Anna answered. As she took a cloth-wrapped package of freshly dug witch hazel from her basket, she saw Peter round the house to see who had set the dogs to barking.

He raised his hand in greeting but turned back to continue his work in the barn behind the house. Everyone was edgy these days, but he did not want to get caught in a conversation with the loquacious Mamma Anna.

"That's very thoughtful of you. Thank you. I'll plant this right beside the mint. Here, let me cut some fresh mint for you. It'll taste good in your tea tonight."

"That would be nice." Realizing that Peter was out of sight and hearing, she put her head close to Barbara's and passed on her secrets. "I wanted to let Hans know before he goes to Schwarzach that the Archbishop is planning to tighten the rules and make everyone swear to be a loyal Catholic. He's bringing in the Jesuits to search every household for Evangelical Lutheran material and to enforce the loyalty oath. He's planning to step up the punishments for not going to mass or not saying the rosary or not wearing a scapular or not keeping the fast days or refusing to confess and pay indulgences. The men at Schwarzach will be in danger of arrest. There are spies everywhere. Don't trust your husband or your sister Eva."

"Eva? Oh, you can't be right. She'd never do anything that would harm Hans."

"I'm just telling you what I heard."

"That's ridiculous. I won't start suspecting my own family. Well, I wouldn't tell Peter, of course, because he's not one of us, like Eva is. But I will try to get a message to Hans. Thank you for bringing the news to me. How did you find out what the Archbishop is planning?"

"I have my ways," Mamma Anna said evasively. She never liked to let people know her sources of information. Sometimes it was merely intuition she was conveying.

"You be careful, too, Mamma Anna. Peter told me that they arrested some herbalist women in the Pongau. Accused them of being witches and casting spells. I worry about your midwifing in the Catholic homes. If someone dies, they might say you'd cast a spell."

"Don't worry about me, child. Everyone knows me and knows I do all I can to help a woman through the pain of childbirth. I've delivered more healthy babies than most midwives. Couldn't do it without the herbs, though. Besides, most of the Catholics are good folks, even Father Jacob. It's just Archbishop Firmian and that crowd in Salzburg who're causing most of the trouble."

"I don't know why you trust Father Jacob. He's been the one enforcing all the new rules."

"I have my reasons. He'll think twice before he'll denounce me, knowing what I know about him." With that tantalizing remark, Mamma Anna turned and started walking toward home.

8

Schwarzach, July 1731

The Protestant women waited anxiously as their men traveled to an inn in the tiny village of Schwarzach, situated on the Salzach River.

Thomas Gschwandl and Tobias Lackner journeyed from the Gastein area, riding their horses through the narrow, winding river valley. Since neither had ever before been out of the Gastein Valley, they approached Schwarzach with much apprehension. Turning north to follow the Salzach River, they joined other travelers. Not being sure of the identity or destination of these strangers, they decided to keep to themselves and not risk saying something to one of Firmian's spies.

Rounding the last bend, they were surprised to see at least a hundred people, mostly men, who had gathered in Schwarzach. The round, green or brown hats of the peasant farmers, miners, and artisans covered the hillside, as the men gathered in groups to talk. Most were dressed in the traditional mountain garb of bloomer pants made from red, green, or blue wool, held up by leather suspenders, with a strap across the chest of their red, blue, or green shirts. Colorful woolen socks met the pants just below the knees.

"I'm surprised so many came," Tobias said. "Must be more than a hundred, and they're still coming."

They looked around for a minute to see if they recognized anyone. "Isn't that Hans and Peter Gruber over there near that rock?" Thomas asked.

"Looks like them."

The two men dismounted and led their horses to a small stream, which ran into the larger river, for a drink. Walking up the hill, they joined Peter and Hans, who were raptly listening to a man addressing a small group. They realized that the speaker was Rupert Stulebner, the smith from Huttau who had spoken to their cave church and invited them to this gathering.

He turned to them and held out his hand. "I'm Rupert Stulebner. Who might you be?"

"Thomas Gschwandl from Hofgastein, and this is Tobias Lackner. We met you before, when you came to our Entrische Kirche. It's good to see what you look like in the daylight." They were seeing a short, stocky man whose face was red from the sun or the heat of the smith's fire. He never seemed to be still but was constantly in motion, even when standing in one place, like a bumblebee hovering over a flower.

"You'll forgive me for not recognizing you. It was very dark in your church, but I could feel the marvelous spirit of the people assembled, even if I couldn't see the faces."

Stulebner greeted them all and moved on to another group of men. He seemed to know everyone.

"What's going to happen?" Tobias asked Peter.

"Stulebner said that Hans Mosegger, a farmer from Hollereck, is going to speak to the crowd in a few minutes; then, the leaders will prepare a statement we can all swear to support."

The great crowd sat down on the hillside when Hans Mosegger stood up to speak. He was an old man, about 70, with white hair and a face weathered by working in the fields and by advancing age. He looked carefully over the congregation of brave Lutherans, many of whom had walked for miles to be there, and began speaking in a compelling voice. He spoke with authority honed by years spent studying the Bible and religious tracts bought from peddlers who had smuggled them from Protestant cities in Europe.

"My dear brothers and sisters! My dear people from far and near!" He spoke loudly in the dialect of the region so that everyone could hear and understand. "We have gathered here today to discuss with one another our crisis of conscience and oppression of heart and soul, and to come to a resolution as to how we will proceed with our lives in the future.

"My dear people, we all believe in the teachings of Jesus Christ and his holy gospel. Christ and his gospel are our salvation and our good fortune; in the name of Jesus lies our salvation; in Him we are saved; and there is no other gospel than that of Jesus Christ.

"The Catholics believe the same as we, but they also believe in that which the Pope and the bishops added. It is their affair if they accept and swallow everything that is presented to them, and it is our affair if we throw out this extra baggage which has been added.

"And it is questionable whether the Pope or the bishops have the right to pluck out pieces of the gospel, to twist it around, patch pieces together, or add pieces to it. Paul said, 'Who fails to abide by the words of Jesus preaches a puffed-up message. Jesus is the same yesterday, today, and forever.'

"Christ said, 'My words will not pass away, and my words may not be distorted; nothing may be added to or taken away from them.'

"Christ gave his apostles the right to forgive sins. Not one word was said about the confessional box. The confessional box is nothing more than an instrument of power on the part of the Pope and the bishops, for control, oppression, and extortion of the people.

"The clergy are themselves full of sins and shortcomings, fornication, drunkenness, usury, covetousness, avarice, and ambition. They have enough to clean up at their own doors.

"Why do they need to know whether and when the young man goes to his girl, whether the farmer drinks a glass too many, or what they read, or cook, or say?"

A cry of approval went up from the people. Thomas and Tobias looked at each other and nodded their heads in agreement.

Hans Burgsteiner and Johann Mosshamer were also in the audience, having ridden their horses from Saalfelden. They were both thrilled to be able to hear the great Mosegger preach. Hans, having tried preaching himself, was impressed at the skill with which this simple man held the congregation's attention. Johann, more the intellectual, marveled at how he organized his thoughts and at his knowledge of the Bible.

"And is there anything in the Holy Scriptures concerning indulgences? No, nothing on this is to be found. This is an invention of the Pope and the bishops to squeeze the last penny out of us, so that they can continually build new monasteries, religious edifices, and churches, and have a mountain of money in addition.

"Who pays the most gets into Heaven first. Can such a teaching be in accordance with the will of our Lord?" Mosegger's voice rose to a shout.

"No!" shouted the crowd.

"No, a thousand times no! Otherwise, the disciples and apostles of Jesus would have been given grace for nothing.

"Christ said at the Last Supper, 'Eat my flesh and drink my blood. Who eats my flesh and drinks my blood has eternal life.'

"And the Pope and the bishops want to take away entirely the cup with the holy blood, against the will of our Lord. Is there anything in Holy Scripture which gives them the right to do this?"

Again the crowd shouted, "No!"

"And the sacrifice of the mass is read in a foreign language, in Latin, which no one understands, never in our own language, German. Why are we not allowed to understand? Because they falsify everything, distort everything. Our hearts and minds and souls remain empty because we understand nothing."

Hans felt the weight of his father's German Bible concealed in his pack over his shoulder. It was his most prized possession, and he had risked bringing it to this important occasion.

Mosegger continued by listing many of the grievances the Protestants had with the Catholics. These included over a hundred fast days the people must observe; serving only the bread at communion; the sins of the clergy; the ban against married clergy; taking money from the poor to build fine churches and palaces; spying on the people to see if they were obeying all of the rules, like wearing a scapular; imposing unreasonable taxes and fines; and locking them in prisons, exiling, and even killing them. He compared the corrupt practices of the Church with the Scripture.

"Jesus preached the new faith, of love and goodness, of forgiveness and forbearance. Jesus gave food and drink to the poor, like a good father, and like a good doctor made the blind to see, the deaf to hear, the lame and the halt to walk upright, the lepers whole, the sick healthy, the dead alive.

"He was good to all, helped everyone in body and soul, consoled all, condemned no one, not even the adulteress or Mary Magdalene.

"But, my dear people, see how it looks today!

"Jesus shed his holy blood for us, but the anointed and sanctified Archbishop forgets about our blood. He had the priest Matthaeus hanged, solely because he preached the gospel; simply because Stoeckl allowed the pastors to escape, the Archbishop had him martyred and beheaded; and during the peasant war, he secretly had twenty-seven farmers in Radstadt beheaded. And he also had the good administrator of Mittersill beheaded because he refused to drive the peasants from their homes and lands. Likewise, Kaspar Vogl and many others as well. And he ordered that the Eschbacher Ruppert and his relatives in Radstadt be driven out with thorn switches because of the gospel, and ordered hundreds and hundreds of herbalist women and casters of spells to be burned as witches. Deer and antelopes mean more to him than our life and blood."

Hans Burgsteiner thought of Mamma Anna, his cousin, who used herbs to heal the sick in Saalfelden. His grandmother had taught her this ancient art. Anger at the injustices the people were suffering welled up in him as he listened to the impassioned preacher.

"Do we find love, goodness, grace with these people as with Jesus? No, they only want our sacrifice, money, and interest payments from us. They make us poor; they take from us our last penny.

"They want to drive us from our homeland, from our lands and our property, to distort the faith, rob us of the cup, steal the gospel. That is what the good pastors of Salzburg do.

"Christ said, 'My commandment is that you love one another. Come unto me all you who are weary and heavy-laden, and I will help you. What you do to my brother, you do to me.'

"And how do the good pastors of Salzburg proceed?" Mosegger began strutting around like a cocky rooster. "They walk about in gold and velvet and silk and taffeta; they pursue riotous living, wear golden chains and brilliant jewels, build beautiful houses and palaces for themselves and their mistresses, pursue theatre, hunting, games, and amusements; looking for new taxes, all sorts of offerings, curiosities, works, services, and compulsory work, new punishments, harassment, irritations. That is the work of the good pastors of Salzburg."

The audience burst into laughter and applause. Mosegger lowered his voice and continued.

"The fruits of the holy gospel and of faith are love and peace, joy and patience, goodness, gentleness, and meekness. But do we find these with the Archbishop, or with the Catholics?"

"No!" the crowd roared.

"No! We see, we detect, no love, no sympathy, and no mercy; for us there is only law and punishment, betrayal, spying, and prison. Everyone is goaded, distorted, betrayed; we are everywhere persecuted, reviled, and cursed. In the Papist church the Holy Scripture and the gospel are ruined; love is destroyed.

"No house, no bedroom, no stable, no shed, no barn or mountain shelter is safe from their spies. Like wolves and murderers the Jesuit fathers and the Capuchins creep into the houses, poke about in every corner, question children and servants, and if you say a word, you are lost.

"Cursed and damned are we. No one dares to trust you, not child, not brother or sister, not father or mother, not servant or neighbor.

"But we can speak with Holy Scripture: 'We are everywhere oppressed, but we cannot be defeated; we can see no future, but we are not without a future; we are persecuted, but we are not abandoned!'

"Where then lies the way for us?

"My dear people, our Lord said, 'I am the way, the truth and the life.' In the gospel is the spirit of truth, and where the spirit of truth is, there is the spirit of God, and freedom and love.

"No matter how it looks in the world, do not go astray; remain with the Lord Jesus and his gospel, and if the Archbishop really does drive us from our homes and our land, if nothing else helps, if we must for the sake of the gospel leave everything behind, then remember: our Lord also had to wander as a small child. He too had nothing, was despised and reviled, persecuted and killed; and when punishment and imprisonment threaten us, when everything is distorted in the Papist church, keep in mind that the Papist church is sick, and that the Lord Jesus has turned away from her.

"I beg you, people. Do not swear an oath to such a faith; a faith that demands you to condemn father and mother who taught you the holy gospel.

"Christ brought the gospel to the poor; the good pastor in Salzburg takes it away; but he can only take away the printed gospel; that which is within, in our breast, he cannot take, and we will not let him take it.

"Christ was above all the savior of the poor. The gospel is the root stock of the tree of Christianity, and the evil people, the evil priests, bishops, Popes, are the mistletoe growth, the death's head, in the tree.

"Yes, my dear people! Love is the greatest commandment, and at the last judgment we will not be asked by the

Lord Jesus whether we belonged to a brotherhood, whether we wore a scapular, whether we purchased an indulgence, or have called upon the saints, whether we went on pilgrimages, whether we have had holy water basins and baptismal water everywhere, whether we diligently prayed the rosary, but rather whether we fulfilled the greatest commandment, whether we have done all that genuine love demands. As the holy Augustine said, 'Love all and do what you will.'

"Therefore, I call upon you, people, I ask you all! Hold together in love and remain true to the gospel; do not abandon our Lord Jesus; betray no one, denounce no one, persecute no one, embrace everyone in love, help everyone, whether friend or foe.

"Now, of course, there is for us no love. Love lies on the bier of death, peace is blown away, joy is burned up; we are persecuted, banned, condemned. Like tigers, the Pope and the bishops attack us, tearing us apart. Many are embittered and wounded. Sleep eludes us, our spirit is sick, tears stream down, our hearts bleed! But we should bear it, people, as our Lord bore the cross. Do not give up; hold fast together.

"It is not a matter of house and land and money and possessions! No! It concerns our bodies and our souls! Hold out, people, hold out, as Christ did carrying the cross. He went to his death for the gospel. His gospel is our gospel; he did not let it be taken away from him, but remained true, and we must do the same."

Thomas thought of his own farm and house and all the animals he was so proud to own. He wondered if he had enough faith to risk losing all that he had for his soul.

"Let that be our resolution! Let no one dare to be a Judas, a sanctimonious scoundrel; stay together in loyalty and love, like the disciples of Jesus.

"Do not sell our gospel, our souls, for the sake of goods and possessions. And as Jesus stretched out his arms on the cross in order to take in all of us, so will he on the last day stretch out his hands to us, and call us to Heaven, if we remain true to him.

"Together with the holy Paul I call to you: 'The God of peace and love, the grace and love of our Lord Jesus, be and remain with us all! Amen.'"

There was a moment of solemn silence, as everyone absorbed the powerful message that had been so skillfully presented.

"He spoke the truth," Thomas said.   "We must stand firm."

"Ja, that's right. Anything less will be wrong."

Hans Burgsteiner was so moved by the sermon that tears ran down his face. Johann put his arm around his friend. "Let's go see if we can meet Mosegger."   As they began walking through the assembly, someone called out to the milling crowd, "Attention, please. My name is Ruprecht Frommer.   Friends, I have a letter here from the Corpus Evangelicorum in Regensburg. As many of you know, the Corpus Evangelicorum is a group of representatives from the Evangelical or Protestant states in the Holy Roman Empire. It is to this group that our brave friends who were expelled from Deferegger and Dürrnberg appealed for help."

Thomas suddenly elbowed Tobias in the ribs and whispered, "Look over there by that clump of larch trees. Isn't that Christian Baumann from Gastein? He's no Protestant. He must be here spying for the priests, to see who came from Gastein."

"Ja, that's him. Maybe he was moved by Mosegger's sermon and will join us."

"I don't think so. He had the priest over for dinner yesterday," Peter said. "I saw him go in the house. I'll bet the priest asked him to come here today to spy."

"How did the priest know about the meeting? I thought it was supposed to be secret."

"You can't keep anything this big a secret."

"No, I guess not."

Their attention returned to the speaker. "And so, dear friends, as the letter admonishes us to remain true to our faith, I for one vow to do just that. I hope all of you will join me in that pledge."

Discussion of what should be put in a statement they could all support began. After a while, the leaders withdrew into a room in the inn to write down the words. As the others waited, different men read Scripture in German and led the group in hymns.

Hans, as a representative from Saalfelden, was asked to say a prayer for the people. He stood tall and straight, honored to be included in the proceedings, even if it did mark him as a leader and increase the risk of punishment.

"O God of all creation, let thy Holy Spirit be felt by all assembled here. Be especially with our leaders, meeting in the other room. May they receive wisdom from you in what we must do.

"We are thankful, O God, for the words of Hans Mosegger and for the support of our fellow Evangelicals at the Corpus Evangelicorum in Regensburg and in all of the Empire. May the religious tolerance that other provinces have be possible here in Salzburg.

"Almighty God, be also in the heart of our ruler, Archbishop Firmian, that he may protect those of us who choose to worship God simply, as the Scripture has described, without the corruption the Pope has added to the faith. Be in our hearts here today. Give us courage to stay true to the gospel of Christ, your Son, even in the face of persecution. We pray in the name of Jesus, our Savior. Amen."

"Who was that praying?" Tobias asked Thomas.

"That was Hans Burgsteiner from Saalfelden," a stranger standing in front of them said.

Next, a group from Goldegg sang one of Hosenknoph's *Sacrae Cantiones*, composed for many voices to sing contrapuntally. Their voices rose like a choir, and everyone fell silent to listen to the interweaving of the words, as each section voiced them at a different time.

The Gastein men, being choir singers themselves, listened carefully, with appreciation for how well the Goldegg group sang, for they were familiar with the music and had sung it in their choir.

While the crowd continued to wait for the leaders to finish writing a statement, Thomas and Tobias urged Peter Gruber to lead the songs familiar to their movement, so everyone could sing. Finally, after much persuasion, he stood and began singing Schaitberger's *Song of the Exile.*

> "I am a poor exile, so must I describe myself,
> I've been driven from my Fatherland,
> Because of God's word...."

Everyone joined in the singing with such feeling and emotion that many eyes brimmed with tears. Peter continued singing all fourteen verses, but most people dropped out much earlier, when they reached the end of their memory of the words.

Thomas kept an eye on Christian Baumann, who must certainly have seen them by now. It was just as well. If they were going to take a stand, it might as well start here.

The leaders emerged from their deliberations, and the men moved into the inn to hear the report. Some stood outside at the windows to hear.

Stulebner called for order. "Gentlemen, after much discussion, we have written a statement we hope all of you can agree to." He cleared his throat and raised the volume of his voice, almost as if in defiance of any objections from the authorities.

"I affirm that I will remain obedient to the authorities in all earthly matters and not be resistant, except for those matters which touch on religion, which belongs not to us, but to God, and a greater obedience is owed by me to God than to men."

Murmurs of agreement and nods of assent were heard and seen as the men listened to the statement.

Stulebner continued, "If we are in agreement on the statement, I need to tell you that we have information that Firmian's commissioners will be meeting in your areas to identify the Protestants. These meetings begin in two days. The Commission consists of the Court Chancellor, Christian von Rall; Court Counsel von Rehling; and Secretary Meichelbeck."

The group groaned at hearing these names, knowing there would be little sympathy for their cause from these people. "They will meet in Werfen, Radstadt, Wagrain, Grossarl, Hofgastein, Taxenboch, and Saalfelden. We need to act with haste to let the people know our decision and publicly declare our position. It will be our responsibility to go back to our districts and inform the people of the statement agreed on here, so that everyone can stand together. Men with swift horses from each area, please gather after this meeting to make your plans for reaching everyone."

Tobias and Thomas nodded to each other, indicating that they would be messengers in the Gastein Valley.

Stulebner continued, "And now, the most solemn part. After the custom of the Smith's Guild, I propose that we all make an oath to stand by this statement by licking the salt." He held up a wooden box of salt for all to see and then placed it back on the round red table. After dipping his hand into the box, he licked the salt from his fingers. Applause followed his act as he waved his salt-free fingers in the air. The other leaders made the same oath, and everyone lined up to commit himself in this way.

As they waited to participate in the oath-taking, Thomas looked around to see if Christian Baumann was still present, but he could not see him. "I guess Christian didn't want to make this oath. He seems to have disappeared. I doubt if we've heard the last of him, though."

"Well, if we can convince everyone to stand together, we have a better chance of success with the Archbishop. There will be safety in numbers," Tobias replied.

They watched as Hans Burgsteiner and Johann Mosshamer tasted the salt.

When it was his turn, Thomas noticed that his hand shook slightly as he reached into the box. He looked at Tobias as he licked his fingers. Tobias returned the gaze as he licked his own salty fingers. Their eyes met as if in pledge to each other to stand firm, no matter what happened. Thomas felt strength in that companionship.

As the men left the room, they began introducing themselves to strangers and shaking hands, as if wanting to seal with friendship what they had pledged with salt.

"Viet Breme, and you?"

"Hans Burgsteiner from Saalfelden."

"Hans Lerchner."

"Johann Mosshamer, County Zeller in Lannthal."

"Martin Hertzog from Schrecking in Pinzgau."

"Schweighofer from Wagrain."

Stulebner charged the men to let all the Protestants know their decision within two days. "If all the Protestants stand by our statement, we have a better chance of success. We must all stand together, agreed?"

"Ja!" was the firm reply from the men.

The four friends from Gastein stood under a giant hemlock tree for protection from a sudden shower, plotting how they would get word of the meeting to all the Protestants in the Gastein Valley. Each took responsibility for notifying certain villages and communities, and discussed who could be relied on in each place to pass along the message. Tobias and Thomas then mounted their horses and kicked them into a gallop along the winding trail, while Hans and Peter Gruber, on foot, began the long walk home.

Johann and Hans started south along the same route the Gastein men took in order to go around the mountain range that separated the Pinzgau from the Pongau region. They traveled south before turning north again to Saalfelden. As they rode, they, too, planned how to get the word to everyone in Saalfelden.

"We'll have to set up a network of trusted people to tell others, if we're going to get the message to everyone in two days. We won't have much time, once we get back, even if we ride all night," Hans reflected, already forming in his mind a list of people who might help.

"Hans, I think we should also have a meeting in Saalfelden, where the people can come together to discuss these matters. I am so much more committed to this cause after hearing Hans Mosegger's sermon and talking with the other Protestants. I think you should preach to the people and inspire them, like Mosegger did in Schwarzach."

"I'm afraid I'm not the preacher Hans Mosegger is. You may be asking too much of me."

"Perhaps, but you could tell the people about what Mosegger and the others said and read them the statement we swore to."

"What about your doing all that? Why me?"

"Because you're the one everyone looks to. You've been our leader since your father died, and, besides, you're an inspiring speaker. Your prayer before that crowd today was very moving. And," he added jokingly, "you're better looking than I am. At least all of the women will pay attention to you."

"A lot of good that does me. I don't even have enough money to take a wife. I can't see how I'll ever be able to marry Maria, whom I love with all my heart. If you hadn't loaned me this horse, I'd be walking right now. It doesn't take much courage for me to defy the Archbishop because I don't have much to lose. It's different for you. You have children and possessions to think about."

"You could lose your life."

"I can think of no better way to die than defending the gospel of Jesus Christ."

9

Saalfelden, August 1731

Mamma Anna's fevered mind continued to dwell in the past, focusing on that sunny hillside meeting Hans and Johann had organized. They had knowingly defied the Archbishop's newest rule, which banned all public meetings of Protestants, and the people followed them. Hans had been eloquent as he preached as much of Mosegger's sermon as he could remember, adding his own thoughts when necessary.

Barbara and her girls were there with the new baby for Hans to baptize, which was also forbidden, but the people were getting tired of being told they could not practice their own religion. Mamma Anna was shocked when she saw Barbara's face covered with bruises and then realized what had probably happened. Anger swelled in her breast, but Barbara's smile helped hide the blue places, as she stood in the golden light.

She had not been smiling that way at the church when the priest baptized the baby last Sunday. Peter had insisted on that baptism, and Barbara had no choice but to go along. Everybody had been ordered to go to mass or risk being arrested, so Mamma Anna was there when they stood up to present the baby to the priest.

Barbara had been so afraid of the priest that it was impossible for her to experience any joy in the service. She had chosen not to wear around her neck the required scapular, which represented one of the religious orders, and she didn't take a rosary. She busied her hands with the baby to keep Father Jacob from noticing, but after the service was over, he stopped her at the door. She held the baby in front of her chest to hide the absence of a scapular, but he was not fooled.

"Frau Rohrmoser, you're not wearing a scapular, and you didn't say the rosary. Maybe with the new baby you've been so busy you're unaware of the new requirements." He spoke louder than necessary, as if wanting the Jesuit priest standing nearby to hear and know that he was trying to get his people to follow the rules. He was bothered by the intrusion of the Jesuits into his parish, as if the Capuchins were incompetent. It was the Jesuits who did not know these people as he did. He had been the parish priest here for years, baptizing, marrying, and burying the people. He knew they could be as stubborn as mules if you pushed them too far. It was better to try to persuade them to be faithful.

"Yes, Father, the baby has taken my mind off everything else," Barbara said meekly, not wanting a confrontation with the priest. Father Jacob then thrust a scapular and a rosary into her hand and said very sternly, "Now you know, Frau Rohrmoser. Let there be no more excuses. You don't want to get your family in trouble. Speaking of your family, I didn't see your brother Hans in church today." His voice became harsh and stern. "Is he back from his trip?"

Barbara was stunned, realizing that Father Jacob must be referring to Hans' trip to Schwarzach. The blood drained out of her face, and she stammered, "I, I, well, I expected him to be here for the christening of his niece. He must not be well."

Barbara looked around for Peter, but he had gone to get the wagon. Maria, who had been listening, moved beside Barbara and took her arm. Catherine and Gertrude circled her on the other side, shielding her from further questioning. Little Hans clung to her skirt, and they moved together away from the church to the wagon, where Peter was waiting.

"Not a word to Peter," Barbara said between her teeth, as the girls silently climbed into the back of the wagon. Barbara, holding the baby, sat up front, beside Peter.

No one said a word, not even the children who had overheard the priest angrily rebuking their mother. The wagon wound its way through the narrow streets of the lovely town. The stately buildings, with brightly-painted decorations, shone in the summer sun. Barbara was usually in awe of the many fine houses and buildings in Saalfelden, but today her eyes were filled with tears, and she struggled to keep from crying. This should be a happy occasion, but all she felt was fear, accompanied by anger and sadness. She longed to get out of the narrow, confining streets and into the open countryside, where she could lift her eyes up to the mountains.

The ordeal at the church had been too much for her in her weakened condition. She hated the inner conflict she experienced, with Peter and the priests on one side, and she and the Protestants on the other. Why could there not be religious freedom in Salzburg, as she had heard about in other places, like Augsburg, where both Catholics and Protestants could worship openly and freely? Oh, how she longed for such freedom.

Barbara knew that part of her anger came from having to submit this precious baby, her little Barbara, to a faith she did not share. Secretly, as she hugged the infant, she vowed to lead her into the Protestant faith as soon as she was old enough. She was grateful that her daughters from her first marriage, Gertrude, Catherine, and Maria, had committed themselves to the true gospel of Christ, but she had not dared teach her Rohrmoser boys to read the German Bible. At least she was not alone in her household. It broke her heart that she could not convince Peter to join the Protestants. She thought he might if it were not illegal. He just could not imagine doing anything against the law.

Peter drove the wagon, also in silence, for about a mile. Then he turned to her abruptly and said, "Where'd you get that scapular and rosary?"

"Where do you think?" Her words betrayed her inner turmoil.

"With the new laws, Father Jacob could have arrested you, you know. He's a kind man, but his patience is running out with you. Those Jesuits are breathing down his neck. Now wear the damn thing," he said harshly, and turned to the others in the back of the wagon. "That goes for all of you."

Tears ran down Barbara's face, but they flowed over a determination set into her features. She reached over the side of the wagon and dropped the cloth scapular and the rosary beads in the dust. Peter was staring straight ahead and did not see her do this. It never occurred to him that she would defy him in this way. Good wives did not do that, and Barbara was a good wife in most ways.

Catherine could not stifle a gasp, as she watched her mother's hand let go of the simple items that had become hated symbols of oppression. Her heart was sad, though, for she knew the price her mother would have to pay at her stepfather's hand when he discovered her disobedience.

Now, just a few days later, Barbara's heart filled with joy, as Hans took his niece in his arms and, reaching into a bowl of water, made the sign of the cross on her forehead, baptizing her in the name of the Father, the Son, and the Holy Ghost. Maria, Catherine, and Gertrude stood on either side of her during the simple ceremony, their arms around each other. It was the ending to a remarkable meeting of Protestants in Saalfelden. Hans dismissed the people with a benediction, and they began to gather up their quilts and picnic baskets to return home. Barbara packed the German Bible under the down pillow in little Barbara's cradle and settled her in it. Maria lifted it, and Barbara put her arms through the straps to carry the cradle on her back.

Horses being ridden very fast from the direction of Saalfelden were heard and then seen when they rounded a curve in the valley. They approached the people still gathered, some of whom sprinted for the trees up the mountainside, while most stood still, first out of curiosity, and then, as the party came nearer, in shock. There were four soldiers wearing unfamiliar uniforms and a Jesuit priest in his long, black robe.

Hans and Johann knew the soldiers must be some of the ones that had recently arrived in the province. Prince Archbishop Firmian had requested them from the Emperor to help put down what he was calling a peasant revolt. With them, also, was the local policeman whom everyone knew, Kaspar Hammerschmidt. The Protestants glared at Kaspar, disgusted that he had aligned himself with these outsiders.

The priest shouted for everyone to stand still. Hans instinctively moved quickly to Maria's side and took her hand. She looked at him with fear and panic in her eyes. He glanced from her eyes to Johann's, about ten feet away. Both men knew what was about to happen and that there was no escape. At least they had alerted the people, whom they were sure would stand firm.

"You all know that public gatherings are against the law," the priest shouted. "We should arrest and fine each one of you."

"Against the law, Father, to have a picnic on the hillside?" someone said. All heads turned to look at Mamma Anna, who dared to challenge the priest and soldiers. "We've always had picnics on this mountain in the summer. We didn't think the law meant we couldn't have a picnic." She sounded like a confused old woman, and the others joined her by nodding their heads and acting surprised at being under suspicion for doing something illegal.

The priest saw a gathering of ignorant peasants who were enjoying the sun in a charming setting, surrounded by tall, majestic mountains. His determination wavered, but then he consulted a list that he removed from his pocket. "I'm looking for two men. You tell me where they are, and I'll let the rest of you go home. But there will be no more picnics or any other meetings of peasants. I need Hans Burgsteiner and Johann Mosshamer."

Everyone froze, not knowing what to do but unwilling to betray Hans and Johann.

The priest looked at Kaspar Hammerschmidt. "Well, you know them. Are they here?"

"Yes, sir, over there." Kaspar pointed to Hans. "That one's Burgsteiner, and this one's Mosshamer." The people stared at Kaspar, and he knew they would never forgive him, but he had to do his duty.

"Seize those men," the priest shouted. Four soldiers grabbed Hans' and Johann's arms.

"No!" screamed Maria. She clawed at the soldier who had separated Hans from her. "No! Stop!" She hung on the soldier's arm, dragging it down with all her weight. The soldier jerked around, knocking her off balance, and backhanded a blow across her face.

"Shut up, bitch!" he yelled. Barbara ran up, holding on to the straps of the cradle, and started kicking the soldier who had hit Maria. Mamma Anna joined her. The surprised soldier let Hans go and ran away from the kicking women.

The other soldiers laughed at him. Furious, he grabbed a rope from his saddle and went back to tie Hans' hands behind his back. He tied the rope to his saddle and proceeded to drag Hans behind him, as he kicked his horse into a gallop.

Screams of protest followed him, as the peasants watched their leader stumble and fall, and felt with him the stones scraping the clothes and skin from his body.

Johann was treated better, being allowed to mount his own horse with his hands tied. A soldier led his horse as the group rode off, with Hans being dragged behind a galloping horse. Cries of "Judas" were heard amidst the yelling, and Kaspar knew they were intended for him.

Maria was on her knees, beating her fists on the ground in helpless frustration, unable to prevent the soldiers from taking Hans away.

"Catherine, take this cradle off my back," Barbara yelled. She struggled out of the harness, ignoring the crying baby, and took Maria in her arms. The women gathered around the prostrate Maria. A few feet away, another clump of women, relatives of Johann, clung together and picked up his three young, already-motherless children, now fatherless, too.

Maria sobbed hysterically. Barbara looked up at Mamma Anna. "Help me," she implored.

Mamma Anna took Maria by the elbow. "Stand up, child, before you make yourself sick," she said gruffly in her no-nonsense voice. Maria was taken aback enough to stand, and Mamma Anna walked her down the hill toward the road. She knew that movement was the best way to help someone get back in control. Barbara, nearly as despairing as Maria after seeing her brother taken, took her other arm. Catherine and Gertrude each picked up an end of the cradle, and the five women walked back along the rocky road to the Rohrmoser farm.

10

On Board the *Purysburg*, 1734

Mamma Anna felt cool wetness on her aching forehead. She opened her eyes when Maria removed the damp cloth from her face. The motion of the ship and the nauseating smell of human waste made her feel sick, and she swallowed to keep from heaving.

"Mamma Anna, are you awake?" Maria asked softly. She placed her hand on the fevered brow to test the intensity of the heat. It did seem to be slightly cooler.

"Is that you, Maria?" Her throat filled with phlegm, and she coughed so deeply that she grabbed her chest with bandaged hands, as pain encased it.

"Yes, Mamma Anna. It's me. Don't try to talk yet. Just rest. Now that you're awake, I'll get Barbara to bring you some soup. You gave us quite a scare. We weren't sure you would ever wake up." She motioned to Gertrude, who stood hovering in the curtained doorway. Gertrude ran off to find Barbara and Catherine.

A spasm of coughing shook her again. Maria recognized the sure sound of pneumonia, and a worried look came over her face. Mamma Anna's old body, already weakened by scurvy, had not fared the ravages of the storm well at all. Maria tried to remember the remedies Mamma Anna had used to cure Gertrude when she had pneumonia. She had watched her prepare the poultice for the chest and the hot teas. She began rummaging in Mamma Anna's basket that hung from a hook until she found the small packages of dried herbs that smelled and looked like the right ones.

"Mamma Anna, you may have a touch of pneumonia. Can you tell me if these are the right herbs to make a poultice, and these for tea?" She held the packages, one at a time, for her to see. Mamma Anna nodded her head in assent to all but one. Maria smiled and returned one of the packages to the basket.

"You just rest, and we'll make you well, just like you did Gertrude. I remember what you said to Gertrude. You told her she had to want to get well. Do you want to get well?"

Mamma Anna closed her eyes as if to think about that one. Did she want to get well? She wasn't sure. Maybe she had lived long enough in this vale of tears. The pastors were right about one thing. Life was a vale of tears.

Not getting a response to her question, Maria said, "Mamma Anna, you've got to want to get well. I don't know what we'd do without you. I couldn't have gotten through that awful time after Hans and Johann were arrested without you."

Barbara rushed in with Gertrude and Catherine.

"She's gone back to sleep."

"Did she know you?" Barbara asked in a whisper.

"Yes, and she was even able to tell me what herbs to use. I think she has pneumonia." Barbara put her ear to the chest cavity and listened to the raspy breathing. "It sounds like Gertrude's did."

"We need to make a tea out of these." Maria held up one of the cloth-wrapped packages. "And a poultice with these."

"That's not easy on this boat. Captain Fry won't let us near the galley. I'll see if Pastor Boltzius or Mr. Zwiffler can help us."

Mamma Anna groaned and tried to say something. She shook her head from side to side. "Not Zwiffler," she managed to say.

The women knew that Mamma Anna had a deep distrust of the apothecary, who had joined the Salzburgers in Rotterdam. She did not agree with his methods of treating the sick with leeches and cupping.

"Don't worry, dear. We won't let him bleed you," Barbara said, relieved that Mamma Anna was conscious of what was happening.

"Deutsch," Mamma Anna said weakly.

"What?" Barbara asked. She turned to the others in the compartment. "What did she say?" No one had understood.

Another coughing spell ended any further attempts to talk, and soon Mamma Anna slept again.

In her worry about Mamma Anna, Maria began to think about that awful time after the arrests of Hans and Johann. Maria had been the one who did not want to live then. She could hardly imagine what terrible things might have happened to them. The only thing Mamma Anna had been able to find out through her network of informers was that the two had been marched to Salzburg, along with other men from the province who had been identified as leaders of the peasant revolt. Everyone assumed they had been imprisoned in the Hohensalzburg, the fortress that towered over the city of Salzburg, but they were unable to find out for sure.

11

Salzburg, September 1731

"So this is Salzburg," Hans thought, as the soldiers marched the prisoners through the narrow streets lined with shops. The buildings seemed to close in on him when he could not see the sky without turning his head straight up.

They reached an open plaza, where richly dressed patrons sat on elegant balconies, drinking coffee and eating pastries. Looming before them was the mountain with the fortress on top, brooding over the city. That gray stone fortress had been visible for hours, as they marched across the country-side toward Salzburg.

People lined the streets, jeering and laughing at the prisoners, who paraded through the plaza. Fine carriages made little attempt to avoid the captives, scraping them as they hurried by.

Undaunted, the men began to sing, "A mighty fortress is our God, a bulwark never failing."

Their feet in heavy, cobbled shoes pounded the stone plaza in the ponderous rhythm of Luther's great hymn of faith. Echoing around the city, the singing gave the men courage to lift their heads and straighten their shoulders. The hymn was a testimony that they were not criminals, but were only seeking religious freedom.

Johann, walking behind Hans, wondered if Martin Luther had this mighty, Salzburg fortress in mind when he composed those words. He hoped God was mightier than that forbidding-looking structure.

"Kill the heretics!" shouted an overweight man with a flushed face, circled by a lace collar and white wig, leaning from one of the balconies. The whole crowd picked up the line, drowning out the singing. A shouting match ensued, with the Lutherans yelling back to their accusers, "You cannot damn what you cannot create. Only God can create."

The chained men began to feel real terror as the frenzied

mob surrounded them. Stones were hurled, but the soldiers made no effort to protect them when the street hoodlums began to push and shove. The men bore the insults with a calm dignity, remembering others who had been so persecuted. Martin Luther himself had been imprisoned and exiled; Martin Lodinger from Hofgastein, exiled; Georg Scherer, beheaded and burned; and in their own lifetime, Joseph Schaitberger had been exiled.

Hans also recalled that Paul had been imprisoned for his faith, and, of course, Jesus himself had once walked through the streets of Jerusalem, jeered by the crowd on the way to his crucifixion. If they had had the courage to stand firm and not waver in their faith, then perhaps he could, too. What better way to be welcomed into Heaven than as a martyr for the gospel?

From the window of his ornately-decorated Residenz, Firmian, both the Prince and Archbishop of the Province of Salzburg, stood with Chancellor von Rall, watching the double line of prisoners file past the Cathedral and begin climbing the stone steps leading up the mountain to the fortress.

"What are they singing?" Firmian asked.

"One of Martin Luther's songs," replied von Rall. "That does not prove they are Lutherans, however. Lutheran ministers have been forbidden in Salzburg for a hundred years. These peasants can't read and write, much less learn a Lutheran catechism or confession. Look how they're dressed in those baggy pants, bright green hats, and blue stockings. They look ridiculous."

"One would expect the leaders of a revolt to look more respectable. Are you sure these are the leaders? I can't imagine anyone following these ragged creatures."

"Your spies at the Schwarzach meeting named the men who swore to resist you. These are the ones who were tracked down and arrested."

"If these arrests don't stop the unrest and dissension, I'll expel all who refuse to give up this foolishness. They must obey the laws of the State and the Church. They must! I'm not having any peasant wars during my reign, and I won't have it on my conscience that I allowed heresy to go unpunished. They'll be obedient, or they'll leave. When you eliminate the leaders, you end the revolt."

"You remember, sir, that, although the Treaty of Westphalia allows the Prince of the land to decide what religion the people will follow, it requires three-years notice before expulsion. How are you going to get around that?"

"I can't wait three years. I mean to do this now. They could start all kinds of trouble in three years. Impossible! I have other things to worry about besides the resistance of a few troublemakers. Read that treaty again, and see if you can come up with some way to circumvent the three-year requirement. If not, I may do it anyway. The Pope can hardly complain, and the Emperor is so afraid that I won't support his pragmatic sanction to permit his daughter to succeed him, that he's no problem. He's already sent his troops to help stop the rebellion, so he's committed. I'm not very worried about the Protestant princes in the Empire, either. They aren't likely to risk war over our peasant uprising. And Friedrich Wilhelm in Prussia has indicated he will take Protestants to farm his land in return for our trade. He's hoping to break the power of the guilds in Prussia."

The dark, Italian-looking Chancellor from the Tyrol leaned over the polished, gold-inlaid table, not daring to sit down while the Prince was standing. "Here's one possibility, your Excellency," von Rall said, looking up from a copy of the treaty. "It only provides a three-year notice for expulsion of Lutherans and Calvinists. Since these peasants have had no Protestant ministers for a hundred years, how can they be considered Lutherans or Calvinists?"

"Brilliant, von Rall, brilliant." Firmian turned away from the unpleasant sight of the dirty prisoners struggling up Monks Mountain. "That's the answer."

He sat down on the red velvet cushion in his elaborately carved chair and tented his hands in his characteristic thinking posture, staring at the intricate gold filigree on the molded ceiling. "Tell the Jesuit priests that I want a house-to-house visitation to find out who the loyal Catholics are. I want the name of everyone who will not swear to keep the church laws. With the leaders out of the way, I think the people will begin to submit. The simple folks have just been excited by some troublemakers. And tell the local administrators to punish every infraction of the church or civil law."

"Yes, your Excellency."

"Is there anything more about this that I need to attend to?"

"Your Excellency, Bishop Michael is waiting to see you. He is creating a howl about your inviting the Jesuits in to order around the parish priests."

"I don't want to see him just now. Let him get the message indirectly that I wouldn't have called in the Jesuits if the Capuchins hadn't been so lenient with the malcontents. They allowed the people to break the church laws right and left. I know the Jesuits; I was trained with them. They'll carry out their duties with strictness and severity. Bishop Michael should be grateful for this help. Let the people hate the Jesuits instead of the Capuchins."

"Good point, your Excellency."

"Also, send around a case of my French wine for the good Bishop. That should smooth his ruffled feathers and keep him occupied while I clean out this rats' nest."

"Shall I travel back to the Pongau to continue the commissions?"

"Yes, but before you do, check to be sure the situation in the Hohensalzburg is under control. I want each prisoner questioned to find out who else is causing this uprising. If they won't talk, tell them to use whatever encouragement is necessary to make them speak. Is that clear?"

"Yes, Excellency. Is there anything else?"

"Order my carriage. I'll be riding out to Klessheim."

"Yes, your Excellency." Von Rall knew that meant he was to send a messenger to Klessheim Palace to notify the nobleman's wife that the Prince was making a visit. He also knew that the lady's husband had been directed to Hellbrun to prepare for a hunt.

* * *

As Hans struggled up the steps to the fortress, he began to feel panic crawl over him like an army of ants. I mustn't be afraid. God is with me, he said to himself, but his body was responding to a fear more visceral than his mind could control. Still weak from the injuries he sustained when he was dragged behind the horse at the time of his arrest, his legs gave way, and he stumbled, rattling the chains. About halfway up, when he failed to lift his left foot high enough to make the next step, Johann, walking behind him, fell over him. As they scrambled to right themselves, Hans noticed tears on Johann's face. He took comfort in the fact that he was not the only one struggling for courage.

He began to think of fear as a physical thing that could be stomped into the stone and pushed down. Concentrating on his feet calmed him. He knew the panic was still there, however, and might return at any minute.

At the top of the steps, the prisoners were herded into a level area that overlooked the city. It was a lovely sight, with the Salzach River winding through the ancient, medieval town. At that moment, the bell in the Cathedral tower just below rang the hour, twelve o'clock. The boom, boom of the bell as it reverberated off the mountain matched the heartbeat Hans could feel in his chest. As he looked at his fellow prisoners, he saw familiar faces. They all looked as frightened as he felt.

"God is with us," he heard himself saying firmly. There were nods of agreement among the men.

"Silence," a soldier said brusquely, and hit Hans in the chest with his fist. Hans did not lose his balance, but he again felt the beginning of panic when his helplessness was made more apparent to him. He lifted his eyes toward the exquisite blue sky. He wanted to drink in that blueness, knowing there would be no blue sky in the dungeon where they were going.

The line of prisoners was led single-file through a lime-
stone passageway that was very narrow, and they descended
a winding, circular stone staircase that made Hans dizzy
when he looked down. As they passed through the passageway, they could hear the screams of someone being tortured.
A heavy door opened, and the men entered the dungeon.
The stench of human excrement hit them in the face like the
force of a solid wall. The room felt like a stinking tomb to
Hans, as his eyes slowly adjusted to the darkness. The walls,
floor, and ceiling were all hard, damp, thick stone. A grate
in the ceiling admitted the only light, along with the sounds
of screaming and moaning.

The dungeon was already filled with men. Hans and Johann looked for a place to sit against the slimy wall but saw
that all available space was taken.   Suddenly, the door
clanged shut, and the bolt slid into place. A chill ran up
Hans' spine when he heard the door slam. He wondered if he
would ever again be free.

After looking around at the staring faces, Hans was overcome with exhaustion, both physical and emotional, as he
realized that he was really in prison. He sat down beside Johann on the floor, wet with urine, and put his head on his
knees. He covered his ears, as the screaming overhead continued, and his body shook involuntarily.

After a long while, he felt a hand on his shoulder. "You
don't get used to the screaming, but you do learn to live with
it."

Hans looked up and saw a face that he recognized but, in
his confusion, could not quite place.

"I'm Hans Lerchner, and the man upstairs in the torture
room is Viet Breme. I believe we met at Schwarzach."

"Ah, yes. So we meet again. I'm Hans Burgsteiner, from
Saalfelden. And this is Johann Mosshamer, also from Saalfelden."

"Perhaps you'd like to join us in praying for Viet. It helps
when you're on the rack to know that the others are praying
for you."

Hans nodded his head. "Yes, of course."

As he looked around, he realized that most of the men against the walls had their eyes closed and were silently praying. They were dressed much like he was, in Alpine peasant attire, but two men in the corner had long hair and beards, with little round black hats on their heads. They rocked back and forth while they prayed.

Then he saw that some of the men in filthy rags were just sleeping. He supposed they must be real criminals.

Hans tried to focus his whirling brain into prayer, and finally he was able to think about Viet Breme and ask God to comfort and give him strength.

Suddenly, the screaming stopped, and footsteps were heard clumping down the stairs. The door squeaked open, and Viet was shoved into the room. He lay crumpled on the floor, unconscious. Hans Lerchner knelt down beside him, carefully straightened out the tortured body, and sat down, with Viet's forehead resting on his leg. After listening to Viet's heart, he nodded his head to the others and whispered, "He's alive."

With his attention focused on Viet, Hans did not notice the soldiers approaching him. Without a word, they grabbed him by the arms and led him out and up the steps to the room above the dungeon.

It was a small room with a wooden wheel on one wall. On the opposite, blood-spattered wall were two iron chains fastened to the stone above head level, about five feet apart. The soldiers pushed Hans' face against the wall, stripped off his shirt, and clamped his wrists in the bracelets at the ends of the chains. His arms were stretched further than they had ever been before, and his feet hung short of the floor.

The door opened, and Hans heard someone enter. "Hans Burgsteiner, do you recant?"

"No."

"Who else is involved in leading this peasant rebellion in Saalfelden?"

"There is no rebellion. We just want to worship God following the gospels, not the Pope."

"Is that all you have to say?"

"Yes."

When his questioner left, a soldier began beating him across the back with a heavy, knotted leather whip.

Hans heard his voice yelling as the leather struck him, but he felt disconnected from that scream. It was as if it were coming from somewhere outside himself. The screaming went on and on.

"Stop! Stop! Please, somebody stop this. I just got here. I'm not ready." He felt each lash like fire burning through his flesh, but his pleading was ignored. His recent fear of imprisonment and torture began to turn into a deep rage as his body endured this punishment, and he ceased screaming. He heard the thud of the cutting leather and the sound of his own blood coursing through his ears against the background of the strains of a hymn floating up from the dungeon below. He remembered that he was here to be faithful to God, and he focused on that, clenching his teeth to silence his voice.

The door opened, and someone came in, but he could not see who, with his face against the wall.

The soldier stopped beating him and took his wrists out of the bracelets. Hans crumpled to the floor in a pool of blood, his and that of others who had preceded him. A tall, gaunt, black-robed priest with dark circles under his eyes stood in front of him.

"Hans Burgsteiner, have you had enough? Are you ready to forget this foolish dissension and become a faithful Catholic?"

Hans was so confused that he made no response.

The priest nodded to the soldier, who slapped Hans across the face, causing a nose bleed to spurt down his chest.

"Hans Burgsteiner, do you recant the Lutheran heresy and accept the Holy Catholic Church as the one true church?"

"No, Father, I don't," Hans gasped, barely able to speak but determined to state his position. "I made an oath to be faithful to the Protestant faith, and no amount of torture will change my mind." He paused, trying to get a good breath of air. "There's no point in wasting your time. Our Lord Jesus Christ went through worse for the love of God. I can do no other."

"You will, my son, you will." The priest turned to the waiting soldiers. "Send him down to think about it. Bring in another one."

Hans was shoved down the steps and back through the dungeon door. He stumbled but did not fall down. Ignoring the men who crowded around him, he lay down on his stomach and rested his head on his crossed arms. He had never been in such misery in his life, or even imagined it.

"Hans, are you alive?" Johann asked. A groan followed this question. "At least he's alive," Johann said brokenly.

"Keep talking to him, son. He'll come around afterwhile. It's always good to hear a familiar voice."

Johann turned to see who was speaking and recognized Hans Mosegger's white hair. "Oh, sir, not you, too. I can't believe they would arrest you."

"But of course they arrested me."

"Have you been tortured like Hans?"

The old man answered quietly, "No, not yet. They threaten me with the torture of others. I don't know which is crueler."

"Johann?" Hans turned his head on the urine-soaked floor.

"Yes, Hans, I'm right here. Rest your face on my leg." He carefully raised Hans' head and cradled it on his lap.

"Johann, I didn't recant. I stood firm."

"Thank God, Hans, and thank God you're still alive."

"You did what God requires of all of us, to be faithful, to never submit to a heretical religion." Herr Mosegger placed his hand on Hans' head, then returned to his place against the wall.

"Do you know who that was, Hans?" Johann asked excitedly. Receiving no response, he went on. "That was Hans Mosegger, the great preacher we heard at Schwarzach." He wasn't sure Hans had heard him, for he seemed to be asleep.

The screeching overhead began again, and the Protestants who were able began to sing. Hans lapsed into unconsciousness, while his wounds continued to bleed on his friend's blue pants. Feeling the warm liquid on his leg, Johann took his shirt and tried to staunch the flow from one deep cut that continued to ooze.

He felt something brush by him and saw a large rat attracted by fresh blood. He spent the next twenty-four hours holding his friend and knocking away the rats. A pot of thin soup made of flour and water was brought in once, but Johann did not get any. It was gone before he could rearrange Hans, borrow a cup, and get to it. He had no appetite anyway, but he knew he should eat to keep up his strength.

Hans stirred occasionally but soon slept again. Johann could feel fever in Hans' body but was helpless to treat him. He almost envied Hans' escape into unconsciousness. His envy intensified when the soldiers came to get him.

As Hans lay on the dungeon floor, dreaming of Maria at sunset, Johann was undergoing his test of endurance. As Hans puzzled over why Maria did not respond to his calls, Johann implored God to give him the strength to resist his tormentors.

12

On Board the *Purysburg*, 1734

"Wake up, Mamma Anna, wake up. I have some soup for you." Maria shook the flabby old woman until her eyes opened. "Pastor Boltzius talked the Captain into giving you this soup."

The women had become very upset when Captain Fry would not allow them to make tea or prepare a poultice for the sick people. He only allowed the Salzburgers to have one meal of tough salt beef or pork, one piece of bread, and two cups of foul-tasting water a day. Commissioner von Reck, a youthful German nobleman, was supposed to make all the arrangements for the Salzburgers with the Captain, but being young and inexperienced and eating well from the Captain's mess himself, he had not presented their case forcefully enough in the eyes of the pastors and the Salzburgers.

The more mature and compassionate Pastor Martin Boltzius, who had seen provisions placed on board for the Salzburgers, decided to intervene, although it overstepped his authority as only the spiritual leader of the group. The Captain's excuse for mistreating the religious refugees was that the Georgia Trustees had ordered him to deliver those provisions to Savannah, and he had stored them where they could not be reached.

Who was right about orders was irrelevant to Pastor Boltzius, as he watched the people become swollen, covered with sores, and weakened with bloody dysentery. Lorentz Huber was even delirious. If their situation did not improve, they would not all survive the voyage.

The Captain had relented enough to provide a flour and water mush for the babies and the sick, and this was the concoction, along with the healing herbs Maria had added, that she was trying to feed Mamma Anna.

Barbara held up Mamma Anna's head, and Maria spooned

in the tasteless mixture, the first food she had eaten in the three days since the storm.

"I have some wine Pastor Boltzius sent you. Now drink some of this."

"The Pastor sent me wine?"

"Yes. He sent wine from his private store to all the sick people, so you won't have to drink that stinking water."

"Imagine that."

The food and drink fully awakened Mamma Anna, and she looked around the tiny compartment sectioned off by dirty gray, canvas curtains.

"How are you feeling?" Barbara asked.

"Terrible. It hurts to breathe. How is everyone else? Is the storm over?"

"Yes, the sun's shining today. Mr. Huber is very sick. Mr. Zwiffler is caring for him."

"What about Catherine? She was lying on the deck after the storm."

"Oh, she's fine, just fretting about a sore on her mouth because it ruins her looks. The girls and almost everyone else are up on the deck enjoying the warm sunshine."

"Where's Deutsch?"

"Who?"

"Deutsch, the sailor who saved my life during the storm. He caught my arm and held me all night. The one with the scarred face."

Barbara covered her mouth with her hand in alarm. "Oh, him. He stopped me on deck and asked about the old woman, but I didn't know what he meant, and he frightened me so that I hurried away."

"He is a sight, isn't he? Scared me, I can tell you, when I opened my eyes and saw that gruesome image staring at me. Thought I'd died and gone to Hell for sure." Mamma Anna began coughing from deep in her chest.

"That poultice didn't work as well without boiling water. I held a cup over the candle, but I couldn't get it to boil. Even so, you're looking better today. Now finish this mush."

"Ugh" was Mamma Anna's response, as she ate another mouthful of the lumpy soup. "Not as good as your potato soup, Barbara."

"I wish I could make some for you, and the rest of us, too, but at least God kept us safe through the storm, and the ship was able to be repaired."

"Yeah, so we could starve to death," Maria said, with uncharacteristic bitterness.

Barbara and Maria sat down on the opposite bunk, and the three women lapsed into silence, each retreating into herself, as each one contemplated the circumstances. Barbara picked up her Bible and began thumbing through it to find a passage that might comfort Mamma Anna and Maria. She selected Luke, who of all the gospel writers seemed to speak to her best. She began with Chapter 13:10 and began to read aloud, squinting to see the words in the near darkness, lighted only by a taper in the passageway.

"Now he was teaching in one of the synagogues on the Sabbath. And there was a woman who had had a spirit of infirmity for eighteen years; she was bent over and could not fully straighten herself. And when Jesus saw her, he called and said to her, 'Woman, you are freed from your infirmity.' And he laid his hands upon her, and immediately she was made straight, and she praised God. But the ruler of the synagogue, indignant because Jesus had healed on the Sabbath, said to the people, 'There are six days on which work ought to be done; come on those days and be healed, and not on the Sabbath day.' Then the Lord answered him, 'You hypocrites! Does not each of you on the Sabbath untie his ox or his ass from the manger and lead it away to water it? And ought not this woman, a daughter of Abraham whom Satan bound for eighteen years, be loosed from this bond on the Sabbath day?'

"He said therefore, 'What is the kingdom of God like? It is like a grain of mustard seed, which a man took and sowed in his garden; and it grew and became a tree, and the birds of the air made nests in its branches.'

"And again he said, 'To what shall I compare the kingdom of God? It is like leaven, which a woman took and hid in three measures of meal, till it was all leavened.'"

"Do you really think Jesus would care about an old, sick woman like me, Barbara?"

"I'm sure of it, Mamma Anna."

"I haven't been too interested in all that pious stuff the pastors are always preaching, but I do admire Jesus. He broke the rules sometimes in order to help people. I like that in a person. It was all those rules the Papists tried to shove down our throats that caused so much misery. I've spent most of my life trying to heal people. I just can't understand what would make a person hurt someone like they did, torturing our boys in that prison in Salzburg."

"They crucified Jesus, too."

"What is it that makes people so cruel?" Maria asked. She started weeping softly, remembering that terrible time after Hans was arrested.

13

Saalfelden, October 1731

Maria and Barbara crunched through a red and gold tunnel of leaves as they walked along the forest path. They soon arrived at Mamma Anna's cottage and knocked on the closed door. No one answered. Barbara opened the door of the one-room log house. She took the heavy cradle from her back and set it down gently, careful not to disturb the sleeping baby.

"She must have been called out on a case," Maria said despondently. "There's no telling when she might return."

Barbara looked around. Mamma Anna's cottage was arranged differently from most Salzburg rooms. The rusty-red table was not in a corner with a crucifix hanging on the wall behind it, but was in the center of the room. Her small wooden bed, covered with a colorful patchwork quilt, stood against the wall opposite the door, and a bench was built along the wall, which turned the corner and stopped at the stone fireplace. The tiny cupboard on the wall opposite the fireplace held a few mismatched crockery cups and bowls, and spoons carved from wood.

A black iron kettle and an iron pot sitting on legs were in the open fireplace, where a few coals still showed a faint red glow. Bundles of twigs and branches picked up in the forest were stacked beside the hearth.

Hanging upside down from the ceiling were bunches of herbs drying, filling the chilly room with a spicy fragrance. The flooring was made of rough boards inexpertly fitted, as if she had laid them herself from odd scraps of split wood. A water bucket and wooden dipper sat on the bench.

The two small windows had no curtains, but a round rag rug made from scraps of wool of different colors was on the uneven floor near the fireplace. The colors blended with the quilt on the bed, patchworked from identical materials. On the table was a dried arrangement of yellow, blue, red, and white wild flowers in an old, cracked porcelain vase, which someone must have discarded. The effect was simple and inviting, though far poorer than the Rohrmoser farmhouse.

"Well, let's make some tea while we wait. She won't mind." Barbara began building up the fire from the hot coals on the hearth. The air was getting colder as the day progressed. They had come this long way to find out if Mamma Anna had heard any news of Hans since his arrest. In her travels from house to house, nursing the sick, she was often the one who heard and passed along information. They had also come for something to help Barbara's tooth, which had been hurting for several days. The toothache was the only reason they had given Peter. He had been angry with them since their return with a prostrate Maria on the evening Hans and Johann had been arrested. They dared not discuss Hans with him.

Maria looked around with some apprehension. She had heard whispers that Mamma Anna was a witch, since she was an old crone who lived alone in the forest and knew the mysteries of the herbs. Barbara had scoffed at such nonsense, saying that she lived alone because her family had all died, and she was a midwife and herbalist because it was the only way she could make enough to live. Still, she was a strange old woman who went around muttering to herself.

As they waited, they talked quietly to avoid disturbing the baby. Barbara carefully took the Bible out of the cradle where she had carried it and began to read aloud. She skipped over the words she did not know, but the story was so familiar that she added what was missing. She read about the Last Supper, the crucifixion, and the women finding the empty tomb. She ended by saying, "If God can give up his son for us, then we must be willing to give up our loved ones for God. Maria, we must accept whatever has happened to Hans as God's will."

"I know, Barbara, and I am praying constantly to have that kind of faith, but I need to know what has happened to him. I wish my faith were as strong as yours. Help me. Pray with me."

The two women knelt on the rug with their elbows resting on their chairs. "O God," Barbara began, "not our wills, but thine be done. Give Hans the courage to stand forever in the faith, no matter what happens. Give us the faith to trust in thee and accept thy will with grateful hearts. We know this life is just a trial. May we gladly pass the test and look forward to life eternal with thee in Heaven. O Jesus, hear our humble prayers. May thy blessing be on all those imprisoned in your name, especially our beloved Hans."

The sun was slanting low in the west when the baby cried, ending their praying and Bible study. It was rare that they had time for such long devotions, for they could not read the Bible when Peter was at home, and there was little time, anyway, with all the work that had to be done.

"We'll have to stay here tonight, but we must go home tomorrow, even if Mamma Anna hasn't come back. Peter will already be upset that we didn't get back today, although I told him we might not. He's very suspicious of me after all that's happened."

Suddenly, Mamma Anna appeared at the door.

"Oh," Barbara jumped with surprise. "I didn't hear you coming."

"I saw someone here and walked silently to see who it was before coming in," said Mamma Anna. "How's that baby? She's not sick, is she?" she asked, smiling at the baby sucking at Barbara's breast.

"She's growing very fast and has not been sick once, but I have a toothache I thought you might help me with."

"I just came from the Schmidts' farm, where their two-month-old baby died. She was sickly from the start. God's will, they said."

Maria could hardly hold back her questions about Hans while Mamma Anna talked about the baby's death. Finally, Barbara, aware of Maria's eagerness and her own, interrupted a pause in Mamma Anna's monologue.

"Mamma Anna, have you heard any news about Hans since his arrest?"

"Now don't you know I'd have come to tell you if I had. All I know is that they held him and Johann overnight in Saalfelden, and then marched them, along with some others, up toward Salzburg. Nobody's heard anything since. I figured you knew that much."

"He was able to walk after being dragged by that horse?" Maria asked, her voice almost cracking.

"I guess so if he marched out of Saalfelden," Mamma Anna replied gently.

"Do you know anyone who goes to Salzburg who could find out where he is?" asked Barbara.

Mamma Anna looked up suspiciously. She was naturally secretive about what she knew, partly to make people think she knew more than she did, but also to encourage people to trust her with their secrets.

"It's not a place most people want to be going these days," she hedged. "No, I don't believe I know anyone headed that way that I would trust. Plenty of priests and soldiers going back and forth, if you want to ask them," she chuckled. She continued more seriously. "I suspect the Protestants are being held in the fortress in Salzburg. I saw it once, sitting high on the mountain overlooking the city and the river. It looked very hard, all that stone. There'd be no escaping from that place."

Realizing that her words had further upset Maria, she said reassuringly, "Come with me, child. We'll get some more wood for the fire before it gets dark." The two women walked outside, Maria pulling on her woolen coat. "I saw a big limb on the ground back this way the other day, but it was too big for me to carry alone. I needed some strong, young person to help me out, and now you've showed up."

Maria followed Mamma Anna into the forest, dodging the branches, since they were not on a path that she could see. The older woman, though, seemed perfectly at home, pointing out where the fox lived and the crows nested.

"There wouldn't be anything else bothering you, would there?" Mamma Anna asked abruptly. "You don't have to hesitate to tell me if you're pregnant or something. You may not want to talk about it in front of Barbara, but I know you and Hans have been sweethearts for a long time, and I know human nature."

"Oh, Mamma Anna, I'm so scared," Maria blurted out, and then started crying.

"So, I'm not far off the mark, am I? Well, if you're pregnant, crying won't change anything. When was your last bleeding time?"

"I'm a month late," Maria said desperately.

"Well, it could be that getting upset about everything has caused you to be late, but it could be the other."

"Mamma Anna, it may sound crazy, but I sometimes hope I have Hans' child growing in me. Then, at other times, I'm so frightened that I don't know what to do."

"Well, child, you're not the first and won't be the last to feel that way, but if you came to me to give you something to kill a baby, if there is a baby, I'm telling you right now, I won't do it. You're strong and healthy and would make a good mother, even in these circumstances. I think Hans would never forgive us if we killed his child."

A sense of relief flooded through Maria when the decision was lifted from her. She had half-wanted Mamma Anna to give her some potion or something.

Mamma Anna went on, "Have you been sick? Have your breasts swelled up?"

"No."

"Well, I'm not always right, but I think it may just be the scaredness that's making you late. You don't have that special look of a pregnant woman. Here's our limb. Grab that end, and let's get back before the sun leaves us completely."

Later that evening, Mamma Anna held a candle and examined Barbara's sore tooth. "All I know to do is pull it, and it's one of your front teeth. It won't help your smile any. Does it hurt that bad?"

"No, I don't think so."

"I'll make a tea that should ease the pain, but it will come back, I'm afraid."

After they had eaten the simple meal of bread, cheese, and cold potatoes, which Maria had brought in her basket, silence settled over the three women. Each one stared into the fire, thinking her own thoughts. Finally, Maria asked hesitantly, "Can you really explain what dreams mean, Mamma Anna, like people say you can?"

"Sometimes, child, sometimes, but there's never any knowing for sure, although occasionally I've been proven right. What was your dream?"

"A few nights ago, I dreamed that Hans was screaming and was lying as if dead in a tomb-like place. I can't shake this dream off. It seemed so real. Then another night, I dreamed that Hans was calling to me, just calling and calling my name. Do these dreams mean that Hans is dead and has passed over into Heaven?"

Maria looked up at the old woman with such pleading in her eyes. Mamma Anna searched her face as if trying to read what was in her heart. Then she shifted her gaze to Barbara, who was watching them.

"Can I trust both of you never to tell a living soul what I say or do tonight?" she asked with great solemnity.

Maria felt an unnatural chill run up her spine, and she looked at Barbara with raised eyebrows, silently asking her how to answer the question. They nodded to each other and then pledged their silence, each expecting to hear news from Salzburg that must be dangerous.

Instead, Mamma Anna began walking around the one-room cabin, sprinkling water and chanting too softly to be understood. She then stood in the center of the room by the table and faced first north, then east, south, and west, raising her hands each time and continuing to chant. In a calm, peaceful voice, she asked Barbara and Maria to sit in a circle with her. They moved their chairs up to the table.

Barbara and Maria were both wondering if perhaps Mamma Anna really was a witch. They were not sure they should cooperate, but neither wanted to break the peaceful atmosphere that had encircled the three women. Even the baby lay quietly in Barbara's arms, watching Mamma Anna.

In a whispery voice, Mamma Anna said, "Maria, Barbara, my grandmother and her grandmother and her grandmother, and all of the grandmothers back to the time the Celtic tribes lived in this valley taught me the old religion. If you're willing, I can ask the old Grandmother to tell us tonight if Hans has passed over into the other life, or is still in this one."

"Who is the old Grandmother? Is she a witch? Why can't you ask God?" Maria asked skeptically.

"I can do what I was taught to do. I don't know who the old Grandmother is, but I know her power. You'll have to go to a priest or a pastor to contact God. I can do only what I was taught. My grandmother, the one who taught me mid-wifing, once told me that I was the one selected to talk to the Grandmother, and she taught me how to do it. Do you want me to continue?"

Maria looked at Barbara. She was sitting very still, her head bowed and her eyes closed. Maria nodded to Mamma Anna to continue.

Mamma Anna placed Barbara's Bible on the table. "Here, put your hands on this if you are afraid of the Grandmother. She won't mind. That way you'll know she's not the Devil."

Maria placed her hands on the Bible, but noticed that Barbara did not. Instead, she softly caressed the baby's arms.

Mamma Anna closed her eyes and began to breathe deeply. She sat that way for a long while as the fire began to die down in the fireplace. Barbara also sat with her eyes closed. Maria looked from one to the other, wondering what to do. She did nothing but felt drawn into the silent circle.

When there were only coals glowing in the fireplace, Mamma Anna opened her eyes. Her face was still and relaxed, like a person just waking from sleep. She looked at Maria with compassion in her eyes, but said nothing.

"Did the Grandmother tell you anything?" Maria asked, after a long wait.

"I'm not sure. She said to listen to your dreams."

"Is that all? Does that mean that Hans is still alive?"

"I don't know. Sometimes messages from the other side are in the form of a puzzle. My advice is to listen to your dreams." Mamma Anna then stood up abruptly and laid quilts, which she took from an old chest, on the rug in front of the fire. Barbara and Maria lay down, with the baby's cradle next to Barbara, and Mamma Anna retired to her bed. In a few minutes, she was snoring.

Maria lay awake for a long time, wondering. Then she slept more peacefully than she had since the arrest.

Barbara woke during the night with a start. She had dreamed that Maria, Gertrude, and Catherine were sitting in a church with a Protestant cross, and she was watching from the outside. It was a flat land, with large trees that had strange, gray hair, like a host of grandmothers, and there was a mist-covered river nearby. She could not shake the reality of the dream or the sense of happiness that pervaded her. She closed her eyes and tried to recapture the dream, but it was gone.

When Barbara opened her eyes the next morning, Maria was on her hands and knees, scrubbing away at a dark red stain on the rug where she had slept.

Mamma Anna's cackle of a laugh sliced the air, and soon all three women were laughing hysterically, though none could say what she was laughing about. Nothing was ever said about the blood on Maria's skirt. Mamma Anna just gave her some old rags, which she put in place, and turned her skirt around so that the stain was under her apron. As they sat around the table, sipping tea with their bread and cheese, Mamma Anna asked, "Did you have a dream last night?"

A look of disappointment moved over Maria's face when she realized she had not dreamed anything she could remember. "No, I thought sure I would, but I didn't."

"Well, I had a strange dream," Barbara said, putting the baby on her shoulder to burp her. "I dreamed that Maria, Gertrude, and Catherine were all sitting in a little, wooden church with an empty cross on the altar. I was flying around outside, but not in the church. There were these tall trees like giant grandmothers with gray hair. A river was flowing nearby. What do you make of that, Mamma Anna?"

"I don't know, Barbara; what do you make of it?"

"I don't know."

Mamma Anna gazed into Barbara's eyes, while Maria watched them in amazement. "You are the one the Grandmother chose to visit with a dream. Remember it carefully. I've often thought you had the spiritual sense, Barbara, just like your mother."

"But it was my father who led the Protestants, and now it's Hans."

"Yes, but she had the gift of spiritual insight, and so do you."

Barbara nodded her head as if a new understanding had come to her.

"Was Hans in your dream?" Maria asked.

"Not that I remember. I only recognized you and Gertrude and Catherine." Barbara paused, then continued, "Mamma Anna, in the dream, I was flying like a bird, with the air lifting me up. I've never felt that sensation before."

Mamma Anna smiled knowingly.

14

On Board the *Purysburg*, 1734

The warm sun was bearing down on Mamma Anna's pasty-white face as she sat protected from the sea breeze. The Kroehr girls had selected a spot for her to sit behind the Captain's bow, sheltering her from the wind with mattresses, hauled up from below to air.

"I could sit like this forever," Mamma Anna said softly, turning her face to capture as much of the sun's heat as possible. "I think I may want to live a little longer after all."

She was surrounded by Catherine and Gertrude, who had been given responsibility to care for her while Maria and Barbara, following the Captain's orders, scrubbed down the compartments below with a mixture of seawater and vinegar. Catherine sat with her hand covering her mouth, hiding an ugly eruption that was rising to a head. Gertrude was restless, wanting to see beyond the mattresses to what else was going on.

Frau Rott stopped by to seek advice from Mamma Anna about her pregnancy. The Rotts were not Salzburgers but had joined the transport group enroute, more interested in improving their circumstances in the New World than in establishing a religious community. They had alienated almost everyone on board ship with their constant harping and complaining. They had tried to further their fortune by buying up raisins and other commodities and selling them to the Salzburgers at inflated prices. Pastor Boltzius had admonished them sternly about making profit on the poor Salzburgers, but to little avail.

"The women tell me you're a midwife. So, what can I do about the nausea that won't go away?" she asked in a demanding voice.

Mamma Anna looked up at this very pregnant woman, wondering if she would deliver before they reached land. Mamma Anna disliked her but knew that she was probably very frightened about having a baby on this crowded little ship.

"Well, I have some dried herbs that might settle your stomach if made into a tea, but I don't have very much, and I don't know if I can replace my supply in Georgia, so the price is pretty high."

Gertrude and Catherine looked at each other and suppressed their giggles as they watched Mamma Anna bargain with the hateful Frau Rott.

"How much? I have some raisins that would taste mighty good in that mush you've been eating."

"Well, let me see. I'd need enough for me and for my friends here. You're going to need more than one cup of tea, so maybe four handfuls of raisins for each cup of tea."

"Four handfuls! Are you crazy? I'm not giving you four for one. Maybe one handful for each cup. That's fairer."

"I don't know. My supply is limited, and lots of people are puking on this boat."

"I'll give you two handfuls for one cup, but that's as high as I'll go."

"Well, since you're pregnant and I feel sorry for any woman who might deliver a baby on this ship, I'll accept that, but it's my hand that does the measuring. You go get your raisins, and I'll swap you the tea when I go back below deck. You come by my compartment."

She settled back with a satisfied grin on her face as Frau Rott teetered off, balancing her cumbersome weight as she crossed the moving deck.

Catherine and Gertrude laughed until they were crying. "Two handfuls for one mint leaf. Mamma Anna, you're the first person on this boat to best Frau Rott in a trade over those raisins of hers."

"I figure there's more than tea involved in her request. She's also going to need a midwife soon, and she can't afford to make me too mad. Anyway, I'll mix in some ginger to change the taste so she won't know it's mostly mint. Besides, I don't know if mint grows in Georgia."

"Anna Burgsteiner, is that you?" The terrible face of Deutsch peered over the mattresses. "I thought I heard that voice. They said you were a goner, but I see that you've come back to life."

"Deutsch, thank God. You're a sight for sore eyes. I've been wanting to see you, but they've had me trapped below deck, and I've been too weak to climb the steps. I wanted to thank you for saving my life, though at times I've been so sick I wasn't sure it was worth it. Come on in this room that the girls have set up for me, and sit down and visit. These two are Barbara's girls that I told you about. This one's Catherine, and the other one's Gertrude. Girls, say hello to my savior."

Catherine and Gertrude were both so repulsed by the mangled face of Deutsch that their expressions of horror were evident, but they managed a shy greeting with averted eyes.

"Well, there's not much to do while we wallow in this damned calm, so until the Cap'n comes back up...." Deutsch sat down on an upturned barrel.

Sensing how uncomfortable the girls were with this uncouth sailor, Mamma Anna said, "Girls, why don't you go help the other women with the scrubbing. And Catherine, drink some of that vinegar before it's mixed with seawater. It might help that lip sore."

They left quickly, glad to be relieved of the obligation to be hospitable.

"Never mind them. They haven't lived long enough to recognize character when they see it. How are those ribs?"

Deutsch lifted his shirt, and they both examined his chest. "They're healing now. Two of them were cracked, I think."

"Must hurt like the Devil." Mamma Anna poked and probed until he jumped away from her. She ignored the glances she was getting from Frau Ortmann, the schoolmaster's wife. She could imagine what that gossip would say about her examining a sailor's chest in broad daylight, but she felt so much better today, she did not care.

"Well, what's been going on among the living while I've been lying around with the dying?"

"We've reached the trade winds, which should blow us all the way to Carolina, and the warm air means we've joined the southern currents, but we'll make no progress with this damned calm."

"Well, I needed the calm, even if you didn't," Mamma Anna said. "First time I've been on deck since the storm."

"Your friend Barbara sent a message to me by that fellow Johann over there, that you were awful sick."

Mamma Anna looked over at Johann Mosshamer, who was helping Mr. Zwiffler hold up a weak Mr. Huber.

"Yeah, I remember when it was Johann who was deathly sick. It was just after he got out of prison. We weren't sure he'd make it, but here he is."

"He don't seem like no criminal who'd be in a prison."

"He never was a criminal, just the nicest fellow, but he did break some of Firmian's laws and got arrested, along with Hans, Maria's fiancé. I told you about them, didn't I?"

"They were the sweethearts, weren't they?"

"That's right. Well, they let Johann out of prison the day before the Proclamation of Expulsion was published on All Saints' Eve. I'm not likely to ever forget October 31, 1731. Firmian published the proclamation on All Saints' Eve because it was the anniversary of the day Martin Luther nailed his ninety-five theses on the door of the church in Wittenburg and started the Protestant Movement, way back in 1517. That fiend Firmian couldn't help but get in another dig at the Protestants."

15

Salzburg, October 1731

The string music floated around Leopold Firmian but did not penetrate his consciousness. The gold filigree on the walls and ceiling glowed in the candlelight, creating an enchanting ambience, but Firmian was oblivious to the setting and the finely dressed ladies and gentlemen. He did not really enjoy social occasions, preferring to think of himself as an ascetic. However, his love of comfort and horses belied this view. The creases in his face were deepened into a scowl. The words and phrases of his proclamation expelling the Protestants kept rolling over in his mind. He wondered if he had covered every point thoroughly enough for its announcement tomorrow. He knew it was harsh to demand that the unlanded peasants leave in eight days, but that way the ones who chose to leave could be out of the country before the worst of the winter snows. It was really the more humane thing to do, he told himself. Chancellor von Rall was probably right when he argued that, with winter approaching, the peasants would think twice about giving up their hearth and home for some deviant religion.

Angelica had dressed particularly carefully for this concert, which she had arranged. The whole idea was to try to lighten Leopold's demeanor, which had been unusually serious since the peasant uprising had begun. None of his strategies had brought the peasants into submission. They still openly defied the laws and refused to obey the Church, even after their leaders were imprisoned. Every new rule just seemed to make those stupid, stubborn people more obstinate.

Her lovely, pale pink, silk dress shimmered in the candlelight but was wasted on Leopold tonight. He was completely inside his own head. Only his body was in the room. She knew he was anxious about the proclamation expelling the Protestants that would be released tomorrow. Well, I'll just have to be patient until this situation is resolved, she thought to herself. She was weary of all the meetings and conversations about what should be done. She was glad a decision had finally been made. Once the protestors had left the country, everyone could get on with happier things.

Suddenly, Firmian looked up, and his eyes swept over the room as if he had just awakened and was surprised at where he found himself. He saw Angelica across the room, glowing in a pale pink haze. As he appraised her appearance, he felt his body react to her presence. She noticed his attention, and a blush spread up her neck and over her cheeks. Ah, she thought, he's finally seen me. Her spirits lifted immediately.

The music ended, and the assembled guests filed into the elegant dining room for a late supper. Angelica skillfully maneuvered the guests and sat beside Leopold. She demurely put her hands in her lap and looked down shyly. The talk at the table was about the music and other lighthearted topics. Leopold did not enter into the conversation but ate solemnly. His gaze turned provocatively on Angelica, and he drank more and more wine.

She felt him take her hand under the table and caress it. She was shocked that he would do such a thing in public, even under the cloth, with her husband just down the table. With one finger, she gently stroked his thumb and then quickly disengaged her hand.

He drank another glass of wine, leaned toward her, and said drunkenly, "Well, my beautiful friend, we'll soon have our land free of rebellious peasants. Fat Friedrich Wilhelm of Prussia will have his workers and be able to beat the powerful guilds, and the Emperor will have two more assured votes for his Pragmatic Sanction." Firmian lifted his refilled glass as if to give a toast to the deal he had made.

Horrified at his improper behavior toward her and his political blunder in mentioning secret dealings with the Emperor and King Wilhelm, Angelica looked around in panic. Frantically, she caught the eye of Chancellor von Rall across the table. The Chancellor jumped up and rushed to Firmian's side as if carrying an urgent message. He knew that the Proclamation should be seen as only a religious issue, not a political one, and the Prince was not thinking clearly. He intercepted the toast and, talking quietly to the Prince, led him out of the room.

The Prince's groomsman, Angelica's husband, scraped back his chair, glared at his wife, and stomped angrily out of the room. Angelica hastily followed him, while the other guests began a buzz of gossip behind their hands.

Angelica knew as she climbed into her husband's coach for the ride back to Schloss Klessheim that she would be severely punished for embarrassing her husband in public. He had encouraged her friendship with the Prince because it was useful to him, but public humiliation was another matter.

Outside Mirabell Palace, where the evening's events were still being discussed, Johann Mosshamer lay against a wall behind a bush. He could go no further. He was barely conscious and knew he might black out at any moment. As he rested, he tried to make sense of what had happened that day. His mind was muddled, and reality merged with frightening images. He knew he had been let out of prison and that he had stumbled down the mountain, away from the fortress. He had walked as far as he could but finally realized that he did not know in which direction he was walking. He had stopped against this wall to wait until daylight. He had heard music but was unsure if it was real or imagined.

He touched his face and felt the heat of fever. His body was shaking with cold, and the sores on his back were throbbing. At last he was out of prison, but he was not sure he had the strength to walk back to Saalfelden.

He had no idea why he and some of the other Protestants had been released. He wondered what had happened to Hans. He had last seen him when the guards took him away a week ago. They had never brought him back. He questioned everyone but learned nothing. Blackness crept over him, and he slept.

When consciousness returned, the sun was shining, and horses' hooves were pounding the ground on the other side of the bush. He stood up slowly, fighting for balance. His head was a little clearer than last night, but his wounded body ached all over. He stumbled out into the road, looked all around to determine which way was south, and began walking.

He paid little attention to what was happening around him, but focused all his energy on putting one foot in front of another. Up ahead, he noticed a large group of people gathered around a proclamation posted on the wall. A crowd quickly gathered, and an official began to read aloud. Johann stopped to listen, horrified at what he was hearing.

"...and who proclaim and adhere to, in public or in secret, the Augsburg or Reformed Confession...are to emigrate from and leave this archbishopric and the lands belonging to it, under threat of heavy punishment, according to circumstances, property, body, and life...."

Johann watched in amazement while bystanders cheered the message that would exile him from the only land he had ever known. Others, though, looked shocked and rushed away to tell their families and friends. As the man continued to read the proclamation, the particulars were spelled out in detail. The poor unlanded peasants must leave immediately, carrying sack and pack. Those with land had three months before they would be forced to emigrate.

Dazed from festering wounds, lack of food and water, and now an uncertain future, he staggered down the road leading out of the city into the open countryside. His mind whirled with what would happen to the Protestants. At least, as a farmer he would not have to leave until spring, but what about the laborers and servants? They had only eight days to leave everything they had ever known and go...where?

After he had struggled for several miles, a man in a wagon stopped to ask where he was going and offered him a ride to Saalfelden. Johann lay down in the back of the wagon and immediately fell asleep. After a long while, the wagon stopped, and the driver tried to arouse him.

The gray sun was barely visible, and a cold drizzle was falling in his face when Johann became aware that someone was speaking to him.

"Wake up, friend, wake up. This is Saalfelden. I'm going on further south."

Johann could barely utter a word of thanks as he painfully pulled himself over the side of the wagon and tried to stand up. The driver drove off, glad to be rid of someone who looked like he might die at any minute.

Looking around, Johann saw the bell tower of the church in the center of Saalfelden and walked toward it. He managed to open the door of the church and collapse face down on the back pew.

It was already dark when Father Jacob came to say his evening prayers and noticed Johann lying on the pew. Turning him over, the priest looked in his face. What he saw caused tears to well up in his eyes. He recognized Johann Mosshamer, whom he had christened as a baby so many years ago. He knew he had been a prisoner in the fortress and why he had been punished so severely. The old priest put his head down and wept at the cruelty of the Church. After wiping his eyes, he dipped his handkerchief in the holy water and tenderly wiped Johann's fevered forehead. He called the sexton, and together they carried Johann into the parish house and laid him on a bed.

As Father Jacob bathed the infected sores on Johann's back caused by the lashings, he wondered what good it did to treat men so cruelly. He doubted that beatings would persuade any man to embrace the Church. Things had gone too far. That dreadful proclamation earlier today and now this. Where would it end? He was certainly not happy having that fierce Jesuit priest breathing down his neck, forcing him to threaten his parishioners.

He knelt beside the bed, his head touching Johann's inert hand, and prayed. He asked God to heal this wounded man and to forgive the harshness of his beloved Church. He prayed for Johann's soul, that he might feel the comfort of God in his pain.

All night, he alternated between prayer, wiping the fevered face with cool water, and covering the shaking body with quilts. In the eerie hour between dark and dawn, when the night sounds had stopped and the day sounds had not yet started, Father Jacob knelt with his head touching Johann's hand. Suddenly, he felt that heated hand caress his brow. He raised his head and saw the face turn toward him, the lips faintly smiling.

As light edged the sky, Father Jacob performed the ritual for the dying. He was exhausted but set about making arrangements for a message to be sent to the Mosshamer farm.

It was midday before Johann's brother's wagon stopped in front of the parish house. The priest helped his brother carry Johann to the wagon and lay him in the back. As the wagon rolled slowly through the streets, the whispered news of Johann's tortured return caused people to leave their work and silently follow the wagon. The message spread quickly, and more and more Protestants joined the procession, like mourners following a corpse. No sound was heard but the crunching of the wagon wheels, the horse, and the people.

Ever since the Proclamation of Expulsion was read in Saalfelden the day before, the Protestants had been in shock. The Protestant men had been ordered into town the day before the reading and forced to surrender their firearms. The officials had collected all the muskets and pistols used to protect the farm animals from wolves and occasionally to kill a deer, a punishable crime, since all game belonged to the Prince.

Peter Rohrmoser had ordered his household to stay indoors in case there really was a peasant revolt brewing. He went alone to hear the reading of the Proclamation of Expulsion and was among those Catholics relieved that the troublemakers were being exiled. Now maybe the women of his house would settle down, he thought.

Mamma Anna watched as the short, rotund Burghermeister read the document aloud. She listened carefully, and for the first time since the trouble began, fear knotted her stomach. She was an herbalist, and she realized that she would be one of those forced to leave unless she embraced the Papist church.

"Lordy, what's a poor old woman like me going to do in a foreign country?" she muttered to herself. She slipped out of the crowd and hurried to the Rohrmoser farm to talk to Barbara and the girls before Peter returned home.

The four women sat around the kitchen table as Mamma Anna recited what she could remember, the crucial points being that landless peasants would be exiled in eight days and landholders, in the spring, allowing them time to sell their land.

Barbara usually heard Mamma Anna's news with some skepticism, knowing she often embroidered her stories to make them more interesting. This time, though, the shock on her old, wrinkled face was too real for disbelief.

"I wish Hans were here to tell us what to do," Maria said. "What's going to happen to the men in prison?"

"I don't know. No one was asking questions except to try to understand what the Proclamation said. Then I got out of there. I didn't want to draw any attention my way. I think it's best if I lie low for awhile."

"Oh, Mamma Anna, they wouldn't send you away. Who'd birth the babies if you weren't here?" Gertrude asked, unable to grasp the changes that were occurring.

"It looks like Firmian's really done it this time," Barbara remarked. "I never thought he'd go this far. Do you think the Protestants will go back to the Papist church rather than go into exile?"

"If Hans comes back, I know he'll leave rather than recant, and I'll go with him," Maria said firmly.

"From the talk in town, it sounded like it's too late for people to change their minds. They'll be forced to leave. You should have seen the number of soldiers in the streets."

"But where will the people go?" asked Catherine plaintively.

Mamma Anna shook her head from side to side. "God only knows the answer to that question."

"Give me your sack, Mamma Anna. If you're going to be staying out of sight, you'll still have to eat." Barbara filled up the dirty linen sack with potatoes, turnips, and cabbages. She placed a freshly baked loaf of bread on top.

"Thank you, love," Mamma Anna said. She never turned down a donation, for they were necessary for her survival, but she always tried to give something in return. She rummaged in her basket and came up with a garlic clove, which she handed to Barbara. Barbara acted delighted with the gift, although a string of garlic hung from the ceiling beam in the corner of the kitchen.

The next day, Eva, Barbara's sister, came riding up in her wagon with the news of Johann's return. Breathlessly, she recounted what she knew. "He's half dead from the beatings, but he's conscious, they say. I heard that Father Jacob found him in the church and took care of him last night, washing his wounds and everything. I always knew Father Jacob was a good man."

"Where is he now?" Maria asked quickly.

"At the Mosshamer farm, although I don't think his brother is very happy to have him back, what with the proclamation and all yesterday. It makes the whole family suspect, having him there, but he couldn't very well turn away his own kin, him being so sick and all."

"Did he say what happened to Hans? Is he coming back, too?" Maria asked excitedly.

"I haven't seen him, myself. I understand that a lot of people followed the wagon from the church to the Mosshamers' farm like mourners in a funeral procession."

"I need to talk with Johann and find out what happened to Hans, but Herr Rohrmoser will never let me go over there. He's ordered us to stay here. Could you go, Aunt Eva, and ask him for me?"

"Maria, I'd do just about anything for you, but not that. It's just too dangerous. I even took a chance coming here. We're all suspects, with Hans having been arrested and being related to us. I never expected the Archbishop to be so cruel as to exile all the Protestants. No, I can't take that chance."

"But Hans is your brother," Barbara said, shocked at her sister's statement.

"He's your brother, too, Barbara. Why don't you go?" Eva retorted sharply. Both sisters felt caught in helplessness, causing them to lash out at each other.

After Eva left, Maria said, with a determination bordering on desperation, "I have to talk to Johann. I'm going tonight after everyone goes to bed. Barbara, you can let me know when Peter's asleep. If I walk all night, I'll be there by to-morrow."

"I'll go with you," said Gertrude, sensing an adventure and getting caught up in the excitement. "You shouldn't go alone."

"Now wait a minute, Gertrude; you're too young to get in-volved in this."

"That's just the point. Nobody will suspect me of doing anything because I am so young."

Catherine sat down on the step with her mouth open, to-tally bewildered by what was happening.

"Barbara, you've been to the Mosshamers' farm. Tell me how to get there."

Without quite realizing it, Barbara found herself helping in the plan. Using a stick, she drew a map in the dirt of the roads they should follow. "It's not as far as the town of Saal-felden from here, but it's southwest."

The women had dropped their voices to a whisper so the younger children could not hear. "You must avoid the sol-diers. If they catch you on the road alone at night...well, you must be careful," Barbara warned.

"I can't believe you're really thinking of doing this," Cath-erine said. "Do you need me to go with you?" She felt that she should offer, but she did not want to go.

"No, Barbara will need you here. Herr Rohrmoser's going to be furious when he discovers us missing tomorrow. He may blame Barbara," Maria said.

"I'll pray for you until you get back," Catherine said, relieved that she did not have to take part in this caper.

The moon lit the road as Maria and Gertrude trudged along, exhilarated by the audacity of sneaking out at night. They walked back in the fields when they were near a farmhouse, and had only one scare, when a dog barked. They were afraid the people in the farmhouse might awaken and check to see what had upset the dog, but they did not.

When they reached the main road south, they became more cautious, for that was where soldiers were more likely to be. They had walked about a mile when they heard horses coming. The girls quickly hid in some bushes beside the road and held their breath until the horses, ridden by uniformed men, passed.

They arrived at the Mosshamer farm before dawn and sat down in a secluded place to wait until it was light. They could make out three buildings and wondered which one housed the sleeping Johann. They were not sure they would be allowed to see him, but Maria was determined to try. They waited until the men left the houses to take care of the animals before approaching the door.

Maria knocked on the door of the first and smaller house. She had seen some of the Mosshamer women at Protestant meetings, but she did not know them well. She also knew the family was divided over the religious issues.

The woman who answered the door looked familiar to Maria. Her eyes were red, as if she had been weeping, and her hair had not been arranged for the day.

"Excuse me for bothering you, but I'm Maria Kroehr, betrothed to Hans Burgsteiner, who was arrested with Johann. I need to talk to Johann. Maybe he knows what happened to Hans. Oh, and this is my sister, Gertrude. Is Johann here?"

The woman squinted her eyes to get a better look. She nodded her head and stepped aside for them to enter. The house was unkempt and more disorderly than Maria and Gertrude had experienced. Barbara ran such a well-organized house, where everything was always clean and neat.

"I remember you, Fraulein Kroehr. I was just feeding him some soup. He's better this morning. Come on back."

Maria followed her to the back room, where Johann was lying on his stomach, his pale, thin face toward the door. He wore no shirt, and his bandaged back showed signs of leaking pus. Maria was shocked at his condition, and tears rolled down her face.

"Oh, Mr. Mosshamer, what have they done to you?"

"They beat him. I wouldn't treat a dog the way they treated him," the woman said angrily. "Johann, you remember Fraulein Kroehr, Hans Burgsteiner's betrothed?"

"Ja." Johann struggled to sit up and managed, with his sister's help, to sit on the side of the bed. He held out his hand to Maria, who knelt by the bed and held his bony, clammy hand in both of hers.

"I don't know where he is, Fraulein Kroehr. I asked everyone, but no one would tell me anything. He was in bad shape from the dirty wounds on his legs, from being dragged behind the horse, and then the beatings." His voice faltered, and he held his head in his other hand. "I tried to take care of him, but I didn't have any medicine or decent food. He was barely conscious when they took him away that last time. He said to me, as they carried him out of the dungeon where we all were, 'I'll never recant.' Then I heard the priest questioning him in the torture chamber above the grate in the ceiling and the whip hitting his back, but I never heard him say a word or scream from the lashings. I figure he was unconscious. But they never brought him back."

"Do you think he's still alive?" Maria asked in a quavering voice, her tormented eyes searching his.

"I don't see how." Great tears rolled down his face as Maria collapsed on the floor in a sobbing heap.

Gertrude sat on the steps of the Mosshamer house, waiting for Maria. Protestant men had begun to arrive and stood around in the yard, hunched over, talking quietly. They all looked stunned. Their world had fallen down on them with the proclamation the day before, along with the news now about the severe treatment that Johann had experienced.

Johann, supported by his sister and Maria, came outside and sat in a chair that had been brought out for him. He spoke to the men, telling them what he knew in a voice that betrayed his weakness.

"They put us in a dungeon in the Hohensalzburg and, one by one, took us to the torture chamber and beat us, trying to get us to tell them the names of Protestant leaders and to swear loyalty to the Roman Church. We could hear the beatings through a grate in the ceiling of the dungeon. We sang hymns and prayed while someone was on the rack. And then, day before yesterday, they released us. I was able to get a ride to Saalfelden, and you know the rest."

"What happened to Hans Burgsteiner?"

Johann looked over at Maria and said, "I've just told Fraulein Kroehr that the last time they took him for questioning, they never brought him back. We think he was unconscious. He had been suffering badly from leg and back wounds that were festering, and he had a high fever. The last words he spoke to me before the guards took him out were, 'I'll never recant,'" Johann concluded in a choking voice.

The assembled men took off their round green hats and bowed their heads in silent tribute to Hans. They contemplated the probable death of this brave young man who had been their leader, and each began to feel the creeping reality of his own mortality and the hardships he faced. These simple men then turned to Johann for guidance about what they should do.

"Johann, exactly what did the Archbishop's proclamation say?" one of the unlettered peasants asked. "I can't quite hold it in my mind. It doesn't make any sense."

"It says that every Protestant must leave the country in eight days unless you own land. If you own land, then you must leave in the spring."

"Eight days! And where are we to go? Does it say that?"

"No, it just says to go."

"But we've always lived here and always been Lutherans. Winter's coming on. How're we supposed to get over those mountains in the winter? I don't even have a horse, and my wife has a nursing baby and three little ones. How could it be done? I don't even know what's on the other side of that mountain there. Do you, Johann?"

"Ja, another mountain."

"What country lies on the other side of the mountains?"

"Bavaria, they say, but I've never seen it. There are supposed to be some Protestant cities in the countries north of Salzburg, but I don't know what they are. Hans knew and told me about them once, but I never paid much attention to him. I never thought I'd need to know about them or not have Hans to ask."

The men continued to talk quietly in disbelief at what had happened to them. They could not imagine living anywhere but where they had always lived. Many had never traveled outside the county of Saalfelden. How would they even know which way to go?

"What are we going to do?" someone asked the group as a whole, but all just shook their heads.

Finally, Johann said, "It looks like we have two choices: either we renounce Luther and swear to be loyal to the Catholic Church, which has been robbing us all these years and which killed Hans, or we leave our homes just at the beginning of winter and walk over those mountains to...." He stopped there, because he did not know what lay over the mountains. "Who knows, maybe life in a Protestant city would be better than here, if we don't starve to death."

Martin Hofer, who had not spoken when the other men had, straightened up and announced with conviction, "Well, as for me and my family, we're going to do what the Lord

God wants us to do. We're going to leave and trust in God to protect us."

"That's what Hans said, and look at what happened to him."

"Then so be it," Martin said firmly. "I won't be the first man to be exiled for his beliefs. If it's God's will for me to leave my home, then I'll leave. And, like Hans, if it's God's will for me to die for my Lord, then I'll die."

"Which way will you go?" Johann asked.

"I don't know. God will have to show the way."

"Some of the men in prison from the Pongau were arrested trying to get to Prussia to ask the Protestant King there, King Wilhelm, to let people come live in his land. It is a land far to the north. They don't know for sure if any of the twenty-two men who were trying to slip across the border to get to Prussia made it. All they know is that three of the men were not arrested with them. Those three might have gotten through," Johann said. He continued, "It seems there are people in Regensburg who are trying to help us. Of course, no one expected the Archbishop to expel everyone, and so quickly. I don't know how to advise you. I'll be leaving in the spring, after I've recovered and settled my property. I have no idea where I'll go, however." Johann finished what for him was a long speech and motioned for the women to help him back into the house.

The talk among the remaining men turned to what a person would take on such a journey and how to sell what they could not carry with them. They began asking about horses and wagons and carts and soon realized that many of them had none of the things needed for a long journey. They had always walked everywhere and carried their possessions on their backs. Before long, they realized that they were all talking as if they had made a decision to leave rather than recant their beliefs.

Gertrude sat on a rock a little aside from the men, watching and listening intently. She felt profoundly that today was somehow a turning point, that her life would never be the same again. She could not imagine what would be different, but she instinctively felt that she could never again take her life for granted and just be happy. She looked around at the hayfield and the mountain rising behind it. A cold breeze swept down, and gray clouds diffused the sun.

When Maria returned, they began the long walk home. Gertrude did not know what to say in the presence of the grief manifested on Maria's face, so they walked in silence.

16

Gastein, November 1731

The Proclamation of Expulsion had been read in the villages of the Gastein Valley, Hofgastein, Badgastein, Badhofgastein, Godauren, and others. As in the rest of the Salzburg Province, in Gastein the Protestant men had been forced to surrender all firearms the day before the Proclamation was read. After all had heard the terrible news, rumors circulated that miners would not be expelled unless they were the leaders of the revolt. Thomas Gschwandl, Tobias Lackner, and others huddled together, wondering who would be considered leaders.

"Well, I guess those of us who went to Schwarzach--Tobias, Peter and Hans Gruber, and me--will probably be considered leaders," Thomas said to the group of men standing around the square in Hofgastein. They had been spared imprisonment, probably because they were needed in the mines.

"Yeah, but Tobias is a foreman in the mine. They wouldn't want to lose him. And you own land, Thomas, so you won't have to leave until spring. It looks like Hans and I might be expelled immediately," Peter said with astonishment, as he realized the personal implications of the Proclamation. "That's just eight days! How can we settle our affairs and plan a new life in another country in eight days? Where will we go? I barely know the names of a few other provinces, and I don't even know where they are."

"Let's meet at the Entrische Kirche to discuss all this. Tonight! Agreed?" Thomas suggested in a low voice. "Pass the word." He did not want to stand in the public square any longer, under the eyes of the soldiers and magistrates.

The men all nodded and separated to tell their families what had happened. Thomas climbed on his horse and rode out of town and up the mountain to his little farm.

Margaretta and Anna Hofer, her sister, continued peeling and cutting up apples for jelly at their kitchen table, while Thomas told them and his son, Little Thomas, about the Proclamation of Expulsion. The shattering news that would cause them to leave their farm on a picturesque Alpine mountainside seemed unreal and out-of-place in such a pristine setting. The brown log and white mortar farmhouse and barn had been built over a hundred years ago. The date was carved in a beam, 1624.

Thomas had inherited the farm when his parents and older brother died. He had been unable to marry his first sweetheart, who did not survive the birth of their son, but he and his mother had raised little Thomas. He had married Margaretta less than a year ago, and their life together had been very happy. She and her sister Anna took over running the house and mothering his son. Margaretta was a devout Protestant and shared his commitment to stand firmly for their beliefs.

It had been Margaretta and Anna who had suffered the repeated questioning by the Jesuits and the searching of their house by the officials. They had even been forced to cook and do menial work for four soldiers who had been billeted with them, enduring their taunts and insults while Thomas was away at the mine. Little Thomas and their hired laborer, Georg Schweiger, had had to sleep in the barn with the animals when the soldiers took over their room. At least the hated soldiers were gone most of the day, but they confiscated Thomas's homemade beer and drank until late at night, disturbing the whole household.

"Oh, Thomas." Margaretta's eyes filled with tears. "Will we have to leave the farm?"

"Not until spring, and there are rumors that the miners won't be expelled at all. Who knows what might happen by spring," Thomas said gently. He knew how much it meant to her to be mistress of her own farm.

"But what about the others who don't own land?" Anna asked. "What about me?"

"You're part of my household as long as you want to be," Thomas said emphatically. "You go or stay with us."

"What about Georg Schweiger, Hans and Peter Gruber, the Hubers, and all the others who don't own land?" Margaretta asked, her voice rising almost to a cry.

"The proclamation said they'll have to leave in eight days or swear loyalty to the Roman Church."

"Oh, Thomas, how awful. What will they do?"

"The men are meeting tonight at the cave to discuss everything. At this point, I don't know."

"Thomas, you can't go to the cave. What about the soldiers right here in our own house? They'll see you and follow."

"I'll be careful. The worst has already happened. There's little else they can do to us."

"They could kill you."

"Don't worry. These soldiers aren't from Salzburg and don't care that much about Firmian's rules. Some of them are even Protestants from other provinces. I'll give them some more beer that they haven't yet found and that'll distract them. I worry more about you and Anna here in the house with them without Georg and me around to protect you. It'll be better if they don't know we've left, so we'll try to slip away unnoticed."

The soldiers returned before sundown, demanding food. Margaretta and Anna dipped up steaming bowls of bean soup and buttered slices of bread. They carried the food into the front room and served the soldiers at the table in the corner. The room was cozy with warmth from the blue tile stove standing against the wall adjacent to the kitchen. The fire in the stove was kept burning from an opening on the kitchen side of the wall. The sun was already setting early, and Anna lit a lamp and set it on the corner stand near the table. Margaretta brought in a large pitcher of beer and four mugs and placed them on the table. She poured each soldier a mug of beer. Their own men were at the kitchen table eating a similar meal, without the beer, so the women were kept busy serving both tables.

"Is this all? Where's the meat?" one rough soldier asked in a dialect of German strange to Margaretta.

"It's a fast day, sir. No meat can be served," she replied. She did not want to get caught breaking one of the food laws with the very soldiers who had been brought in to enforce them.

"I don't give a damn what day it is. Bring me some meat."

"Leave the girl alone. She's doing what she's supposed to," an older soldier said. He had been very polite to Margaretta since they first came, but sometimes he could not control the raucous behavior of the others.

"Well, then, bring more beer." Margaretta picked up the pitcher and refilled it. She continued to refill it many times until all the soldiers were drunk and singing loudly.

Thomas decided it was time for Georg and him to leave. He went in to tell the soldiers goodnight, and he and Margaretta retired to their room. He slid a chest against the door so the drunken men could not bother Margaretta, then climbed out the window, where Anna was waiting. He boosted her through the window so that the two sisters could wait together for his return, then joined Georg, who held two horses on the other side of the barn.

A light snow began to fall when they reached the top of the mountain and entered the cave. The world outside reflected the light of the moon in unearthly loveliness, but left a path of footprints to the entrance of the cave. The enchantment of early snow disappeared as Thomas and Georg stepped across the entrance of the Entrische Kirche. Word of the secret meeting had spread rapidly, but many men had difficulty avoiding the scrutiny of the soldiers, who seemed to be everywhere tonight.

"Were you followed?" Tobias asked, holding up a lantern.

"No, I don't think so, but those footprints leading here make me uneasy."

"What the snow reveals, it also covers up," Tobias replied.

Thomas lit his lantern, and they made their way back through the cold, dark passageway to the chamber within. Lanterns faintly illuminated Luther's Bible and a cross. The flickering light also fell across the pale, shadowed, grim faces.

Tobias addressed the group. "The Burghermeister told me today he didn't think the miners would be expelled yet, because the Archbishop wanted time to bring in other miners before he sent us out. He can't afford to shut down the mines. So it looks like some of us are safe for awhile. The farmers and servants will have to go now, if they don't own land."

"Those of us with land have until spring to sell our property and leave," Thomas said harshly. "If everyone starts selling their land at the same time, it will be worthless. Who will buy it? Unless, of course, the Protestants decide to become Catholics. I don't see that happening. Everybody's too fed up with Firmian and his terrible laws. Hundreds of people signed the petition that went to Regensburg, refusing to swear to be loyal Catholics. It's probably already too late to change our minds, even if we wanted to."

"My land's been in my family for hundreds of years. You don't just sell land and move away. Where would we go? I've never been further from Gastein than St. Johann," a gruff voice said from the darkness.

"At least you have land," Hans Gruber said. "As a servant, I own nothing and must leave in eight days. Where will I go? I don't know. Winter's coming. Where will my sons and I find shelter and food if we leave?"

"How old are your sons? I heard that no children under twelve would be allowed to leave with their parents. My sister, who is a servant in the inn, overheard the Jesuits talking, and they're planning to take all our children to the nuns and raise them as Catholics. They're going to steal our children."

"No, they wouldn't do such a thing," Thomas said in disbelief. "No one would be so cruel."

"If the Archbishop is cruel enough to expel all of us with nowhere to go, with winter coming on, I'll believe anything," Peter Gruber said. "This is really a test of our faith. Firmian knows he has us caught in a terrible situation. If we leave, we risk dying of cold and hunger. If we stay, we must deny our faith. I say we leave and put our trust in God."

All of the heads in the chamber turned to look at thirty-two-year-old Peter Gruber as he spoke those steady words. The anxiety and confusion that had been almost suffocating Thomas since first hearing the Expulsion Proclamation began to dissipate, and a powerful calm and determination swept through him.

He spoke to the group from his heart. "You're right, Peter. This is our trial. How do we stand the test? Do we hold firmly to the Lord Jesus Christ, or do we bow in shame to a corrupt Papist Church that we despise. That's the choice that Luther and Lodinger had to make, and now it's our turn. It's awfully hard to think of giving up my family's farm. I've so often felt the presence of God while on my farm that I'm afraid I sometimes thought the farm was God. But God is not my little piece of land and my house. God is eternal love, to be lived out now and for all eternity."

Tobias filled the silence that followed Thomas's remarks. "I say we bow our heads and pray for God's guidance. That is the best source of strength." As everyone fell to their knees, Tobias prayed, "O God in heaven, look down on us this night, and fill our hearts with your love and wisdom. Guide us to do thy will, even if we must suffer for it. We are thankful for this opportunity to show our faithfulness."

Back at the Gschwandl farm, Margaretta opened the shutters and gazed out at the snowy night for the hundredth time. She caressed the window frame with her hand as if trying to make a permanent imprint of the grains in the wood on her brain. She was weak from crying and disgusted with herself for caring more about leaving their house and farm than about being faithful to God. She pulled the shutters closed and sat on the bed, wrapping the down covering around her freezing body. She was still sitting that way when Thomas returned near dawn and rapped on the window.

17

On Board the *Purysburg*, February 1734

"Is that when you left Salzburg?" Deutsch asked.

"No," Mamma Anna said, "it was a little while after that, but thousands of people had to leave then. It was the saddest thing I ever saw. I won't ever forget it as long as I live. Soldiers were pushing and shoving people, some of them old and sick, and some just babies. They separated families, stealing some of the children to give to the nuns to rear as Catholics. People were hiding their little ones in wagons to keep from losing them. Most of that first group didn't even have wagons or horses or anything. Some pushed quickly constructed carts. But most just walked out of Saalfelden with a sack slung over their shoulder, holding everything they would have to live on for the rest of their lives."

"Where'd they go?"

"Well, at the time we didn't have any idea where they were going. They didn't know either. It was a real mess. It was the saddest sight, but, in another way, it was the grandest thing I ever saw, too."

"How could it be a grand thing, all those people treated so mean?"

"Well, here were the poorest people in our valley, defying the priests, the bishops and the Archbishop, the Pope, and all the other rich, important men, walking proudly out of Saalfelden. They sang hymns and held their heads high. It touched even my old, worn-out heart to see such courage and strength. I never believed that so many people would actually hold firm to their beliefs. I figured when it came down to giving up everything they had, people would give in and obey the Archbishop. But, I was wrong. It was the same all over the province, I'm told. Lots of folks didn't have any choice but to leave by then, because they had refused to swear to be loyal to the Church. The priests were still trying to get some of them to change their minds and swear, but not many would. It was a remarkable thing, I can tell you."

"Why didn't you leave then?"

"I thought I'd have to. I'd gathered up what I could carry with me, but a rich merchant in town who lived in one of those big houses came to get me to look after his wife, who was having twins. He talked the authorities out of making me leave. I never did swear to be loyal to the Church, though. Too much had happened by then. I just couldn't do that. Neither could the others.

"Some of that bunch from Gastein left that November. I've heard them tell their stories. The Gruber brothers, Hans and Peter, and the Huber family. Old Mr. Huber never has recovered from that ordeal. He's the man over there that Johann is holding up. He's been sicker than I have. Can't eat anything without getting the bloody flux. 'Course, with some decent food, I think I could get his stomach straightened out, but all that Hungarian apothecary Zwiffler's done is bleed him with leeches. I never put much faith in leeches. It doesn't make sense to me that, if he's losing blood from his bowels, it's going to help him to lose more blood from the leeches. Does that make sense to you?"

"I guess I never thought about it. Got into some leeches in Africa once, and I don't think I felt any better for it."

"Africa. You've been to Africa? What were you doing in Africa?"

"Shipped out on a slaver once. Biggest mistake I ever made. Got into the fight of my life, jumping ship in the West Indies."

"Is that when you cut your face?"

"Well, I didn't cut my own face. The bastard that did that got his throat cut, but that ain't generally known around here, so keep your mouth shut about it." Deutsch gave her a look so fierce that, if Mamma Anna had not already known what a kind man he could be, would have scared her terribly.

"I won't tell, Mr. Deutsch. You can count on that. I've got a few secrets myself that don't bear repeating. I've been telling you my stories, but you haven't told me much of anything about yourself."

"I ain't much of a talker, and I'd rather listen to yours. Then I have something new to think about when I'm on a lonely watch. Your telling about how the folks had to leave reminded me of how they captured the Africans and forced them on the slave ships. But I can't think about that. It was too awful, even for an old salt like me." He shook his head sorrowfully, then looked up at the slant of the sun. "I've got a while longer before my watch; tell me more about the leaving."

18

Gastein, November 1731

Peter and Hans Gruber were eating breakfast with their father, their brother Michael, and Hans' two sons, ten-year-old Johann and thirteen-year-old Peter. The four unmarried Gruber sisters were cooking and serving the men. The table was too small for everyone to sit at the same time. Their custom was for the men to eat first, then the women. The cooking fire felt good in the sharp, clear, November air.

"What's going to happen now?" Wilhelm, the father, asked.

"I don't know, Father. The Proclamation said that all Protestants without land would have to leave yesterday. That includes Hans and me, but, since nothing happened yesterday, maybe something's been worked out," Peter said.

"I didn't think they would act that fast. Something will be worked out. The Archbishop knows how many Protestants there are now. He surely doesn't want all those people to leave. Who would work his land and mines?"

"What about all the soldiers? If we didn't have so many people crammed into this tiny house, we'd be housing soldiers like everyone else. They must have been sent in for some reason," Michael said.

Silence fell as heavy footsteps were heard approaching the house.

BAM, BAM, BAM! Fists pounded the door.

The family members froze. Finally, Michael rose and opened the door.

"Everyone outside," a big, rough-looking soldier in an imperial uniform shouted.

The whole family walked out and lined up as directed. Hans put his arms around the shoulders of his two sons. Two soldiers, who looked to be no more than eighteen or nineteen, swaggered into the house and threw clothes and even kitchen utensils on the floor, searching for contraband books and pamphlets. They found a book of Protestant songs, including all the verses of *Song of the Exile*, which Peter had been memorizing, concealed under a straw-filled mattress on the floor upstairs. The soldiers brought it outside and set it afire. Tears came to Peter's eyes as he watched the flames curl the precious pages.

"Who has the lease on this place?" asked the big soldier, who was older and seemed to be in charge.

"I do, and my eldest son Michael after me," Wilhelm Gruber said.

The soldier looked at a list in his hand. "Name the household."

"Well, there's me and Michael and my four daughters, and Peter and Hans and his two sons, Johann and Peter."

"Peter and Hans Gruber?" he asked, pointing to the two men.

"Ja," they both replied.

"You are on my list. Let's go."

The soldiers turned to proceed down the road. They motioned for Hans and Peter to walk ahead of them.

The family stood in shock when they realized what was happening. "We'll all go together," Michael said. "We're all Protestants. Just give us time to get our things together."

"You should have been ready," one of the young soldiers said.

"No one leaves today except Peter and Hans Gruber. Those are my orders," the soldier with the list said. "The rest of you will leave in the spring."

"But we're a family. We stay together, no matter what happens," Wilhelm cried gruffly.

"Be quiet, old man. You two," he said, pointing to Peter and Hans, "come on now."

"My two sons will come with me," Hans said firmly.

"Leave them. Now move along," the soldier said, in a voice accustomed to command.

Hans embraced his two sons, who were awkward at such a show of affection. The whole family began hugging, and the sisters cried, crowding around Peter and Hans. "We'll come back for you or get a message to you about where we are, so that you can join us," Hans said.

"Where will you be going?" Wilhelm asked desperately, realizing he might never see his sons again.

"I don't know," Hans replied. "We'll try to let you know."

Peter started back into the house to get things he and Hans would need for the journey.

The big soldier stopped him with his gun and motioned him down the road. "It's too late for that. Let's go; we're behind schedule."

"But we don't have any food or heavy clothes. Is the Prince going to feed and clothe us?" Peter asked.

The two young soldiers took Peter's last remark as an insult to the Prince, and they grabbed him and dragged him back to the road. Peter did manage to snatch two walking staffs that were leaning against the house outside the door. He handed one to Hans.

The two brothers accepted the inevitable and began walking down the road, carrying with them only the clothes on their backs.

They joined other groups of people being escorted toward Hofgastein by soldiers. A crowd of more than a hundred peasants, looking stunned, mingled together in the small village when they reached Hofgastein. Slowly, the soldiers herded the dazed servants and laborers westward toward the road to Goldegg. Hans and Peter stuck close together to avoid becoming separated in the huge crowd.

People along the roadside called out, and many tried to go along with the exiled group, but the soldiers pushed them back. The Grubers saw Thomas Gschwandl beside the road, motioning to them. They edged over to him.

"Here, take these provisions that Margaretta and Anna have prepared for those who had to leave today."

"God bless you, Thomas, and many thanks. They wouldn't let us take time to get anything."

The soldiers pushed along the men. Peter and Hans each carried one of the sacks Thomas had given them, not knowing what was inside. The crowd included many whole families. Some women carried their infants on their backs in heavy wooden cradles with straps around their shoulders. Young children were carried or held by the hand. Old and infirm people were helped along by others. A few families had carts pulled by horses, but most were poor servants with no such possessions, walking only with the help of a staff. Some carried packs of provisions, but others, like Hans and Peter, had nothing with them.

The mingling horde of people kept looking to see who else was leaving with them.

"There's Georg Schweiger and his mother over there," Peter said. Eighteen-year-old Georg was carrying a heavy pack. He and his mother must have been prepared to leave. They saw Simon Reiter, with his father, brother, and six sisters, all talking at once. The sisters were as elated as if this were a wonderful holiday celebration. Nothing so exciting had ever happened in their drudgery-filled lives.

"Where's the rest of the Gruber family?" Peter heard from all sides, as the Reiter sisters, moving in a pack like a flock of birds, surrounded him.

"The soldiers wouldn't let them come," Peter answered, blushing at so much female attention. "Only us. They wouldn't even let Hans bring his boys."

"Oh, no!" chorused the six sisters at once.

"We'll send for them as soon as we get settled somewhere," Hans said grimly. "Perhaps it's better this way. They'll have time to get things in order before leaving, and Peter and I can establish a place to live." The normally cheerful, optimistic Hans began to look for the good in what was happening, but Peter could see the pain on his face and hear the catch in his voice. The six Reiter girls moved on like a wave when they spotted twenty-nine-year-old Balthasar Fleiss up ahead.

Peter and Hans watched Balthasar as he was engulfed by the Reiter girls and could not help laughing at their excitement and exuberance.

"Which one is which?" Peter asked Hans.

"I don't know. I never could keep their names straight," Hans replied.

They overtook Lorentz Huber, with his wife and four young children. He had a bandage on his leg and was limping slowly.

"What happened to your leg?" Hans asked.

"It's just a bad cut. Did it with my ax. Don't need to be walking on it this much, yet."

"Here, give me your pack and rest your weight on Peter," Hans said.

Lorentz leaned on Peter, who put an arm around him and half-carried him.

"Thanks, Peter. That's much easier."

"You must have been ready to go. You had your provisions packed," Hans said, noticing that everyone in the Huber family carried large packs.

"No. The soldier that came let us pack a few things before we left. He didn't seem to like his job. Said he was a Protestant himself," Lorentz replied.

"Where are your brother Paul and his family?" Hans asked Lorentz.

"They weren't allowed to come. What about Michael and your father and sons?"

"The same thing. Once Peter and I get settled somewhere, we'll send for them," Hans replied.

"It's a shame to break up families," Lorentz sighed, "but God's will must be done."

"Ja, and this must be God's will. Just look at the Protestants that stood firm for their faith, even when it meant leaving their homes at the beginning of winter."

"Ja, it's an amazing thing. Only God could have brought about this wonder."

The men gazed in awe at the mass of humanity walking along with them. The sun became warmer as they walked northeast beside the Gasteiner Ache rippling by on the left side, the mountains rising on the right. The six Reiter girls doubled back, looking for their father and brothers again.

"Where are they taking us?" Lorentz asked.

"To Salzburg, I guess. At least this is the road to Salzburg. I've never been there. Have you?" Peter asked.

"Me? Nein. I've lived all my fifty-two years right here in Gasteiner Tal."

The path became narrower and steeper as they approached the pass in the mountains. The small children and old people slowed down, and the soldiers began prodding them along.

Peter looked back at the Gastein Valley, with the river winding between the two mountain ranges. The pure, crisp air sparkled in the November sun. The view was breathtakingly beautiful. His heart filled with unaccustomed pain as he thought of the loss of his homeland. He noticed the trail that led to the Entrische Kirche, their cave church, and he began to sing the *Song of the Exile*. Others joined in, and Peter led them through the verses he remembered.

As each group reached the highest point of the pass, they looked back across the valley before moving down the other side. Salty tears streamed down their faces.

Clouds built up when they turned northward. Now the river on the right was the rushing Salzach, and the mountains on the left were unfamiliar to most. Without the sun, the wind through the valley was cold. Those with heavy coats in their packs pulled them out and put them on. The others just hugged their arms around themselves and braved the wind.

Peter was a strong, young man of only thirty-two, but he began to feel the burden of supporting Lorentz. He and Hans swapped places, and Peter carried the packs, while Hans helped Lorentz.

"I'm sorry I'm so much trouble," Lorentz said, "but I don't know how I'd make it without your help."

"I'm glad we can help. You'd do the same for us," Hans replied.

The sun was slanting from the west when they reached the road that led to Goldegg. It was jammed with more Protestants being marched north toward Schwarzach. The two groups crushed together as the soldiers forced them to merge.

Cold and weary from walking all day, the people were astounded to see more streams of marchers being led onto the same road. Many of them had also been walking all day.

"Maybe we can stay the night in the inn in Schwarzach," Hans said.

"Are you crazy? There won't even be room for the soldiers in that tiny inn," Peter replied sharply.

"Surely the women and children can't stay outside. It may rain, and it's going to be too cold."

"Do you really think the authorities care what happens to us?" Peter scoffed.

The two brothers looked around at the huge crowd. Their hearts were overcome with sadness for their plight and pride in their dedication. All of these pilgrims had risked exile and death to stand firm in their faith.

The authorities at Schwarzach tried to organize the people as night approached, but none of them had ever faced such a task, and no one knew what to do. Mostly, family groups just fended for themselves as best they could. There was no shelter for anyone. Fortunately, the rain held off, but the cold wind blew even colder.

Peter, Hans, and the Huber family cleared the rocks from a place in the road and sat down. Peter and Hans looked in the packs that Thomas had handed them and found bread, cheese, and quilts. They shared their supper with others around them and lay down, attempting to sleep. Although they were exhausted, sleep was impossible.

As the night wore on, Peter lay on his back, looking up at the sky. No stars were in sight, and the soupy moon was barely visible. There was much milling around as family members tried to find each other in the dark. Children whimpered, and cold, hungry, wet babies cried. Every time he closed his eyes, he saw the mass of peasants leaving the Gastein Valley and the fleeting faces of family members left behind. He wondered what further trials God had in store for them.

The next day, the Salzach River supported a continuous line of canoes, jostling each other while inexperienced men tried to maneuver them downriver. At dawn the soldiers had begun pushing the Protestants into canoes to travel north through Salzburg to the Bavarian border. Many had never been in a boat and were frightened to leave the land.

Hans and Peter managed to get themselves and the Hubers into the same overloaded canoe. Lorentz found the canoe more comfortable than walking, but he worried about the freezing, misty rain that had begun to fall, forming an icy sheen on the clothes of his wife and children when the mist froze. So far, Hans and Peter had been able to keep the canoe upright, even though some of the passengers were nervous and continued to rock the boat, trying to see what was happening up ahead or behind them.

"Sit still, please, or you'll turn us over," Hans warned several times.

"I'm looking to see if my sister and her family are in another canoe," a woman called out.

As they watched, a canoe just ahead of them tipped over. Men, women, and children all began floundering in the water. A baby was dropped, and the mother screamed, "Help! Save my baby." Someone retrieved the baby and, with considerable splashing, made it to the shore. The young mother grabbed Peter's oar. He held her afloat until Hans could maneuver the canoe to the shore. She scrambled up the bank and held her baby to her breast, crying hysterically.

The canoe was righted, and the people climbed back in. Their wet clothes and hair became stiff with ice in the freezing wind. About midday, the canoes passed the city of Salzburg, but they were not allowed to stop. The shores were lined with people curious to see the exiled peasants pass by.

The rain stopped, and the gray clouds whitened when a little sunlight managed to penetrate the air and bring some much-needed warmth. From the canoe, they could see a steady procession of Protestants walking north, following the river. By late afternoon, the reluctant sun had drifted behind clouds again, and a chill wind blew down the river valley.

When they came ashore for the night, Peter and Hans checked to see how the baby who had almost drowned was doing. They found the mother sitting on the ground, holding a stiff, blue baby. She was shaking but would not release the dead child. Peter gathered some fallen limbs and started a fire close enough to warm her. As the warmth seeped into her consciousness, she finally allowed her husband to take the baby from her arms. They had no choice but to bury the child beside the river. A small group of Protestants prayed and read Scripture over the tiny grave.

Exposure to the cold without adequate clothing was the most immediate problem the exiles faced. Almost everyone became sick or felt on the verge of sickness. During the night, others died. There was no escape from their misery. Groups huddled together for warmth and companionship.

"It's worse than I thought it would be," Peter said to Hans. "I didn't count on being out on the river all day in the freezing rain."

Hans nodded his head in agreement. "I think I have a fever. We'll all come down with pneumonia under these conditions."

The sun shone brightly over a new snow the next morning. Spirits lifted with the sun and the freshness of a white world. Up and down the river, several graves were dug. The dead were laid in them, and then the canoes were filled with the living to continue their journey down the river.

When they reached Tittmoning, at the Bavarian border, there was a crush of people waiting for passes to leave the

Salzburg Province. Hans and Peter helped the Huber children up the bank and joined the throng.

After they had found a place to sit by a tree, Peter directed, "Everybody wait here while I try to find out what's happening. But please don't move, or I might never find you again."

After an hour had passed, Peter returned. "It seems that the Bavarian government will only let people across the border if they have a pass, and they will not issue this many passes. I guess they don't want us either."

"Do you suppose they'll send us back home?" Hans asked.

"I don't know. There seems to be a lot of confusion."

A soldier came by, and Hans asked, "What's happening?"

The soldier responded, "I don't know. Just stay where you are until you're given further orders."

The cold, hungry travelers milled around, looking for sustenance wherever they could find it, as they waited day after day. Some were given passes and crossed into Bavaria, but most were kept waiting. They spent their time talking, trying to plan for an uncertain future. Rumors ran through the idle crowd quickly. Cities were identified where Protestants would be welcomed, but warnings given of Catholic cities. The foreign names were bewildering to those who had never before left their homes.

"I hear that we can go west to Memmingen," Peter said to Hans and Lorentz.

"I was thinking we might try Augsburg," Hans replied. "I've at least heard of it before."

"Are they near each other?" Lorentz asked.

"I don't know where either one is exactly," Peter replied.

"What will we do when we get there?" Hans asked.

"Well, we've worked hard all our lives. I guess we can find some kind of work." He looked around at the thousands of people camped around him and realized that all of them would be looking for work. They were enough for a whole city themselves. How could any city absorb that many workers?

"It isn't going to be easy, though. We have no money," Peter continued.

"We have our God. God will provide. In that we can trust," Hans said quietly.

After about two weeks, Hans, Peter, and Lorentz were languishing under their tree. Lorentz's leg had healed considerably during the long wait, although he still had a deep, rattling cough. His wife and children, although miserable, had survived the ordeal fairly well. They had not yet run out of food.

"Let's go," a soldier called out, and people began scrambling for their belongings as they rushed toward the border. Hans and Peter hurriedly grabbed their packs to join the melee, but slowed down to assist the Hubers and their children. When they finally reached the border, they were handed a pass and walked into Bavaria, following the crowd in front of them in a westerly direction, not knowing where they were being led.

19

On Board the *Purysburg*, February 1734

Gertrude came to get Mamma Anna but hesitated when she heard her talking to Deutsch. She was surprised that his face did not seem so frightening when he was listening to Mamma Anna's story. She waited until Mamma Anna dropped her voice as if reaching a stopping place before she interrupted. "Mother thinks you've been in the wind long enough. She wants me to bring you and your mattress down. Everything's been scrubbed."

"The sun's still warm, and I can breathe better up here. The air's so foul below. Sit down a minute, Trudi, and tell Deutsch about what happened in Saalfelden when the poor people got expelled with winter coming on. I was too busy with those twins to do more than watch from the window occasionally."

"Well, Mr. Deutsch, it was an awful time. We didn't know for sure what had happened to Uncle Hans, but we had to assume he was dead. Maria took that news very hard. She cried all the time."

20

Saalfelden, November 1731

Maria woke up early, and numbness covered her soul. She slapped her arm to know that she was alive, shivered, and pulled the down comforter up to her chin. A cold wind was blowing around the window. Winter was coming.

Winter, she mused. I feel like winter. No life. Frozen. The uncontrollable tears began again, like a constant flood spilling over. She closed her eyes, and fleeting visions of Johann's tortured body, with Hans' face attached to it, flashed before her. She opened them quickly and stared at the boards in the ceiling. The familiar knots and patterns of the wood comforted her.

Catherine moved beside her, and she heard the baby cry from another room. Gertrude, on the small bed under the window, stood up on her knees to see through the crack in the shuttered window.

"At least it's not snowing yet, but the sky is gray with clouds," Gertrude said. She sat on the edge of the bed and began pulling on her bright blue woolen stockings. "These stockings are getting too small."

"I'll help you make a new pair," Catherine said. Catherine was accomplished at spinning the sheep's wool, dyeing, and knitting it into whatever the family needed. She took great pride in her work and welcomed an opportunity to do something she loved.

"Thanks, Catherine. How's Maria?" Gertrude's voice dropped to a whisper.

"I'll be fine, Gertrude. You don't have to whisper like I'm sick or something. Just give me a little more time," Maria answered, with breath shivering through her voice.

"We'd better get up if we're going to say goodbye to the people who leave today. I've made a scarf for Martin. I want to give it to him. Do you think I should?" Catherine asked Gertrude with some hesitation.

Gertrude giggled. "Martin. I wondered who you were knitting that scarf for."

"Today may be my last chance. I'll probably never see him again, so I guess it doesn't matter what he thinks of me. Do you think he likes me?"

"I don't know. I never even thought about it. Oh, I have to hurry. I must go early to Greta's house. She's been my best friend for years. If she has to leave, who'll be my best friend? I wonder where they'll go. Do you think we'll leave someday? If we have to go, I'd rather go with everyone else." Gertrude was working herself into quite a state as she finished dressing and yanked a comb through her long blond hair.

"Slow down, Trudi. You'll break that comb," Catherine yelled at her.

Gertrude threw the comb down on the bed, raced out of the room with her untied apron strings and unbraided hair streaming behind her, and ran headlong into her stepfather. "Slow down, Gertrude. What are you in such a rush about?"

"I have to go say goodbye to Greta. Her family may have to leave today. I don't want to miss her."

"They don't have to leave, young lady; they chose to leave. If they'd come to their senses and do their duty, they could go on with their lives like they always have." Peter's voice rose in indignation as he spoke. He couldn't understand why people wanted to disrupt their whole lives over religion. One religion was just like another one as far as he was concerned. He certainly was not giving up his land for such foolishness.

Gertrude dashed out the door. She did not want to get into a discussion with her stepfather. Ever since Hans was arrested and the Proclamation of Expulsion was published, there had been tension in the house. Her mother supported the Protestants, and her stepfather did not. Silence was like a wall between her parents.

Gertrude ran across the fields to the road and started up the hill. The road was steep, and she was soon out of breath.

The sun began to come up, and the sky streaked with pink as she sighted Greta's house up ahead. It was a small house with two rooms, where Greta, her mother, and five brothers and sisters lived. The cottage was on the land of a wealthy landowner. Her mother was a servant, and Greta, at thirteen, ran the house and cared for her younger brothers and sisters. Gertrude sometimes helped her when she could get away from her own chores.

As she came nearer, she saw two soldiers on horses, holding guns in their hands. She stepped behind a tree to watch. One soldier swung his leg over the side of the horse and gracefully jumped down. He was young and handsome, with an arrogant swagger. He knocked on the door with the butt of his musket.

Gertrude could see the fear on the face of Hannah, Greta's mother, when she opened the door and saw the soldiers. The two soldiers pushed her aside and entered. They began searching the house, overturning mattresses and quilts, looking for contraband material. Evangelical pamphlets fluttered out of a sewing basket when the handsome soldier shook it upside down.

Gertrude could see the younger children huddled around their mother, while Greta cringed behind the table.

"Whose are these?" the soldier shouted, picking up the pamphlets. "Filthy heresy," he said, tossing them into the cooking fire.

"They're mine, sir," Hannah said firmly, finding strength in the anger she felt at seeing her house torn apart.

"Where is your husband?"

"My husband died two years ago. I'm a servant on the Mohler farm. You're keeping me from my work. They'll wonder why I'm late."

"There's no need to fret about that," the young man laughed cruelly. "Give me the names and ages of each of your children."

As Hannah pointed out each child and told the age, the other soldier motioned for them to go outside, where they stood together in a huddle. When she named Greta, who was thirteen, the young soldier leered at her and made an obscene comment under his breath to his companion, who laughed. Hannah ran to Greta and stood between the soldiers and her daughter.

"It's too bad we're in such a hurry, but we have orders to clean out this section of the county before noon, and this is the first house. Tie up the children," he said to the other soldier. "They'll go to the convent to be raised in a proper way. You'll thank me some day, madam, for saving your children from the fires of Hell."

"No!" screamed Hannah and Greta at once. They both ran out of the house and encircled the children in their arms.

The wailing children, the screaming mother and older sister created such a disturbing uproar that the soldier was enraged. When he shot his musket into the air, they all fell silent at the deafening report.

"Now stand back, woman. You and the older girl start walking down that road and straight out of this province. You and your kind are not welcome here." He jabbed them with the point of his gun until they began stumbling down the mountain road, missing their footing when they looked back at the five crying children, tied together.

Gertrude watched in horror as a wagon came up the road, and the children were put in and driven away. By then, Greta and Hannah were out of sight. She turned and ran back home as fast as she could, avoiding the road swarming with soldiers.

She ran frantically into the house, grabbed a sack of potatoes, dumped half of them on the floor, snatched up a round cheese wrapped in cloth and added it to the sack, together with apples and a loaf of bread that had been cooling on the table. Barbara came into the kitchen as she was dashing out.

"What on earth are you doing, Gertrude?" Barbara shouted.

"The soldiers took the children, and now Greta and her mother are on the road headed out of Saalfelden. I've got to catch them. They didn't even get to take any food." Gertrude did not wait for a response, but dashed across the yard to the road. She ran frantically up and down until she finally saw Greta and Hannah.

The mother stumbled along in dazed silence. She did not look to left or right, but straight ahead. Her face was stony, her step dogged. The road was becoming crowded with families, some walking, others pulling carts or riding in wagons. Each was loaded with as much as could be carried. Soldiers on horseback rode around the straggling line of peasants walking down the road.

"Greta, Greta," Gertrude called, when she saw her friend. "I was afraid I'd miss you. Here, take this food." She thrust the sack into the girl's hand.

"Trudi, they took the little ones," Greta said, disbelief still in her voice.

"I know, Greta. I watched from behind a tree, but I couldn't think of anything to do to stop them. I saw them put the children in a wagon and drive away."

Barbara had followed Gertrude to the road, fearful that the soldiers might get her confused with the others. She frantically searched the procession for Gertrude, who finally appeared when Hannah and Greta reached the Kroehr farm. Gertrude was walking along with her arm around Greta. The two young girls were crying.

"Gertrude! Gertrude! Come here," Barbara yelled. A soldier pushed her back. "That's my daughter. She's not supposed to go. Gertrude!" Barbara screamed at the top of her voice.

Gertrude heard her mother and turned to leave. She hugged Greta goodbye, took off a small, crudely carved, wooden cross from around her neck, and placed it in Greta's hand. "Remember me."

"I will."

The soldier paid no attention when she joined Barbara at the side of the road. Barbara embraced her as if she were back from the dead, then chastised her for taking such a chance as they hurried back into the house. As the day wore on, hundreds of peasants walked by their house on the way to the main road.

After promising not to leave the yard, Gertrude sat down on the big stone outcropping in front and watched the continuous procession of people walking down the road. She was transfixed and could not move. She noticed that her mother and Catherine began giving people food to carry with them as they walked by. She did not move to help but sat there all day, as if in a trance.

As the shadows began to lengthen and the wind turned colder, Maria joined Gertrude on the rock and threw a quilt around her.

"You'll freeze to death sitting out here all day," Maria said softly.

"Where are they all going, Maria? What will they eat? Where will they live?"

"I don't know, Trudi. They'll just have to trust that God will provide."

"Do you believe that, Maria?" Gertrude asked earnestly.

"I honestly don't know." Maria sighed deeply and struggled to maintain her composure. She was so weary of crying. It was time to stop drowning herself in tears over the loss of Hans and see to the living. Today's parade of brave neighbors marching by the house had snapped her out of her own grief. She knew that, if Hans were still alive, he would be in that line of refugees, too. She knew she would have gone with him, no matter what the future held, but she was afraid to leave until she knew something definite about what had happened to him.

"I'm tempted to join them," Maria said softly. "I no longer want to live in this place where people like Hans are tortured and killed, and good people are exiled. All day I've been trying to decide whether or not to put my clothes in a basket and join the others."

"Oh, Maria, no!" wailed Gertrude. "You wouldn't leave us, would you?"

"I haven't yet," Maria answered, "but surely you understand my feelings."

"If you go, so do I," Gertrude said firmly.

"We may all have no choice in the matter if the soldiers decide we must go."

"But Herr Rohrmoser's a loyal Catholic. They won't make us leave as long as we live in his house, will they?"

"I don't know. Everything's so confused. I don't know what will happen."

The two young women sat huddled together on the rock, staring at the road where a few people were still walking along.

"We'd better go take care of our chores, Trudi. The cow still must be milked, even if our whole lives are changing." Slowly, they walked into the house, wrapped together in the quilt.

21

On Board the *Purysburg*, February 1734

Pastor Boltzius sat on the storage compartment on the deck of the *Purysburg*, the same structure that had sheltered Mamma Anna and Deutsch during the storm. He was writing in his journal as he did every day. What a methodical man, Mamma Anna thought. She'd never known a man who was more of a mystery to her than Pastor Boltzius. She'd been watching him closely, but from a distance, since he and his assistant, Pastor Gronau, had joined the Salzburgers in Rotterdam. She sensed that he did not approve of her; yet, he had sent her a bottle of wine when she was sick and had prayed at her bedside every day.

He was certainly winning the hearts of the other Salzburgers. Barbara and the Kroehr girls were completely under his spell. They would not hear any criticism of him and made sure they did not miss a single prayer meeting. They spent every free minute reading the Bible and talking about what each passage meant. They were also reading other tracts that he had given them. And everybody was constantly discussing religion. Mamma Anna could not understand why it took so much studying to know God. The others acted like they had never practiced their faith right until they had a pastor to show them how. She was mystified.

She remembered when they needed no pastor to interpret the Bible. Barbara would read it to them, and they seemed to understand it perfectly well without all those fancy words.

22

Saalfelden, February 1732

Crystal snowflakes drifting down cushioned every surface with a downy covering. Barbara held the baby on her shoulder, which was thrown back in stiff, unspoken defiance, and gazed at the white world through a small opening in the shuttered window.

"I put up with your brother Hans betrothing my stepdaughter and then making a martyr of himself, but I'll be damned if I'll let my wife invite those heretics into my house for illegal meetings. No! Absolutely not!" Peter stormed at Barbara's back. "And don't think you've fooled me about hiding that illegal Bible, either. I've tolerated it because I don't think it should be illegal, but I don't appreciate your risking my farm for your religious nonsense. This is the Rohrmoser farm. I'm in charge here." Peter grabbed his coat from a peg in the wall and stamped out.

Tears came into Barbara's eyes, but she refused to cry. There was truth in what Peter said. She felt torn between loyalty to her husband and loyalty to her Protestant beliefs and community. She had not expected the Protestant women who remained after Hans' death and the fall exodus to turn to her for leadership. Of course, she had assisted her father and later her brother Hans in organizing the Protestant meetings. Now the women expected the family to continue to organize them. How could she, with a Catholic husband? And, yet, how could she not?

She had just asked Peter if the Protestant women could have their meetings here. It would be a fairly safe place. Since Peter was a Catholic, the authorities would not be as suspicious. Now, she would have to find another place. It was hard in the winter, when they could not meet outside. She hated putting any family in danger of being arrested. The authorities had already meted out so many cruelties. Her last hope was Mamma Anna. At least Mamma Anna could make her own decisions, and no one else would be affected, since she lived alone. Her tiny, one-room cottage was not really big enough, but it seemed to be the best possibility.

I need to go ask her and set a time, she thought, and then she remembered the baby. I can't take the baby out in the cold, and I can't leave her here, since I'm nursing. A familiar surge of frustration plummeted through her body, but she refused to give in to it. Obstacles can be overcome if I will trust in God. I'll just have to ask the girls to go to Mamma Anna's and make the arrangements for me, she determined.

Barbara went into the kitchen, where Gertrude, Catherine, and Maria were making candles. Maria was pouring melted wax into the molds, while Catherine adjusted the wicks on the rod, which Gertrude held while she dipped it up and down in the melted wax. Six-year-old Hans was sitting on the floor, breaking old candles into smaller pieces to be melted.

"I guess you heard?" Barbara asked. All of the heads nodded solemnly.

"We'll have to ask Mamma Anna to let the women meet at her house. I can't take the baby out in the cold, so someone else will have to go to her house and make the arrangements."

"We'll go," the three girls all said at once, eager for a chance to get out of the house.

"Can I go? Can I go?" Little Hans asked, jumping up and down.

"I guess so, but you must all be back before dark, and that comes early. If she's not home, don't wait," Barbara said firmly.

"We won't; don't worry," Maria assured her.

The four put on coats, knitted scarves, hats, and mittens, and took along sleds to coast down the hills.

Barbara set the baby down on a quilt on the floor and continued the candle making. When the job was finished, she cleaned up the mess and began cutting potatoes for dinner. She put water on to boil and mixed dough for dumplings. She was lost in her own thoughts when Peter came in from the barn.

"Where is everybody?" he asked gruffly.

Risking the truth because she did not like deceiving him, Barbara said, "I sent them to find another meeting place."

"You stupid woman!" Peter shouted, throwing down his wet coat in anger. "I thought you understood. I don't want you or my children involved with those people anymore. You are my wife. You must do as I say."

"Yes, I'm your wife, Peter, and it hurts me to go against your wishes, but God must come first, even before you," Barbara said, straining to keep her voice controlled.

"How do you think I feel when men laugh at me because I can't control my own wife. By God, you will do as I say from now on, or pay the consequences."

As he shouted his threats, Peter slapped her across the face, grabbed her wrist, and twisted her arm behind her back until she bent over with the pain. Holding his walking stick in the other hand, he beat her across the bottom.

Barbara steeled herself and refused to cry out. She struggled to get away, but Peter was so strong that she could not free herself. While bent over, she looked at her baby girl on the quilt, and tears came to her eyes as she realized that she, too, would have to submit to those stronger than herself.

When Peter's anger and frustration diminished, he released her and sat down at the table, his head in his hands.

"I did that for your own good, you know. I don't want them to arrest you or force you into exile. I don't want to lose you."

Barbara knew he wanted her to go to him, comfort and forgive him, but she would not. She stood with her back to him and took long, shuddering breaths.

Only days later, the Lutheran women squeezed into Mamma Anna's one-room cottage. Barbara did not remove her scarf, hoping to hide the black eye that was still visible from Peter's beating.

Maria rushed immediately to Mamma Anna, who had arranged for someone to go to the Hohensalzburg to ask about Hans.

"What did he find out?" Maria pleaded.

"Nothing. They said he isn't there. That's all he learned. They wouldn't tell him anything about where they bury the dead. It's time to give up hope, Maria. Hans is surely dead. You've got to figure out how to live your life without him." Mamma Anna put her arms around the grieving young woman and patted her back as if she were a child.

As the meeting began, Gertrude, Catherine, and Maria surrounded Barbara. Maria held a candle, while Barbara read the Twenty-third Psalm aloud. "The Lord is my shepherd; I shall not want...."

When she finished reading, she looked at the other women without a man to escort them to the Protestant meetings.

"Dear friends, we are risking our lives to worship together this evening," she said. "Let us pray together." She paused while she formed the words in her mind. "Almighty God, be with your humble servants gathered here in secret tonight in your name. Be with our exiled brothers and sisters and provide them shelter and care in a foreign land. Give us courage to be faithful, as they have been. O Jesus, join this group tonight. Be in our hearts as we face expulsion in the spring. We know this life is just a trial for our future life with you after death. Help us to stand that trial without flinching." Barbara's voice dropped almost to a whisper. "And, loving Jesus, soften the hearts of those who despise and persecute us. In your name we pray. Amen."

Other women in the room added their prayers to hers. Barbara became so lost in her private thoughts that she hardly heard what was said. When she joined in the singing, she was overcome with emotion and had to stop. She had been strong at home, but in the midst of this group, her pent-up feelings came to the surface, and she found herself crying. She wept for herself and her painful dilemma; she wept for the dear people who were in exile; and she wept for the people gathered, who would also be banished soon, giving up their homes and native land for their beliefs. She also wept for Hans, whom she missed so much and whose presence she felt so strongly in this gathering.

Barbara suddenly looked up, startled, as the group froze in fear, hearing horses' hooves approaching the house. Then steps and talking were heard.

"This must be the place. Look at all those footprints in the snow."

The door was pushed open, and two soldiers entered. The women in the room stared mutely at the snow-dusted men. It was too late for running or hiding.

"Which one of you is Anna Burgsteiner, the midwife?" the tallest soldier asked.

"I am," said Mamma Anna, relief evident in her voice, for she was used to such requests. "I'll get my things."

"Never mind your things. You're under arrest. All you other people go home. I should arrest you all, but tonight only Anna, the witch, will be arrested."

"This is a Protestant meeting and Mamma Anna's a Protestant," Barbara said in a clear voice, rushing to Mamma Anna's side and taking her hand. She knew that to be accused of witchcraft might mean death. To be a Protestant was not as serious an offense.

Mamma Anna turned and hugged Barbara, whispering in her ear, "The Grandmother prepared me for this. Don't be afraid. Take my basket with you."

Barbara stepped back, and their eyes met in deep wonderment. Turning to the soldier, Barbara asked, "Where are you taking her?"

"To the jail in Saalfelden. I don't know what will happen after that. Now, everyone tell me your names. I must know who is present."

The women obediently gave their names. The shorter soldier took the Protestant books and pamphlets. Barbara looked around to see what had happened to her Bible. She didn't see it anywhere, and neither did the soldier.

"Now move along. Go back to your homes."

Maria, Gertrude, and Catherine all hugged Mamma Anna, and with Barbara, put on their coats and walked outside. Gertrude was walking very stiffly and taking small steps. The moonlight on the snow made the night bright enough to see the path home. As they stopped to look back, they saw Mamma Anna, walking along beside the soldiers. She did not look back.

When they were out of hearing, Barbara asked, "What happened to the Bible?"

"I have it," Gertrude said, "under my skirt, between my legs. Is it safe to take it out yet?"

They all turned to look at her and burst out laughing. "How did you do that?" Barbara asked.

"Well, I was holding the Bible when I heard the horses, and I just pushed it under my skirt between my legs. I thought sure I'd drop it when I started walking, but I didn't."

"They're out of sight now. You can drop it," Maria said. Gertrude let it drop into the snow, then cried in alarm when she saw bright red blood on the precious Bible. More drops of blood spotted the snow between her legs. Gertrude began to cry. Barbara put her arms around her daughter. "Don't worry, Trudi, darling. It's just your first bleeding time. You're a woman now. It's nothing to be afraid of."

Catherine picked up the Bible and began wiping it off with her apron, which was wet with snow. "See. Most of it is coming off. No one but us will ever know."

"I don't want to be a woman if it means this bleeding," Gertrude said vehemently.

The other three women laughed gently. "It's not a matter of what we want. It's the way God made us, and it makes it possible for us to have babies," Barbara replied. "You'll get used to it. Now let's go home and get you cleaned up."

"What will they do to Mamma Anna?" Catherine asked.

"I don't know. We can hope that they only send her into exile. My fear is that they will accuse her of witchcraft. Hans told me about some herbalist women in the Pongau who were killed by the authorities."

"Oh, Mother, they wouldn't really kill her for healing people, would they?" Gertrude asked in astonishment. "Let's go tomorrow and tell them she's just a midwife and healer."

"Absolutely not, Gertrude," Barbara said sternly. "It's far too dangerous. We're in enough trouble for having been there when she was arrested. We don't want witchcraft added to the charge. There's no telling what Peter's going to do to me when he hears about this. He may send us all away. We must not interfere. There is nothing we can do that would help Mamma Anna, anyway, except pray for her to have courage."

"She should have left when the others did. I wish I had," Maria said quietly. "Barbara, we really must prepare to leave in the spring. Life here is becoming impossible."

"How can I leave, Maria, without Peter and the children? I've tried so hard to convert Peter to our religion, but he will not even let me bring up the subject anymore. I think he's unwilling to consider any course that might mean he would have to leave his farm. Sometimes I think the farm is his religion."

Maria remarked plaintively, "After tonight, none of us may have a choice in the matter."

23

On Board the *Purysburg*, February 1734

From a distance, Mamma Anna watched a group of Salz-burgers sitting in rapt attention, listening to Pastor Boltzius lead them in a study of the Psalms. Barbara had her Bible propped up on her knees so that both she and Gertrude could follow the words as he read. Barbara's face showed a tense-ness, almost a desperation of spirit, as if expecting Pastor Boltzius' next word to make her pain go away. She had never forgiven herself for leaving her husband and babies.

Pastor Gronau was sharing his Bible with Catherine and another young woman, both girls looking more pious than necessary to memorize a Bible verse. Mamma Anna sus-pected they were more interested in impressing the young minister than they were in pleasing God. She chuckled at the picture.

The small group included Margaretta and Thomas Gschwandl and their little daughter, and Anna Hofer and Georg. She thought about their tales of leaving Gastein. She knew the journey to Salzburg and on to Bavaria must have been awful for that great crowd of people.

She had been separated from Barbara and the others after her arrest and did not know their fate until later. During that short time, Barbara had changed from a vibrant, young mother to an old, sad woman with white in her hair. She was so filled with regret about what she had left behind that she had trouble thinking about what was ahead. Gertrude, who had been a carefree young girl in Saalfelden, was now a quiet, sober person, staring for hours at the sea as if search-ing the horizon for the meaning of human existence. Cath-erine had become afraid of everything, it seemed, and needed constant reassurance that they would survive. Maria's jour-ney had been different. She had begun the march in grief but had emerged as a strong, loving woman whose smile and hand brought comfort to the sick and frightened.

24

Gastein, April 1732

Spring-scented air drifted through the open window of Thomas and Margaretta's bedroom, where they lay exhausted from packing and making arrangements to leave their farm and Gastein the next day. Tomorrow, they would also have to say goodbye to young Thomas, who was not allowed to emigrate with his father because he was a bastard. They had been told that no children under twelve who were not legitimate would be allowed to leave. Young Thomas had been born before his father inherited the farm. His mother had died in childbirth, before they could be married. The boy had always lived with his father. They had selected a Catholic relative of the boy's mother for him to stay with, the Wallners, who would be kind to his son, Thomas thought, but he feared he would never see him again.

"Thomas will be well cared for at Michael Wallner's in Hinterstarff. They're a good family, and later you'll be able to send for him," Margaretta said, trying to comfort Thomas.

"I can't imagine leaving him and this farm. I've always lived here, and my father, and his father, and his father. It's been in our family for at least two hundred years, and I expected my Thomas to live here. But losing the farm isn't half as hard as leaving Thomas behind."

Margaretta put her arms around her husband and held her body close to his. His face rested on her firm, young breast. It was unusual for her to reach for him. She had been a shy and modest bride. Even in his sadness and exhaustion, Thomas responded to her comforting caresses. I'll make him a new son, Margaretta thought, innocently thinking one child could replace another.

The next day, Thomas closed the door to his house for the last time. He took the reins and began leading the horse and wagon down the mountain, away from the farm. Instinctively, as he passed the fields, his mind turned to what needed to be done for the next harvest. He shook his head to force reality into it again. There would be no next harvest.

Young Thomas walked beside him. He had hardly said a word since he found out that he would be left behind. He moved stiffly, like a machine.

"I'll send for you as soon as I can," Thomas said, "but I don't know where we are going, exactly. Peter and Hans Gruber sent word that they are in Memmingen, in Bavaria. I expect we will go there, too, if we can." They walked along in silence, looking at the familiar shapes where the mountains met the sky. "You know I wouldn't leave you if I had any choice, Son," Thomas continued. "The authorities say I have to leave and that you must stay. I never thought they would break up families." Thomas paused again. He was uncomfortable expressing deep feelings to those he loved, but he knew this might be the last chance he would have with his son.

"Remember, Thomas, that God loves you and will protect you. And, Son, I'll never forget you, no matter what happens. Don't forget you have a father."

"Yes, Father."

Margaretta and Anna walked beside the wagon. It was piled high with household goods, non-perishable food, tools, and clothing. There was even a wooden box containing flower seedlings. Margaretta was not sure what flowers grew in foreign lands. These would remind her of her window boxes, which always spilled over with bright red geraniums. They were leaving behind so much. Her mind reviewed the list: Young Thomas, the farm, one cow, twelve sheep, one hog, one horse, and several foals. They were not allowed to take all their money with them, and Thomas had left money with friends, hoping that someday they could send it to him.

When the family reached the main road to Hofgastein, all four turned to gaze back up the mountain for a last look at the farm. Thomas flicked the reins and moved forward. The road became crowded with other exiles as they approached

the village. Many had carts or wagons and were better prepared for a long journey than those who had been forced out
in the fall.

At Michael Wallner's house, where young Thomas would
stay, the sad party stopped. Thomas hugged his son, shook
hands with Michael, and left quickly. He was so near tears
that he could not bear to speak. Margaretta walked beside
her husband, her arm around his waist. When he looked at
her sternly with red eyes, she removed her arm. He was
afraid that any tenderness would cause him to cry. If he began, he might never be able to stop.

They passed house after house that stood empty. Almost
every family was leaving. "Who will be left?" Margaretta
murmured, as they passed another empty homestead.

"The Catholics," Thomas replied bitterly.

In Hofgastein, soldiers, Catholic deputies, and priests
moved the people along, but the confluence of hundreds of
wagons, horses, dogs, and people made the scene chaotic. In
the confusion, Tobias Lackner approached Thomas and put
an arm around his shoulder.

"I'll be following as soon as Firmian can replace the miners. Where are you planning to go, so that I can try to join
you?" Tobias asked.

"Hans and Peter Gruber sent word that they were in
Memmingen, in Bavaria. We'll try to go there, but I'm not
sure exactly where that is or even if we will be allowed to go
there. I haven't been able to find out much information that I
feel is reliable, although there are plenty of rumors. Some
are saying that the King of Prussia is welcoming people into
East Prussia, wherever that is. We'll just have to wait and
see. I'll try to let you know something, and if you can bring
Thomas with you, I will be forever grateful."

"I'll try, but the priests are very strong on raising the children as Catholics. I doubt if they'll let Thomas go. I'll keep
an eye on him, however."

"Thanks, Tobias." The two men shook hands. As Tobias left to return to the mines, he turned to Margaretta and Anna and tipped his hat to them.

The Gschwandl family moved slowly westward out of the Gastein Valley, through the pass near the Entrische Kirche, and north toward Salzburg. The road was so crowded with people that movement was slow and clumsy. When they neared the turn-off to Goldegg, the road was so clogged with people and carts that the procession stopped. It was several days before they were able to resume their journey northward.

The little family group established a routine as they trekked slowly north. They were so amazed at the sacrifices so many people were making that they were moved to thank God for such faithfulness. They sang their Protestant hymns and the *Song of the Exile*. The singing lifted their spirits and provided rhythm for the walking.

25

Saalfelden, April 1732

"These are the people from this household who must leave." The heavy soldier seemed to fill the front room of the Rohrmoser farmhouse as he haltingly read from his list of Protestants who must emigrate. "Barbara Rohrmoser, wife of Peter Rohrmoser; Maria Kroehr; Catherine Kroehr; Gertrude Kroehr."

The family stood in silence for at least thirty seconds. Then Peter said gruffly, "My wife and daughters should not have to leave since I am a Catholic and the head of this household."

The soldier turned and called out the door to the Catholic deputy who had been assigned to him. "Rohrmoser says he's a good Catholic, and his wife and daughters should not have to leave. Know anything about this case?"

"I sure do," the man said gruffly, stamping into the front room, his polished boots making staccato reports on the wooden floor like a round of gunshot. Barbara saw that it was Hammerschmidt, the man who had pointed out Hans and Johann when they were arrested. He gave her a haughty look and continued. "This man's wife is one of the main organizers of the Protestants, and her stepdaughter was betrothed to Hans Burgsteiner, that firebrand who preached heresy all over the county. These four women were also with Anna Burgsteiner when she was arrested. The authorities definitely want them to go, but they must leave behind the children under twelve."

"Surely you don't mean the baby, sir. I'm still nursing her," Barbara said, as if for clarification. "My daughters and I have been notified that we must leave and are ready to go. I'm prepared to leave Herr Rohrmoser's sons, but this baby girl might die without her mother's milk."

"All children under twelve. That's the order," the soldier replied.

"But she might die. No one would be so cruel as to separate a nursing baby from her mother," Barbara cried, incredulous.

She held the baby to her breast and sat down on the bench built onto the wall of the room. Tears ran down her face as she hugged little Barbara close to her. "O God, I didn't expect this. I was prepared to leave, but not the baby." Five-year-old Hans ran to his mother, and she took him on her lap, too. She wept as she held the two children, rocking back and forth.

The big soldier brushed tears from his own eyes as he witnessed this sad parting. Not wanting to prolong the ordeal, he said brusquely, "Let's go. Get your things. We must go now."

Maria, Catherine, and Gertrude each in turn kissed the other children. Gertrude picked up little Hans and hugged him. He clung to her, his arms around her neck and his legs around her waist. Maria and Catherine gathered the bundles they had been carefully preparing for weeks.

Abruptly, Barbara, carrying the baby, went up the steps to the room she had shared so many years with Peter, and then, with each baby in turn. She sat on the bed, opened her bodice, and offered her breast to little Barbara for the last time. The baby nuzzled in contentedly and began sucking her mother's milk.

Barbara looked down at the rosy child and wondered, How can I leave her? I can't do this. I simply can't.

Voices from below invaded her consciousness. "Go get her or I'll have to," the soldier said. Peter's slow, deliberate footsteps sounded on the stairs. He came to the door and looked despairingly at his wife and child.

"I can't leave her, Peter. I can't," Barbara said, looking up at him. "Do something, please. Come with us."

The soldier suddenly appeared at the bedroom door, startling both of them. He strode over, took the baby from Barbara, and thrust her at Peter. Barbara heard the pop as the baby's mouth broke the suction from her breast. She automatically covered her exposed body. The soldier grabbed her arm, pulled her from the room, down the stairs, and out the door, where Maria, Catherine, and Gertrude were waiting with the bundles.

Dazed, Barbara began to walk with the others down the road toward Saalfelden. Maria was carrying Barbara's load as well as her own. Peter had refused to give them a horse and cart. Finally, Barbara reached out for her burden and carried it. As they neared the hillside where the Protestants had met the day Hans and Johann were arrested, they saw a great crowd of exiles gathered. They had stopped for a last worship service. The four women stood, their arms around each other, and sang the hymns, prayed the prayers, and listened to the preaching that had led them to this disruption in their lives.

26

Goldegg, April 1732

"Look at all the Protestants!" Gertrude exclaimed, awe in her voice. The road and surrounding hillsides were jammed with people, carts, horses, and bundles, all jostling for room to move along. Gertrude's excitement was shared by Catherine and Maria, amazed at the number of people who had chosen religious freedom as an exile. "God is surely with us. This is a miracle." Gertrude began singing the familiar words of the *Song of the Exile*: "I am a wretched exile here and now must tell my story, for I was banished from my home to spread God's Word and Glory...." She heard the song grow ahead and behind her as others joined in, until the music sounded like a choir processing in church.

They had been walking for two days and were now approaching the intersection where the road to Salzburg meets the road to the Gastein Valley. Even the hillsides were cluttered with people when the exiles from the Gastein Valley, Rauris, Goldegg, and all the villages along the way converged on the road to Salzburg. Soldiers on horseback tried to keep things moving, but there were so many people that movement was slow and clumsy.

Gertrude's excitement was reflected in the faces of Catherine and Maria, but not in Barbara's. Barbara had withdrawn into herself and moved along mechanically, stains from milk seeping unattended on the front of her blouse. She looked at the smiling faces of the three young women, shocked that happiness shone there. For a moment, they seemed to be strangers to her.

How can they be happy? she thought. We've left half of our family behind. She felt a sob forming in her chest but did not allow it to surface. Her sadness was burrowing into her core, beneath an ocean of tears. How will I ever bear this pain in my heart? she asked herself. She turned her mind toward prayer, which had been her lifelong custom. O God in Heaven, O Jesus, help me, she prayed. I feel like this pain in my heart is as heavy as the cross you carried on the road to Golgotha. As her mind wandered, it suddenly stopped on the familiar Scripture in John 3:16, "God so loved the world that he gave his only begotten Son, that whosoever believeth in him should not perish but have everlasting life."

A deep sigh went through her body as she grasped, for the first time, the pain God must have felt when he sacrificed his child for the world. Her pain was no greater, for at least her children lived. The least she could do for her God was to bear this pain of separation. Barbara suddenly fell down on her knees and clasped her hands in prayer, muttering, "Thank you, God. You did help me. Through my pain I can better know your pain and the pain of the Blessed Mother. Thank you, merciful God, for my reward will be with you."

"Mother, what's wrong?" Catherine cried, trying to keep Barbara from being trampled by the people following close behind them. The girls had constantly worried about her because she was so devastated at leaving Peter and the children, especially the baby. She had barely said a word since their departure. They had just led her along with them.

"Catherine, I understand now," she said, tears streaking her face through the accumulated dust. "I was just thanking God for the pain in my heart. I now understand better God's grief when he sacrificed his Son for the whole world. My sacrifice is not as great as that. This life is just a test for the life to come. I must stand my trial and trust in God."

Several heads nodded in agreement when nearby travelers overheard her words to Catherine.

"God be praised," a wiry young man said, kneeling beside her and taking her hand. "I'm Johann Mosshamer from County Zeller, near Saalfelden. Are you Barbara Rohrmoser?" he asked politely.

"Ja." She looked up into a face that was familiar, but she could not quite place him.

"You and your brother, Hans Burgsteiner, are well-known to all Protestants in the Saalfelden area."

"You knew Hans?"

"We walked this very road together last summer, going to the Salzbund in Schwarzach."

"Barbara, you remember.   This is Johann Mosshamer, who was arrested with Hans," Maria said, moving up beside Barbara and putting her free arm around her.

"Of course, Herr Mosshamer. I'm afraid I'm a little distraught. I should have recognized you immediately."

"That's understandable, Frau Rohrmoser," Johann said, then looked across the bent-over Barbara into the face of the beautiful young woman holding her other arm.   "Your brother was a great inspiration to me."

"This is my stepdaughter, Maria Kroehr. She was betrothed to Hans," Barbara said, noticing the open admiration reflected on Johann's face as he gazed at Maria.

"Ja. We met after I was released from prison. She was kind enough to visit me." He looked down, remembering the grief on her face when he had given her the bad news about Hans. "Have you had further word about Hans, Fraulein?"

"No, nothing. Have you?"

"I would have told you immediately if I had. I fear that there's no hope."

"It's God's will," Barbara murmured. A silence engulfed them as they felt again their loss of Hans.

"You seem to have recovered your health," Maria said.

"Ja. I'm glad God allowed me to see this day. Hans would have been thrilled to see the faithfulness that this great exodus represents, don't you agree, Fraulein Maria?"

"Ja. I was also thinking as I walked along how Hans would have loved seeing the conviction of God on the faces of so many people," Maria said softly. "He always wondered if the Protestants would stand firm when tested. In a way, he gave his life for this to happen."

"Ja, that's true, Maria, and we must not fail the test. We must do God's will and grasp the opportunity of exile to worship God freely."

"I am grateful that my daughters will have the opportunity to worship God without fear. I will always grieve, however, for those we left behind. But I can't read the mind of God; perhaps they're needed here," Barbara said.

The four women and Johann walked along in silence again, listening to the tramping of many feet and the squeak of gritty wagon wheels. Behind the noise of the march could be heard the water of the Salzach River rushing over rocks on its way north.

Gertrude looked up at the unfamiliar mountains and saw the snow still on the peaks. Green from the grasses and trees was like a pale web on the hillsides. She then looked around at the faces of the people. Never before had she seen so many people together, and she began to wonder where they were from and how they had lived.

Catherine's thoughts drifted, and she tried to imagine what kind of life lay ahead for them. Would they be desperately poor, forced to beg in the streets of a strange town? Would she ever marry and have children? Was it true that there really were whole cities of Protestants? Would she have to be a servant in someone else's house? She tried not to be afraid for the future, but she kept imagining possibilities.

Maria ached for the absent Hans. She had felt his presence more since they had started this trek than she had in months. She became aware that Johann was watching her when he thought she would not notice. She realized she was pleased, in spite of herself.

Barbara walked in sorrowful peace. She began to carry on imaginary conversations with Peter, offering new arguments that might have convinced him to accompany them. But she always came up against his square, determined face, with its locked, pulsating jaws. She could never have persuaded him. Still, she felt a sense of failure that she had not found a way to convince Peter, who had once loved her, and she, him. Well, it's too late now. I must live out my fate, she thought, and heard herself sigh deeply.

Johann broke the silence as the sun slanted from the west. "That's Schwarzach up ahead, where Hans and I came to the Salzbund." He turned to Maria. "Would you like to see the place where the oath was taken?"

"Oh, could we?" Maria replied quickly.

"Come with me."

As Johann and Maria led the way, Catherine, Barbara, and Gertrude followed. When they approached the inn, soldiers were lounging on the steps.

"Could we go in for a moment?" Johann asked.

The soldiers looked surprised that one of the Protestants would seek entrance to an inn.

"No. Move along now."

"We only want to look inside."

The soldier was irritated at this second request. "Get on out of here before I have to force you."

The little group turned and joined the line of marchers, reminded again that, as long as they were in this country, they were not free.

When they stopped to camp for the night, the four women sat in a circle around their fire as usual. They prepared their plain meal of bread and cheese and warmed themselves against the chilly night. They each sensed that Johann was not far away, but he stayed out of sight, allowing the women their privacy.

"How long before we get to Salzburg?" Gertrude asked.

"Two days, perhaps three," Maria answered. None of them had ever been to Salzburg.

"I wonder what it looks like and if we'll see Archbishop Firmian?"

The other three women laughed. "I doubt that such a rich and important man will be out looking at us," Barbara said.

"What will we eat when our food runs out?" Catherine said.

"God will provide. We must have faith," Barbara said softly.

27

On Board the *Purysburg*, February 1734

Martin Boltzius turned to his companion as they walked around the deck. "I'm concerned, Pastor Gronau, that some of the people in our party are not attending our services or studying the Scriptures with us. We must find a way to bring them into the fold. Our new settlement will not be a blessed community of believers if some members are reluctant Christians."

"I've been struck by the pious attitude of most of the Salzburgers, sir. Take Frau Rohrmoser and her daughters, for instance. They couldn't be more serious in their studying of the Scriptures and their longing for the way of our Lord."

"Yes, that's true, but what about the woman they call Mamma Anna? She's certainly a peculiar person. The people seem to hold her in high regard, due to her being a midwife, but I find her resistant to our preaching and teaching. She sits on the edge of our meetings and never sings the new hymns that the others have learned. She makes no effort to improve her knowledge of God."

"I think she listens to Frau Rohrmoser when she teaches the children. Perhaps her faith is more childlike than the others," Pastor Gronau replied gently, looking for something kind to say about the woman. He rather enjoyed her, even though her behavior was not exactly proper all the time.

"I don't like to repeat the gossip of a woman like Frau Rott; I even admonished her to cease telling lies about people, but she told me about one disturbing incident involving Mamma Anna."

"What was that?" Pastor Gronau asked.

"She said she saw Mamma Anna rubbing the naked back and chest of that sailor she's always talking to, the one who saved her life the night of the great storm. She was doing this in public, where everyone could see her."

"Surely she was applying an ointment or something."

"Well, that's another thing that bothers me. We have Mr. Zwiffler with us to tend the sick. I don't trust some old, ignorant peasant woman, who may be an herbalist," Pastor Boltzius said, shaking his head. "I shall pray about this situation and wait for God to provide an answer. Meantime, keep an eye on her and report back to me what you observe. It is our duty to be vigilant with the souls of our charges."

"Yes, of course."

28

Salzburg, April 1732

As Archbishop Leopold Firmian strolled through the gardens at Mirabell Palace in Salzburg, he noticed that only the early bulbs were blooming. He stooped, broke off a narcissus, and held it to his nose, enjoying its fragrance. The grounds of the palace sloped toward the Salzach River, offering a lovely view of the city, with the Hohensalzburg, the fortress, towering on the mountain on the other side. Marring that tranquil view was the seemingly endless parade of exiles being led north along the edge of the river to Bavaria or beyond.

Archbishop Firmian stopped and fixed his gaze on the struggling procession. Most of the ladies and gentlemen of the court mingling in the garden appeared oblivious to the file of emigrants, although a few were actually uneasy about the large numbers of people passing through Salzburg on their way north. They were heard whispering behind their hands. "Who will be left to farm the fields and dig the mines?"

"Our beloved Archbishop has carried religion too far this time, don't you think?"

"I've lost my best servants to this stupid expulsion."

"You know what they are calling the Archbishop now?" one clever courtesan asked the group gathered around her, but out of range of the Archbishop.

"No, what?" they eagerly responded, looking for some good gossip to pass along.

"They're calling him 'Lead me on' because it sounds like 'Fuer mi an,' a play on his name. It's certainly an appropriate name for those poor, exiled creatures to call him, don't you think?" she asked with a smirk.

Across the way, Chancellor von Rall approached Firmian and fell into step beside him. He did not like for the Prince to watch the fleeing Lutheran exiles. Firmian might decide that von Rall's policies had been too stringent. Who would have guessed that there were so many Protestants in the Province, or that so many would refuse to capitulate? He had been busy arranging for Firmian to make an official visit to Vienna for a hunting party with the Emperor, hoping to get his mind off those poor wretches.

"The Emperor will meet you at his favorite hunting lodge."

"Can you arrange for me to take my own horses? I wouldn't want to be at a disadvantage by having to ride strange horses."

"Yes, your Excellency."

"I would also need to take some members of the court."

"There are ten barges available, sir, which can be outfitted to accommodate quite a large party in great comfort."

Firmian turned back toward the palace, his spirits lifting in anticipation of the planned adventure. It would be a grand expedition. They all needed to relax and have some fun after the strain of the last year. Now that the heretics were finally leaving, he would no longer worry about an insurrection. One nagging problem still bothered him, though.

"Von Rall, who is going to farm our lands and work our mines with so many people leaving?"

"With your permission, Excellency, I'll bring in good Catholic workers from the Tyrol area. They will be most loyal and make fine servants and farmers."

"Yes, that's the answer. Do that."

On the other side of the river, Gertrude's wide blue eyes glittered, trying to see everything at once. Her plaited, blond hair that had been coiled over her ears had fallen down, and the braids swung back and forth under her broad-brimmed green hat, as she repeatedly looked from side to side.

"Look at that castle on the hill, Catherine!" she said, with a gasping intake of air.

"That's no castle, young lady, that's the Hohensalzburg, where they've tortured some of us Protestants, poor souls," a rough-sounding man interjected.

"Oh, Maria, look! That's where Uncle Hans was in prison!" Gertrude cried, pointing to the fortress on the mountain.

Maria lifted her eyes to see the fortress looming on the hill above the spires of the Cathedral. She stopped to stare, but the crowd of people pushed her forward. Barbara nudged and guided her along.

"Do you suppose we could try to find Hans?" Maria asked Barbara wistfully.

"Now, Maria, others who knew who to ask have already tried to find out something with no success. There's no chance that a group of women would get anywhere. Besides, the soldiers aren't allowing us to leave the road. Let's just pray for his soul as we walk through this place where his soul must have left his body and joined our God in Heaven."

"Look, Catherine!" Gertrude said for the tenth time, pointing at another wonder.

"Yes, Trudi, I see," Catherine answered, as awed as Gertrude at finally seeing the city that had dominated their imaginations all their lives. Crowds of people lined the narrow streets, watching the emigrants. Some laughed and jeered, but others reached out, pushing food or other useful items into the hands of the exiles.

"There's Firmian!" someone shouted. A man was pointing at the palace across the river. Gertrude dropped her bundle and scrambled up on a low stone wall beside the river to gaze at the palace. She saw several finely dressed men and women, but she could not tell which one was Archbishop Firmian.

"Come back down here, Trudi," Barbara called sharply, as the crowd suddenly surged to one side of the road when a coach with four horses clattered down the narrow street.

The abrupt movement of the crowd forced a man with a baby's cradle on his back against the river wall. The wooden cradle knocked Gertrude off balance, and she fell into the Salzach River, six feet below.

Barbara saw her fall, but the jam of people blocked her movement. "Gertrude!" she screamed. "Somebody help! My daughter fell in the river!"

Heads turned to watch a broad-shouldered blond man leap up on the wall and jump into the river.

Gertrude was wildly flailing her arms, barely managing to stay afloat as the water carried her north. The man swam toward her, gradually gaining on the current. When he grabbed her, Gertrude was so panicked that she fought against him. He clutched her dress, and the two of them went under. The crowd watched from the riverbank in stunned silence.

"Thomas!" screamed a young woman over the noise of the crowd as she saw her husband disappear under the muddy water.

Barbara, Catherine, and Maria stared in gray-faced horror at the spot where Gertrude and Thomas had gone under.

"There they are!" someone yelled, pointing downriver where the current had taken them. Thomas's blond head emerged, and he pulled the limp Gertrude toward the bank. Others ran to help. By the time her family reached her, Gertrude had been revived and was sitting up. Barbara knelt on the ground, hugging Gertrude to her breast, weeping and rocking her back and forth. "Thank God, you're alive. I couldn't bear to lose another child. Oh, thank God."

"Thank you for saving Trudi," Maria said to the blond man, who was struggling to his feet. His wife Margaretta slid down the bank and approached him. He opened his arms, and she hugged him fiercely.

"Oh, Thomas, I thought you were gone!" Margaretta gasped.

"I'm fine," he muttered weakly, then turned toward Gertrude. "How is she?"

"I'm alive," Gertrude said weakly, but her face was white, and she shivered in her wet woolen clothes.

Barbara turned to Thomas. "Oh, thank you, sir, for saving my child. Who are you so that we can thank God for you?"

"I'm Thomas Gschwandl from Gastein, and this is my wife Margaretta," Thomas said shyly.

"God bless you. How can we ever thank you enough?" Barbara said, taking his hand.

"It must be God's will that she survived," Thomas replied.

"Why would God care that much about me?" Gertrude asked.

"Only God knows the answer to that," Thomas replied.

While the Kroehr women introduced themselves, Johann Mosshamer joined the group.

"What happened? What happened?" he asked everyone at once.

"Gertrude fell into the river, and this man, Thomas Gschwandl, saved her," Maria answered.

A look of recognition passed between the two men.

"I believe we met in Schwarzach at the Salzbund," Johann said. "I'm Johann Mosshamer from near Saalfelden, and you're from Gastein, I believe."

"Ja, Thomas Gschwandl here," Thomas replied, wiping water from his face. "And this is my wife Margaretta and up there, holding my horse and wagon, is her sister Anna."

"Johann, could you go back and find Gertrude's bundle, by the wall where she fell in?" Maria asked.

"Yes, of course, Maria." Johann ran off, disappointed that he had missed an opportunity to save Gertrude and be a hero in front of Maria, but at least he could help her now.

The little party, with two dripping people, moved up the bank toward the Gschwandl wagon. Anna draped a blanket around Gertrude and handed another one to Thomas.

Soon, Johann returned with Gertrude's bundle. The women formed a circle of blankets, shielding Gertrude while she stripped off her soggy woolen clothes and donned her other set. She had no other shoes, but she was able, at least, to wear dry stockings.

When she was redressed, she tried to raise her bundle to continue the march, but she was too weak to lift it.

Thomas took it from her hand and heaved it on top of his loaded wagon. "Can you walk, child?" he asked.

"Yes, sir, I think I can," Gertrude replied.

The group rejoined the slowly moving procession, prodded along by soldiers shouting for people to move along and punching them with their guns when they walked too slowly.

The marvels of Salzburg had dimmed in all their eyes. As they moved past a monastery whose bells were tolling the hour of four, a mourning dove brushed Maria's hat, causing her to look up at the gray stone monastery, where she caught the eye of a nun staring down at them from a high window. She found herself weeping, partly in relief that Gertrude had been saved, but also in a parting grief that Hans would be lost to her forever when they left Salzburg. She realized that, even if he were alive, he would never know where to find her. Johann moved up behind her and put his free hand around her waist. She leaned toward him, feeling comfort from the warmth of his body.

"Should I try to do something else to find out what happened to Hans before we leave Salzburg? All that time in Saalfelden, I thought, if I could only get to Salzburg, I could find out something. But now I'm here, I don't know what to do. Who could I ask? Where could I go?" She looked up into Johann's face for answers, anguish squeezing her voice.

"There's nothing you can do, Maria. Many people have tried, with no success. Besides, the soldiers will not let us go anywhere in the city."

Catherine and Barbara held Gertrude's still-shaking hands, pulling her along into the open countryside. The little party stayed close to the Gschwandls' wagon. Margaretta and Anna began to get acquainted with the Saalfelden women as they plodded along the churned-up road together.

At dusk, Maria and Catherine scouted about for dry limbs. When they had built a fire, Gertrude lay on a blanket nearby, her wet clothes draped on sticks, steaming as they dried. A few yards away, the Gschwandl family built their fire and settled in for the night.

Johann and Thomas sat talking about what had happened since they were together last July in Schwarzach.

"Your companion, Hans, what happened to him? Is he in this great crowd somewhere?" Thomas asked.

"No, he was arrested and tortured in that fortress in Salzburg. We think he later died from his wounds. That was his niece you saved from drowning today. Barbara is his sister, and Maria was his betrothed," Johann answered quietly.

"Ah, so much loss. He was a handsome young man and prayed so eloquently. God's will is hard to understand sometimes," Thomas replied.

"How about your friend, Tobias, I believe?" Johann asked.

"Tobias Lackner, yes. He's still in Gastein. He's a foreman in the mines, and the Prince still needs him to keep the mines operating. I'm hoping he can bring my son when he comes. I had to leave him behind."

Johann shook his head in recognition of Thomas's sadness.

"I have children I left in Saalfelden, also," he said quietly. "They're in the care of my sister and brothers. My sister has been raising them since my wife died. I feared this journey was too dangerous for them. When I get established somewhere, I'll send for them." Johann felt sadness creeping over him as he thought about his children. He suppressed the guilt that had been growing since he had become involved with Hans in organizing the Protestants. His brothers had often enough pointed out the folly of his actions and their adverse effect on his children. He had stubbornly gone his own way, causing a rift within the family. Now, he bore the added guilt of leaving his children in the family's care.

After a while he continued, "Well, we must believe all our hardships are God's will. Frau Rohrmoser left behind a husband, and two little ones, too. It must be doubly hard for a mother to leave her children, particularly a nursing baby."

This time, Thomas nodded without speaking. The pain of the partings settled over the two men, and they sat in silence, feeling the smoldering embers of their hearts and watching the burning limbs diminish.

In a monastery back in Salzburg, the nun who had watched the Protestant procession from the second-story window spooned potato soup into the gray mouth of her patient.

"How is he?" the Mother Superior asked, leaning over the bed of the pale, gaunt man.

"About the same. His stump is healing from the amputation, but he still doesn't speak," Sister Theresa replied. The man swallowed the soup, but no flicker of life was apparent in his vacant blue eyes.

"What a pity," the Mother Superior said, as she knelt beside the bed and began her ritual prayer for the sick. When she had finished, she rose and placed her hand on Sister Theresa's arm. "You're doing a fine job of nursing him, my child. I never thought he would live when they brought him to us."

"What had happened to him, Reverend Mother? His wounds looked like he'd been beaten. If I knew something about him, maybe I could get him to talk to me."

"That's not something you need to know. As servants of God, we just humbly nurse the poor, sick wretches God sends to us." The Mother Superior did not want the sisters under her care to know that they were nursing a Protestant who had been tortured on the orders of the Archbishop. She feared that their tender hearts would not understand the need for such cruelty, and they might question the Church's actions. They needed protection from such conflicts of the soul. Caution was necessary, or the prison authorities might let them die instead of bringing them to the sisters. She rather doubted that the Archbishop and his Chancellor knew that Father Michael was sending the poor Protestant wretches to her convent after they collapsed under torture. He had told her to tell no one, not even the sisters.

Sister Theresa put the bowl down and wiped the lips of her patient. She gazed at the ashen face that might once have been handsome, with its high cheekbones and deeply set blue eyes. She allowed her hand to caress the sunken cheek and push back the oily, blond hair that was flopping over his forehead. She broke off a small piece of hard bread and placed it in his open mouth, but he made no effort to eat it.

"I'll make you well, sir; just relax and trust in God," she crooned. She removed the bread, fearing he might choke on it. When the tower bell struck four, she quickly straightened the pale linen comforter on the plain wooden bed and turned to the small window opening in the smoky stone wall. Below, the clamor of thousands of passing exiles almost drowned out the deep bass tones of the bell.

A mourning dove perched on the stone sill as if escaping from the vibrations of the bell and the noise and confusion of the street. Soldiers shouted orders; cartwheels ground on the road; horses thudded by; children cried; and feet shuffled along. Absentmindedly, she crumbled up bread for the dove as she watched the endless procession of Protestants. The birds also seemed to mourn the suffering humanity passing below. Where did they all come from? Unconscious tears ran down her face. The sister closed the shutters, plunging the room into near darkness before hurrying away to attend to her other duties prior to evening prayers.

29

Tittmoning Road, April 1732

As the sun rose, Gertrude lay wrapped in quilts, shivering from the chill morning air and from fever that had visited her during the night. She remembered watching the stars blur as her vision wavered.

She struggled to stand up, but sat back down abruptly. It had been two days since she had fallen into the river, and she had become sicker each day. Barbara stooped down, placing a hand on her forehead to gauge the fever. Feeling the heat, she involuntarily shook her head.

Maria stirred up the fire, while Catherine went to the river to fill the kettle with water. All three women were tired, dirty, and worried about Gertrude.

"Barbara, what was that tea that Mamma Anna used to make for colds in the chest?" Maria asked.

"I was just thinking about Mamma Anna, wishing she were here to help us with Gertrude. I've heard nothing since they took her away that terrible night. Do you suppose she's in this great crowd of people somewhere?"

"It's possible. Some of the others who were arrested have been exiled and are marching with us."

The two women looked again at Gertrude, whose pasty white face surrounded blue eyes glittering with fever. Barbara placed a cool, wet cloth on her forehead, took it away, and felt the heat that had been absorbed on the linen.

"Is the water boiling?" Barbara asked.

"Yes. Should I make some herb tea?" Maria asked.

Barbara opened a small wooden box and unfolded a cloth pouch. She took a pinch of dried herbs and put them in a cup. Maria poured in the steaming water. Gently, they held Gertrude up and helped her drink the mixture.

"What herb did you use?" Maria asked Barbara.

"I'm not sure, but Mamma Anna prepared it for me to give the children when they had a fever." Barbara looked around to see what was happening with the others and saw that they were preparing to continue their journey. "I don't think the soldiers will let us stay here until Gertrude is better. We'll have to carry her somehow."

Maria walked over to the Gschwandl family nearby. Soon, Thomas returned with her. He lifted Gertrude and carried her to his wagon. Margaretta and Anna rearranged the household goods and made a place for her to lie down, high up on the pile.

After the two families had begun their slow trek again, Barbara touched Thomas's arm. "Again you have helped us when we needed it most. God has been good to send you to us."

Gertrude lay on top of the lumpy, makeshift bed and bumped along with the rhythm of the plodding horse pulling the wagon. She slept fitfully, but when she was awake, she stared at the outline of the mountains against the blue sky. She watched clouds roll in and blot out the sun, putting a chill on the long afternoon.

There were times when she wondered if she would live. She began to think about what it would be like to die. Would she go to Heaven to be with God? Would she see Uncle Hans or her father, whom she could barely remember? Her mother always said this life was just a trial for life after death. She wondered if she had been good enough in this life. She began to weep over all the bad things she remembered doing. Even jumping on the wall to see across the river had been a bad thing. Now she was being punished.

"O God," she prayed, "I'll try to be very good. I don't think I'm ready to die yet. I haven't really started living my life. Dear Jesus, if you let me live through this illness, I'll learn to read the Bible better and pray every day. I'll be good to other people and work hard. I don't want to die yet. I haven't been good enough yet to go to Heaven. I'll do better, I promise, if you'll just let me live."

Gertrude's mind rambled, the jostling of the wagon causing her head to pound with each bump. The wagon stopped,

and she tried to raise herself to see over the bundled household goods, but she flopped back. "What's happening?" she
called weakly.

"There's a bridge up ahead, and everyone's been stopped,"
Barbara answered. "How are you feeling, Trudi?"

"My head hurts, but I'll be good," Gertrude said, tears
running down her face.

Soldiers rode down the road, yelling, "Pull over for the
night. You can cross the river into Bavaria tomorrow."

Thomas took Gertrude in his strong arms, set her down,
and laid her on the quilt Barbara had spread out under a tree.
Her face was pale, with red splotches where she had been
crying.

"Why are you crying, child?" Barbara asked. "Does your
head hurt that much?"

"No, Mother, I'm crying because I haven't been good
enough to go to Heaven if I die."

"Gertrude, don't be silly. You have been good enough.
You love God and even left your home to please God. Be-
sides, you're not going to die. You're young and strong.
You'll survive this illness and be a stronger person for it."

"But, Mother, how do you know I won't die?" Gertrude
sobbed in unusual desperation.

Barbara was becoming very alarmed at Gertrude's state of
mind. She held her head in her lap and gently stroked it with
a wet cloth. In a low voice, she crooned, "There, my darling
child. It's just the fever making you so afraid. Did I ever tell
you about the dream I had about all of us, and especially
you?"

"No, I don't think so."

"Well, that night when Maria and I, with little Barbara…." Her voice cracked a little when she said "little Barbara," but she bravely continued. "That night we stayed over
at Mamma Anna's house, the time when Maria tried to get
news about Hans, well, Mamma Anna prayed with us, and
then I had the strangest dream. I dreamed that Maria, Catherine, and you were all sitting in a church in a strange place

where the trees had long gray hair. You were a very important lady and had children sitting beside you."

"Where were you, Mother?" Gertrude asked.

"Well, I don't know exactly. You know how dreams are, but it seemed like I was floating around outside, looking in the church."

"Was this church in Heaven, Mother?"

"No, I don't think so, child. It seemed more like the future in this life. So I think you still have a long life to lead with a husband and children. Why don't you sleep now?"

Gertrude relaxed and drifted off to sleep. Barbara sat still, with Gertrude's head resting in her lap. She looked at the mountains in the distance and said in her mind, "I will lift up mine eyes unto the hills, from whence cometh my help. My help cometh from the Lord, who made Heaven and earth."

Later that evening, after Gertrude had eaten some soup and gone back to sleep, Barbara joined the rest of the group sitting around the Gschwandls' fire.

"How is Gertrude?" Margaretta asked.

"She's quiet finally and able to sleep. We can only pray for her now."

"Will we really leave Salzburg tomorrow?" Catherine asked.

"Ja, it looks that way," Thomas replied.

"Does the land in Bavaria look like the land in Salzburg?"

"None of us have ever seen any land but Salzburg, Catherine," said Johann, who also sat under the big tree, as close to Maria as he respectfully could. "I walked ahead today to see what was there. We have to cross the bridge at Tittmoning; then we will be in Bavaria. I guess we can go where we please after that, except not back into Salzburg."

"Where do you advise us to go, Johann?" Barbara asked.

"I don't know. I've heard that the King of Prussia has invited families who owned land in Salzburg to settle in Prussia. He's a Protestant. I don't know where Prussia is, however, or how to get there."

"Imagine, a Protestant king," Barbara said in amazement.

"Where do you plan to go, Thomas?" Johann asked.

"Well, others from Gastein are in a city called Memmingen, which isn't far from Augsburg, I'm told. My friend, Tobias Lackner, is expecting us to go there. He plans to join us when he leaves. I'm hoping he can bring my son. I need to find the way to Memmingen. Do you know where it might be, Johann?" Thomas asked.

"I heard someone say that it's west of here. Just follow the road west."

"If you folks want to come along with us, we would be pleased. Margaretta and Anna enjoy the company of the Saalfelden women," Thomas said, knowing that the women needed help if Gertrude was to be cared for. After pulling Gertrude from the river, he felt especially protective of her.

"Oh, Herr Gschwandl, we would be most grateful to continue our travels with your family. You have already saved our Gertrude twice. Four women traveling alone can use the help of another family," Barbara replied. "We have been thankful for your protection, too, Johann."

Color came into Johann's cheeks, and he nodded his pleasure in being included with the group.

"It's settled then. Tomorrow we head for Memmingen. Will you be traveling there, also?" Thomas asked Johann.

"Perhaps," Johann replied.

Later, before they retired for the night, Maria took a wooden pail down to the river to get water for bathing. Johann, who had been hoping for a moment alone with her, away from the others, followed her.

"Oh, you startled me," Maria said, when he walked up behind her.

"You should be cautious about walking alone in the dark, Maria. I don't trust these soldiers. I've seen how they look at you."

"I was just getting some water," Maria said defensively.

"Actually, I wanted to talk to you alone for a minute."

"Maybe you're the one I should worry about," she said almost flirtatiously. She suddenly realized she had not spoken with a man like that since Hans. Guilt at being unfaithful to him twinged her.

"Maria," Johann said, changing to a serious tone, "a new life starts for us tomorrow. Only God knows what is in store for us."

"That's true, Johann."

"I know you still miss Hans. So do I. I was honored to be his friend and companion in God's work, but he's gone, and we're left. Do you think you could ever think kindly toward me?" He paused, then continued when she did not answer immediately. "I need to know if my chances with you are impossible. If they are, I'll part company with you and your family after we leave Salzburg. If not...."

"Johann, I do think kindly toward you," Maria said, and she turned to put a hand on his arm. "I'm glad you knew Hans, too. It will help you to be patient with me. I'm very glad you're traveling with us, but there's still such a mountain of sadness in me. Only time will help that. If I just knew for sure what had happened to him."

"He's dead, Maria, just like my wife. It's time we both accepted that and begin to plan for the future."

"Perhaps you're right, but I need more time. Our whole lives are in such turmoil right now."

"Yes, I understand."

During the night, the wind changed. Wet clouds moved over the tired clumps of exiles, as they spent their last, restless night in the Province of Salzburg. A light rain began sifting down, and their woolen clothes were soon soaked to the flesh.

Barbara and Maria held a woolen blanket over Gertrude, trying to protect her from the rain, but the ground was soon soggy with water, and the down comforter under Gertrude became sodden. She fretted and tossed. All they were able to do was keep the rain from falling directly in her face. All around, groups of people gave up trying to sleep and huddled under trees inadequate to shelter them.

The willows hanging low over the greenish-white water of the Salzach River slowly became visible, as Thomas knelt to wash mud from his hands. He stood awhile, watching the sky lighten and staring at the wooden bridge that was their passage into Bavaria and the unknown. Slowly, the dark blur sharpened into the brown log beams of the Tittmoning Bridge. His gaze turned toward the mountains already left behind, but they hid themselves in the dense gray air.

"God, help us," Thomas prayed. He knew that Margaretta and Anna depended on him to provide for them, and now the four women from Saalfelden needed his help, also. He leaned against a willow tree and prayed, his eyes focused on the land across the river.

"My trust is in thee, O Lord. Thou hast brought us to this place. I don't know what's in store for us, but may I serve thee bravely and without fear. This is a miserable trial, but I only ask for strength to stand it." Thomas became distracted from his prayers when the awakening noises of the crowd intruded on the morning quiet.

He returned to his wagon, where Margaretta and Anna had laid out bread and cheese with his beer.

"Thomas, should we share our food with others who weren't able to bring as much? The Saalfelden women are already running out of food. What should we do?" Margaretta asked nervously.

"Yes, we must share with them. Someday we may be without, also. We'll then be relying on someone to share with us. God will provide, Margaretta. Trust in the Lord," Thomas replied.

The gray dawn was a relief after the wet, sleepless night. Barbara, Catherine, and Maria ate some stale, moldy bread and drank some weak tea. Barbara lifted Gertrude's head and held a cup to her lips. She tried to swallow, but this brought on deep coughing from her chest. When the coughing had subsided, Barbara insisted that she drink the herbal mixture. "You must at least drink something, or you'll become too weak to fight this illness," she said to Gertrude sternly.

Gertrude looked up in surprise. Her mother was usually kind and gentle when she was sick.

"You've got to fight the illness, Gertrude. Don't give in to it. You must decide to live. Do you understand me?" Barbara said, almost harshly.

"Yes, Mother," Gertrude replied weakly, "I'll try." She gulped down the tea and stood up, with help from Barbara.

"Here, lean against this tree while I wash your face and hands," Barbara said, leading her to a hemlock tree and gently bathing her.

Maria and Catherine packed up the wet, down comforters and blankets and shoved them into their packs, preparing for the day's march. Catherine could not resist worrying about the future.

"Mother, what will we eat when our food runs out?" she asked.

"Don't whine, Catherine," Barbara replied sharply. "The Lord will provide, or we'll die. Come help me with Trudi."

The two wet and miserable women led Gertrude to the Gschwandl wagon, where Margaretta and Anna helped her into the place they had prepared for her by restacking their provisions.

"You look like you could use a ride today, too," Margaretta said to Barbara.

"I'm fine. It's just the rain. It makes us all look worn out," Barbara said.

Johann came back from checking on what was ahead. "Our names are on the list for entry today," he said.

"You mean they actually have our names on a list?" Thomas asked.

"Yes, I gave them our names yesterday. They only permit a certain number to enter Bavaria each day. We go today."

Johann, in his excitement, put his arm around Maria and twirled her around. "We start our new life today. Even the weather is improving," he said, looking up. The rain had stopped, and the clouds were beginning to break up.

Johann's excitement infected everyone in the group, and they began stepping a little more lightly as they walked towards the bridge. Gertrude pulled herself up and looked over the side of the wagon, as the wheels rumbled across the wooden bridge. The sun suddenly shone through the clouds, making shafts of light on the river. The sparkle on the water caused her to squint her eyes, and she gazed south, searching for the mountains in the distance, but they were still shrouded with mist. I'll never see those mountains again, but maybe there will be others in this new land, she thought to herself.

They were stopped at the border, and their names were checked off the list. People behind them began singing the *Song of the Exile* while they waited to cross.

The sun shone intermittently as they went through the gray stone gate at Tittmoning. Gertrude, lying back in the wagon, could see the onion-shaped church steeple as they creaked over the stone street through the little village and passed through the gate at the other end of town.

"Which way is Memmingen?" Johann asked the silent people who stood by the road, watching the exiles. He received shrugs in response. The whole multitude of exiles was following the road west.

The procession stopped at midday to rest and eat. The sun was warm, and they spread out their wet belongings to dry. The men were going from one party to another, discussing where to go.

"There is land available for us in Prussia," one man said.

"Where is Prussia?" asked Thomas.

"It's to the north. You should turn north towards Augsburg to go there," the man said excitedly.

"How far is Prussia?" Johann asked. He was very interested in land. He had been the youngest brother in his family and had, therefore, never owned land of his own. He had been like a tenant on his older brother's land. He longed for his own farm.

The man had a crude map, which he laid out on the ground. "This is Augsburg," he said, pointing to a dot on the paper, "and here is Königsberg. It's a long way, but the King of Prussia has invited us to come to his land. Just imagine, a Protestant king offering us land. Thousands of people who left Salzburg in November have already gone there."

"If thousands have already gone, is there still more land for us?" Johann asked.

Thomas and Johann looked at each other, doubt covering their faces. Their experiences living in Salzburg under the Catholic Prince Archbishop did not make it easy to believe in the generosity of any king, even a Protestant one.

"How do you know he invited us?" Thomas asked.

"The word is being passed down the line, but be sure not to turn north towards München. That's a Catholic city, and we're not welcome there. God be with you," the stranger said abruptly, and turned to spread his news to the next group.

"Well, what do you think of that?" Johann asked Thomas.

"I don't know. Do you suppose it's true?"

"I would like to have some land of my own, but that looked like a long way. I don't think Gertrude could make such a trip just now. Maria will never leave her family, and they may need me. I'll go wherever they decide. What about you, Thomas?"

"I told Tobias Lackner I would wait in Memmingen in case he can bring my son with him. The Hubers and others from Gastein are already there, I think. That's where we'll go for now." He paused and scanned the sky with his eyes. "Of course, you folks don't have to go with us. But, as you said, Gertrude needs our wagon to ride in until she improves."

The two men joined the six women, who were combining their food for the midday meal. Gertrude was sitting up against a tree. She coughed deeply, clutching her chest in pain, but she was able to eat and drink. Her eyes were still bright with fever, however.

Barbara asked the men, "What did that visitor have to say?"

"He said the King of Prussia has invited the Salzburgers to his country, and he will give them land. He showed us a map, and Prussia is a long way north, much further than we have already come. He said we should turn north towards Augsburg," Johann replied.

"I plan to continue west toward Memmingen," Thomas said. "The Hubers and the Grubers from Gastein are expecting us, and Tobias Lackner and others from Gastein will follow us there. If Tobias should be able to bring my son with him, I would miss him if I turned north."

Everyone except Barbara looked down at their food at the mention of Thomas's son. No one else except Barbara still held out hope that the children of the exiles might be released.

"If Peter should change his mind and bring my children, it would be better not to be as far away as Prussia," Barbara said. "Besides, Gertrude's not strong enough to make such a journey. We must stop somewhere nearer and find a place for her to get well again. I think we'd better go on to Memmingen with the Gschwandls. What do you think, Maria?"

"Yes, of course. Gertrude can't walk yet. After she's well, then we can think of other possibilities," Maria said. She glanced at Johann to see what his reaction might be.

"I'll travel with all of you," Johann said.

"Thank you, Johann. We need your protection," Barbara said, "but we don't want to stand in your way of having land of your own, if the man's story is true."

"People are more important than land," Johann said, as he stood up and walked away from the group.

After eating, they continued their procession in a westerly direction.

30

Memmingen Road, May 1732

Anna Hofer, Margaretta Gschwandl's sister, walked beside the wagon with Catherine Kroehr. The two were becoming good friends and found that they enjoyed each other's company while they trudged along in the endless procession.

"I wonder what Memmingen will be like," Catherine said. "Mother won't let me ask her anymore. I guess I do worry too much about what will happen to us. I just can't help it. She says I don't trust in God enough. It's hard to believe that God will provide, and yet, when we were running out of food, your sister and Herr Gschwandl shared their food with us. I suppose God did provide. But what happens when your food runs out?"

"I don't know," Anna said. She liked having someone to talk to besides Margaretta. She loved her younger sister, but it was awkward being dependent on her and Thomas. Still, the adventure of this great journey was exciting to her. She had never been much of anywhere before. "The land is so different, isn't it? There are no high mountains, just rolling hills, and sometimes it's flat. It makes it easier to walk, but I miss the mountains and the river."

"It would be a whole lot easier if I didn't have these awful blisters on my feet," Catherine whined. "Nothing I do seems to help because they open up again every day with this endless walking. Don't you have blisters, Anna? You never mention it."

"Of course I do. Everyone does, but there's nothing we can do, so what's the point of talking about it. It just reminds me that they hurt."

"Now you sound just like my mother," Catherine said, scrunching up her face in disgust. "Don't complain. It just makes things worse," she said, mimicking her mother's voice.

Anna laughed conspiratorially.

While the girls were talking, Margaretta paced herself beside Barbara, who was walking along reading her Lutheran Bible.

"What are you reading?" Margaretta asked.

"I was just reading about Moses leading the children of Israel into the Promised Land. This is also a great exodus, and God will provide for us, too. God led us to you and Thomas, who have helped us so much. We are deeply grateful. I hope someday I can do something for you," Barbara said.

"Perhaps you can now, Frau Rohrmoser. As you know, I'm newly married, and I'm not sure, but I may be having a baby. You've had many babies. Tell me what it's like, so that I can be sure. Thomas doesn't know yet." She hesitated. "I don't have a mother to ask. I hope you don't mind."

"No, my dear, of course I don't mind. Have you missed your monthly bleeding?" Barbara asked.

"Yes," said Margaretta shyly. She ducked her head to hide her cheeks that had turned red with embarrassment.

"Now don't be bashful. Having a baby is God's way to bring people on this earth. Babies are a blessing. But it will be difficult without a home. We'll take care of you, though, and get you through this. Maria has helped me have my babies, and now I can help you. Don't you worry. By the time the baby comes, you may have another home. When do you plan to tell Thomas?"

"I hate to discuss this with him at such a time. I'll wait until we get settled somewhere. He has so much to worry about right now. I don't want him to worry about me, but I just had to tell someone."

"Your secret is safe with me. Are you sick in the mornings?"

"Yes, sometimes."

"I'll give you some tea to settle your stomach," Barbara said sympathetically, patting Margaretta's arm. "I've been through it many times."

"I guess I'm just a little afraid."

"Of course you are. I can remember how frightened I was with my first baby, Catherine. Mamma Anna helped me with that delivery. It was a lot harder than the last one, I can tell you. The first time is the scariest. You don't know what to expect, but try not to worry. We'll take good care of you."

"Thank you. I feel better now. It's hard holding such a secret inside you. You begin imagining all sorts of horrible things. It doesn't seem so terrible now that I've talked with you." Barbara put her arm around the young woman's shoulders and felt her trembling.

Maria and Johann were walking ahead of the wagon with Thomas. The three were in animated conversation.

"Life may be better for me in a Protestant city," Johann said. "All my life, the Catholic Church has been an obstacle. Being the third son, I had no inheritance, and life as a servant is so poor. I could never own land and was a servant in my own house. I may have to be a servant in Bavaria, but at least I'll be able to worship God openly as an Evangelical and not have to worry about being punished for it."

"It must have been very hard for you to leave your farm, Thomas. I hope someday you'll have another," Maria said.

"Ja. I had always lived on that land, and all my family for many generations. I still can't believe I'll never see it again. It wasn't an easy life, but...." Thomas let his voice drop and failed to finish the sentence.

After a lengthy pause, Thomas continued, "But the hardest part was leaving young Thomas. I have to remind myself of Abraham being willing to sacrifice his son for God. And, of course, Jesus was God's sacrifice for us. Still, it's hard to think of Thomas growing up with Catholics."

"All Catholics aren't bad," Maria said softly. "Father Jacob was very kind to Johann when he was hurt. The sexton told me that he sat up all night praying over him."

She turned to Johann, walking on her other side. "Isn't it strange that Father Jacob would take care of you, Johann, when it was the Church that had tortured you? It makes me think that all Catholics aren't so bad, just some." Maria paused as they listened to the hundreds of feet walking along the road.

Johann nodded his head in agreement.

Maria continued, "But I agree, Thomas. It's the people we left behind that are the hardest part. I know it broke Barbara's heart that she could never convince Herr Rohrmoser to join us in the ways of Luther. And then having to leave the baby...." Maria's voice choked. "I don't know if Barbara will ever get over that. But, in the end, the soldiers would not let her stay, or the children come. She had no choice. She doesn't seem like the same person to me. She wears her sadness in all that she does."

"Barbara is a strong woman," Johann said. "She stood up to Peter's family in the midst of criticism, and she led the people after Hans was taken. She has always been an inspiration to me and to the other Protestants of Saalfelden. She told me that her pain has deepened her faith. She is very steadfast in her faith."

"That's true," said Maria. "She's the one who always leads us back to God when we begin straying away into our own concerns."

Ahead, Gertrude lay on top of the Gschwandls' household goods, sleeping intermittently. When she opened her eyes, she watched the fluffy white clouds move across the blue sky. Occasionally, she pulled herself up to gaze at the horizon. The land is so flat, she thought. How strange for there to be no mountains. She watched the endless procession of exiles snake along the road, ahead and behind their own party. Some, like her mother, were proudly reading German Bibles and other religious pamphlets, which they had never been allowed to read in Salzburg, as they stumbled along, leaning on walking canes carved out of trees from their ancestral villages. The panorama swam in and out of Gertrude's fevered mind as she was uncomfortably jostled on her lumpy, improvised, swaying bed.

As the day waned, the travelers began to realize for the

first time that no soldiers were riding up and down the line shouting orders. They could stop when they wanted and go where they wanted.

"We don't have to worry about Firmian's soldiers anymore," Johann said. "We should get to the road that goes north to Augsburg soon. I expect most of this great crowd will turn north, don't you?" he asked Thomas.

"Ja, probably. The possibility of land and protection in Prussia is tempting. Are you sure you don't want to turn north, Johann?"

Johann looked at Maria. "Not yet, Thomas; not yet."

When a hemlock forest with a stream running through it appeared on the right, Thomas led his horse off the road and into a small clearing. "We all need some rest," he said, "especially Gertrude. Let's stop early. I'm also afraid of wearing out my horse."

Margaretta and Barbara began planning a good dinner of ham and dumplings, pooling their provisions to make the meal. Barbara offered Margaretta one of her tea mixtures to help her morning sickness.

Thomas and Johann began constructing a crude shelter, not wanting to repeat the discomfort of being drenched like the previous night. Johann's eye followed Catherine, Anna, and Maria, who set off following the stream into the forest. His mind went with them, but he dared not go. The girls found a quiet, secluded pool and, removing their clothes, bathed themselves in the cold water. They washed their hair and underclothes with the precious soap they had brought with them.

Gertrude lay in the slanting sun and watched as the procession of exiles continued to trudge west. Many were carrying heavy, round wooden cradles on their backs with babies in them. One wagon passed by jammed with old people and children who could not walk. Some pushed round vegetable carts, their belongings stacked on top where their produce used to ride. One woman pulled a small hand wagon in which a young child with a bandaged leg rode. But most just walked, leaning wearily on walking staffs and often singing hymns as they passed.

Gertrude wondered who was left in Salzburg. Being part of the procession, she had not realized how many exiles there were, but watching this crowd clumping by, she began to understand the magnitude of the exodus. Even in her weak state, she was awed by what they had all done in the name of God. She lay back, closed her eyes, and felt that her fate was in God's hands. If God had more in store for her, she would be healed of this illness. If not, she would die. She felt very peaceful as she drifted off into sleep.

31

Memmingen, 1732

As the Gschwandl wagon followed the procession of exiles through the gate into the town of Memmingen, the weary Protestants were surprised to see townspeople lining the streets, cheering them and thrusting gifts into their hands. The church bells were pealing, bouncing off the buildings encompassing the square. The Pastor of St. Martin's Evangelische Lutherische Church stood greeting the men with handshakes.

The women from Saalfelden looked around at the spectacle, their mouths hanging open in amazement. They were so surprised to be welcomed to Memmingen in this way that they could not speak. Catherine noticed the beautiful clothes of the ladies, with skirts that fell all the way to the ground. She realized that the coarse woolen, Alpine dress of the Salzburgers was very different from what these fine people wore.

She began to feel conscious of her dirty peasant clothes and concerned about what these people would think of them. The men and women all looked so different from the Salzburgers, yet seemed to be happy to see them.

"What's this all about?" asked Maria. "Why are they cheering for us?"

"I don't know," Barbara answered. "Let's listen to the speakers and find out."

"Ladies and gentlemen, we welcome you with open arms to this Protestant city. You have renewed the faith of all of us as you have made your witness against a Catholic tyrant, suffering exile for the sake of your faith. We are a small town, but we open our hearts to you."

The Salzburger emigrants gazed at the beautiful square surrounding them. The speaker was standing in front of the stately, white city hall, with two onion-shaped domes on each side and fluted walls meeting in the center, forming a higher, central dome. Flowers were blooming in boxes under each window. At the other end of the square was a gray stone church. Barbara was amazed to see such a big Protestant church. She had never seen a Protestant church before. Along one side of the square was a beautiful pink building painted in similar style to the lovely painted buildings in Saalfelden.

The man continued speaking for quite some time, quoting much Scripture and praising the actions of the Salzburgers. Then several other men spoke. Barbara lost track of who they all were, but each one praised the Salzburgers for their courageous faith in God. Tears ran down the faces of many of the emigrants, who stared in disbelief and relief. They had been persecuted for so long that they had difficulty understanding such a welcome.

When the speeches ended, the Salzburgers spontaneously began singing *A Mighty Fortress is Our God*. The townspeople joined them, and Luther's hymn sounded as firm as the gray stone of the church in the square.

Townspeople began inviting the exiles into their homes. The weaver's wife, in German that was strange sounding but understandable to Barbara, beckoned for her to come into her house.

"There are four of us," Barbara said, "and Gertrude is sick."

"Come, come, all four of you," the grinning woman said.

"Johann, we're going with this good woman," Maria called in the midst of the confusion.

"Ja, I'll find you," Johann called back. A lady was handing him a basket of food.

The Gschwandls were ushered off to another home.

Barbara helped Gertrude into the front room beside the weaver's shop. It was small, but there was a bench where Gertrude could sit down. In the center of the room were a table and chairs. Gertrude began a deep, painful cough that caused her to double up, gasping. Everyone was afraid the weaver's wife would send them away when she heard Gertrude coughing so.

"Let's get that child to bed," she said instead, and led Gertrude up the stairs to a wooden bed with a feather mattress. Gertrude slowly lay down on the first bed she had seen since leaving the Rohrmoser farm in Saalfelden so long ago.

"Thank you, kind lady," she said weakly.

"God bless you, child. Now go to sleep."

"Why are you being so kind to us?" Barbara asked, her voice catching in almost a sob.

"I am a Christian," the lady replied, "and my heart has been warmed by what you Salzburgers have suffered. We have come to take our faith for granted. We haven't had to suffer persecution. The least we can do is welcome those who have."

Barbara took the woman's work-roughened hands and kissed them.

"Oh, none of that, dearie; I'm just a simple woman."

"What is your name?" Barbara asked. "I want to remember it always."

"My name is Brigitte Scherraus. My husband is the weaver. And who are you?"

Barbara introduced herself and the others and began to relate their story.

"Is there someone who could help Gertrude?" Barbara asked hesitantly.

"Why, yes, as a matter of fact one of the Salzburgers who came earlier is a wonderful healer." She leaned out the window and yelled to a blond boy about twelve years old who was coming down the street, "Uli, fetch the healing woman. Go quickly."

"Yes, Mother. Who's sick?" he called back.

"Just hurry. You'll find out later."

A few minutes later, Barbara looked out the window and saw a familiar figure hurrying down the street with Uli. She was fat and disheveled-looking and was carrying a big, full basket.

"Mamma Anna," Barbara cried. "We thought you were dead! How did you get here?"

"Oh, my goodness! Look who's here--Barbara, Catherine, Maria. I can't believe it. When did you arrive? Where's Gertrude?" Mamma Anna asked, hugging everyone.

"Gertrude is very sick. This good woman has put her to bed upstairs. That's why she sent for you. Imagine our surprise when we saw you coming down the street. I know you can help Gertrude, but how did you get here? The last time we saw you was when the soldiers dragged you away that terrible night last February."

"I'll tell my story later. First, let me see Gertrude. I brought that child into the world; I don't want to lose her now."

Brigitte led the way up the stairs, and everyone else followed, crowding into the tiny room.

"Everyone out except Barbara," Mamma Anna ordered.

Catherine and Maria looked at each other and laughed. They remembered Mamma Anna's bossy ways. They both felt relief, knowing Gertrude was in her hands. She knew how to heal people. They trusted her.

They turned to go back downstairs. Frau Scherraus looked startled at being ordered out of her own room. Maria turned to her. "She will call us if she needs anything. She doesn't want to be distracted when she's examining a sick person. She says it makes her miss things that might be important," Maria explained.

Mamma Anna felt Gertrude's forehead and left her hand there to absorb the amount of heat. "Her fever is high. How long has she been this hot?" she asked Barbara.

"Well, since she fell in the Salzach River in Salzburg. She almost drowned and swallowed a lot of water. She began with a cold and fever, and then this terrible cough deep in her chest started. She has been getting weaker and weaker. Her throat has closed up, and she can't eat much."

"How did she walk in such a condition?"

"The man who saved her from the river had a wagon, and she has been riding in it since she got sick. I'm so glad you are here to heal her. She drank the tea for fever that you gave me, when I could heat water to make it. Sometimes it wasn't possible."

Gertrude opened her eyes. "Mamma Anna? Mother, is this really Mamma Anna?" Gertrude asked weakly.

"Yes, Trudi. She is here in Memmingen. She's going to take care of you and make you well again."

"Oh, Mamma Anna, I'm so glad. I don't want to die yet," Gertrude said.

Mamma Anna opened Gertrude's clothes and examined her throat and chest. Gertrude's deep cough brought a frown to her face as she put an ear to her chest.

"That rattle sounds like pneumonia. Thank goodness she's usually strong and healthy," Mamma Anna said to Barbara. She reached in her bag and rummaged around until she came up with a cloth package. "Go make some tea with this. Be sure to boil the water a long time before steeping the tea. Ask for some rags. I want to make a plaster for her chest."

Barbara left the room. Mamma Anna sat down beside Gertrude on the bed. She took her hand and said in a firm voice, "Trudi, do you want to get well?"

"Oh, yes, I do," Gertrude said solemnly.

"Then you must do everything I say. You must trust in God that you will get well. The first thing is for you to lie back and rest. You are all worn out from traveling. Just rest."

Later that day, after Gertrude had been doctored and was asleep, Barbara, Maria, and Catherine sat around the table in the front room and listened while Mamma Anna told her story.

"Well, you were there that night they arrested me. They carried me through the snow to the jail in Saalfelden. Lordy, I was cold and freezing. There wasn't any heat in that filthy place. They threw me in with the men, some of them thieves and murderers, I guess. I was plenty scared, I can tell you. Anyway, when morning came, I saw the jailer and recognized him. He was a Rohrmoser, Barbara, one of Thomas's sons."

"Which one?" asked Barbara.

"This one was Michael. Well, as I said, I remembered him. I had helped save his wife from a difficult birth. She was bleeding something awful when they came for me. They hadn't called me at first, but this was an emergency. Nobody else could get the bleeding stopped. So I worked on her for the longest time, and finally the bleeding stopped. She was mighty weak, but she lived. So did the baby."

"So what did Michael Rohrmoser do?" Maria asked, trying to get Mamma Anna back on track. She knew her tendency to go into the details of every birthing.

"Oh, yes, well, I said to Michael, 'How's that baby doing, and your wife?' and he said, 'Mamma Anna, what are you doing here?' So I said, 'They arrested me last night. See what you can do about saving my life like I saved your wife's.'

"Well, he looked so sheepish I knew he'd do what he could, but he never has been very smart. Excuse me, Barbara, talking about your kin this way," Mamma Anna said, aside to Barbara. Barbara nodded her head in approval. "Anyway, I wasn't sure he'd be able to think of any way to help me, even if he wanted to. I decided I'd better think of something myself, so I says to him, 'Michael, go tell Father Jacob I want to see him.'

"'You want to convert back to the church?' that idiot asked.

"'I need a priest, Michael, but be sure it's Father Jacob,' I said firmly. Sure enough, before long here comes Michael with Father Jacob. Now the Father is surprised that the soldiers have put a woman into the same jail with the men.

"'What's she doing in there with the men?' he asks, outraged.

"'I guess there wasn't anywhere else to put her. We don't get many women prisoners,' Michael answered back.

"'Well, get her out of there,' the priest said.

"So anyway, they let me out, and then no one knew what to do with me. I suggested that they just send me into exile and get it over with. I'd have to go in the spring anyway. I figured if I didn't leave the country quick, they'd mess around cooking up stuff about me and kill me.

"So, lo and behold, they bought my plan and exiled me. They were afraid to send me walking. Afraid I'd go home or something, so they set me on a horse and sent a soldier with me all the way to Tittmoning. He was a good-looking fellow, too. So I got a ride out of Salzburg, and I walked the rest of the way. There were a few stragglers still on the road from the November crowd, and I joined up with them and came to Memmingen. It's a nice town. The people have taken us in, and I've been kept pretty busy delivering babies and taking care of the sick."

"It's a miracle that you're here, just when we need you so badly," Barbara said.

"The Holy Spirit works in mysterious ways," Mamma Anna replied.

32

On Board the *Purysburg*, 1734

Barbara, Catherine, Gertrude, and Mamma Anna lay in their stacked bunks, talking after the candle in the passageway had been blown out for the night. It was so dark in the crowded, stinking cubicle that smell, touch, and hearing became the only senses that were usable.

"I'm so glad that you're feeling better, Mamma Anna. You're like a second mother to me. It would have broken my heart to have to lose you," Barbara said into the darkness. "I'll never forget how relieved I was when you came trotting down that street in Memmingen following Uli Scherraus. I was about out of my mind from worrying about Gertrude."

"Well, you can be sure I was just as happy to see all of you. I didn't think I'd ever find anyone again that meant anything to me. Even though I was busy and the people were friendly, I was lonesome to the bone for someone from home," she answered from the lower bunk.

"Mamma Anna, when Gertrude was so sick and then you got sick, I realized that none of us knew what to do," Barbara said. "I'm so glad you taught Maria and Johann some of what you know, but I'm surprised that what you do is so different from what Mr. Zwiffler does for the sick."

"Well, I've just always tried to remember what my own granny taught me, and then what has helped people over the years. I've lost a lot of people, my own family among them, so I guess there's more to know than I've learned."

"Pastor Gronau says that you will die when God wants you to die and not before. Does that mean the medicine doesn't matter?" Catherine asked.

"Well, I don't know the answer to that one, Catherine. I just try to make people feel better. Surely God doesn't want people to suffer more than is necessary."

"Pastor Boltzius said that we should rejoice in adversity and stand the trial of this earthly life, knowing that our reward will be in Heaven," Gertrude said.

Mamma Anna chuckled, "Well, Trudi, my love, I expect by now we've all earned our place in Heaven if a life of hardship is the key. We've already experienced enough of that to open a door or two, I expect."

"But, Mamma Anna, you've got to be faithful to God and live a devout Christian life along with the hardships in order to get into Heaven," Gertrude replied earnestly.

"You sound like you're worried about my soul, child. I am who I am, and I don't know how to be anybody else. I just do the best I can, and I don't hold much to being judged by anyone else. 'Judge not that you be not judged,' I believe the Scripture says," Mamma Anna replied, in a voice that showed some irritation. She was getting tired of people trying to change her ways. She knew what she knew, and that was that. It was enough that the pastors and all the other pious Salzburgers were always trying to get her to pray with them. She certainly didn't need a child she'd known since infancy to act more knowledgeable about life than she was.

"I think it's time we all went to sleep," Barbara said diplomatically. She was also concerned about Mamma Anna's nonconformist ways, but she knew better than to try to preach to her.

33

Memmingen, 1733

"Do you know the whereabouts of Hans or Peter Gruber?" Thomas Gschwandl asked a lady hurrying with her market basket across the square in Memmingen. He had resorted to asking anyone he met for the whereabouts of his friends from Gastein. He had been in Memmingen for months now and still had not found either the Gruber brothers or the Huber family. Margaretta was so distraught with the new baby that he thought it would comfort her to see friends from Gastein.

"Hans and Peter Gruber, you say? Hmmm. I can't say that I do. There've been so many of you Salzburgers, I can't learn all the names. Sorry," she replied.

"How about Lorentz Huber?" Thomas asked again.

"Sorry, sir," she said, as she hurried off.

Thomas strolled down to St. Martin's Church at the other end of the square. He had asked the pastor many times about his friends, but he did not know where else to turn. He had been surprised that the Grubers and Hubers were not in Memmingen as they had promised. Perhaps they had moved on or had never come here at all. It made him feel very lonely. He had expected to see these old friends again.

He cautiously opened the heavy door and stepped inside the church. It was cool and quiet. In the dim light he could see no one, and he turned to leave.

"You looking for the pastor?"

"Ja. Do you know where he is?"

Thomas was addressing a little wizened man who was using a hoe to cut down the weeds around the church.

"Just saw him headed for the blacksmith."

"Maybe you can help me, sir," Thomas said. "I'm looking for some friends from Gastein. I thought the pastor might know where they are."

"Is this Gastein part of them Salzburgers?"

"Ja."

"Thought as much. Well, I know lots of them. Who you looking for?"

"Hans and Peter Gruber and Lorentz Huber and his wife and four children."

"Four little ones, huh?"

"Have you seen them?"

"Maybe. I'm not sure of the name. It wasn't easy to find a place for that many. You see that building there?" he said, pointing down the street. "Well, turn right there and go 'til you come to a big oak tree with a well under it, and turn left. After a ways you'll come to an old stone cottage. They might be there. Nobody was living there, and the town's letting a family live in it. It might be Huber."

"Thank you, sir," Thomas said hopefully, and set out to follow the directions. Disappointment soon followed, for the family he discovered in the cottage was not the Hubers.

"I'm looking for the Huber family from Gastein," he said politely to the sad-looking woman who came to the door.

"Don't know that name. We came from St. Johann."

"I'm sorry to bother you. My wife just had a baby and wanted to see her old friends. Someone thought this might be the family."

"We've already lost one of our babies," she said despairingly. "The two-year-old died during the winter. We had to leave in November, you see, and it was so cold. The little one couldn't stand the cold. We're grateful for a place to live. It's small and tumbledown, but it's a roof. God has helped us some, at least."

"Ja," Thomas said sympathetically, remembering his own son lost to him. "I'll just keep looking for the Hubers. You don't happen to know the Gruber brothers, do you?"

"No, but I seldom get into town. There's so much to do."

As Thomas walked back towards town, he saw a line of Salzburgers walking beside a wagon loaded with felled trees. He knew they were Salzburgers because they were dressed in Alpine clothes. As he stopped to watch them, he suddenly saw two men whom he recognized, walking together.

"Peter, Hans," he called excitedly, waving his hands.

The two men looked around simultaneously.

"Thomas, is that you?" Peter asked.

The three men slapped each other on the back. "I've been searching for you for months," Thomas said. "I'd begun to think you weren't still here in Memmingen."

"We've been off in the forest to the north, cutting trees for the lumberman. We're just coming back. We didn't know you had come, or we'd have tried to send word."

"Have you seen the Hubers?"

"Ja. They moved on to Augsburg, hoping for a better place to stay. There wasn't enough room for six people anywhere," Peter replied.

"Tell us about Gastein. Did you see my sons?" Hans asked eagerly.

"They're fine, but they can't leave. I'm hoping Tobias can bring my son when he comes, but I don't know." Thomas's voice trailed off.

A heavy sadness surrounded them as they remembered their lost families.

Thomas felt better than he had in a long while, seeing these old, comfortable friends. "We have a new baby born just last week. Margaretta was wishing for some familiar faces; that's why I went off looking for you and the Hubers today. The sight of you two will surely cheer her up. We're staying at the Gnann place. When can you come by?"

"We'll have to unload these wagons first, but after that we are due some free time," Peter replied.

* * *

The next morning, Maria and Johann followed Mamma Anna on her rounds.

"I'm not used to having helpers," Mamma Anna said, "but there are so many sick people that I can't stay with all of them. I'm not going to live forever, either. Someone needs to know what it's taken me a lifetime to learn. Others taught me."

"Mamma Anna, I've always been interested in healing and impressed with the way you can help sick people. I'm honored that you'll teach me. Besides, if I weren't working with you, I'd have to be a servant," Maria said. "This work is much more interesting, and I feel like I'm serving God in a special way when I take care of a sick person."

"Well, I never expected to be teaching a man," Mamma Anna said with a chuckle, turning to Johann. "The women will never let you be their midwife, you know, Johann, but the men will be more comfortable with you in some of their ailments. So stick with me, and I'll teach the both of you what I know. You can lift old man Fetzer for me. He's too heavy for me to handle," she said, turning into a cottage with a barking dog.

Johann went up to the dog and petted him until he wagged his tail in greeting.

When Maria and Mamma Anna left a while later, Johann stayed with the old man, since he lived alone and wasn't doing well.

"I never saw a man so good at taking care of sick people before. He certainly has the instinct for it. I've seen it in lots of women, you, for one, but never in a man. God works in mysterious ways.

"Now, Maria, let's you and me go look in on Margaretta and that new baby girl. She had a hard time giving birth to that baby. Some women's bodies just don't seem to be made for childbirth. The hips are too narrow and don't want to open up properly. Thank the Lord the baby was small. I'm not sure she could have survived a big baby. The ordeal wore her out and caused awful swellings to come. It'll take her a long time to recover, and that small baby will be harder to care for than a big one."

"Mamma Anna, I wonder if I'll ever know what to do in all of the different circumstances that come up, like you do."

"I don't always know. Sometimes, I'm just guessing and using common sense. Sometimes, nothing I do works, and people die. You have to accept that and not be afraid the next time."

The makeshift bedroom the Gschwandls had fashioned for themselves in a stall in the Gnanns' barn was a poor place for a new mother and a week-old baby. When the women arrived, they found Margaretta sobbing inconsolably, holding the little screaming baby in her arms.

Mamma Anna quickly took the baby and walked outside with her, while Maria knelt down and put her arms around Margaretta to comfort her.

"She just cries and cries," wailed Margaretta. "I can't get her to stop. I feed her, and she just keeps crying. What am I doing wrong? Is she going to die?"

"Mamma Anna will take care of her," Maria said calmly. "When did she start crying like this?"

"Last night. She cried for hours. I couldn't get her to stop for the longest time." Margaretta's body shook as she sobbed on Maria's shoulder.

"Everything's going to be better now. Lie back and let me wash your face. Where are Anna and Thomas?" Maria asked, gently wiping her face with a damp cloth.

"Thomas went looking for the Grubers and Hubers, folks from Gastein. He was trying to find some way to cheer me up because I was crying for my dead mother. Maria, I'm so ashamed of myself, but I can't quit crying. I'm as bad as the baby."

"Where's Anna? She shouldn't have left you alone like this."

"I was so worried about the baby, I sent her to look for Mamma Anna. She didn't know what to do, either."

Mamma Anna came back into the barn, the baby in an exhausted sleep in the crook of her arm.

"What's wrong with her, Mamma Anna?"

"Well, she seems to be growing so she must be getting enough milk. After she passed some gas, she settled down. I think she just has a gassy stomach. She's such a little baby still. I've noticed that the really small babies often have a gassy stomach until they grow bigger. She seems strong and healthy otherwise."

Mamma Anna put the sleeping baby in the wooden cradle that Thomas had made and then turned to Margaretta. "Now then, let me examine you to be sure you are healing properly. Is there much pain?"

"I don't want to complain," Margaretta started, but then her voice broke into a sob. "I just hurt all the time."

"Yes, child, I know," the old midwife said compassionately. "Can you tell me exactly where it hurts the most."

The restless baby began crying again, drawing up her legs and waving her tightly balled fists.

"Maria, pick the baby up and hold her bent over, with your hand on her stomach. That seems to help the pain," Mamma Anna said quietly.

Maria did as she was told, and the baby stopped crying.

"Is that all I needed to be doing to get her to stop crying?" Margaretta asked.

"Well, it won't keep the baby from having gas pains, but it does relieve her for a minute. It can also help to keep her stomach next to yours. The warmth from your body eases the cramping and relaxes her." Maria held the baby across her stomach and swayed back and forth until she calmed down enough to close her eyes.

"Now, Margaretta, most of your hurting is coming from some swelling. You need to stay in bed and not move around. I'll mix up a wash to put on the swelling that will make it feel better. Where can I boil some water?"

Anna came rushing in. "I've been looking everywhere for you. Barbara said you were probably coming out here, so I came back. We didn't know what to do," she said desperately.

"Anna, you and Thomas should not both leave at the same time. Someone needs to stay with Margaretta all the time," Mamma Anna said sternly. "She's not strong enough to handle the baby by herself. Now, go boil some water for me."

"Yes, Mamma Anna, but the baby was crying so. I didn't know what to do."

"I'll show you what to do. Now get that water."

Calm replaced chaotic confusion when Mamma Anna exerted control. Maria noted that her bossy ways seemed to make everyone relax and trust her. She wondered if she would ever have enough confidence in her own knowledge of healing to engender such trust from others. She knew that healing was her new mission in life.

Maria watched carefully while Mamma Anna mixed the boiling water with the herbs, let it cool, and then, using a cloth, washed Margaretta's swollen, painful area with the soothing solution.

"Mamma Anna, I never knew having a baby was so hard," Margaretta said. "I've been thinking so much about Mary, who had Jesus in a stable, like I had my baby. I'd never known before, when I heard the Christmas story, how painful that must have been for her. Why does God make women suffer so?"

"I don't know, child. Maybe it's because God is a man and doesn't understand about childbirth," Mamma Anna replied, an edge of bitterness in her voice.

"But I thought God understood everything."

"Humph," sniffed Mamma Anna. Then she said calmly, "Now quit worrying about such things and go to sleep, while you're feeling better. We'll look after the baby." She herded Anna and Maria, who was still holding the baby, out of the barn.

"Anna, I'll stay tonight so you can get some much-needed sleep. Maria, you arrange for someone to be here tomorrow to help out for another week or so. Barbara, Catherine, and you can take turns. Also, Maria, I need to add to my supply of herbs. You and Johann meet me at first light, and I'll show you how to find them in the forest, unless there is an emergency. Learning the medicines is the hardest thing about healing."

"Yes, Mamma Anna, first light," Maria called to her.

As Maria walked back to town alone, she realized her life had taken on new focus since she had begun working with

Mamma Anna. Part of the new focus had come, she knew, because Johann was working with her, too. They made a good team, she and Johann. She didn't love him with the kind of passionate abandon that she had loved the handsome and gallant Hans, but she realized that she did love Johann. It was a deep, quiet, gentle love. She seemed destined to love poor men who could not afford to marry. Maybe she would never marry. At least she had something useful to do with her life now.

When Maria returned to the Scherraus cottage, she went immediately upstairs to check on Gertrude. Since she had been working with Mamma Anna, she knew better what to do.

Gertrude was lying in bed with the Bible open in front of her. She was reading aloud to Catherine, who was sitting nearby, sewing. She stopped reading when Maria entered.

"You look better every day, Trudi," Maria said.

"Yes, I can read aloud without coughing. My chest doesn't hurt anymore. I'm still very tired, though. Reading is about all I have the energy to do. I promised God that, if I got well, I would read the whole Bible. I've started at the beginning. I'm afraid I don't understand it all, though."

"What are you making, Catherine?" Maria asked.

"I'm doing some sewing for Frau Scherraus. I'm making an apron. I'm learning to spin the wool much better, too, after working with Herr Scherraus. He taught me some techniques I had never known. I get to watch as he weaves. I believe I could be a good weaver if he taught me. But he's trying to teach Uli. I'm afraid Uli isn't very interested in learning. He's too careless sometimes. At least I get to sew."

"Where is Barbara?" Maria asked.

"She's probably cooking. She's working very hard to help out. She worries about imposing on the Scherraus family. Where would we go if they put us out?"

"Now don't start worrying again, Catherine. Let's just be grateful for their kindness. God will take care of the future."

"We're going to have to help Margaretta and Anna with the new baby for a while longer. Anna doesn't know enough to do it alone. Can you go out tomorrow, and then Barbara and I can take turns?"

"Yes. I can do this sewing while I'm out there."

Johann stopped by just before dark. Maria went down to talk with him. They sat on the front step.

"How is Gertrude?" he asked out of habit.

"Much better. Her coughing and fever are gone. She is still very weak, though. It will take awhile for her to be stronger. At least she's getting enough food and rest."

"I saw Thomas Gschwandl today. He'd finally found two friends from Gastein. They had been off cutting trees for the lumberman."

"Well, that's good news and should bring some happiness to them. Margaretta and Anna are having a difficult time with the new baby. It is crying too much, and Margaretta is healing slowly. Mamma Anna wants us to meet her at first light tomorrow to go into the forest to select roots and herbs for medicines."

"Good," Johann said, "that should be interesting."

"Did you get any supper?" Maria asked. Johann did not have a home to stay in. He was sleeping wherever he could. She pulled a roll out of her apron pocket and gave it to him. The roll was filled with cheese and sausage.

"This will do nicely. Herr Fetzer gave me some eggs. I'll eat them later."

They looked up at the summer sky where the stars had begun to appear. Johann took Maria's hand and squeezed it. "I'd better go. See you at first light."

"Good night, Johann," Maria said softly.

After Johann left, she remained sitting on the steps, where Catherine joined her.

"Why do the men always like you, Maria? You always seem to have a man interested in you, and I never do. Is there something wrong with me?" Catherine asked. "Tell me honestly."

"Poor men, you mean. Somehow I never get interested in a man who can marry me. They are always too poor," Maria said. "And there is nothing wrong with you. You are very pretty and accomplished. You just have to wait for the right one. You are still young. What I'm discovering, Catherine, is that happiness doesn't always depend on a man. I think I could have a satisfying life if I knew how to heal people and bring babies into the world. Even if I marry, I think I'd like to be able to do those things, although with a family of my own it would be difficult."

"But, Maria, I don't think I could ever want to do those things."

"No, Catherine, that wouldn't be your way. You'll have to find your own thing that makes you happy, like your hand-work. Now that's something I'm not much good at, and you're so talented."

"I do enjoy figuring out how to make something beautiful. Just knowing I thought up the design out of my head and then made it with my own hands and, when it's finished, hearing other people praise my work. Yes, that is satisfying, but I still want more out of life than that. I want a husband and children and a house to make pretty things for."

Maria put her arm around the younger girl, and they both stared at the stars.

"Our lives will not be easy, Catherine, but we are having interesting experiences, aren't we? Let's go to bed. We both need to be up early."

34

Salzburg, 1733

Gray wavered through his tentative vision as he slowly opened his eyes. A line where the wall and ceiling intersected stood still and formed a place to focus. Where was this line? Was it a prison? A tomb?

Hans slowly turned his head. In the dim light he saw the outline of a small window. He closed his eyes, trying to remember where he was, when he heard footsteps approaching. A hand caressed his forehead, and he opened his eyes and stared into the light of a lantern.

The hand jerked back instantly. "Oh, you're awake!" Sister Theresa had become accustomed to her patient's being unconscious and had forgotten that he might awaken. She reacted to his open eyes as if the dead had returned to life.

Hans searched her face for something familiar and was frightened by her wimple. He closed his eyes and then looked again. She was a nun. Where was he? He tried to sit up, but his throbbing head caused him to fall back on the pillow.

Sister Theresa recovered her senses and placed her hand on his chest. "You mustn't sit up yet. You're too weak. I'm Sister Theresa, and you've been my patient for a long time. You are in a convent hospital in Salzburg. Welcome back to this life."

Questions swirled in his brain, but Hans was unable to make his mouth ask them. The effort exhausted him, and he sank into a deep sleep. The next time he awoke, sun was shining through the window, and a mourning dove on the sill was keening to its mate. Sister Theresa was bathing his face and arms with warm water. She smiled down at him. Instinctively, he smiled back. "Have you been taking care of me?" he asked.

"Ja, sir. You've been very sick. How are you feeling today? I have some soup for you to eat." She dried him carefully and, after placing a pillow behind his head, began to spoon the soup into his mouth. "Even while you were unconscious, you never stopped eating. God must want you to live."

"How long have I been here?" Hans asked.

"I can't remember exactly, but it's been many months."

"How did I get here?"

"I don't know. You were just brought into my ward, and I have cared for you ever since. That is my duty to God, to care for the sick." She paused and continued feeding him. "When you are stronger, perhaps you can tell me how you were hurt, but you need to rest now." She removed the extra pillow and moved away to feed another patient.

Hans lay still, trying to recall what had happened to him. Pieces of images floated by, images of the dungeon and the torture room. Other images of sunlight on the mountains and faces of remembered people also began to flood his brain. He tried to sort them out, but soon fell asleep again.

35

Memmingen, August 1733

Two hundred and fifty more people recently expelled from Salzburg filed into St. Martin's Church. Thomas, Margaretta, and Anna twisted their heads around, searching for familiar faces among the newcomers. Barbara, Catherine, Gertrude, and Maria sat next to Johann on the row behind the Gschwandls. They were also carefully studying the new arrivals.

"Tobias," Thomas called, "Tobias Lackner." Thomas waved his hand and beckoned his old friend, who was wearily trudging down the aisle.

"Thomas, oh, Thomas, my old friend. How good it is to see you." They embraced each other, and Tobias moved into the seat next to Thomas.

"You've just come?" Thomas asked.

"Ja. We've been on the road eighteen days. We are all tired and dirty. They led us straight into the church without a chance to clean up."

"Did you see my son Thomas? Is he with you?" Thomas asked.

"I saw him and tried to bring him, but the authorities would not even consider letting him come with me. There's nothing you can do, Thomas. Some came back to try to get their children, but none succeeded," Tobias said.

Disappointment flooded Thomas, although he had really given up hope of ever seeing his young son again. "Was he well when you last saw him?"

"Ja. He's grown a foot taller, it seems. He works hard on the farm, but they feed him good."

"I'm so glad to see you, old friend. Who else came from Gastein?"

"Mostly a bunch of us miners that Firmian finally decided he could afford to get rid of--after they brought in some Catholics from the Tyrol to work the mines, that is. I'm not too sorry to be out of Salzburg. Just about everybody I cared about had already left."

The people finally seated themselves, and quiet smoothed over the assembled group. The pastor of the church stood up and welcomed the Salzburgers who had just arrived. Their faces registered amazement and relief to be welcomed in a Protestant church.

"And now, please give your attention to Mr. Schorer, who is representing Pastor Urlsperger from St. Anne's Church in Augsburg."

The Salzburgers all knew of Pastor Urlsperger and the work he had done to help them.

Mr. Schorer stood up and began speaking in a formal voice. "The Reverend Samuel Urlsperger, Pastor of St. Anne's Church in Augsburg, announces a transport being organized to Georgia in North America. The King of England needs settlers in his new colony, and through the Society for Promoting Christian Knowledge, an English missionary society, the King is sponsoring this transport for Salzburg emigrants who want to go." A great murmur pervaded the church when the people heard the news and turned to speak to their friends and families.

"Provisions will be made for your journey to Georgia and until you can raise your first crop. Each man will receive a grant of land. The Society will provide a pastor and a teacher to accompany the group. The Indians in the area are friendly and in need of the civilizing influence of Christians like yourselves. A good man, The Honorable James Oglethorpe, governs the colony. This is a generous and benevolent offer from the King of England, who admires your courage and devotion in refusing to cooperate with Catholic tyrants.

"The transport is hoping to leave as soon as possible. Therefore, I need to know today if you are interested in joining the transport to Georgia. We need to leave day after tomorrow for Augsburg, where the transport is organizing. There will even be a commissioner accompanying the group to make all the arrangements. Traveling with this transport will be nothing like the haphazard way you were forced out of Salzburg. All your needs will be taken care of."

"Would we be separated into distant places when we received our land?" a man asked.

"You would be in the same area, I am told," Mr. Schorer replied.

"How can we trust that all of these promises will be kept?" another man asked.

"You have the word of the King of England. What more do you need?" Mr. Schorer replied. "The English king has already provided great sums of money for the aid of the Salzburgers. This king provided the money distributed to many of you by Pastor Urlsperger. He is a Protestant and, along with all of Protestant Europe, has been deeply moved by your sacrifice."

"Is the journey across the great sea safe?" another asked.

"Ships make the journey safely every day," Mr. Schorer responded.

"I've heard that the Tirnbergers who went to Holland were treated poorly by the local people and were laughed at because their language was different. Will the people in Georgia speak English and laugh at our German?" a man asked.

"Well, you must remember that King George of England is himself from Hanover and speaks German. It's not likely that an English colony will laugh at German," Mr. Schorer replied, with some impatience slipping into his voice. He needed to organize the people quickly and get them to Augsburg before the transport filled.

"I realize there are many questions in your minds about such a long journey. You should know that months of work and correspondence between Pastor Urlsperger and the English Society for Promoting Christian Knowledge have taken place to organize this transport. Pastor Urlsperger has worked tirelessly trying to arrange places for you Salzburgers to settle on your own land and start a new life in a Protestant state. This is a wonderful opportunity that you should not turn down. Although no one will be forced to go against his will, many of you already know there is no land available for you here."

Margaretta and Thomas Gschwandl looked at each other. Margaretta was holding their baby daughter in her arms.

"Oh, Thomas, a chance to have our own farm again. I do hate working as a servant. I know you do, too."

"It's a long journey, Margaretta. Are you sure you want to try it?"

"I'm sure. We need to build our own life. There's no room for us here."

"And you, Anna?"

"Yes, Thomas," Anna answered, without hesitation.

The church was buzzing with conversation as family groups discussed the possibility of joining this transport to Georgia.

Johann looked at Maria. He whispered to her, "If I go to Georgia, I'll be granted land. Would you be interested in going to Georgia, Maria? It might mean that I could afford to marry."

"I think we should consider this opportunity," Maria said quietly.

"Would you marry me if I am a landowner?"

Maria was flustered at his sudden proposal of marriage in the midst of this great crowd. She hesitated. "Let's discuss that later, Johann. First, we need to be sure this is something we want to do."

Johann realized that she probably would not make a decision to go to Georgia without the other women. "Do you think Barbara and the girls will want to go?" he asked.

"I don't know. Let's go outside and ask them."

Groups of Salzburgers drifted outside and stood in small knots, talking intently. The women and Johann gathered under a tree.

"Barbara, Johann thinks this transport to Georgia may be the opportunity for a better life that we have been praying for. Since we missed the chance for land in Prussia when we decided to go to Memmingen instead of Augsburg, perhaps this is what God had in mind for us. Will you and the girls come if we go?" Maria asked.

Barbara looked surprised that Maria had spoken so boldly. Then she smiled when she saw Johann take Maria's hand. "Together, Maria?" Barbara asked, with a sparkle in her eye.

"I've asked Maria to go to Georgia with me, and to marry me," he added quickly. "Maria hasn't decided yet."

Barbara felt an unexpected twinge of pain, realizing that Maria had finally given up on seeing Hans again. But she smiled brightly, hiding her own sense of loss.

Catherine and Gertrude hugged Maria and squealed with delight.

"Let's go, too, Mother," Gertrude said. "I'm well now, so you don't have to worry about me."

"We need to stay together, Mother," Catherine said. "If Maria and Johann go, we should. Maybe in a country where men have land, there will be a chance for Gertrude and me to have our own homes. I would rather not be a servant all my life, unless it's God's will, of course," Catherine said wistfully.

"Catherine, aren't you worried about how we'll survive such a long trip?" Barbara asked teasingly.

"But he said the King will provide all we need," replied Catherine, before she realized she was being teased.

"Well, it looks like everyone is eager for this opportunity. I've resisted leaving this area because I kept hoping for a way to unite our whole family again, but I guess I owe it to Catherine and Gertrude to give them this chance for a better life. But I still don't know how we'd live. Will they give land to women without husbands?"

"I'll ask that question of Mr. Schorer. Even if they won't give you land of your own, you and the girls can always be a part of our household," Johann said.

"That's very kind of you, Johann, but when you have your own family, you may regret your generosity."

They looked around and saw people crowded around Mr. Schorer. Thomas was one of the men giving his name.

"Look, the Gschwandls are going," Catherine said, looking toward Margaretta and Anna. She ran to them, took the baby, and danced around with her. After giving the baby back to Margaretta, she and Anna walked off with their heads together, watching to see which single men were signing up.

Anna pointed out the men from Gastein, mostly miners who had just arrived in Memmingen. "That's Tobias Lackner, the tall, pale one. He's a great friend of Thomas. The young man with the wavy brown hair talking to his mother is Georg Schweiger. He's from Prembstall near Gastein." She blushed as she spoke about Georg.

"Is he someone you're interested in?" Catherine asked.

"Well, I might be, if he had land."

They watched Georg turn and walk toward Mr. Schorer. "Oh, he's going, Catherine," Anna said, squeezing Catherine's arm. "Look, he's giving his name."

"Thomas is shaking his hand. Now he knows you're going, too," Catherine said. "Why don't you go speak to his mother; then, when he rejoins her, you'll get to talk with him?"

"Oh, I couldn't. That's much too obvious."

Georg turned from his conversation with Thomas and looked over at Anna and Catherine. He blushed and looked embarrassed, and Anna quickly turned away.

"He looked at you. Why did you turn away?" Catherine said, giggling.

"I'm shy around him," Anna said. "Besides, I don't see you talking to any men."

"I don't know any of them. All the single men seem to be miners from Gastein. Who are some of the others?"

"Well, there's Balthasar Fleiss from Godauren, where Thomas is from. I don't think you'd like him very much. He's rather slow."

"Who are those two men with Thomas now?"

"Oh, that's Hans and Peter Gruber. Now Peter would be a good match for you. He's just thirty-four."

"He keeps looking at Maria," Catherine said. "Oh, I forgot to tell you, Johann has asked Maria to marry him and go to Georgia. I don't think she's decided yet. She's probably waiting to see if all of us go."

"When did this happen?" Anna squealed, delighted. "I knew he loved her, but I wasn't sure how she felt. She was very much in love with your uncle who was killed, wasn't she?"

"Yes, but they've both been helping Mamma Anna take care of sick people and have grown very close," Catherine replied. "Maria was afraid they would never be able to marry, however."

"Maybe things are going to work out for us after all, Catherine. It's so exciting. Just think, crossing the sea to Georgia. I wonder what it will be like."

While they were talking, an old man began addressing the crowd. "Folks, you're making a mistake going to Georgia. If you don't die on the trip across the great sea, you'll be killed by savage Indians. I've heard about terrible, fierce animals in the forests there. The land is all wilderness. You'll starve while you clear the land, before you ever get to plant a crop, if the savages and the animals don't get you first. Three hundred Salzburgers died on the North Sea going to Prussia. Now that's not half as long a voyage as it is to Georgia. This is a mistake. Don't believe this man. The King of England just wants other people to face those dangers before he sends his own subjects."

Some men hesitated and fell into more deliberation before giving their names.

The newcomers from Gastein gathered around Thomas.

"What do you think, Thomas. Is he telling the truth?"

"Well, I trust Pastor Urlsperger in Augsburg. He's been responsible for more charity for us here in Memmingen than anyone else, and that charity came from England. I believe the King is truly concerned for us. Besides, Englishmen already live in the Colony of Georgia. If they can live there, why can't we?"

Heads nodded as they followed the logic of Thomas's remarks.

"Besides, I've been here longer than most of you, and we will never own farms here. I'm ready to take the chance. God will take care of us. That's been proven many times." Heads nodded again.

Johann joined the men deliberating in clumps. Maria put her arm around Barbara, and the two women walked away from the others. "What should we do, Barbara?" Maria asked. "I don't want to go to Georgia without you and the girls."

"If Catherine and Gertrude are ever to have a husband with land, this may be their best chance. I'll never have that again, so where I am matters little, as long as I'm with you girls. You're all the family I have left. But Mr. Schorer said that only men would get land. What will we do in Georgia without land? We'll have to be servants there as well."

"If I marry Johann, you'll always have a place with us."

"But do you love Johann?"

Maria patted Barbara's arm. "Not in the same way that I loved Hans, but I do care for him. I can't spend the rest of my life waiting for Hans, who is probably dead. It's been too long." Maria sighed deeply, and then continued, "Besides, one of us should marry to gain a man's protection if we go to this wilderness in Georgia. Would you rather Catherine or Gertrude marry one of the Gastein miners?" The two women looked over at Catherine and Anna, giggling together as they watched the men sign up.

"No. They look like rough, ignorant men. Catherine and Gertrude might have better chances in Georgia. It's just that it seems like your marrying Johann means we've given up on ever finding Hans again. As you know, that's hard for me, but you're probably wise to marry Johann. He's kind and intelligent and will make a good husband, and he's from Saalfelden."

Maria and Barbara walked back and rounded up the girls. "Well, Catherine and Gertrude, what do you think we should do?"

"I think we should go, Mother," Gertrude said. "I'm not sick anymore, and it feels like an opportunity God has given us to carry Christianity to the savages." Barbara was startled at Gertrude's reason for wanting to go to Georgia. It was hard for her to admit that Gertrude was no longer a child and had such serious thoughts.

"And you, Catherine?"

"I wouldn't want to be left behind to be a servant all my life. The Gschwandls are going. I think we should all stay together. There's little hope for us here; perhaps Georgia will be better."

36

On Board the *Purysburg*, 1734

Mamma Anna and Deutsch stood at the deck railing, watching the sunset. "All my friends from Saalfelden decided to go to Georgia and live in the wilderness. I thought at the time, I'm too old to make such a journey and start over again in the wilderness. Then I thought of those three young women who would need me when they married and had their babies. Maria's learned some about midwifing, but she hasn't seen all I've seen. So here I am, not knowing what's ahead. What's Georgia like? You've been there, haven't you?"

"No, not quite. I've been to Charlestown, which is north of Savannah, in the Carolinas. It's a right good size town."

"Did you see any savages?"

Deutsch laughed. "Well, it all depends on what you mean by savages. I never saw any Indians, if that's what you mean. It seemed to me like mostly Englishmen and slaves from Africa. By now, the African slaves probably outnumber the Englishmen. It's a nasty business, hauling slaves. I ain't gonna do that no more."

Deutsch gazed at the horizon and remained quiet for awhile. "I don't generally leave the ship when we're in Charlestown. Never know who might see me and try to force me back on a slaver."

"You mean you cross this ocean, and then don't even touch land when you get there?"

"Ja. I prefer the water to the land, anyway. I fit in here. I don't fit in on land."

"I don't know how I'm going to fit in with this new town they're planning. Pastor Boltzius keeps trying to make me into something I'm not. He's kind about it, but I can see he isn't pleased with me. He hasn't lived through what I've lived through, with the church always trying to get me to believe something I don't believe. It naturally makes me suspicious when someone else starts making up new rules to follow. They aren't written down yet, but they're there. Attend every service; learn these new hymns; read this pamphlet; learn Bible verses." Mamma Anna shook her head. "It makes me nervous. I can't talk about this to the others. They're all as happy as can be with the new pastors, and go around repeating every word they say."

After a silence in which they both drank in the warm breezes that pushed the ship westward into the blazing sky, she added, "Tell me something, Deutsch. You've sailed all over the world and seen a lot of people. Why do some people always try to tell everyone else what to believe, like they're the only ones who know God?"

"I never thought about it. It just always seemed to me like some folks were in charge, and some folks weren't. I ain't never been in charge, so I don't know how those folks think."

37

Memmingen, 1733

Two days later, the people who had given their names to go to Georgia, only about twenty-five in all, gathered on the road to Augsburg and began the first part of a long journey.

They looked to Thomas to lead them, and his wagon pulled out at the head of the procession, with Margaretta walking beside him, carrying baby Margaretta in a cradle on her back. Anna and Catherine followed, with Barbara and Gertrude behind them, followed by Maria and Johann.

Brigitte and Uli Scherraus had come out to say goodbye. The Saalfelden women had hugged them and thanked them for the hundredth time, promising never to forget them.

"Maria, have you seen Mamma Anna?" Barbara asked, her eyes searching the group of people gathered.

"No, not this morning. She's planning to come. Where do you think she is?"

"Probably looking after some sick person."

"Johann," Maria said. "Go tell Thomas to wait until we find Mamma Anna." She handed her bundle to Barbara and hurried away. Soon she returned with Mamma Anna, who was carrying several baskets and rushing along, her hat askew and her stringy gray hair flying everywhere.

"You were about to get left behind," Barbara scolded. "You can't carry all that stuff. Maybe you can put it on Thomas's wagon. What is all of this, anyway?"

"It's my healing stuff. I've been up all night trying to get everything together that I might need. Whew, I'm too old for this."

The group fell into a familiar rhythm, walking and singing, as they made their way north to Augsburg. Thomas was thinking, Augsburg. Finally I'll see Augsburg and St. Anne's Church, where Martin Luther first had his Augsburg Confession presented. That Confession has changed my life. Augsburg.

38

Augsburg, September 1733

The Reverend Samuel Urlsperger, Pastor of St. Anne's Church, relieved his frustration by pacing back and forth in the hallway outside the Privy Council Chamber. He was a handsome man, with fine facial features surrounded by an immaculate, white curled wig. The stiff white ruff around his neck was perfectly pleated and contrasted sharply with his long black robe.

Inside the room, the Magistrates of the Privy Council were meeting to decide whether or not to approve Pastor Urlsperger's memorial to allow the Protestants he was assembling for the transport to Georgia to enter the city of Augsburg. They were to be housed at the Evangelical Hospital and in the homes of Evangelical burghers. The Privy Council in this divided, but usually tolerant, city consisted of both Catholic and Protestant magistrates. The two religious factions took turns running the city. Unfortunately for Urlsperger, the Catholics were in charge this week.

Urlsperger heard the clock in the tower next to the city hall strike twelve. He turned mid-pace and walked out of the city hall, across the square, past the elegant homes of the merchants and burghers of Augsburg. His path led him through the open market, where farmers were selling fresh produce. Ignoring the calls to buy fresh cabbages, he hurried through the market and approached the side door of St. Anne's Church.

He was no longer in awe, as he had once been, of his role as the senior pastor of this historic church. Recently, however, he had made a practice of visiting the upstairs room where Luther had been imprisoned for his own protection during the church trial precipitated by his courageous stand against the corruption in the Catholic Church. Since his involvement with the Salzburgers, Urlsperger had felt that history was repeating itself two hundred years after Luther's battles with the Roman Church. The same old battles were being fought again, and he had refugees to take care of. He found himself seeking Luther's counsel often, searching for ways to relocate these brave peasants, who had sacrificed everything they had for the sake of their faith.

Even though a midday meal with his staff waited, he paused for a moment to quiet the turmoil in his soul, pausing briefly in the cool, quiet sanctuary. Even this holy place reflected the division of Augsburg and the Christian Church, as well as its tolerance, or at least the tolerance of its benefactor, Fugger. Fugger, a wealthy banker and merchant, had built a Protestant altar at the opposite end of his family's private Catholic altar. Fugger's vision was for both branches of Christianity to exist under one roof. Of course, the original chapel next to the larger hall had been built centuries ago by the early Roman conquerors. Urlsperger reflected on the scope of Christian history that St. Anne's Church embodied. His participation with the Salzburg emigrants was just another piece in the mosaic of that long story.

As he stood looking at the crucifix at one end and the mural of Christ and the babies at the other, Urlsperger recalled Fugger's wise vision of unity. The painting of Christ in the midst of mothers holding their babies, even holding one himself, which was hanging behind the Protestant altar, made a shiver run through his body. He thought about the Salzburgers, camped with their babies outside the city wall, waiting for the Privy Council to approve their entry.

After sitting down to eat with his staff, Urlsperger continued to brood over the exiles. Knowing all that was on his mind, his assistant pastor and the clerks remained reserved in their comments, and the meal proceeded in near silence.

"How many have arrived?" Urlsperger asked his assistant.

"The group from Memmingen has not arrived, but there are several small groups already here, perhaps about fifteen people in all."

A servant entered the room with a messenger. "A message from the Privy Council, Your Reverence," the messenger said.

"Humph," Urlsperger said, holding out his hand for the note. He broke the seal and read it.

"They have denied permission for the Salzburgers to enter the city." He hit the table with a balled fist, making the dishes rattle. Gaining more composure with effort, he said to his staff, "We will just have to wait until the Protestant magistrates are in charge." Turning to his assistant, he instructed, "Make sure the people are settled as comfortably as possible on Schauer's land outside the city. They will be much less comfortable there, but there's nothing else we can do. Make the arrangements with Schauer. I'll come later to conduct a service with them."

Urlsperger studied the paper intently. "This message makes several untrue allegations against the Salzburgers, such as the fear of misconduct once they are allowed to enter the city. I'll be in my office composing a response." Urlsperger walked swiftly from the table without finishing his meal.

As the party from Memmingen met other Salzburgers traveling towards Augsburg, they discovered that they, too, were considering joining the transport to Georgia. Some were just arriving from Salzburg.

"What's it like in Salzburg?" Thomas asked Paulus Zittrauer from Flagau.

"Firmian's men are still persecuting everyone who confesses to being Protestant. We heard about this opportunity for land in Georgia and decided to leave. It was hard leaving our farmland, but it became more impossible every day to stay. We were about the last Protestants to leave our area. We had no friends left after my wife's mother died. She was too ill to travel, and we could not leave her alone. How have you fared for these months?"

"The good people of Memmingen took us in, but there was no future for us there. We've come to Augsburg to go to Georgia. At least we can start over again with some land. I'm worried about taking my wife and child on the long voyage across the sea, though, but Margaretta wants to go. She doesn't like being a servant on someone else's farm. Neither do I," Thomas answered.

Soldiers wearing elegant, powder blue and white uniforms rode up to the travelers from the north.

"Are you the Salzburgers headed for Augsburg?" the officer in charge asked.

"Yes, we are," Thomas answered for the group. "Is there something wrong?"

"No, indeed not. We have been sent to escort you to Augsburg."

"An escort for us. That's very surprising. You must be Protestants then," replied Thomas.

"Yes, but some of my men are Catholics. The Privy Council asked us to escort you to the Bird Gate."

A caution fell over the group as they walked behind the soldiers on horseback.

"I can't imagine friendly soldiers," Paulus Zittrauer said to Thomas. "Can we trust them?"

"I hope so. There's not much we can do about it if we can't. God will protect us."

As they saw the city come into view, Thomas called back to Tobias, "Lead us in song, Tobias. Let them know who is coming."

Tobias began singing the *Song of the Exile*, and soon all the people were singing while they walked.

Tears ran down the faces of the group of local Protestants who had come to meet the Salzburgers at the Bird Gate. They were overcome with emotion when they heard these courageous, persecuted Protestants singing as they approached Augsburg.

The soldiers stopped to talk with the delegation of men and then turned to face the Salzburgers. "I'm sorry, but you cannot enter the city of Augsburg today," the officer in charge said. "The Catholic magistrates will not allow you entrance."

"Why not?" Thomas asked.

"Augsburg is governed by both Protestants and Catholics. You have arrived on a day that the Catholics are in charge. They will not permit you to enter. The Protestants will vote differently when they are in control; then you may enter."

A man with a white ruff around his neck and wearing a long black robe stepped forward.

"I am the assistant to Pastor Samuel Urlsperger, senior pastor of St. Anne's Church. He has made arrangements for you to stay in the garden of Mr. Schauer, outside the city wall. Please follow me. Pastor Urlsperger will hold a service with you after you are settled."

"It's because of Urlsperger that I'm here," Zittrauer told Thomas. "He sent the message of the transport to Georgia by a merchant, who also distributed Protestant literature until he was captured. I've wanted to see this famous pastor for a long time."

"Let's all try to stay together," Barbara said to Catherine and Maria, holding on to Gertrude's arm. The four women found a tree and put their sacks of belongings on the ground. They collapsed in weariness, then looked around.

"Should we try to stay in the barn?" asked Catherine, seeing the Gschwandls headed that way.

"Let the people with babies have the barn," Maria said.

"Oh, I guess you're right," Catherine said. "I didn't think about that."

"At least I'm not sick anymore," Gertrude said. "The last journey was so terrible because I was so sick. I pray we all stay well during this long journey."

"Yes, Gertrude," Barbara said. "I was so afraid we would lose you when your fever was so hot, but, thanks be to God, you survived. Just look at how healthy you are now. It must be God's will."

Later that day, Maria and Johann stood together listening to Pastor Urlsperger speak to the group, using as his text the story of Joshua leading the children of Israel into the Promised Land. He read to them from the last chapter of the Book of Joshua, in a strong, sincere voice. "'And I gave you a land on which you had not labored, and cities which you had not built, and you dwell therein; you eat the fruit of vineyards and olive yards which you did not plant. Now therefore fear the Lord, and serve him in sincerity and in faithfulness; put away the gods, which your fathers served beyond the River, and in Egypt, and serve the Lord. And if you are unwilling to serve the Lord, choose this day whom you will serve, whether the gods your fathers served in the region beyond the River, or the gods of the Amorites in whose land you dwell; but as for me and my house, we will serve the Lord.' Then the people answered, 'God forbid that we should forsake the Lord, to serve other gods; for it is the Lord our God who brought us and our fathers up from the land of Egypt, out of the house of bondage, and who did those great signs in our sight, and preserved us in all the way that we went, and among all the peoples through whom we passed; and the Lord drove out before us all the peoples, the Amorites who lived in the land; therefore we also will serve the Lord, for he is our God.'"

The heads of the Salzburgers nodded, comparing their situation with the story of the children of Israel. God had brought them out of bondage and was giving them a new land, too. Johann took Maria's hand, looked into her eyes, and said quietly, "As for me and my house, we shall serve the Lord."

Maria's eyes filled with tears, and she nodded, choking back unsorted emotions.

"I'll speak to Pastor Urlsperger after the service about marrying us," Johann said. "He has done so much for the Salzburgers; I would like for him to marry us before we leave Augsburg. Would you like that?"

"Yes, Johann." Relief flooded Maria when she committed herself to an immediate marriage, putting to rest all her hesitations, making the practical decision. Johann would be a steadier husband than Hans ever would have been. He was quieter, more interested in making her happy and building a home. His faith had a depth of understanding that she had never before seen, even in the passionate Hans. She was grown up now. She could live without that wild passion, which had both fascinated and frightened her.

"Pastor Urlsperger, Pastor Urlsperger," Johann called after the pastor, who was walking quickly back toward Augsburg, accompanied by several well-dressed gentlemen.

"Yes, are you calling me?" Urlsperger stopped and turned to face Johann.

"Yes, sir, if you don't mind."

"What is it? How can I help you?" the pastor asked, recognizing the shyness of the simple Alpine peasant.

"I wondered, sir, if you would marry Maria Kroehr and me," Johann said faintly, almost losing his courage in the presence of this famous man.

"You want me to marry you?"

"Ja, if it's not too much to ask? Since I'll be getting land in Georgia, we can get married. We've been waiting a long time, and we would like a Protestant wedding, here in Augsburg."

"Yes, of course I'll marry you. If you can wait until next week, I'll marry you in St. Anne's Church, inside the city."

"Ja! That will be perfect," Johann said, his countenance changing immediately, a smile taking over his face.

"Good. Then it's settled. One week from today. By then all of you will be allowed into Augsburg."

"Sir, I have no money to pay for a wedding," Johann said.

"Then I'll make the arrangements. You have already paid a much greater price than I'll ever be called on to pay. At least I can see you well married. Where is your bride?"

"Wait here," Johann said. "I'll get her." He was in such a state of excitement that he hardly felt his feet touch the ground as he ran back to Maria. He grabbed her arm and pulled her after him back to Pastor Urlsperger.

"This is Maria," Johann said proudly. "Maria, he's going to marry us a week from today in St. Anne's Church in Augsburg!" he exclaimed, all out of breath.

Maria looked up at the amused Pastor Urlsperger and

watched his eyebrows lift with unexpected interest when he saw her face. She was accustomed to men reacting to her beauty, and she quickly lowered her eyes and ducked her head, saying simply, "Thank you, sir."

On Sunday the Salzburgers marched into Augsburg to attend services at St. Anne's Church. They passed through the Bird Gate and up the street to a corner, where the procession turned left. First, they entered the Barefoot Church of the Franciscans, where a brief prayer service was held in the bare stone sanctuary, decorated only by a simple wooden crucifix. The vaulted plainness of this church calmed Maria's agitated spirit.

After leaving the Franciscans' church, they walked solemnly toward St. Anne's Church. People lined the streets. Rich ladies in their long silk dresses dabbed their eyes as the Salzburgers sang the *Song of the Exile*. Wealthy burghers stood in the doorways of their impressive houses and cheered the procession.

One by one, they passed through the massive iron door and congregated in a courtyard lined with graves. Pastor Urlsperger greeted them, pointed out the window of the room where Martin Luther was once imprisoned, and told them of his admiration for the Salzburgers, who had also suffered imprisonment and exile in order to remain faithful to the Augsburg Confession, which was first presented in this very church. Gertrude stood with her mouth slightly open, trying to understand the significance of what she was experiencing. She didn't feel important in any way and had trouble comparing the people she knew from Saalfelden to the great Martin Luther.

The group filed reverently into the sanctuary and was seated on the Protestant side of the church. The seats had backs that could be used to face either the Protestant altar or turned toward the center of the sanctuary, where a high pulpit hung from the ceiling. Today, the seats faced the pulpit, which meant that the Salzburgers looked toward the Catholic altar, where a stone crucifix gazed down on the people.

Carved into the altar railing, built by the Fugger family for infant baptisms, were stone babies, curved and fat.

Music from the enormous organ chilled the Saalfelden women. Even Mamma Anna visibly reacted to the swelling sound that filled the spacious room. Gertrude's eyes instinctively lifted toward the ceiling, as if searching the heavens for the glorious sound, and saw pink and gold flower-shaped designs.

Protestants from Augsburg took every available seat, and many stood against the walls. They stared at the Salzburgers, excited by their strange way of dressing and the stories of their brave sacrifices for the faith. During the service, Pastor Urlsperger praised the faithfulness of the Salzburgers and asked for God's grace to be with them on their journey to Georgia in the New World. He entreated them to continue their obedience to God, and take their faith to their new land.

After the service, Barbara and the girls explored the sanctuary. Barbara knelt at the Protestant altar, tears blurring her vision while she stared at the painting of Jesus holding an infant, surrounded by women with their babies. In that moment, the reality of never again seeing her own little ones swept over her. The tenderness in the face of Jesus reopened the wound in her heart, causing her to feel movement in her milk glands, and she collapsed in tears.

"Barbara, you must surrender your grief to Jesus and leave it here," Maria said, putting her arm around her stepmother.

"I know you're right, Maria, and I thought I had, but...."

"We must accept the fact that we'll never see the others again. When we go, there's no coming back. Along with leaving behind Peter and the children, we are also abandoning any hope of ever finding out how Hans died."

Mamma Anna, Gertrude, and Catherine joined Barbara and Maria, and they all prayed together for faith strong enough to help them face their new lives.

The women clung together for a moment, composing themselves as they would many times in the future, finding strength in their bond with each other.

They then followed the other Salzburgers into a hall, where tables had been set for a feast. They were ushered to their seats and served excellent food and drink by the elegantly dressed ladies and gentlemen of Augsburg.

"We should be serving you," Thomas Gschwandl said in astonishment. "We are the servants."

"Today, you are our honored guests," the people replied.

Thomas leaned over to Tobias. "What do you think Archbishop Firmian would think about our being treated so handsomely?" The Salzburgers all laughed heartily at his remark. Soon, everyone was laughing at the contrast between the rich servants and the poor guests, and how their fortunes had turned.

The next day, Pastor Urlsperger, his warm hand covering theirs, stilled the trembling of Maria and Johann as they stood before him. Maria wore her weathered, broad-brimmed, green wool hat, a red skirt and blue apron, a white linen blouse and a black laced-up vest. Her blue hand-knitted stockings were a gift from Catherine. Barbara, Catherine, and Gertrude stood beside her.

Johann held his green hat in one hand, while he clutched Maria's hand with the other. His face was scrubbed clean above the red shirt under his brown coat. He had carefully brushed the dirt from his brown bloomer-like pants, which fastened just below his knees and were held up with V-shaped, leather suspenders. Thomas Gschwandl stood by his side.

The couple did not miss marriage finery but were grateful that, with the promise of becoming a landowner, Johann could finally afford to marry. They gazed into each other's eyes and said their vows, shyness softening their voices.

The bride and groom were served a wedding supper by the Augsburg ladies, and one offered them the use of a room in her house. Maria's face reddened when Johann accepted the offer.

"Well, now, a toast to the bride and groom. May you be

faithful to your marriage vows and to your God. If so, then you will be together through all eternity."

Later that evening, Maria and Johann slowly ascended the staircase to the bedroom that had been loaned to them. After looking around, Johann blew out the candle, and they were surrounded by darkness.

Feeling her way around the bed, Maria nervously took off her clothes and climbed in, pulling the down coverlet over herself. Her body was stiff with the fear of rejection when Johann discovered she was not a virgin. She had told no one about her experience with Hans in the forest, but when she closed her eyes, she could still see the trees interlaced over her head.

She heard Johann's coat hit the floor, then his pants and suspenders. She could not hear his shirt. The bed creaked when he sat down to remove his shoes and stockings.

"Johann," she said, in a small, panicky voice.

"Yes, Maria?"

"I'm afraid..." she started her confession, but her voice caught, and she could not finish.

"Don't be afraid, my darling. I'll always be kind to you," Johann said tenderly.

He hesitantly reached for her and held her close. She trembled with confused emotions. Her body warmed to his, and he stroked her and quickly completed the act of love, sighing contentedly before falling asleep. She lay awake a long time. As she released pent-up feelings, tears ran down her face, and she let go of her past love for Hans and her sense of guilt for betraying him. The tears were also of happiness in anticipation of her life with Johann.

39

Saalfelden, 1733

The pale, gaunt, one-legged man hobbled down the road, propped on a crutch. His blue eyes burned with tears when he recognized the shape of the white-topped mountains against the blue sky. He rested against a tree, feeling the emotions of the exile finally returning home. No one who cared about him was still in this place, but the familiarity of the scenery caused tears to run down his scraggly face. There was the mountain where he had made love to his beautiful Maria, whose remembered face he had held in his mind constantly since his arrest two years earlier. He wondered if he would ever find her again. He could not allow himself to think that she might not love a one-legged beggar. Finding her again was the only thing he had to live for. When he closed his eyes, the image of her brown eyes became an icon to him, like the eyes of the Madonna that had hung on the wall near his bed in the monastery.

Peter Rohrmoser had said that Maria left with Barbara, Catherine, and Gertrude in the great expulsion in the spring of 1732, months ago. "What about Barbara's baby?" he had asked. Peter had pointed to a little girl, shyly hiding behind the door.

"My sister came to live with us to care for the house and children," Peter had explained. Although he never invited Hans into the house, he did say before Hans left to send word if he found them. "The children ask where their mother is."

When the peddler's wagon came into view, Hans moved to the center of the road in order to force him to stop. Hans knew the peddler would eventually head back north to Bavaria to get a new supply of goods. Without much hesitation, the peddler agreed to let Hans ride along with him.

40

On Board the *Purysburg*, 1734

Mamma Anna was uncomfortably mashed between Barbara and Thomas Gschwandl on a bench in the tiny room
Captain Fry reluctantly allowed Pastor Boltzius to use for his
daily services. With no water to bathe, the collective odor of
so many bodies in so small a space was stifling. She had decided to attend the services in order to stop everyone from
worrying about her soul. She was not worried about it, but
she was tired of being prayed over every night by Barbara
and the girls. She knew they were also concerned about the
kind of impression she made on the pastors. She figured
Barbara had her eye on those two single pastors for her girls
and was trying to make sure nothing blotched their reputa-
tions. Sharing a compartment with Mamma Anna, who did
not always attend services, was not exactly helping that
cause. For the girls' sake, she was sitting here in this
cramped place, listening to Boltzius drone on and on, instead
of relaxing on the deck, talking to Deutsch. He was the only
one she could be honest with. He just listened and never
judged her. She had never known a man before who did not
try to tell her what to think.

Later that evening, Mamma Anna, unable to sleep, went
up on deck to get some fresh air. She was stronger now, and
the wind was warmer. The light of the moon dipped in and
out of the rippling water, where an occasional fish jumped
up. Some of the sailors were singing what was probably a
bawdy song, judging from the way they were laughing, but
she could not understand the English words. Her own
thoughts crowded out the noise, and she hardly heard the
singing.

"You shouldn't be up here alone at night," someone said
in a drunken voice, right next to her. She jumped in surprise
and turned to see Deutsch, swaying against the railing. "One
of these sailors is likely to jump you."

She drew slightly away from her friend and laughed. "They won't be interested in an old bag like me."

"I wouldn't be so sure. I've seen them swoon over a big fish. You look better than a fish, I can tell you that." He leered at her, a grin contorting his disfigured face.

Having had many years of experience with drunken men, she said firmly, "Sit down, Deutsch, before you fall overboard and drown yourself."

Without considering her command, he obeyed it and crumpled up beside her, his head against her leg. She sat down, too, and laid his head in her lap, leaning back against the railing.

"How'd you get here anyway, Anna?" Deutsch asked slurringly, before he started snoring.

Not realizing he was asleep, Mamma Anna thought for a minute before recalling that morning in Augsburg when they had all given their names to the clerk and declared their intention to join the transport to Georgia.

41

Augsburg, October 1733

"All of you who are resolved to go to the English Colony of Georgia come stand here and be counted." The Salzburgers gathered around, answering when their names were called.

"Come forward and give information concerning those people who might follow after you. We will try to give them information about you, so that you will not be lost to them. Hans Gruber, are you here and still desiring to go?"

"Ja. Here, sir."

"Give me your age, place of birth, and occupation, and I will write the information in this ledger."

"Hans Gruber, born in Hoff in Gastein."

"Are you married?"

"No. I could never afford to marry."

"Age?"

"About forty-five, I expect."

"Occupation?"

"I was a servant, sir. A laborer."

"Do you expect anyone to follow you?"

"Well, I've left behind my father and mother, four sisters, and one brother, who might follow." He listed their names and then said with special pleading, "I'm most anxious about my two sons, Johann, age ten, and Peter, age thirteen, in case they are let free and sent after me. They wouldn't let me bring them."

"Did you leave behind any estate or money?"

"Ja, some money was left. Two-hundred-and-twenty guilders with Michael Gruber at Dorff in Gastein, one-hundred guilders with Wilhelm Gruber, my father; and with Balthasar Schafflinger, a peasant in Unterlarasteig, twenty guilders."

"That's all," the clerk said importantly. Hans awkwardly stepped aside, and the clerk called the next name.

"Paulus Schweighofer?"

Paulus walked up to the table. "Here, sir." Having heard the questions asked of Hans, Paulus just began giving the information.

"I'm Paulus Schweighofer, a weaver, about forty-five years of age, born in Mittersill on the Mühlbach in the Valley of Pinzgau, and this is my wife."

"Slow down. I can't write that fast," the clerk said. Paulus repeated the information slowly, while the clerk painstakingly wrote it down.

Margaretta Prindlinger with her three children was next. The children, ages seven, four, and one, were hanging onto her skirt as she stood before the table. Writing about her, the clerk wondered how she would manage in the wilderness with three young children and no husband.

Next came Lorentz Huber, from Gastein, who was fifty-four years old, and his wife and four children, whose ages were thirteen, ten, eight, and five.

"And who do you expect to follow?"

"I expect my brother's son and daughters, who are with the Great Transport to Memmingen. Their names are Paul, Barbara, Magdalena, Margaretta, and Christina Huber."

"Do you have any estate left behind?"

"No, only household goods."

Thomas Gschwandl was the sixteenth name on the list. He went forward, along with Margaretta and their one-year-old daughter. Margaretta's sister, Anna Hofer, followed behind them.

"Thomas Gschwandl here. I'm from Hoff in Gastein and am thirty-nine years old. I'm a farmer and a miner. I expect to follow me, a cousin, Hans Schock, and my wife expects her other sister, Maria Trigler, and her bastard. If they won't let her bring the child, she may not come."

"And what have you left behind, Mr. Gschwandl?"

"I desire that my bastard son, Thomas Gschwandl, age eleven, gotten by Heiglein and baptized in Hoff in Gastein, follow me if they will let him out. They wouldn't allow him to come with me. He is lodged with Michael Wallner in Hinterstarff in Gastein."

"What property have you left behind?"

"I left behind four-hundred guilders from my estate called Niederberg in Bodauner in Hoff, now in the possession of Hans Kohler. I also left to him all movables, including one cow, twelve sheep, one hog, a one-year-old horse, and several foals, which I desire to be sold and the money sent me."

Thomas went on, "My brother, Blasius Gschwandl, also owes me one-hundred guilders, an inheritance from my father and mother."

Barbara and her daughters stood with Maria and Johann in the sunlight for warmth, waiting for their names to be called. They watched with interest as those who would be their friends and neighbors for the rest of their lives filed past. Anna Hofer joined them after she was finished and Margaretta had gone to the barn to feed her baby.

Catherine kept asking Anna who the different people from Gastein were. "We are the only ones from Saalfelden, and there are so many from Gastein. I hope they won't treat us like strangers."

"I'm from Gastein, and you're my best friend," Anna said.

"I didn't mean you, Anna, or the Gschwandls, but all of the others who just came."

"After we've traveled together and established a community in the wilderness, I expect we'll feel very close to all of these people, regardless of where they were born," Barbara said. "After all, we're all exiles for God. Each one of these people has suffered just as we have. That should make us all close in the Spirit."

"Yes, Barbara, I know you're right, but...." Catherine let her voice drop.

"She's worried that the single men from Gastein won't like her," Gertrude said.

"Oh, Gertrude, that's mean," Barbara said. "Apologize to your sister."

"I'm sorry," Gertrude said with a smirk.

The twenty-first name called was Johann Mosshamer. He stepped to the table.

"Johann Mosshamer?"

"Ja."

"Profession?"

"Servant, sir."

"Married?"

"Just newly, sir, to Maria Kroehr."

"Age?"

"Thirty-four."

"Who do you expect to follow, and what did you leave behind?"

"Nobody, unless my brother-in-law, Martin Thum, living in Harham in the Jurisdiction of Lichtenberg, and my brother Matthias, living in Lannthal in the Jurisdiction of Zeller, would change their minds and embrace the Protestant religion. I have sixty guilders with this brother-in-law and twenty guilders with my brother. I expect to inherit from my cousin, Rupert Piberger, four-thousand guilders."

"And your wife, Maria Kroehr?"

"Ja, I'm here," Maria answered.

"Are you expecting anyone or leaving anything behind?"

"I'm not expecting anyone, but I left behind one-hundred guilders and twenty-six-and-a-half kreutzers."

"That's all," the clerk said, completing the entry in his ledger.

"Next, your stepmother, Barbara Rohrmoser." Barbara walked up to the clerk, with Catherine and Gertrude beside her.

"I'm Barbara Rohrmoser, wife of Peter Rohrmoser, who is still in the Province of Salzburg with our small children. I was born in Oberkehlbach in the County of Saalfelden."

"How old are you?"

"Thirty-seven years old."

"And what did you leave behind?"

"I left, with my husband, Peter Rohrmoser, at Stockham on the Heath in Saalfelden, three-hundred guilders."

"Do you expect anyone?"

"Perhaps my two sisters, Gertrude Eps or Eva Hirsch-bichler."

"And these girls are your daughters?" he said, looking with interest at Catherine and Gertrude on either side of their mother.

"Ja, Catherine Kroehr, who is eighteen, and Gertrude Kroehr, fifteen."

"Thank you. Next, Georg Buecher and his wife and six children."

Later that afternoon, after the roll call was finished, the exiles, who were to compose the first Salzburger transport to the English Colony of Georgia, lifted their faces to Samuel Urlsperger, who stood on a small hill addressing them. Several families had already dropped out of the transport due to sudden illnesses or for other reasons. The Gschwandls, Mosshamers, and Kroehrs stood together. Excitement filled them as they prepared to leave the following day.

"Dear friends," Pastor Urlsperger began, using his most serious tone, "you are embarking on a long journey. His Majesty, the King of England, is your sponsor. He has entrusted to me monies for your needs on the journey. Please come forward when I call your names and receive His Majesty's generous gift of four guilders, twenty kreutzers for each family. Please declare how much money you have with you so that your leaders will know who may have needs in the future."

The first name on the list was Hans Gruber. He stepped up and reached out his hand to receive the money. He bowed his head in humble gratitude.

"How much do you have in all?"

"Forty guilders," he replied.

"Paulus Schweighofer and family, one-hundred-and-thirty-three guilders."

"Lorentz Huber and family, fifty-four guilders."

"Thomas Gschwandl and family, fifty guilders."

"Tobias Lackner, twenty-nine guilders."

"Johann Mosshamer and wife, ninety guilders."

"Barbara Rohrmoser, nineteen guilders."

"Catherine Kroehr, six guilders."

"Gertrude Kroehr, four guilders."

The company became familiar with each person's name and circumstances as the list was read.

"Next, we must assign chests to each family to pack your belongings. The chests will be carried up the river on a barge. You must decide what items you will need with you on the journey to Rotterdam, where you will board ship to England, and then to North America," Samuel Urlsperger said, skillfully organizing the people into groups assigned to each chest. "The chests will be marked with letters and numbers specifying what persons have belongings in the chest."

Chest number two was marked "S.R." and included the baggage of Stephan Riedelsperger, Johann Mosshamer, Barbara Rohrmoser and her children, Anna Burgsteiner, and Christian Leinberger.

Chest number six was a red trunk belonging to Thomas Gschwandl and his family. Included also were Anna Hofer and Leonard Rauner.

Barbara and her group scurried around, sorting their meager belongings into two piles, things to pack in the chest and those to carry by hand. Ladies from Augsburg went from group to group, distributing linens and other garments of clothing.

"Everyone make two piles," Barbara said, "one pile to pack in the chest and one pile to carry. We won't always have access to the chest, so we must take everything necessary by hand."

"Will we have to sleep outside?" Gertrude asked, as she folded her down comforter.

"I don't know. I hope not often, but perhaps we'd better take our bedding with us," Barbara replied.

"Will we have to cook on the way?" Catherine asked.

"I imagine so," Barbara said, placing her cooking pot in

the pile to carry by hand. She picked up the Kroehr Bible that she had carried all the way from Saalfelden and placed it in the pile to carry.

"Mother, that's awfully heavy. Won't it be safer from the rain in the chest?" Catherine asked.

"I think we might need it on this trip. It's further to Rotterdam than we have already come. We may need to be close to God's Word."

"We'll have the protection of Commissioner von Reck on this trip. It won't be like last time."

"Commissioner von Reck cannot give us the protection of God, Catherine; only God can do that."

"Would you like some new linens to wear on your trip?" a finely dressed lady from Augsburg asked, approaching Barbara and the girls.

"Oh, yes," Catherine said, reaching out to touch the linen garments. "Thank you so much. Look at this fine linen, Trudi. And you've embroidered flowers on it." Catherine was so excited over the gift that she impulsively hugged the lady. "Oh, I'm sorry," she apologized.

"I'm glad our gift has made you happy."

"Oh, yes."

"Here, give some to your sister and mother."

"I have another sister, Maria. Can she have some, too?"

"Catherine!" Barbara said sharply, "we do not ask for handouts. We only accept what God has mercifully given us."

"Of course. Here, take this set for your other sister."

The ladies turned with their basket of gifts and went to another group of women packing to leave.

"Mother, we should take a bath before we start this long journey. Let's see if we can fill one of the troughs in the barn and wash ourselves and our hair before we leave."

"Well, we're almost finished with the packing," Barbara said, looking down at the small piles that constituted all that they owned in the world. "Gertrude and I will take this stuff and pack it in the chest. We'll join you in the barn. The sun's warm, so we can still get our hair dry before dark if we hurry. Keep out the soap, Gertrude."

Barbara and Gertrude carried their belongings in a quilt over to chest number two. They carefully packed their extra clothes and bedding, along with their few possessions, including seed corn that Johann had purchased. The chest was nearly full, and everyone's things had not yet been packed.

Mamma Anna rushed up with a wooden box full of dried herbs and roots. While Barbara rearranged things to accommodate the box, Riedelsperger arrived with his possessions and saw that there was not room for everything.

"Frau Burgsteiner, you'll have to remove that box. It takes up too much room."

"But I've worked for weeks to collect and dry these medicinal plants. We'll need them on the trip."

"I understand that there will be an apothecary on the trip. I'm sure he will provide us with whatever medicines are needed."

"An apothecary?"

"Yes, so you won't need this box," he said haughtily, and lifted out the box of herbs, handing it to Mamma Anna.

"Well!" she said in consternation, "I believe I'm allowed to have as much room as you are. If I choose to carry herbs in my space, that's my affair." She plopped her box back into the chest on top of Riedelsperger's bundle.

Riedelsperger was completely taken aback, unused to being challenged by a woman. "We'll see about this," he said, stomping off to consult with the men who were organizing the transport. The women could hear him demanding to be put in charge of his chest or to be given space in another one. He did not want to share his chest with an old herbalist who insisted on carrying her Devil's potions. They watched him point at Mamma Anna and declare in a loud voice, "She shouldn't be allowed to travel with decent Christian men. Her presence will put us all in danger."

It seemed that the eyes of every person who was packing a chest froze and stared at Mamma Anna and the other Saalfelden women, who stood around chest number two.

Barbara's hand flew to her mouth in horror at the accusation. Instinctively, she put her arm around her old friend to protect her.

Undaunted, Mamma Anna mumbled, "That stupid, mean-hearted old goat. He's the one not acting like a Christian."

"Hush, Mamma Anna. Don't say another word. Let me get Thomas. He'll work things out." Barbara ran over to the red chest and said desperately, "Thomas, do something. You know these accusations are untrue. She's a respected midwife. Where would Margaretta have been without her?"

Thomas nodded his head and, with great dignity, approached Riedelsperger and the gentleman he was addressing. "Excuse me, sir, but I think you have been misinformed. Frau Burgsteiner is a respected midwife and needs her medicines in order to treat the fevers of childbirth. She tended my own wife, who would not have survived without her care."

After much discussion, a compromise was reached. The herbs would not be packed in the chest, but Mamma Anna could take them with her.

The women went together to the barn, where in a frenzy of energy, Catherine had enlisted most of the transport women in heating water and filling the scrubbed-out trough. The women stood guard while each took a turn in the water. Barbara washed Catherine's brown hair and then Gertrude's yellow hair. When the accumulated oil was scrubbed off Gertrude's hair, it shone like sunshine.

By the time it was Barbara's turn in the bath water, small bugs floated on the surface. She scooped up as many as possible and threw them out. Looking at her naked body for the first time in a long while, she saw that she had added some weight since her last bath, a good sign that she had had more food to eat. The people of Augsburg had been generous to the Salzburgers. Catherine scrubbed her mother's hair and saw gray streaking the dark blond. She had not thought of her mother as old enough to have gray hair.

The women sat in the sun, bent over, combing their hair

over their heads to dry the underside in the afternoon sunshine.

By eleven o'clock the next morning, the Salzburgers had assembled to begin their trek north to Rotterdam in Holland. When Barbara had rushed to add one more thing to the chest, Stephan Riedelsperger was taking his things out. He had decided at the last minute to wait on a friend and go with him on the next transport. Barbara hurried to tell Mamma Anna, who brought her wooden box and placed it in the chest. The Zittrauer and Schweighofer families also decided to wait for the second transport. Urlsperger then added to the group a few people who were not Salzburgers but who wanted to go to the English colony for free land.

"My dear Salzburgers," Samuel Urlsperger began, as he stood to speak to the departing group, "this gentleman here is the nobleman von Reck. He has been assigned by the Council in Regensburg to be your commissioner on the trip to Georgia."

Von Reck, a handsome young man standing beside a fine black chaise pulled by a beautiful black horse, smiled self-consciously and nodded to the group. He hardy looked older than Catherine. His servant was standing behind him.

"Commissioner von Reck will make all necessary arrangements for your journey. Also traveling with you to Rotterdam is Pastor Schumacher. He will be your spiritual guide until the two pastors accompanying you to Georgia arrive. Their names are Pastors Boltzius and Gronau. They are leaving from Halle Seminary and will meet you in Rotterdam. They have agreed to be your pastors in Georgia.

"Also joining your group is Andrew Zwiffler, an apothecary, to take care of your physical needs, and, as promised, a schoolmaster, Mr. Ortmann, and his wife, will join your party later.

"You will travel today to Donauwörth, then on to the Protestant towns of Ebermergen and Harburg. You will go through Dinkelsbühl, Rothenburg, Marktbreit, and Marktsteft, then on to Würzburg, where you will board a ship on the Main River via Wertheim to Frankfurt. From Frankfurt you will go by ship down the Rhine River to Rotterdam, from which you will embark to Dover, England. There, the ship will be provisioned for the journey across the sea to Savannah, Georgia. When you arrive, Trustee Oglethorpe will assign land to you, and you will begin establishing a Christian community in the wilderness.

"Great planning and effort have gone into your safe journey to Georgia and into the establishment of your new community. Let us pray together for God's blessing on this venture."

All of the gathered people bowed their heads.

"O Holy God, you have brought these, your servants, safely this far, after many hardships. May your great mercy go with them on this long journey and protect them for your service in the New World. May their hearts be ever mindful of your presence and accept humbly your will. We who are staying behind are grateful for their example and sacrifice, and we shall continue to pray for their well-being. Grace, mercy, and peace be with them on their journey. In Jesus' name we offer our prayer. Amen."

Tears were streaming down Samuel Urlsperger's face when he finished the prayer and began shaking the hands of the men in the group. With von Reck's chaise leading the way, followed by the chaise containing the other gentlemen, Pastor Schumacher and Andrew Zwiffler, the procession began. The older people and the children traveled in wagons, while the others walked. Thomas Gschwandl led his own horse and wagon, with Margaretta and the baby riding. The others fell into line, walking to the rhythm of the *Song of the Exile* as they steadfastly started off.

"I wonder if that young man has ever been to Georgia?" Thomas asked Tobias, cocking his head toward von Reck.

"He's awfully young to be in charge of this group. I hope he knows what he's doing," Tobias grumbled back.

"Well, with God's help, I guess we can take care of ourselves if we have to," Thomas replied.

"Ja, that's true," Tobias chuckled.

"At least this time planning has been done on our behalf. It's not like the confusion when we left Gastein. It's good to have you and the other men from Gastein along. I know I can count on the Gastein miners when there is work to be done, and there will be hard work to be done, clearing a wilderness and building a community."

"We should have enough Gastein manpower to get the job done. There's you and me and Hans and Peter Gruber, Balthasar Fleiss, Simon Reiter, and young Georg Schweiger and Lorentz Huber, although, at fifty-two, he may be too old and burdened with too many children to offer much strength to the effort."

"Then, of course, there are other men who should be good workers, like Matthias Mittersteiner from Goldegg and Martin Hertzog from Schrecking. Johann Mosshamer from Saalfelden is a good man. We traveled together to Memmingen after Gertrude had her accident. And then there's Simon Reuschgott from Salzburg. Do you know anything about him? He just joined up at the last minute."

"No, and I don't know about this Swabian, Leonard Rauner, yet. It seems strange taking along others besides Salzburgers. Perhaps the years of persecution have made all of us Salzburgers more humble and grateful to God for our deliverance."

"Well, we mustn't judge people too harshly. God must have a reason for their coming with us."

"Imagine having our own Protestant pastor to accompany us to Rotterdam. Remember how we longed for a Protestant pastor and church in Gastein? We are truly blessed on this journey."

"I believe this transport is in God's hands, with two pastors going with us to Georgia. We're very lucky. We'll never again be persecuted for our religion. It will be up to us to establish a pious community as an example to all in this new land."

"Yes, and a schoolmaster. Just imagine. The children

244 ♦ *Rose Shearouse Thomason*

will be educated," Tobias said.

"Ja. I'm very happy about that. Our sons will be educated landowners. Have you selected a bride from the single women along?" Thomas asked with a smile.

"Well, I've been looking," Tobias said. "A man will need a wife on a farm to help with the work and make a home." He paused and then said, "Johann Mosshamer's already wed the prettiest one."

"You mean Maria. Being pretty caused her a heap of trouble from the soldiers along the way. She took to walking with her head down, so they couldn't see her face. But she has two half-sisters, Catherine and Gertrude."

"Ja, but their mother would probably never let them near a rough miner like me."

"Well, there's always Anna Hofer, but you'd better act fast. Georg Schweiger is interested in her. There's Maria Schweighofer and her close friend, Catherine Piedler, although Stephan Riedelsperger seems interested in Catherine. Too bad he didn't come along. He said he'd follow on the next transport. Then there's Maria Hierl from Saalfelden."

"You've really done some research, haven't you? Remember, there are more single men than women. Some of us will get left out. I'll just wait until it feels right and that land I'm going to get is really under my feet."

"You always were cautious," Thomas said.

They processed through the walled town of Donauwörth, singing their Protestant hymns. People came out to watch them, but, being Catholic, did not invite them into their homes. They passed through the gate on the other side and continued on their way north. The weather was warm for the last day of October, but, when the sun began to wane, the air became chilly.

Margaretta Gschwandl nursed her baby sitting on the wagon seat. When the child was satisfied, she fell asleep in the cradle in the wagon. Margaretta jumped down to walk with Anna and Catherine.

"I'm sure glad we have this wagon. I'd hate to be carrying

that heavy cradle on my back," she said to the girls walking beside her.

"I just saw Georg while I was back down the line, and he asked about you, Anna," Catherine said, catching up with the others.

"Did he really?"

"Yes, really."

"If he's so interested in how I am, why doesn't he come ask himself?" Anna said with a toss of her head.

Catherine and Margaretta laughed at Anna's embarrassment over the attentions of Georg. They both knew that Anna was pleased that Georg was interested in her, but she was unsure of how to act.

"Catherine, there are more single men than women in this transport. Have you decided who you'll marry?" Margaretta asked.

"No. So far, no one has interested me. Mother keeps telling Gertrude and me to wait until we get to Savannah. There may be a gentleman looking for a wife. There won't be as many women there, either."

"Well, I don't think I'd want to marry an Englishman," Anna said. "You couldn't even talk to him. And besides, after all we've been through, I'd want to marry someone who had lived through the same experiences. That way we'd understand each other better."

42

On Board the *Purysburg*, 1734

"That whole long way across Europe, the young men and the young women looked each other over," Mamma Anna laughed. "And we were hailed as heroes in most towns we passed through. You'll find this hard to believe, but the burghermeisters came out and made speeches, and the people put us up in their homes. It was something to see. I'll never forget it. It kind of made up for all the persecution we had suffered under Firmian.

"I remember when we got to Rothenburg. Have you ever been to Rothenburg, Deutsch?"

"Nein, I lived in the north of Germany," Deutsch replied, having roused from sleep to listen to Mamma Anna's story.

"Well, Rothenburg was one of the prettiest cities we saw. It was a brisk day in early November when we approached the gate and gathered under a sea-green clock with gold hands glistening in the sun. As usual, Tobias and the Gruber brothers began the singing. This time, they had chosen Luther's hymn, *A Mighty Fortress is our God*, to herald our entrance into the city. The Protestants lined the streets, with some people running to be sure that they did not miss the spectacle of the Salzburgers' coming. We had become famous by now. The singing sounded strong as we wound through the narrow streets, passed the gray stone church, and came to a stop in front of the large, impressive city hall, with its colonnade of stone arches and its balcony. To the side was a tall clock tower with a glockenspiel.

"After all the speechmaking, the townspeople began inviting us into their homes. Barbara, the girls, and I went with an old lady followed by a longhaired dog. She led us through the twisting streets to number one Judenstrasse.

"'That's my house,' she said, and pointed to a peaked white house with three brown beams separating three floors. There were two windows with green shutters and a door in the middle on the ground floor. Attached to the main house was a thatch-roofed stone cottage. That's where we stayed. She said it had been built somewhere around 1100.

"She brought our supper and breakfast to us, and she was a good cook. Gave us some hard rolls to take along with us. We enjoyed having a place of our own. She had a number of children living in her house, but she kept them away from us, so they wouldn't bother our rest.

"We were invited to the royal gardens the next day. I'd say our short stay in Rothenburg was the best place we'd been since we left home. It was certainly better than what happened to us in Marktbreit."

"What happened there?" Deutsch asked, hoping she'd continue her tale.

"Well, as we were getting near this town, a horseman came galloping toward us and gave orders to Commissioner von Reck that we were to turn around. He was a messenger with orders from the Catholic bailiff telling von Reck to take his party outside the territories of the Prince of Schartzberg, which meant going around Marktbreit.

"We got an idea of what a hot-head our young commissioner was that day. He refused to obey the order and marched us straight for the gate of Marktbreit. He told that messenger that there was no other way to go except through the city, since we were boarding a ship in Marktsteft, just on the other side of Marktbreit, and that he had no intention of rerouting his party.

"I was plenty scared, I can tell you. I didn't know whether to be proud of our leader or to denounce him as a fool."

"Why did the prince want you to avoid Marktbreit? Was it a Catholic city?"

"What we found out was that the authorities were Catholics, but the poor peasants were Protestants, just like in Salzburg. The peasants had lined the streets waiting for us, and the authorities got scared, afraid we'd have a bad influence on the peasants.

"Anyway, we sang as we marched into the city, two by

two. By this time, we'd gotten pretty good at making an impressive entrance into a city. Sure enough, the poor people cheered us, and two of them went up into the bell tower of the church and sounded the trumpets. We had quite a celebration with those people."

"Did the bailiff arrest any of you?"

"No. I think he decided the best thing to do was just let us pass through the town as quickly as possible, which we did. It really lifted our spirits, though, to give hope to the peasants in Marktbreit. He may have arrested some of the poor people; I don't know about that.

"Anyway, we walked along the Main River to Marktsteft, where a small sailing ship was waiting for us. We had to unload all our things from the wagons and carry them on board. Von Reck sold the wagons and told us we'd travel by ship the rest of the way to Georgia. It felt good to sit down and let our blisters heal, but the wind did a poor job of moving us. We'd made faster progress on foot. We went through Würzburg and finally stopped in Wertheim for supplies.

"Pastor Schumacher started in teaching the catechism to everyone, just like we'd never heard of it. He said we had to be able to answer the questions perfectly before we met our new pastors in Rotterdam. That seemed important to most people, and they spent their time on the boat practicing the right words.

"It was in Wertheim, I believe, that the Rott family decided to join the transport to Georgia. They pretended to be so moved by the story of the Salzburgers, which Pastor Schumacher told in a service, that they decided to go with us. Actually, I think they were probably running from debtors and hoped to gain some free land by joining the Salzburgers. I knew from the beginning that they were a bad sort, and her expecting a baby, too. I hope she doesn't have that child before we get to Savannah. It'll be hard going on this ship, I can tell you.

"But von Reck sometimes can't see what's right in front of him; he was always inviting people to join us. Why, even in

Frankfurt, he took Thomas Gschwandl with him to try to talk the Tirnbergers into going with us to Georgia. Did you ever hear about the Tirnbergers?"

"No, who were they?"

"Well, poor things, they were another group exiled by Firmian, who were sent to Holland to live, but the people in Holland hated them and treated them badly. They finally came back to Frankfurt, most of them sick and dying from malnutrition, Thomas said. They couldn't join our transport because they were too sick. I don't think they'll ever trust anyone else's promises again. Sometimes I wonder if we can trust the King of England to live up to his promises. We were told we'd have sufficient food on this voyage across the ocean, but Captain Fry is starving us. I'm afraid it may be that way in Georgia, too.

"Lordy, look at that light streaking the sky. I've sat out here and talked all night. I'd better not be caught up here by Pastor Boltzius, with a sailor's head in my lap."

Deutsch laughed heartily as he stood up stiffly. Mamma Anna scrambled down the stairs, quickly got into her bunk, and turned her face to the wall. When the others awoke, she feigned illness and stayed in bed most of the day.

* * *

Gertrude stood leaning on the rail of the *Purysburg*, letting the wind blow through her yellow hair, the breeze having worried her hat until she took it off. She glanced about to see if Barbara was watching and, not seeing her vigilant mother, relaxed into her own drifting dreams. She loved these moments alone, staring into the water and imagining all the creatures that might live below its dark, rolling surface. Then, lifting her eyes skyward, she imagined heavenly life in all its glorious forms. Floating on the sea made the world simple; the heavens met the waters, and the ship with its inhabitants sailed between the two. She envisioned God sitting on a cloud, blowing the wind, and speeding her toward her destiny.

Gertrude was unaware of the picture she made, the trade

winds pressing her clothes to her coatless young body, her golden hair streaming in the sunlight. Several pairs of masculine eyes watched her, but none dared approach. Tobias Lackner had noticed her habits and tried to be on deck when she was, but kept his distance. He knew from Thomas that Barbara had forbidden Gertrude to speak to him alone. Even the earnest Pastor Boltzius glanced up from his journal writing now and then, his face softening slightly when he gazed in her direction.

* * *

She had first begun loving the water when she stood at the prow of the small craft they had boarded in Frankfurt to sail down the Rhine River to Rotterdam. She remembered the wind and current carrying them slowly past the castles perched high on the hills rising from the river. Each turn in the river revealed another such vision, like turning the pages in a fairy tale book. She had been dreaming that she was a princess in one of those castles, wearing a pale pink, silk ball gown, trimmed with embroidered rosebuds, her neck encircled by jewels.

She had imagined dancing with a handsome prince, who would marry her and take her to live in that next castle which was becoming visible as the boat glided around a curve.

As the cold November wind blew down the river, she had pulled her coat tighter and hugged herself. Her mother and sister had gone below to stay warm, calling her to come, but she had stayed, not wanting to miss seeing the castles. Eventually, she had become aware that someone was standing beside her and, glancing sideways, saw that it was Tobias Lackner, one of the miners from Gastein.

"Those castles are very beautiful, aren't they?" he said softly, his words almost swallowed by the wind.

"Yes, they are," Gertrude replied, casting her eyes downward, her cheeks blushing with embarrassment. Her mother would not like her talking with a man alone. She looked behind her but saw no one.

"Your thoughts seem to be in another world," Tobias

ventured. He was surprised at himself for having the courage to talk to Gertrude alone, since he was usually shy with women. He had not planned this encounter; it had just happened.

"Another world?" she replied, surprised that he seemed to have read her mind. "How did you know?"

"Your face reminded me of a beautiful princess in one of those castles, like in the fairy tales."

Gertrude looked at him, startled at how his words matched what she had been thinking. In her innocence, she did not consider the compliment to be flattery, for she almost never thought of her appearance. She had not looked in a mirror in months and still visualized herself as the child reflected in Saalfelden.

Gazing at him full in the face for the first time, she saw merriment in his bright, green eyes, as though he might be teasing her. Gertrude found herself laughing and said, "I was dreaming of what it would be like to live in a castle; were you?"

"No, not really. I guess I'm too old for such dreams about myself."

"It's very foolish of me to think of such things, but I never expected to see real castles. I expected to live my whole life in our valley in Saalfelden, but God has led us on this great journey, and I'm always surprised at the new sights we see. The world is much bigger than I realized, and there are so many amazing people and things in it. If we hadn't been exiled, I would never have known these wonders."

The low sun shone on her face, causing her skin to glow with excitement. Her fragile, youthful, but unconscious beauty stunned Tobias. He felt warmth spread over his body, even though the wind was cold.

"Do you feel the same way?"

Now it was his turn to blush, and he tried to remember what she had been saying. He must not let her know what he was really feeling. He shifted his gaze toward the water ahead and answered softly, "Ja, me, too."

"Trudi, where are you?" Barbara called loudly from behind them. "Oh, there you are. Come below, child, before you catch cold." Barbara looked from Gertrude to Tobias, and realized that she had interrupted their conversation.

After an awkward moment, Gertrude turned abruptly and walked across the deck, deliberately avoiding her mother's disapproving face. Looking sternly at Tobias, Barbara hesitated but said nothing when he met her gaze without wavering. Finally, she turned and followed Gertrude down the ladder. At the bottom she grabbed Gertrude's arm and turned her around. "What were you doing with that man?" she whispered intently.

"Oh, Mother, he was just talking to me about the castles. Quit worrying. After all, he's a good friend of Herr Gschwandl."

"Did anyone else see you alone with him?"

"I wasn't alone with him," Gertrude said defiantly.

"You must be more careful, Trudi. Men have started looking at you like a woman. I don't want you to get involved with a rough, uneducated miner."

"He seemed very nice."

"Be careful, Gertrude. I have other plans for you."

"What other plans?"

"Just be patient and wait on the Lord," Barbara replied piously. "Now come with me. Pastor Schumacher has started his instruction."

* * *

As Gertrude turned around on the deck of the *Purysburg* on this March morning, she saw Tobias looking at her again. She often noticed him staring at her. A slight thrill of danger passed through her, and she boldly returned his gaze. Her eyes flicked quickly across the deck at Pastor Boltzius, who was watching them. She quickly fled below when Tobias started walking toward her, but, in that brief moment, she had been shocked by the angular bones of his cheeks and jaw almost protruding through his skin. He must be sick. She wondered if lack of food had changed her face that much.

43

Halle, Fall 1733

"Excuse me, sir. Who in Halle can tell me which Salzburgers have passed through here on the way to Prussia?" Hans asked the collared cleric in front of the seminary.

"You probably should ask Pastor Boltzius, over there at the orphanage. He led a party of Salzburgers to Prussia. Are you one of the exiles?"

"Ja," Hans said. "I'm trying to locate the people from my village."

"Oh, you poor man. God will surely bless you in Heaven for your great sacrifice for the faith." He reached into his pocket, took out a coin, and placed it in Hans' hand. "I'm sure Pastor Boltzius will be delighted to see you. He and Pastor Gronau are preparing to lead another group of Salzburgers to the English colony of Georgia. He's most committed to helping the Salzburgers."

"Thank you, sir. I'll ask him. Over there?"

"Ja. Just ask for Pastor Boltzius."

After some delay, a dignified man with a prominent nose and florid cheeks hurried toward Hans, holding out his hand in greeting. "What can I do for you? I'm in something of a hurry, since I'm leaving tomorrow on a long journey."

"Someone told me that you led a party of Salzburgers to Prussia. I'm trying to locate people from the village of Saalfelden. My sister Barbara, my two nieces, and my fiancée, Maria Kroehr. Do you remember them?"

"There were some people from Saalfelden in the party I led to Königsberg, but I can't be sure they were your family. I do remember a Maria, I think, but that's such a common name, and it's been more than a year. I really am not sure. The records in Königsberg should be accurate. I suggest that you travel there and check. How long since you've seen them?"

"I know they left Saalfelden in the spring of '32. I was in

prison at the time and then ill."

"I'm sorry I can't be more help. Would you be interested in traveling with us to Georgia? I'm meeting a party of Salzburgers in Rotterdam. I believe most of them are miners from Gastein who were just recently expelled."

"No, I think I'd better go on to Königsberg. Thank you for your help." Hans waved his hand and continued north, walking painfully with a crutch and the new wooden leg he had carved.

44

On Board the *Purysburg*, February 1734

Catherine sat as close to the center of the *Purysburg* deck as she could get, afraid to look into the water. Every day on this ship was torture for her. It seemed they would never get to land again. She had first experienced this trapped feeling when they arrived in Rotterdam last November and were not allowed to leave the boat. She had been so frustrated to be docked, yet unable to touch land. As the ship creaked and groaned, she remembered how the people had stood on the deck of the small ship tied up at the docks in Rotterdam.

That November day, the gray sky had blended into the black water of the Maas River, and the damp, wintry wind caused them to hug their arms around themselves to find extra warmth. Barbara had squeezed over toward Thomas and Margaretta, who were trying to shield little one-year-old Margaretta from the cold wind.

"What's the delay?" Barbara asked Thomas.

"I don't know. Von Reck, Schumacher, and Zwiffler haven't come back from the magistrate's office yet. They've been gone a long time."

"Something must be wrong. We've been waiting here for hours," Barbara said.

"I'm sure there are many details to arrange," Thomas replied. "We'll just have to be patient."

"Ja. Of course, you're right. I don't mean to complain. It's just so cold." Turning to Margaretta, Barbara said, "How's the baby?"

"She has a cold. I'm afraid she may have a fever. What do you think?" Margaretta said.

Barbara felt the baby's forehead and nodded. "Yes, a little perhaps. Mamma Anna might have something to help her feel better."

Margaretta looked embarrassed and whispered quietly, "Thomas wants me to wait for Mr. Zwiffler to treat her."

"Oh, I see," Barbara replied. She knew other people had turned to the apothecary with their illnesses, but she was surprised that the Gschwandls would question Mamma Anna's healing.

Two hours later, von Reck and several other gentlemen returned to the boat.

"My dear colonists," von Reck shouted over the wind to the people gathered on the deck, "the magistrate of Rotterdam has refused your entrance into the city. However, the City Council has offered to try and arrange billeting for you in two locations. We were unable to persuade the recalcitrant magistrate. But we did rendezvous with your new pastors. May I present the two distinguished clerics from Halle who will be joining our party, Pastor Johann Martin Boltzius and Pastor Israel Christian Gronau."

The Salzburgers buzzed with excitement at seeing the two pastors for the first time, but shyness prevented their greeting them. They were handsome gentlemen, both in dark wool coats, carrying Bibles in their hands. They wore white wigs and, visible under their coats, the high necked, white clerical collars of Protestant pastors, with two sheer, straight ends protruding three or four inches down the front and flapping in the wind.

Pastor Boltzius had a long face, which had turned red in the cold wind. His straight, prominent nose was even redder. Large, heavy-lidded brown eyes that never seemed to quite open all the way were set under a high forehead. His lips were slightly curved in a small, dignified smile. When he surveyed the gathered Salzburgers, his eyes filled with tears, and compassion was visible through his reserve. He and Pastor Gronau looked at each other, both of them blinking, overcome by emotion but unwilling to show it publicly.

The Salzburgers viewed the two men with awe. They were amazed that these educated gentlemen were willing to spend the rest of their lives with them in the wilderness of Georgia.

Boltzius looked at the cold, travel-weary people in their

once bright but now faded green hats and colorful woolen mountain clothes and was touched to the core of his being when he thought of the tremendous sacrifice they had made in order to be faithful to God. After an awkward moment of mutual staring, he knew he must do something to begin knowing the people who would be his flock for the rest of his life. He had rehearsed in his mind what he would say, but, seeing their calm, happy faces, instead of speaking, he began walking among them, greeting each one personally and shaking the hands of the men.

Gronau, seeing the senior Boltzius greeting the people, did likewise. He was much shyer and more diffident, but seemed equally kind. As the people introduced themselves, their Salzburg mountain accents sounded strange to the Halle pastors, but pleasantly exotic. Barbara, with Catherine and Gertrude on either side, bowed her head when Boltzius approached her.

"God bless you, sir, for making this journey with us," she murmured.

"It is God who has brought us all thus far, and God who will lead us to our new home," he replied.

Gronau joined them at the moment Boltzius asked their names. Barbara stammered in her nervousness, "Oh, sir, I'm Barbara Rohrmoser, and these are my daughters, Catherine and Gertrude," she replied, pointing to the wrong girls as she said their names.

"No, Mother, I'm Gertrude and that's Catherine," Gertrude said, laughing. They all joined in the laughter, and Boltzius and Gronau both bowed slightly toward each of the girls. Catherine blushed under the brief gaze of the ministers before they moved on to greet Maria and Johann Mosshamer, who were next.

Thomas approached von Reck, who had just finished talking to the ship's captain. "Sir, would it be possible for us to at least move to the new ship and get established there?" Thomas asked.

"I've already checked with Captain Fry of the *Purysburg*,

and he refuses to have you aboard until he is ready to launch, sometime next week." Von Reck pulled out his watch and, seeing the time, looked impatiently at the two pastors, still greeting each of the Salzburgers.

"Pastor Schumacher," von Reck said, turning to the traveling chaplain, "we have a dinner engagement with Pastor Lowther of the English Church here in Rotterdam. We need to leave shortly because I first need to meet with Mr. Ortmann, the schoolmaster, who will serve as my interpreter."

Taking the hint, Pastor Schumacher addressed the group. "Dear friends, your new pastors are delighted to meet you, but they have other appointments to keep. You will see them again soon. I will bid you farewell tomorrow, and they will take over the responsibility for your spiritual guidance on the following day."

"Why do we have to stay on this boat? Can't we at least walk around on the land?" Catherine asked Thomas.

"No. We were told that we might not enter Rotterdam. After seeing the condition of the Tirnbergers, I'm relieved not to be spending much time here in Holland. These people have little sympathy for our cause, and we do not speak their language," Thomas replied.

Shifting the conversation, Barbara asked, "Thomas, what do you know about these two pastors?"

"Mr. Schumacher told me they were educated in Halle, which is the seminary in northern Germany where Spener and Francke teach. He's been instructing us in some of their papers. They were working in the famous orphanage at Halle when they agreed to come with us, and they are said to be devout men, true pietists. Pastor Schumacher believes they will be good spiritual leaders for us." Thomas paused for a moment and then added, "And they also look young and strong, which may be very important in the wilderness."

"Are their families coming with them?" Barbara asked.

"I understand that they are coming unattended, leaving behind their parents, brothers and sisters, and friends, just as we are." Again Thomas paused and then added, with a smile

and a wink at Barbara, "And they are neither one married."
Several people giggled at his insinuation, but Barbara was
shocked, turned her back, and walked away.

"That's what you get for being so nosy," Maria said, putting her arm around Barbara, whose pride had been wounded
by Thomas's joke.

"He embarrassed me, implying that I'm interested in one
of the gentlemen. Everyone knows that I have a husband
and am not free to marry. Anyway, I'm older than both of
them. I can't believe Thomas would do that with everyone
watching. I thought he was a good and pious man."

"He is, Barbara. He was just having fun. Besides, everyone also knows you've been protecting Catherine and
Gertrude from the single men among us. After all, Tobias is
his best friend, and you told Trudi not to talk to him. There
are few secrets in a group like this," Maria said.

"I must quit being so forward," Barbara lamented. "It always gets me in trouble. Having the responsibility for Catherine and Gertrude alone, I sometimes forget I'm just a
woman and can't talk and act like a man," Barbara said.

"You're not alone, Barbara. Johann and I are here, and
we're all family. Johann will help you with whatever you
need," Maria said.

"Yes, I know, but I hate to have to depend on him. I
know I should not be covetous, but I am upset that I won't
get any of the free land in Georgia, even though I am head of
my family, just because I am a woman," Barbara went on.
"Of course, I'm grateful for Johann's protection."

"It doesn't seem fair, but I guess a woman couldn't work
the land without a man," Maria said. "Johann says that's the
reason for the English law."

"And what man can manage a home without a woman?"
Barbara added. "But they don't deny a home to a man with
no wife."

"Well, there's not much we can do about it. We can just
be grateful for any land, and you know Johann likes the idea
of being the head of this family, all of us. The new pastors

looked kind. I'm sure they will make sure we are all provided for."

Barbara smiled, as though in agreement, but secretly
wished she could head her own family, and not have to rely
on her stepdaughter's husband or the kindness of the pastors.

"It looks like all the single people have begun to pair up.
The women know they must have a husband in order to get
land, and the men know they need a wife to help establish a
home. I expect there will be a lot more weddings before we
get there. You may be making a mistake protecting Catherine and Gertrude. They may lose out," Maria warned. "You
don't really think those two educated gentlemen pastors will
marry the daughters of poor Saalfelden peasants, do you?"

"I've been praying about this, and I still feel that God has
something more in store for my girls than being wives of
Gastein miners. That's why God has sent me on this journey
with them. I have to believe that, otherwise my sacrifice has
been too great." Barbara stopped, surprised at what she had
just said. "I didn't mean to say that, for no sacrifice is too
great for God. After all, God gave his only Son for our sins,"
she murmured contritely.

Later that evening, at the back of the boat, Anna Hofer
stood talking to Georg Schweiger. Most of the people were
below at the evening prayer meeting, where Pastor Schumacher was giving his farewell sermon. All but a few of the
sailors had gone ashore, and the others were in the mess.

Anna turned and looked at Georg, who was staring out at
the black water. No moon or stars were visible through the
heavy cloud cover, and the only light was from a flickering
lantern in the prow of the boat. Nearby, Simon Reiter and
his cousin Maria were in deep conversation, with Simon doing most of the talking and Maria nodding her head occasionally.

Georg turned to Anna and put his arm around her waist,
pulling her to him. "We should stand closer for warmth," he
said.

Anna liked the feel of the hardness of his body as she absorbed some of his heat. They fit together nicely, though he was a little taller. She had never been held by a man before, and it was a delicious feeling. She wondered what Margaretta and Thomas must have thought when they realized that she and Georg were not at the prayer meeting. When he had taken her hand, leading her up the ladder, she had just followed. It was the first time he had ever done such a thing.

"I've been wanting to talk to you alone," he started, "but there are always so many people around, and no way to get away from them."

"Ja, it is crowded," she answered a little breathlessly.

"I don't want you to think that I'm not grateful for all that has been done for us, but this journey is uncomfortable in some ways," he said rather stiffly.

"In many ways, actually." Anna laughed nervously. "But it's so much better than when we first left Gastein. That was a real nightmare."

"I guess it wasn't as difficult for those of us who came later, although those last two years in Gastein were pretty awful. We were always afraid of being arrested for something. The Catholics kept up the persecution." He paused, shaking the bad memories from his mind. "You don't think ill of me for keeping you from the evening prayer meeting, do you?"

"I suppose I should, but it's the only time to be away from the others," Anna said. Realizing she probably should not have been so bold, her hand instinctively flew to her mouth. "Oh, I'm afraid you'll think me too forward," she added hastily.

"No, I think you are just right. Sometimes shy and sometimes forward," Georg murmured, and tightened his arm around her. "I've been admiring you for a long time."

"I've been admiring you, too," Anna replied, with a catch in her voice. She could not believe this was happening to her. She remembered that, at one time in her life, she had feared that she would never be married. Maybe she would after all, and to Georg, the most promising single man from

Gastein.

Hearing a noise, they both looked over to Simon and Maria and could faintly tell in the dark that they were kissing. Both of them turned back abruptly, embarrassed.

Georg wanted to kiss Anna, but since this was the first time they had been alone together, he didn't think he should. It might frighten her, but then, she seemed to like him. He held back. He did not want Thomas to think he had taken advantage of his sister-in-law. He had already risked Thomas's disfavor by skipping prayer meeting and bringing Anna up here. Thomas seemed to be the most respected of the Salzburgers and the one everyone turned to for advice. He had realized for some time that it might help his own prospects if he were a part of Thomas's family.

Anna shivered, partly from the cold wind and partly from happiness. Georg, afraid she was chilled, turned her to him and put both arms around her, pulling her body to his. They stood that way, both hearts pounding under their heavy woolen clothes. Anna's face was mashed into his shoulder and neck; their round green hats were knocked askew.

After a while, she lifted her face and looked up at him. Without further hesitation, he covered her mouth with his, softly at first and then more firmly. They were both swimming in their own thoughts.

The next evening, the twenty-ninth of November, Pastors Boltzius and Gronau came on board with the other gentlemen in the party to conduct their first service with the Salzburgers. They had the people gather on the deck, since the weather had improved and there was not much wind. It was more comfortable there than in the much smaller space below.

Everyone was present except Mrs. Huber and her children, who were sick. Margaretta was holding little Margaretta, who was fretful, ready to leave if the baby really started crying. Anna and Georg sat beside her.

Boltzius spoke with a North German accent that was different from Schumacher's and was nearly incomprehensible to the Salzburgers. They listened politely, straining to understand this impressive man of God and showing signs of happiness when they recognized something he was saying.

Barbara was not sure whether her difficulty in understanding was due to his accent or because what he was saying was strange to her. Her faith had been so simple back in Saalfelden. She had never realized that such extensive explaining was necessary in order to understand God. There was so much she did not know, but, at least now, she and her girls would be able to learn these things. She stroked the Lutheran Bible, which had been her father's and then had belonged to her brother Hans, and thanked God for this chance.

After the service, Boltzius and Gronau went from family to family, questioning each person on Luther's Catechism. The pastors were pleased that the people knew the correct responses and gave them enthusiastically. Gertrude was relieved, once they had examined the Kroehr-Mosshamer group, that she had not made any mistakes. It had frightened her, reminding her of being questioned by the priest back in Saalfelden. This time, at least, she believed the answers that were expected.

Seeing that so many of the people had Bibles, many of which had been given to them in Augsburg, Boltzius called them together again and began instructing them on how to find the different books in the Bible.

Barbara, Gertrude, and Catherine already knew where each book was located, for they had been studying the Bible all their lives, so they began to help the others who had only recently acquired a Bible. The activity turned into almost a game, and there was much happiness at learning something very practical that would help open the doors to reading and understanding the Bible.

"Just think," Hans Gruber said to his brother Peter, "the people back home in Gastein will never even have a chance to see a Bible in German, and here we are being taught how to read it. It's hard to believe our good fortune."

"Ja, and there's no soldier or priest trying to arrest us, either," Peter replied.

The next day, the people were moved to two houses, which the City Council had arranged. One of the pastors stayed in each house. The Kroehr and Mosshamer families were sitting in the kitchen of their house, talking with the Gschwandl family, which now included Georg Schweiger, who had been welcomed by Thomas as a suitor for Anna. Thomas had admonished Georg not to miss morning or evening prayer meetings again, however. He had also had Margaretta speak to Anna about proper behavior. Margaretta had told Anna what Thomas had said, but then they laughed with delight while Anna shared her confidences with her sister.

As they sat at the kitchen table, little Margaretta started crying. Maria reached over, picked up the baby from her cradle, and held her face against her own to gauge her temperature. "Does she have dysentery?" Maria asked Margaretta quietly.

"No, just a cold. I think her ears might hurt," Margaretta replied.

"I'll make her a cup of special tea," Maria said, and passed the crying child back to Margaretta. Then she hesitated. "Unless you would prefer to have Mr. Zwiffler look at her."

"No. He's at the other house. Mr. Huber and two of their children are sick, and he's staying there with them," Margaretta replied. "Besides, I'm not sure his doctoring is better than yours and Mamma Anna's."

"I would like to learn from him, but I'm afraid to ask," Maria said wistfully. "He probably wouldn't want to bother with me. He's been kept pretty busy with one thing and another."

Maria brewed a weak tea from dried willow bark and warmed a stone on the hearth. She placed the warm stone against the baby's ear and spooned the tea into her mouth, sip by sip. After that process was over, little Margaretta fell asleep and rested peacefully in her cradle.

"She's soon going to outgrow that cradle," Maria said, smiling at the sleeping baby.

Earlier that morning, Catherine had organized baths for the women, and she now sat before the fire, while Gertrude combed her sister's long, light-brown hair, holding up each combfull of strands before the fire to dry it. The door opened, letting a draft of cold air into the stuffy room as Pastor Gronau entered. Catherine jumped up, not wanting the pastor to see her with her hair wet.

"Please, girls, you don't have to leave on my account. I know how crowded it is here." He sat down on a bench and began talking to Thomas, Georg, and Johann, who were gathered in the far corner of the room. Gertrude continued to comb Catherine's hair, which shone in the firelight. They made a pretty picture of womanly domesticity, with Catherine bent over her sewing. Israel Gronau's eyes kept drifting back to them while he talked to the men.

"When will we leave, and how long does it take to sail to England?" Thomas asked Gronau.

"We'll probably leave on Wednesday," Israel said, "but that depends on everything being ready, and on the wind and tides."

"It'll be good to finally get on the ship that will take us across the ocean," Thomas said. "How long will we be in England?"

"I'm not sure. We're supposed to land in Dover and be met there by members of the sponsoring parties, The Society for Promoting Christian Knowledge and the Georgia Trustees. Then the ship will be loaded with the provisions that will be needed to sustain us for a year. I understand some English settlers will also be boarding the same ship."

Gronau consciously tried to keep his eyes averted from Gertrude and Catherine across the room. Once Catherine glanced up, and their eyes met. She immediately looked down at her sewing again. She seemed to be mending something, perhaps a stocking.

45

On Board the *Purysburg*, November 1733

"Mr. Ortmann, what did Captain Fry say?" von Reck asked impatiently. He was beginning to doubt the schoolmaster's ability to translate the English Captain's words into German.

"He says that the pastors will have to bunk with the Salzburgers, sir, that there's no room anywhere else," Ortmann replied with a sly grin.

"But that's preposterous! These gentlemen can't be sharing bunks with the peasants," von Reck said indignantly. "Tell him that is not acceptable. The Georgia Trustees who hired his ship would never approve those arrangements."

Ortmann spoke again in English to the Captain, who laughed scornfully. "He says if them fine gentlemen are going to be missionaries, they might as well start now. He says his cabin is promised to another family that's coming aboard in Dover. It's full up. He says to tell this von Reck fellow, if he's in charge of that queer-looking group, to assign bunks to his people and hurry up about it. He's got work to do." Captain Fry turned his back and walked away to supervise the loading of provisions.

Such was the welcome the Salzburgers received on the *Purysburg*, the sailing ship that would take them first to Dover, England, and then on to Georgia.

Von Reck sketched out the compartments and numbered them. He assigned the family groups first, then the single women, and finally the single men. He placed the two pastors with the single men.

Each compartment consisted of four narrow bunks stacked on top of each other. There were no doors, but canvas curtains covered the openings. Fresh air never reached the depth of the ship, and it smelled of human waste, with an overlay of vinegar.

Barbara, Gertrude, Catherine, and Mamma Anna were assigned to one compartment. They began to work out how they would sleep and store their meager belongings. They would seldom change clothes, and they learned to avert their eyes and leave the compartment out of courtesy to each other when privacy was needed.

The four people in the compartment agreed among themselves not to complain about the cramped quarters or any other hardships they might experience, but simply to thank God and pray for a safe voyage.

The next morning, they set sail, moving slowly out of the Rotterdam harbor, with the Salzburgers on the deck singing a hymn. While Pastor Boltzius offered a prayer, they could hear the sneers and swearing of the sailors, but, not understanding English, they were not offended.

They ran aground on a sand bar while still in the Maas River and floundered for several days, waiting for help. While the ship was stuck, Pastor Boltzius took the opportunity to begin his instruction to the Salzburgers. The Saalfelden women stood together as he taught them.

"We must use this time to penetrate the heart of God more closely, preparing ourselves for the hardships we may encounter in our journey, for whatever happens is God's will. This life on earth is a trial for the life to come in Heaven. We must stand our trial with complete trust in God."

Boltzius seemed to gain strength from his own words. He lowered his voice to a pitch that vibrated more deeply and prayed loudly in a rhythmic cadence that the people found startling but effective in calling up the feeling of God's presence with them. "Heavenly Father, we ask your mercy on these your faithful servants. Make the waters rise so that we can continue on your mission to spread the gospel of Jesus Christ into the New World. Help us to use all adversity to learn more about your will for us, we pray in the name of our Lord and Savior, Jesus Christ. Amen."

Mamma Anna overheard Ortmann, the new schoolmaster, say to his wife, "I don't know if I'm going to be able to stand these sanctimonious people and all these prayer meetings."

She had laughed in reply. "Well, we've signed on with them, so we have to go. You had no better prospects here, and maybe this adventure will prove to be profitable. At least you'll have your salary from the SPCK, and our passage will be paid, as well as a land grant with provisions for a year. We can put up with a few prayer meetings for that. It's certainly better than what we could expect here."

"You always were the practical one," the schoolmaster had replied. "We'll just go along with the religious stuff and not do anything that will upset von Reck and the pastors. After we get to Georgia, we can work out things to suit ourselves."

As the two pastors sat on the deck planning their religious instruction for the Salzburgers, Boltzius asked the younger man, "Well, Israel, what do you think of our flock?"

"They're very pious, sir, but lack training. However, many of them can read and write and have some knowledge of the Bible and other religious material."

"They have welcomed us most enthusiastically," Boltzius said.

"Oh, no doubt about it. They seem to be kind, sweet, obedient people, people who love God and are eager to learn."

"Commissioner von Reck says that Thomas Gschwandl is looked to as their natural leader, especially by the men from Gastein, and he is a good, devout man."

"Yes, and Johann Mosshamer and his family are well-informed also. While in residence with them in Rotterdam, I was impressed with their devoutness and the way the women care for everyone's needs in a godly way."

Boltzius nodded in agreement. "Remember how we used to question the boys in the orphanage about the Bible verses that were assigned to them? I think that might be a good way to handle the evening prayer meetings. That way we would have proof, explanation, and application that the people are learning how to locate the books and chapters of the Bible. They would also get practice in reading the Scripture, which they badly need," Boltzius said, becoming excited by his idea.

"Yes, and it would also help us to understand their dialect if we hear them reading a common text. It will have more meaning for them, too."

"Well then, let's organize it that way," Boltzius continued. "I'll talk to them about a selected Scripture and then ask questions of the children and adults to see if they understand the meaning. That way, any misinterpretations can be cleared up immediately. Otherwise, we will not be sure what they understand." He paused, continuing to think. "We can assign several verses for the people to look up and read between sessions. We then can question them about the verses at the next session."

"That's a splendid plan, sir," Gronau said.

"I think you and I will make an excellent team," Boltzius said, patting Gronau on the shoulder. "Why don't you select the Scriptures that are to be assigned. I shall be discoursing on the sixth chapter of John, where Jesus performs many miracles, such as the feeding of the five thousand people."

Both men became absorbed in their tasks and failed to notice that the waters were beginning to rise, lifting the ship from its sandy mooring before help from Rotterdam had reached them.

They looked up, startled, when they heard one of the sailors yelling, "Heave ho!" The raised sails caught the wind, jerking the ship through the water. A great shout went up from the passengers on the deck. The Salzburgers began singing a hymn of praise, while the sailors looked at them and laughed. Everyone's spirits were lifted at being on their way again.

Catherine remembered well when the *Purysburg* reached the North Sea on November the nineteenth, for she became violently ill from the rolling sea. As she lay in her bunk in misery, heaving into a pail, she failed to notice that almost everyone else was sick, too.

Later, she stood stoically at the side of the ship, holding

tightly to a railing, unable to stand the stench of vomit below. Her knuckles were white with the strain of her grip, and her face matched that whiteness. As she fixed her gaze on the black water rising in swells, she was terrified at the rolling sea and the tossing of the ship, which seemed so small and insubstantial. All she could think about were the poor Salzburgers who had been shipwrecked in the North Sea on their way to Prussia. Hundreds had been lost. She was horrified at the thought of a watery death.

Catherine had vowed not to complain, and she worried that she would be considered weak or without sufficient faith if she expressed her paralyzing fear, so she said not a word to anyone.

Three days later, standing on the deck with Gertrude, watching the white cliffs materialize through the blowing rain, she finally admitted, "If I ever get back on land, I don't think I'll be able to get on a ship again." Barbara overheard Catherine and said sternly, "We agreed not to complain, Catherine. You'd have to stay in England the rest of your life if you never got on a ship again. Don't be absurd."

Catherine closed her lips in a firm line, determined not to say anything else. She had not shared her fear while the ship tossed on the open sea, but the experience had badly frightened her. She did not see how she could bear to be on the ocean for the months that it would take to reach Georgia. She had never imagined it would be so difficult.

As the Salzburgers watched from the ship, Captain Thomas Coram, one of the Georgia Trustees, spoke to Baron von Reck, Pastor Boltzius, and Pastor Gronau. "Welcome, gentlemen. The Georgia Trustees are delighted that you are conducting this transport to Georgia. I have with me King George's court chaplains, Mr. Butienter and Mr. Ziegenhagen." The chaplains greeted them in German, which was the language of King George. This was a great relief to von Reck and the pastors, whose English was still poor. "We have made special arrangements for the comfort of the Salzburgers, beginning with a meal, where they will meet many important Englishmen who have been supporting this transport. You will also meet other colonists from England who will be traveling with you on the *Purysburg*. These people have been carefully selected from the poor of London, all persons of practical skill and good character, willing to work hard to build a new life in Georgia."

Baron von Reck then led the Salzburgers, two by two, through the streets of Dover to the house where a meal had been prepared for them. They created quite a sensation as they paraded through the town. Boltzius and Gronau, who followed at the end of the procession, were thrilled at the dramatic impression the Salzburgers were making on the local English people, comparing it to their own powerful response two years ago, witnessing earlier Salzburgers marching through Halle on their way to Prussia. Boltzius had been so moved by the sight that, after leading a group on to Königsberg, he had answered the call to be pastor of this group of Salzburgers going to the wilderness of Georgia. Both men felt very humble to be a part of the procession this time.

Before eating the food set for them, the Salzburgers sang several hymns of praise and thanksgiving. This display of religious fervor greatly pleased the high-ranking personages who were attending the meal, even though most of them did not recognize the German words to the songs.

Chaplain Butienter pointed out to Boltzius another table of people who were watching the Salzburgers curiously. "Those people are English emigrants to Georgia and will be joining you on the *Purysburg*. The Trustees have carefully selected them to settle with Oglethorpe in Savannah. As you may know, the Georgia experiment was organized to help the poor people of London. Mr. Oglethorpe, a Member of Parliament, became interested in the poor when a friend of his was thrown into debtors' prison. He was appalled at the treatment his friend received. He has worked diligently, along with the churches and the missionary societies, to rescue deserving people before their fate is sealed.

"This group has been handpicked by the Georgia Trustees as hardworking, devout people who will make good citizens if given a chance. They also represent crafts that are needed in the colonies, such as carpenters and coopers."

The English colonists, who were not as well-behaved as the Salzburgers during the meal, were quite surprised as they observed this strange group from Europe, singing and praying before and after the meal. In response to questions about the group, Captain Coram told them briefly the story of the religious persecution of the Salzburgers and their trek across Europe. They shook their heads in astonishment.

Catherine felt better after she had eaten a well-prepared meal, changed out of her wet woolen clothes, and rested on a real bed. Still, she began planning a way not to have to return to the ship for the rest of the journey. She knew she could never discuss her fears with her mother, who she knew would not understand and would chastise her for her lack of trust in God.

Their welcome in Dover had been impressive. The court chaplain had given everyone over eighteen years of age, including herself, one pound sterling. She held the coin up to the light, but could not make out any of the symbols. She had no idea how much a pound sterling was worth. In her mind, she counted her other money, sewn into her clothing for safekeeping.

Catherine had secretly enjoyed parading through the Protestant towns since leaving Salzburg, hearing the praise that important people poured on them, although, like the others, she had behaved very modestly. She was grateful for all that had been done for them and did not want to leave the group she truly loved, but she did not see how she could control her fear of the sea.

I am so tired of traveling, she thought, as tears rolled down her face. I'm tired of being dirty, cold, hungry, and crowded up with so many people. This is the first time I've been alone in weeks. She rubbed her hands luxuriously over the feather mattress and smooth linen sheets she was lying on. It seems we've been traveling forever, and there's still so far to go, further even than we've come.

Gertrude and Barbara came bursting in, faces aglow. Gertrude greeted her with excitement. "Catherine, can you believe how well we're being treated here?" She extended her arm to include the attractive room in which they were lodged. It was only a tiny garret room with one bed, but only the three of them had been assigned to it. It had wallpaper with pictures of pink violets, and a ceramic washbowl and pitcher. There were even curtains at the windows.

"I confess I was never really sure about the English, but they are taking such good care of us. We are being supported by the contributions from so many good people of England. Imagine that! God has truly blessed us." Barbara looked over at Catherine and realized that she had been crying.

"Why, what on earth is the matter?" she asked, taking Catherine's hand. "Are you sick?"

"No, Mother, I'm fine."

"Then why have you been crying?"

"I don't really know. It's nothing. Don't let me spoil your happiness."

"Well, if you aren't sick, you'd better get ready for prayer meeting. Mr. Butienter is preaching. We mustn't be late. It's a public meeting, and Pastor Boltzius expects a number of Englishmen to be present."

"Yes, Mother," Catherine said obediently. She got up, put her damp skirt back on, and washed her face in the washbowl, enjoying the smell of the scented soap.

Boltzius and his assistant, Gronau, were kept busy for the next days while they waited for the *Purysburg* to sail. They not only had to prepare for the morning and evening prayer meetings, which many Englishmen attended, but there were numerous people to see and arrangements to make.

Captain Coram showed them, along with Baron von Reck, the abundant stacks of necessary victuals that were being loaded on the ship for the Salzburgers' first year. He told them that the Trustees hoped they would arrive in time to clear enough land of trees the first summer to plant a crop to supply them with food for the next year.

When they returned to their rooms, Mr. Butienter was waiting for them. "Now, gentlemen," he said to the two pastors, "I have something else for you." He presented Boltzius and Gronau with the vestments of their office, an altar cloth, and a chalice.

"Oh, my dear sir, you are too generous," Boltzius said, truly overcome with the gift.

"We're most grateful," Gronau said, trying on the vestments.

"Now, let me show you how these might best be used in your services to conform to the Royal German Court Chapel in London. As German clerics in an Anglican country, we have adapted to the Church of England without, I believe, sacrificing anything of importance from the Lutheran tradition. Since you will be in an English country, you will not want to alienate your countrymen." Boltzius and Gronau listened carefully to the instruction that was offered them.

On December twenty-fifth, at morning prayers, Boltzius explained to the Salzburgers that it was not yet Christmas in England, since England used the Julian calendar instead of the Gregorian calendar of Europe. He said they would celebrate Christmas with the English, now that they were to become citizens of England.

"Imagine the days being set down differently," Johann said in amazement to Maria. "Isn't that remarkable?"

All day, the people seemed quieter, their thoughts drifting back to the celebrations of Christmas in their Alpine homes.

Catherine wandered alone out to the seaside, hoping that praying beside the water might help her conquer her fear. She sat down on the top of a white cliff, high above the slapping waves. She had told no one, not even the inquisitive Gertrude, what was troubling her. She was too ashamed.

She sat with her knees pulled up, forming a shelf for her folded arms and resting head. She cried softly, trying to pray for courage to face death. She was appalled at her weakness. Gertrude had actually almost drowned in the Salzach River; yet she wasn't afraid. She remembered how awful it had been, watching Gertrude disappear beneath the water.

"Aren't you cold out here in the wind?" a voice asked her. Catherine lifted her tear-wet face and saw Pastor Gronau standing beside her.

Seeing her tears, he hesitated, and then asked, "Are you sad remembering Christmas at your former home?" Without waiting for an answer, he continued, "I've been remembering many happy times and missing my family, whom I may never see again."

As she stood up, the wind caught her red skirt, filling it like a sail. She hurriedly brushed at her face to remove the tears and said haltingly, "Oh, I had forgotten it was Christmas at home."

"Then what is distressing you so, Miss Kroehr?" he said, in what he hoped was a pastoral manner. "Is it a spiritual problem?" he continued, feeling that was a safer topic for him to be discussing with a young woman than another kind of personal problem.

"Yes, I guess it is. I lack sufficient faith, sir," Catherine mumbled, tucking her head.

"But I don't understand. You and your family seem so strong in the faith. You've sacrificed so much for God."

"Yes, the others have enough faith not to be afraid of the sea," she said, gazing out over the cliff at the water of the English Channel, "but my faith is so weak, I'm afraid to get back on the ship."

She turned to him abruptly and said with desperation, "Can't I stay here in England, sir? The people have shown such kindness to us. Surely someone would help me if I stayed."

Israel Gronau was so startled at her outburst that he took her hands in his and looked into her eyes. "God will protect you, Catherine. Everyone has some fear of facing danger, but you will not die until it is God's will for you; and if it is

God's will, there's nothing you can do to avoid it."

He said this with such calmness and assurance that she found herself almost believing it. "Are you familiar with Gerhardt's hymn, *Give to the Wind Thy Fears*?"

"No, sir."

Gronau began softly singing the hymn to her, but continuing to hold her hands in his:

Give to the wind thy fears;
Hope and be undismayed.
God hears thy sighs and counts thy tears,
God shall lift up thy head.

Through waves and clouds and storms
God gently clears thy way,
Wait thou God's time; so shall this night
Soon end in joyous day.

Leave to God's sovereign sway
To choose and to command;
So shalt thou, wondering, own that way,
How wise, how strong this hand.

Let us in life, in death,
Thy steadfast truth declare,
And publish with our latest breath
Thy love and guardian care.

New tears began to stream down her face.

"Perhaps we should go back and discuss your fear with Pastor Boltzius," Gronau said, with a voice that had suddenly lost its resonance.

"Oh, no, please, sir, I wouldn't want anyone else to know of my weakness. Please don't tell anyone. You are the only one who knows," she pleaded with her voice and eyes. "Besides, I'm feeling much better now."

"Excellent, Miss Kroehr, but you cannot stay in England.

Then everyone would know."

Catherine felt calmer after having finally shared her secret fear, and she experienced a renewal of strength. She smiled at him for the first time and said, "God has answered my prayer for courage through you. You are a true man of God."

Together they bowed their heads in a prayer of thanksgiving for God's tender mercy toward her, then walked slowly back to their lodging. Israel, shaken by the unusual emotions that he had experienced during their encounter, felt relief and gratitude that he had, nevertheless, successfully ministered to her.

On December twenty-first, according to England's calendar, the citizenship ceremony was held. The Salzburgers gathered, along with Captain Coram, deputy for the Trustees, Captain Tobias Fry, Captain of the *Purysburg*, and William Sale, an English merchant. Baron von Reck stood before them, looking very noble and important in his finest clothes.

"Ladies and Gentlemen, you should be very grateful for the benevolence of your English sponsors, the Trustees of the Colony of Georgia and the Society for Promoting Christian Knowledge. I urge you to be obedient to your new country, which has offered you asylum."

Captain Coram stepped forward and through a translator said, "Will you raise your right hand and promise to be subject to the English government, your present authority, and, as subjects, to show obedience in your enjoyment of the rights and freedoms of the land. If you so agree, raise your hand and say, 'Yes.'"

With a loud response, the people said, "Ja!"

Thomas looked over at Tobias, Johann, and the others, remembering the salt oath they had sworn in Schwarzach over two years ago. What a long way that oath had brought them. He wondered what this oath to England would bring. As he reflected on that earlier oath-taking, he hardly heard the words that were being read about the freedoms and privileges they were to enjoy and the duties that would be expected in their new land.

All their names were written on the bottom of the proclamation, and each was required to touch the paper and pledge to honor it. Thomas reverently touched the paper and responded, "Ja," and made way for the next person. As he shook hands with Coram, his heart was full. He intended to abide by this oath, just like the Salzbund, forever.

Immediately after the morning service on the English Christmas Day, Pastor Boltzius performed the marriage of Simon Reiter and Maria. Everyone joined in the happiness of the simple wedding. The couple had invited Georg Schweiger and Anna Hofer to stand up with them, causing the congregation to wonder if Georg and Anna might be the next couple to wed.

On the twenty-seventh, Boltzius and Gronau had an opportunity to meet Mr. Pury, founder of Purysburg, the closest town to Savannah, just across the river in Carolina. Pury assured them that James Oglethorpe was a kind and honest man who would treat the Salzburgers well. Baron von Reck joined them, and the four men spent a pleasant afternoon listening to Pury describe the richness of the soil, the endless game and fish available, and the warm climate of Georgia. He was the first person they had encountered who had actually been to Georgia. He assured them that the land was a paradise filled with all they would need to sustain life.

"What about the savages who live in the forest?" von Reck asked.

"The Indians in that area are friendly and welcome the settlers. There's no reason for alarm. Their chief, Tomochichi, has become a great friend of Oglethorpe."

"Are any of the Indians Christians?" Boltzius asked.

"No, not that I know of, unless Mary Musgrove is. She's a half-breed married to a trader and speaks both the Indian language and English. You'll be the first Christian ministers to be in Georgia. But I must warn you that the Indian language is devilish to decipher."

"How much land do the Indians own?" von Reck wanted

to know.

"These people don't think in terms of owning the land. They don't stay in one place very long. They move around, chasing the game. Anyway, there's more land than we can ever fill up. It's all wilderness, you see."

46

On Board the *Purysburg*, January 1734

As he came into the lodging of the Salzburgers, von Reck called, "Get your things together; we're boarding the ship!" It was the seventh of January 1734, and they were finally to be on their way.

Barbara, Gertrude, and Catherine ran up the three flights of steps to their garret to gather their belongings. "Do you have our money?" Gertrude asked her mother. Barbara felt the secret pouch in her petticoat.

"Yes." Turning to Catherine, she asked, "And how about you?" Catherine had insisted on carrying her own money this time and had sewn a secret pocket to hold it. Barbara had been reluctant for her to do that, but she was eighteen years old. It was hard for Barbara to realize that her little girl had grown up.

It did not take long for them to bundle up their belongings. The chest had been repacked days ago and was already on board the ship. Barbara took special care of her Bible and the pamphlets recently given to her by the pastors. They had recognized her strong interest in learning more about the writings of the German pietists. They also noticed that she taught her children and others what she learned from her reading.

"Are you ready?" Maria called up the steps.

"Ja, we're coming," Barbara answered.

The Salzburgers retraced their steps and processed, two by two, back to the ship that would take them from Dover to Savannah.

Captain Fry was more courteous this time, having been chastised by Captain Coram for his harsh treatment on the trip to Dover. The pastors were given better quarters and invited to eat at the Captain's table. Baron von Reck again assigned the Salzburgers to their quarters below deck, giving them priority over the English settlers who were also making the voyage. But the distinctions made little difference, since all of the compartments were wretched.

He organized them into groups and designated one person as leader. This person was responsible for the candle and for making sure it was extinguished at night or when the seas were rough. This was an important job, because a fire would be disastrous for all. The times that the candle could be lit were strictly regulated, and orders must be followed.

Johann was selected to lead a group. This privilege made it possible for him and Maria to have their own compartment.

Barbara and the girls were next door with Mamma Anna. They would live in stinking darkness for the two-month crossing, with rats scurrying around on the floor, sometimes venturing into the beds. They put away their belongings hurriedly and returned to the deck.

"Why aren't we leaving?" Barbara asked Thomas.

"The wind. It's blowing in the wrong direction. We have to wait for it to turn east before it is strong enough to move the ship through the Channel, according to that sailor over there who speaks German."

The next day, everything was frozen. The Salzburgers stood on the deck in the freezing wind that blew from the north, watching the ship slowly ease out of the harbor of Dover and into the Channel. Immediately, the rocking of the ship caused the people to become sick. Catherine hung her head over the side in despair. She was so embarrassed to be sick in front of the others, but, when she raised her head, she saw that almost everyone was in the same predicament, even the pastors.

Their progress depended on the winds which, they believed, blew at the whim of God. The next day, they were blessed with a southeasterly wind that helped them sail smoothly through the three-hundred-mile channel in two days. Philip von Reck sat with his drawing book and sketched the needles at the Isle of Wight as they sailed past. Later, he drew Land's End, their last sight of England before entering the Atlantic Ocean. He had a great interest in the flora and fauna of the New World and had brought along paints in order to record his findings with drawings.

Boltzius sat nearby, writing in the journal that he had kept meticulously since leaving Halle. He wanted to preserve more than the details of their lives; he wanted to record their spiritual journey as well. He felt a strong responsibility to assure both Pastor Urlsperger and the faculty at Halle Seminary of the spiritual progress and religious training of the Salzburgers. That had been the mission they had entrusted to him, and he took it very seriously. The spiritual welfare of these people was in his hands. He must be diligent in their instruction in the way that would lead them to eternal life.

He stopped in his writing to ask for God's guidance in this important mission. The souls of his people rested heavily on his heart, for they would face many dangers on the crossing. As he watched the black water of the vast ocean, he thought of all the tales of shipwrecks that he had heard. He was beginning to know his flock well enough now to be especially concerned about the souls of particular individuals.

His daily routine was becoming comfortable. He led the morning prayer meeting, with Gronau's assistance, in the little room that Captain Fry had given them. It was small and uncomfortable, but the Salzburgers did not complain. After breakfast, he and Gronau walked the deck for exercise and fresh air. Then he visited the sick before settling down for serious study and journal writing. After the noon meal, he rested, then met with the children to hear their catechism. Time was also reserved to talk with the Salzburgers about their concerns. The evening prayer meeting followed supper. It was a busy day, but that suited him as long as he could establish a regular schedule. His compassionate heart, however, invited many interruptions, since he made himself available to anyone with spiritual concerns.

On the night of January eleventh, the wind increased so much that the stay, a large rope holding the main mast, broke. The ship was in temporary danger, but no other harm was done, and life on the ship soon fell back into the routine that had been established. By the twenty-fourth, they had picked up the trade winds, which pleased the sailors very much. They said that these winds would take them all the way to Carolina.

Maria Mosshamer, looking agitated, sought out Mamma Anna one cold January morning. She found her huddled out of the wind in a sunny corner. "Mamma Anna, I dreamed about Hans last night. I dreamed we were in Saalfelden, sitting on that hillside where he was arrested. Remember that place?"

Mamma Anna nodded.

"I was so happy, and it felt so real. All morning I've been trying to forget the dream, but it won't go away. What does it mean?" Before Mamma Anna could answer, she continued. "I'm a terrible person," she moaned, "married to Johann and still dreaming of Hans. How can I control my dreams? Do dreams come from God?"

"I'm no authority about what comes from God, but I have paid attention to dreams. Sometimes they give us messages, but the message is hard to understand. It's in clues. Sometimes, I think, dreams are just reminding us of what we've lost, so we don't forget. I used to dream of my dead husband and children, just like they were still alive. As the years have gone by, that doesn't happen as much."

"Do you think it's a message that he's still alive?" Maria asked, a quiver in her voice.

"I don't know, child. That's something we'll probably never know. It's not likely he'd ever find us where we're going. My advice is to put Hans behind you and concentrate on being a good wife to Johann." Mamma Anna patted her arm to soothe her.

"I thought I had done that until the dream. It just seemed like I had come home again, and everything was fine. Should I tell Johann about it?"

"What would be the point of that? I imagine he has his own dreams. After all, he lost a wife and left children behind. He must be saddened by that."

"Yes. He becomes quite melancholy when he thinks too long about his children. He refuses to talk about them. I think he feels guilty about leaving them with his sister."

"Or he misses them. Just because we've pushed off from the land doesn't mean we don't carry our past with us."

As the two women gazed at the endless water, Maria continued, "Something else is bothering me, Mamma Anna."

` "What's that, Maria?"

"What do you think of Mr. Zwiffler's medicine?"

"I haven't seen much of it yet."

"I was wondering about asking if I could learn from him. What do you think?"

"I think you should learn all you can about healing. There is always more to know," Mamma Anna said carefully.

"Aren't you curious to find out what he knows?"

"Maria, I figure, with him along on this trip, I'll just be a midwife and let him handle the other illnesses. He seems like the kind of man who wouldn't appreciate what I know. I've seen him looking at me in a strange way. Since that fool in Augsburg called me a witch in front of everyone, I think I'd better stay out of his way. I don't want any trouble."

After a thoughtful pause, she continued. "I'm more concerned about the people getting enough food. If they don't start feeding us more than one sorry meal a day, we'll all die of starvation. I think the bloody flux everyone is suffering is probably caused by the bad food, but there's nothing we can do about that. Even Pastor Boltzius hasn't been able to get Captain Fry to give us the food that was sent for us. I'm especially worried about Lorentz Huber and Tobias Lackner. They're getting weaker and weaker every day. Zwiffler bled them, but they seemed worse afterwards, not better."

"How is Frau Rott? She seems about ready to have her baby."

"Ja. Let's hope she waits until we get to Savannah." Mamma Anna reached into her apron pocket, pulled out a handful of raisins, and offered some to Maria. "At least she pays me well with raisins. On this ship, food is more valuable than money. You can't eat money. Take some for Johann, too. He's not looking well, either."

In another part of the ship, Barbara sat with little Magdalena Huber in her lap, her older brothers and sisters sitting nearby, and began telling a Bible story to entertain them. Their father was sick with the bloody flux, and their mother was busy nursing him. Every day the children looked paler and more listless. Barbara wanted to weep at their sad faces, but instead she smiled and told them the story of Joseph and the coat of many colors. Soon, other young children were gathered around, listening raptly. As Barbara acted out parts of the story so the children could understand, Boltzius and Gronau watched with amusement.

"It's good to use this time to teach the children. We should ask the schoolmaster, Mr. Ortmann, to begin classes with them. I'll do that right now. There he is over by that lifeboat." Boltzius walked over with a smile on his face, sure that his request would be well received.

"Mr. Ortmann, see how attentive the children are to Frau Rohrmoser telling a Bible story. It occurred to me that this would be a good time to begin giving them lessons, while we have so much time on our hands."

"Begin classes on the ship?" Ortmann asked, with surprise in his voice.

"Yes," Boltzius continued, "don't you think that's a good idea?"

"Well, frankly, sir," Ortmann stammered, stalling for some way out of having to work during the voyage. His mind raced through some possible answers. He could say that he was not expected to start until a proper school was built, but he knew that would fail to satisfy Boltzius, who had become something of a zealot where the welfare of these Salzburgers was concerned. Suddenly he thought of his excuse.

"But, sir, all of the school books are packed away. With what would I teach them? Perhaps it will be better, since we are just beginning with them, for you to continue teaching them the catechism and the Bible. That's more important for their souls, which may be in imminent danger." Ortmann was pleased with his response but kept a soulful look on his face.

"Yes, I see your point. I will continue with the catechism classes, and perhaps we can make Frau Rohrmoser's Bible stories a regular thing."

After the children had dispersed, Boltzius approached Barbara. "Frau Rohrmoser, you told the story very well. The children seemed to understand it quickly."

Barbara was immediately embarrassed. "Oh, Pastor Boltzius, I didn't realize you were listening. Did I make any mistakes in telling the story? I wouldn't want to teach them wrong."

"I heard no errors. Perhaps you could tell Bible stories to the children every day," he said.

"Every day? Oh, sir, I'm not sure I know that many. It would take a lot of preparation," Barbara answered, very pleased at being asked. "Perhaps you or Pastor Gronau or the schoolmaster would be a better choice."

"The children might find it hard to understand us, but you speak the language as they do. I'll help you in selecting stories and explain the lesson to be learned from each one. Then you can read and prepare to tell them to the children."

"With your help, I'll be honored to try. Gertrude and Catherine, my daughters, are good storytellers, too. Perhaps they could share this responsibility, and you could teach all of us."

"They can come to the preparation sessions, and then I'll decide when they are ready to teach the children."

"Thank you, Pastor Boltzius. They'll benefit so much from your teaching. Thank you."

"Yes, well then, why don't we meet immediately following the midday meal," he said, before realizing that only those who ate at the Captain's table had a midday meal. Embarrassed that he ate better than the others did, he stammered on, "That way I can share my food with you and your daughters."

Barbara, ashamed at being in need of food, simply looked down at the floor. She did not turn down the offer, however, knowing her girls needed both the instruction and the food.

* * *

Israel Gronau stood at the rail, watching the sunset. The colors reflecting on the water were every shade of pink and orange, all shimmering together. He had never seen such sunsets and had made it a practice to watch them each evening. If God could create such beauty, how much more beautiful God must be, he thought.

Von Reck joined him. He often sought out Pastor Gronau, since they were the same age and were both educated Germans, although the similarities ended there. Gronau was no nobleman, and Philip was far from a minister.

"It's quite lovely. I wish I could capture such colors with my paints," von Reck said.

"I was just thinking that, if God can create such beauty, how much more beautiful God must be," Gronau responded.

"Ah, yes, a lovely thought. It is fortunate for my soul that I am traveling with you two pastors and the Salzburgers. I've never prayed so regularly before, and I can see a change coming over my life."

As they stood watching the sea, von Reck remembered how he had felt following the great storm that had almost destroyed them earlier in the voyage.

* * *

At the prayer service held after the great storm, Pastor Boltzius praised God for their purifying trials. He was pleased, he said, that the pious Salzburgers had prayed, sung hymns, and quoted Scripture for comfort, while other passengers screamed and wailed in fear.

He then read the story of Samuel to the people: "As Samuel erected a pillar which he called Ebenezer, so do we all need to erect in our hearts an eternal memorial of divine favors." During the discussion following the Scripture reading, Thomas Gschwandl had suggested that, since God had spared all of them during the terrible storm, they should erect a pillar in their new town and call it Ebenezer, just as Samuel had done. His suggestion was received with great enthusiasm, for God had protected them thus far.

The next day, as von Reck stood on the deck surveying the considerable damage to the ship caused by the storm, Israel Gronau came over and stood beside him.

"What is that in the water, Pastor Gronau?" von Reck asked.

"It looks like land. Maybe it's an island," Israel said. Several people saw something on the horizon that was unusual, but it did not look like a ship. There were no sails.

The sailors called to the Captain, who had a boat lowered and ordered several sailors to investigate. He knew there should not be an island and feared that they might have been blown off course by the storm.

When the sailors returned, they reported that it was a capsized ship, but they could find no signs of life. All the lifeboats were gone, however, which meant that people may have survived.

Everyone on the *Purysburg* felt the impact of this news, for they all knew it could well have been their ship that had capsized in the dreadful storm. Although they searched earnestly for possible lifeboats, none were found.

Von Reck later approached Pastor Boltzius, filled with emotion. "Pastor Boltzius, I'm sure that God protected us during the storm because of the Salzburgers and you two ministers. I feel so grateful that a merciful God has vouchsafed to send me with you. I can feel the presence of God in a way I never have before. Thank you for your guidance." He hugged the minister in gratitude.

"This life is just a trial for the life to come. I'm glad for the storm, for it caused you to place your trust in God," Boltzius responded, obviously moved by the Commissioner's confession.

* * *

As von Reck once again stood discussing his spiritual condition with one of the pastors, he reflected on that earlier exchange and his spiritual debt to the Salzburgers. Unaccustomed to discussing spiritual matters, though, he soon became bored with that line of conversation, turned his back to the railing, and surveyed the other people on deck.

"There are no women on this ship appropriate to my station in life," he said wistfully. "More's the pity. How do you control your bodily needs in the presence of so many unattached women, Israel? Are minister's needs different from those of other men?"

"I think we're made just like other men. We Protestant ministers do not deny the flesh, like the Catholic priests. Luther himself married."

"But who can you marry in Georgia? There will be no German girls from good families, only Salzburg peasants and poor English lasses."

"God will provide for all my needs. I trust in that. Remember the Scripture passage about the lilies of the field, that neither toil nor spin?"

"Yes, yes, I remember," von Reck said impatiently, tiring of pious talk, "but don't you feel restless when you see a woman like that one?" He nodded toward a group of women that included Gertrude, Catherine, Maria Mosshamer, and Maria Hierl.

"Which one?" Gronau asked somewhat apprehensively, not trusting the way von Reck was leering in their direction. He suddenly felt protective of the women.

"That dark-haired beauty who's laughing."

"You mean Maria Mosshamer?" he asked, feeling relieved. "Commissioner von Reck, you must be careful. She is a married woman."

"Don't be shocked, Pastor. I'm just looking."

"But God knows what's in your mind, also."

* * *

On March fourth, the Captain ordered a sounding at six in the morning and drew Carolina sand. The water took on a yellowish color, reflecting a shallower bottom. A scow was sighted bound from Charlestown to Pennsylvania, and when it passed, a crewman told the Captain that the ship was ten leagues from the shore.

"Look, there's land!" Gertrude yelled, and everyone took up the cry. It was March fifth, almost two months since they had last seen land. Peter Gruber began singing *Te Deum*, and soon the Salzburgers were sounding like a choir, singing praise to God for their safe passage. The coast slowly emerged, and large pine trees could be seen lining the shore. A contrary wind kept the ship from reaching Charlestown, though. On the sixth, they lost sight of land altogether, greatly disappointing everyone aboard. They did learn from a passing English ship that James Oglethorpe, the Trustee of Georgia in charge of managing the new colony, had arrived in Charlestown the night before on his way to England.

Von Reck, with youthful impatience, fretted to Boltzius and Gronau about the delay in making port. "It looks like there should be some way the sails could be turned to move the ship back toward Charlestown. I'm afraid that Mr. Oglethorpe will leave before we get there. Who can assign land for our community without him? Captain Coram said he's the only Trustee here."

"I'm sure he made all the arrangements before he left Savannah. God has brought us safely thus far; I trust that our welfare is in his hands. Do not forget whose mission we are on," admonished Boltzius.

A pilot arrived from Charlestown on the seventh at nine in the morning, and the Captain cast anchor. At ten Captain Fry, von Reck, Boltzius, and Gronau boarded the pilot's boat, arriving at Charlestown by one in the afternoon. Realizing that they would not be permitted to go ashore in Charlestown Catherine watched the small boat leave with tears of frustration running down her face. She balled her fist and hit the railing. "It's not fair," she said fiercely, but no one heard her.

47

Königsberg, Prussia, January 1734

Hans drove his peddler's cart into Königsberg, home to many of the exiled Salzburgers. He drove until he saw an Evangelical Church and stopped. Inside, he asked the pastor about his family and fiancée and was sent to examine the church records. He sat poring over the names of thousands of people who had passed through Königsberg on their way to settlement in Prussia. It took him several days to decide that their names were not listed. He had found the names of others from Saalfelden he knew, including a distant cousin, Martin Burgsteiner, who had stayed in Königsberg.

Hans visited Martin and his large family at home that evening. "Hans, what an honor to have you in our home. We thought you were dead. When Johann Mosshamer came back from prison without you, we assumed you were dead. How did you escape?" Martin asked.

"I was beaten unconscious and left suffering from infection in my leg. I woke up in a monastery, where the sisters nursed me back to health. They would never tell me how I got there. I think they were secretly trying to save the prisoners without the authorities knowing. Months later, when I was healed, they arranged for me to slip out at night. Without their care, I would have died."

"So the Catholics tried to kill you, and the Catholics saved you," Martin said, shaking his head. "It is a strange world."

"I'm here trying to locate my sister, Barbara Rohrmoser, and my betrothed, Maria Kroehr. Do you know where they went when they left Saalfelden?" Hans looked at Martin with such yearning in his eyes.

"Well, let me see. It was a very confusing time. Soldiers forced many people to leave in the fall of '31, but I believe they left when we did in the spring of '32. Seems like they were in the crowd at that last service we held on the hillside where you and Johann had been arrested. They marched us south around the mountain, then north towards Goldegg. There was such a crush of humanity on the road when the people from the Gastein Valley joined us, and the people from St. Johann and Wagrain, too. We all got separated, and the Saalfelden people did not stay together. I don't remember seeing them again. Did you check the list at the church?"

"Ja. I've spent three days searching that list. That's where I found your name."

"Many people are lost from each other," Martin added quietly, "and many died along the way. Did you check the list of those who were on the ship that sank in the North Sea?"

"Ja. I forced myself to read that long list. They were not on it. Surely all of them would not have died."

"They might have married and changed their names. It's been two years. All of Saalfelden thought you were dead. I thought I'd seen a ghost when you came in tonight."

"Well, I guess I have to know. I'll just keep on looking. They had to go somewhere."

"I see you're a peddler now."

"Ja. That way I can support myself as I travel around looking for my Maria," Hans answered. "Thank you for your information."

"I'm afraid it wasn't much help. It's always possible that someone's name was left off the official lists."

"Ja. I'll look around here awhile and then head back to Augsburg. I met a pastor who was taking a transport to the English colonies in America. I'll find them if it takes the rest of my life."

"You may not like what you find, Hans. Maybe it would be better to settle down here and make a new life for yourself, instead of trying to find the old one," Martin advised. But Hans just waved his hand in a salute and climbed up on his wagon.

48

Charlestown, March 1734

The three men stepped on the soil of Carolina and felt it solid beneath their feet. They were disoriented for a few minutes but gained confidence as they walked, observing the flat land with its wide streets and clapboard houses. For the first time, they saw men and women from Africa, with their dark skin and strange hair. These Africans seemed to be everywhere, doing the manual labor around this port city.

Von Reck left the ministers to explore Charlestown while he went to call on the Governor, Robert Johnson.

"Baron von Reck, Commissioner of the Salzburger transport," he announced stiffly to the man who greeted him at the Governor's offices.

"Ah, yes, Baron von Reck, the Governor will see you immediately. This way, please."

Von Reck was ushered into a simple but elegant room, where sunlight streamed through the large glass windows, lighting up the area but blotting out the features of the Governor, whose back was to the window.

"Baron von Reck, your Excellency," the clerk announced.

"Welcome, Baron," he said, and turned to his clerk. "Go notify Mr. James Oglethorpe that his settlers are here."

"Yes, your Excellency," he said, leaving the room.

"Did you have a safe crossing?" the Governor asked, after offering von Reck a chair.

"Yes, your Excellency, no lives were lost, and very few are sick."

"That's good news, indeed, and rare, I might add, that no lives were lost on such a long voyage."

Mr. Oglethorpe came rushing in, carrying rolls of maps under his arm, beaming his delight at seeing the Commissioner of the Salzburger transport. "Ah, you've made it! How many were lost? Did you have a good crossing?" He hurled his questions enthusiastically.

"All have arrived alive, sir, though a few are sick," von Reck repeated. "The crossing was rough at times, but we were not wrecked. God protected us even through the storms."

"I'm so delighted to hear that good news," Oglethorpe said. "And I'm delighted that you arrived before I left for England. That's why I'm in Charlestown at this time. I'm long overdue to report back to England on the progress of our settlement. Perhaps you can come to my rooms, and we can discuss the details of selecting land for the Salzburgers."

"Yes, of course, sir," von Reck said, and the two men bade the Governor farewell, after accepting an invitation to dine with him that evening.

Oglethorpe and von Reck left the Governor's office and strolled around Charlestown, while Oglethorpe made arrangements to send a steer, a barrel of wine, and a load of vegetables to the settlers waiting on the *Purysburg*. Von Reck was fascinated by this new city, with trees already blooming in March and fresh cabbages, turnips, radishes, and lettuce piled in the carts in the marketplace.

"I notice that Charlestown has no wall surrounding it. The threat of attack from the Indians or the Spaniards must not be serious."

"No, attack from Indians is not likely, and the Spanish are much further south. But an attack from the thirty thousand African slaves in Carolina is indeed a danger. These poor, miserable people were captured and chained in ships, brought here and sold into slavery, and are now forced to work long hours in the hot sun on the plantations for no wages. Only a few are allowed to earn money for their work on Sundays." Oglethorpe paused, shaking his head at the cruelty of the slave system. "There have been insurrections on the islands of St. Thomas and St. John."

"Are they Christians, sir?"

"No effort is being made to make Christians of them that I can see. They do not even marry, but are bred like beasts. I have decided that there will be no Africans imported to

Georgia. I have no stomach for such cruelty, and I wish to create a colony where we do not have to live in fear, one where each person is paid for the work they perform."

"I'm much relieved to hear that, sir. Your reputation for benevolence toward the poor of London is well known to us. Captain Coram of the Georgia Trustees told us of your wonderful experiment in selecting worthy, hardworking, poor people as settlers in Georgia. Indeed, we have traveled with some of these people, but unfortunately we could not converse with them very readily."

When they reached his rooms, Oglethorpe spread out a map on the table and offered von Reck the opportunity to select the land for the Salzburg settlement.

"The land available is north of the Ogeechee River here," he said, pointing at the map, "and south of the Savannah River. Perhaps this area would be good. There are large streams that flow into the Savannah River which would make travel to the area easier."

"Are there mountains or other obstacles to farming in the area?"

"No, all of the land is quite flat. I've been through this area following an Indian trail, and the forest is thick, indicating a fertile soil once it is cleared. I also noticed springs in this area," he said, pointing to a particular spot.

Von Reck selected an inland section of land on a large stream, twenty-one miles from Savannah and thirty miles from the sea, with clear brooks from cool springs.

That night, the party from the *Purysburg* dined with Governor Johnson and James Oglethorpe.

"And how do you like our little city, gentlemen?" Governor Johnson inquired of Boltzius and Gronau while they enjoyed a delicious oyster stew served as the first course.

"There are many surprises," Boltzius replied.

"Oh? And what might those be?"

"Well, the city has no walls, and the population seems predominantly African." Boltzius stopped to slurp more of the milky stew. "I'm also amazed at the warm climate and the early growing season."

"Very different from northern Europe, huh? You're from Halle, I believe?"

"Most recently, yes, your Excellency."

The black servants came in with the main course of wild turkey and venison, served with a variety of vegetables and rice. A gasp of delight came from the travelers when they surveyed the feast spread before them.

"Please tell us what we are eating," von Reck asked his host. "It is most delicious."

"This bird is a turkey and is one of the wild birds in the region. The meat is venison. Deer are very plentiful in Carolina, and in Georgia, too, I'm told. Meat is readily available for the hunting. Are you a hunter, sir?"

"I've had little opportunity in Europe. The game parks are the sole preserve of the princes, and only once was I honored by an invitation to a royal hunt."

"What a pity. Oglethorpe, you must assign someone to teach these settlers how to hunt the game in the forest. That way they will never go hungry."

"I've already made such provisions, sir. Indian hunters have been asked to assist the settlers when they arrive."

"Indian hunters? Is that safe?" Boltzius asked.

"Oh, they are quite friendly and will be eager to help you any way they can. You will have to become familiar with their ways, of course, for they do not understand the idea of private property and may carry away something that interests them. They do not think of that as stealing, as we do."

"We have a great deal to learn about our new land and its people," Boltzius said. "I hope there will be an opportunity to make Christians of the Indians. Do you speak their language, sir?" Boltzius asked Oglethorpe.

"Only a little. I use an interpreter for serious negotiations. Mary Musgrove is an Indian woman married to an Englishman, and she speaks both languages. I depend on her."

A very rich pie covered with nuts called pecans was served as the dessert. Gronau, who had eaten heartily at every course, had difficulty eating the piece served to him, but it was so tasty that he could not resist eating all of it.

"You seem to enjoy our Carolina food, Pastor Gronau," Governor Johnson said congenially.

"Yes, your Excellency, it is quite grand," Gronau replied.

"Good. Well, gentlemen, here's to your successful settlement in Georgia," Johnson said, raising his wineglass to von Reck and the pastors. "And here's to your safe voyage to England, Mr. Oglethorpe."

"And to your good health, sir," Oglethorpe said in return.

On March ninth, von Reck, Boltzius, Gronau, and Captain Fry returned to the *Purysburg*, and the sails were set to proceed southward toward Georgia. The Salzburgers and the English settlers lined the deck when the coast of Georgia was sighted the next day. They cast anchor at the mouth of the Savannah River and waited for high tide. At about eight in the evening, the ship entered the river.

The people from Saalfelden stood on deck that night with the other Salzburgers, too excited to sleep, trying to decipher the shoreline. The light of the moon was dispersed in a cloudy sky, casting a pale, silvery light. Stars were visible intermittently in the overcast sky. Fatigue eventually overtook each family, and they felt their way in the darkness to their bunks below.

"I wonder where we'll sleep tomorrow night," Gertrude whispered to Catherine.

"Probably right here," Catherine replied bitterly. "They'll probably make us stay on this ship even after we get to Savannah." She was still fretting over not being allowed to go ashore in Charlestown.

They rested a few hours, but by sunrise most of the passengers were back on deck. Slowly the ship moved up the river against the tidal current.

Barbara, Gertrude, and Catherine again stood at the railing, watching the brownish-red water edged by softly waving grasses. Beyond the marshy grass, they saw trees as tall and as old as creation. The songs of thousands of birds filled the morning air.

"I've never heard such birds," Gertrude exclaimed. "This really is a paradise." A flock of white egrets rose from the marsh and soared gracefully down the winding river.

Looking into the water, they could see numerous fish swimming. "Oh, look at all the fish!" Gertrude exclaimed, clapping her hands together in excitement at all the wonders that surrounded them. In her haste to see this new world, she had not secured her yellow hair, and it flowed down her back, catching the glow from the morning sun. Her childlike excitement caused several of the single men to watch her as much as the scenery.

Pastor Boltzius, noticing where the attention of the men was focused, moved over near Gertrude, edging out Tobias Lackner, who was similarly attracted to this young girl.

"Oh, Pastor Boltzius, hasn't God made a beautiful world? What kind of fish are these?" she asked, without waiting for an answer.

"I'm told those are sturgeon, and the river is filled with oysters, too," he said, in a voice he used to teach the children.

As they rounded a bend, the forest grew nearer the edge of the water, and they were able to see great trees with large limbs in convoluted designs that rose and then dipped back down to the water. Gray mosses hung from the branches like grandmothers' hair.

Barbara gasped, and her hand flew to her mouth. She called out, "The trees! See the trees!" The others paid little attention to her outburst, assuming that she was just excited by the unusual trees. Barbara's face was drained of all color, as if she had seen a ghost. "Those trees with the gray hair, I saw them in a dream two years ago!"

The people within hearing distance, including the two pastors, looked at her with curiosity.

Maria, standing nearby, said, "Do you mean the dream you had that night at Mamma Anna's house?"

"Yes. I remember dreaming about the grandmother trees.

God spoke to me in a dream, just as he spoke to Joseph. Oh, Pastor Boltzius, I have been truly blessed. It is God's will that has brought my girls and me to this land," Barbara exclaimed.

"This is but another manifestation of our gracious God, who bestows good on those who trust in Him."

"It's like I've been here before, although I've never seen such trees except in my dream. God must have planned all along for us to come here." Barbara was trembling, but continued to stare at the trees until the forest receded behind more grassland.

Maria spotted Mamma Anna talking to that ugly sailor she had befriended, and hurried over to tell her about Barbara's dream coming true.

"You'll sail away again on the *Purysburg*, I suppose," Mamma Anna was saying to Deutsch.

"Ja. We'll be in port awhile to take on timber and provisions for the crossing, but I'm not likely to spend much time in Savannah. It depends on what ships come in. May not be any others coming to this backwater. Where will you be going once we land?"

"Thomas said that Oglethorpe and von Reck chose land for us further on up this river and then up another stream. It looks like that's where I'll be. I don't have anywhere else to go, although I don't know how welcome I'll be there."

"You could stay in Savannah. They probably need a midwife, with all these English women coming over."

"I don't speak English, and Barbara and the girls are my only family. They'll need me when they marry and have babies. I'll stick with them."

"Then we'll probably not see each other again unless...."

"Mamma Anna, did you see those trees with the long gray hair?" Maria asked breathlessly, ignoring Deutsch. "Barbara says they're like in that dream she had at your house in Saalfelden. She says God spoke to her in a dream, just like he spoke to Joseph."

"Humph," Mamma Anna snorted. She waved Deutsch

away. After he was out of hearing distance, she said in an irritated voice, "If you remember, Maria, it was after I spoke with the old Grandmother that she had that dream."

"You mean the dream came from the old Grandmother?" Maria asked, shocked.

"And she sent you something that night, too, if I'm not mistaken." Mamma Anna said, looking sternly into Maria's eyes. Maria blushed, remembering that her late blood had flowed that night.

"Mamma Anna, don't talk like that. These people would never understand," Maria said, looking around to see who might be listening. Fortunately, only English settlers were nearby, and they did not understand German.

"Perhaps they wouldn't, but you must understand. You're going to need to be able to summon help from many sources in order to survive in that wilderness out there," she said, waving her arm to encompass the panorama of the marsh and forest. "You mustn't forget from whence cometh your help."

"Me?" Maria asked, shocked again. "What about you? You'll be with us, too."

"Not forever, Maria. I'm an old woman, weakened by this long voyage. You'll be the one."

"Oh, Mamma Anna, don't say such things. I'd be terrified to think the women would have no one but me to get them through childbirth."

"You'll learn as you go along. That's what I did. But they'll look to you for more than just midwifing, Maria. You'll also be consulted on the mysteries of life."

"You mean people will come to me the way we've always gone to you?" Maria asked, incredulous. "But I don't know anything about the mysteries of life."

"You'll learn. You just have to think about things in your own way, staying as close to what you know is true as you possibly can." Mamma Anna paused and gazed at the forest, which hugged the river again. "When your mind starts cluttering up, and you can't think straight, go off by yourself, and let your soul blossom like a flower."

"Mamma Anna, you're scaring me."

"Don't be afraid, Maria, She'll be with you."

"Who? Do you mean the Virgin Mary or the old Grandmother?" Maria turned her fear and anger on Mamma Anna. "I refuse to be a part of your old religion. We've sacrificed everything to be free to worship God in this new land. That's the God I serve and go to for help."

"Don't be disturbed, my child," Mamma Anna said, laying a comforting hand on Maria's arm. "They're all the same spirit."

"But Pastor Boltzius says that the only way to know God is through Jesus. And the Bible says 'Thou shalt have no other Gods before me.' Are you saying that the Bible and Pastor Boltzius are wrong?"

"I'm not saying anyone is wrong. I'm just saying you should think about things in your own way and stick to what you know is true."

The two women stood together in silence while the ship slowly made its way against the current. A snake meandered toward the shore with slow dignity. Mamma Anna smiled at the snake, remembering that her grandmother had once told her that a swimming snake was a sign of good luck. In her mind, she thanked the Grandmothers for this sign that she had done the right thing to pass on her wisdom to Maria. She knew she had frightened her, but she also knew she would never forget their conversation.

Maria finally turned to Mamma Anna and asked quietly, "Why me, Mamma Anna?"

"Ah, I've asked myself that question many times."

While the two women were talking, Catherine was becoming flustered. When Baron von Reck and Pastor Gronau came over to join Pastor Boltzius, she blushed when Israel Gronau greeted her with a nod of his head.

"The Savannah is aptly named," von Reck commented. "The grasses look like pictures of the savannah of Africa."

"It's a wider river than the Rhine," Boltzius remarked. "It's supposed to be sixteen to twenty-five feet deep. That should be deep enough for our ship."

"The depth changes with the rising and falling of the tides," Gronau added. Then looking into the water, he said, "There are so many fish I believe I could catch one with my bare hands."

A loud scratching sound convulsed the *Purysburg*, followed by the cursing of the sailors. The ship jerked to a halt when it struck a sandbar.

"Confound it!" von Reck shouted over the noise. "We're so close to the town of Savannah and now we're stuck. What rotten luck." He stormed off to see the Captain to find out how they could get off the sandbar.

A German carpenter who had come aboard in Charlestown volunteered to take a small boat to Savannah for help. "I can be there in two hours. You need someone who knows the river and where the sandbars are located," he told the Captain.

"Ask for a pilot to navigate this river, then. In the meantime, we'll lighten the ship and wait for the tide to raise the water." Turning to his crew, he said, "Pour all the drinking water overboard. We don't need it anymore." The sailors immediately began dumping out barrels of water.

Von Reck paced the deck impatiently. He indicated some irritation that the Salzburgers remained so calm during the delay, when they were so close to Savannah.

Thomas Gschwandl sat reading Scripture, while Margaretta played nearby with their daughter. "How can you be so content when we have to wait like this, stuck on this stupid sandbar?" von Reck asked him in a tight voice.

"Sir," Thomas answered slowly, "we are in no danger. The ship appears undamaged. We have come such a long way, led safely by God, that this impediment must be his will. I do not question his will; I only try to obey it."

Von Reck was somewhat taken aback by this thoughtful response from Thomas. He turned and did his pacing on another part of the deck.

"I hope he didn't take offense at your words," Margaretta

said, watching von Reck's red face.

"He addressed me. I only answered his question as truthfully as possible," replied Thomas. "Besides, that young man has a lot of growing up to do. I'm a little tired of his tantrums." Tobias, sitting nearby, smiled and nodded his head in agreement.

"Thomas, you must be careful what you say," Margaretta said reproachfully.

The two men laughed at her impudence in telling Thomas how to behave. Her face reddened, and she picked up the baby and walked away to join a group of women.

The pilot from Savannah arrived as the tide rose higher than usual. By eleven in the evening, the ship was dislodged from the sandbar. The captain anchored it in a deeper part of the water for the night. The following morning, they proceeded up the river, arriving in Savannah before twelve noon.

Part II

Ebenezer

49

Savannah, March 1734

"Boom! Boom! Boom!" sounded the guns from the *Purysburg* when the town of Savannah became visible. A great cheer went up on the left side of the river, and the passengers on the ship saw what must have been every inhabitant of Savannah, including the Indians, lining the shore on the high bluffs overlooking the river.

"Boom! Boom!" answered the guns from Savannah, greeting the new arrivals. When the ship was anchored, Captain Fry, von Reck, Boltzius, Gronau, and the pharmacist, Mr. Zwiffler, disembarked in small boats and were met on shore with great pleasure. Even the Indians reached out to touch them in welcome.

The Saalfelden women stood with the other Salzburgers and settlers on the deck, delighting in the festivities. Catherine longed to set her feet on land again, but she controlled her impatience at once again being left on the ship. The travelers were surrounded by their bundles of belongings, having brought them on deck in anticipation of leaving the ship forever.

"I can't believe we're actually here," Barbara kept saying over and over again. "It was so long ago in Memmingen when we first heard about Georgia, and there it is."

"Those savages look friendly, don't they?" Gertrude said cautiously. "They're touching the pastors. I wonder what they feel like. Their skin is so dark, and their hair is odd-looking."

"Maybe they're just dirty," Catherine said.

"Their clothes certainly are strange," Gertrude continued.

"That's what people said about us when we left Salzburg. Remember in Augsburg how people stared at us," Barbara reminded them.

"Yes, I guess my yellow hair looks just as strange to them as their black hair does to me."

"Probably stranger," Catherine teased.

The small boats began returning to the ship, and, slowly, the English settlers and the Salzburgers were taken to the shore. There they climbed wooden ladders to the top of the bluffs for their first view of Savannah.

"Let's try to get in the same boat," Barbara said. "Where are Maria and Johann? We should be with them."

The three women looked around and saw Maria helping Mrs. Huber and Johann practically carrying the weak, emaciated Mr. Huber. He had never recovered his strength, and she had succumbed to the same illness. The four children were pale and sick-looking, also. They were trying to prepare them to descend into the boats for the trip ashore.

Barbara and the girls joined them, and each one took a child by the hand. "It's a miracle we lived to see this day," Mr. Huber said.

"You'll feel much better once we get on land again," Maria comforted him.

"Yes, if it's God's will," he replied softly.

Before coming up on deck, Maria had bound both Hubers in rags to catch their uncontrollable, bloody bowel discharge until they could reach the shore. The horrible smell dissipated somewhat in the fresh air.

"We'll go on board with the parents if you will come with the children," Johann said to Barbara.

"Where's Mamma Anna?" Barbara asked.

Gertrude looked across the deck and said, "She's helping Frau Rott. She started having labor pains last night." Gertrude also saw Peter Gruber practically carrying Tobias Lackner, who was too weak to walk alone.

The joy of first stepping onto the soil of Savannah was clouded with caring for the sick. What better way to start our new life than ministering to those in need, Barbara thought.

Catherine, holding Magdalena Huber, stepped out of the small boat into the shallow water. She struggled through the mud to the slippery round rocks dumped on the shore by ships that no longer needed them for ballast. She clambered for the ladder and slowly made her way up the bluff. At the top, she set the child down and looked around. Women came over to greet her, but she could only smile in response to their words, for she knew no English. Her head began spinning, and she leaned against a tree to keep from fainting. The child ran to find her mother.

I made it across the sea, she thought; I'm actually on land again. She sat down and placed both hands on the ground. She just wanted to touch the earth. Tears filled her eyes and slid down her face. The land seemed to rock back and forth, just as the ship had on the water.

Israel Gronau walked over and bent down to see what was wrong.

"Are you ill?" he inquired politely.

"Why is the earth moving?" she asked.

"It's not moving. You just haven't adjusted to land yet. It takes time."

"Oh." She tried to stand, and he took her hand to assist her.

"Thank you, sir. I can't believe we're actually here, on land again. You said in Dover that I could make it across the sea if I trusted in God, and I did. If I can do that, with God's help, I can do anything required of me."

"Remember that when we face hardships in the wilderness," Israel said. "God will always be with us." He reached out and wiped the tears from her cheeks. Catherine looked up at him and smiled, her hazel eyes searching the depths of his brown ones. He wanted to take her in his arms, but he dared not. Instead, he abruptly turned away and rejoined Boltzius and the other gentlemen.

After settling the Hubers in a protected place under a tree, Barbara went to examine the gray, hair-like moss that hung from the trees. She held long strands of it in her hands, wondering about this fulfillment of a part of her dream.

Martin Boltzius and Philip von Reck followed the men who had spent the past year building Savannah, listening as they showed off their work. The town was laid out in large squares. Buildings surrounded the squares with land left open in the center for the common use of all who lived around it. The clapboard houses were simple, without glass in the windows. Oiled paper or cloth covered the openings.

"Where is Mr. Oglethorpe's house?" von Reck asked.

"Oh, he still sleeps in a tent. He wants to be sure everyone else is sheltered first before he is. He is a most generous person."

That is an example I must remember, Boltzius thought.

As they walked, swarms of small black insects circled their heads. "What are these pesky things?" von Reck wanted to know.

"You might as well get used to the gnats and mosquitoes. The only thing that they avoid is smoke from fires. We often build fires upwind to keep them away while we work outside." The people were constantly waving their hands in front of their faces to keep the insects out of their eyes and nose.

The men were shown an experimental garden, ordered by King George, to see what plants would flourish in this new land. All sorts of vegetables were healthy-looking, and other cash possibilities, such as flax and indigo, were doing quite well.

"Was this area covered with huge trees like the surrounding forest?" von Reck asked.

"Yes. It took much hard work to clear enough land to build the town. You will face the same task in the wilderness."

"Where do the Indians live?" Boltzius asked.

"They have a village about a hundred paces from town. They move around often, however, chasing the game. We'll take you there tomorrow, but first we'd better see to providing shelter for the Salzburgers tonight."

As the party returned to the storehouse where the Mayor managed affairs in Oglethorpe's absence, they discussed the arrangements for the newcomers. The two pastors would be housed in Reverend Quincy's house while he was out of town. Soon, von Reck and his guides would leave to go to look at the land designated for the Saltzburgers' community.

The Gastein miners and the other Salzburg men helped the Englishmen construct a large tent for shelter while they were in Savannah. The residents shared food with the newcomers for their evening meal.

Gertrude tried to sleep that first night, but the buzzing of biting insects in her ears kept her awake. She was also bothered by the loud noises of the forest, just beyond the town. The constant cacophony of the crickets, tree frogs, and other night creatures was spooky and strange. Peter Gruber had killed a snake crawling through the grass right at dusk. She was afraid that more snakes might be crawling around. The tent did not have a floor, and they lay on blankets on the ground.

Dawn was a relief for her. She felt like she was crawling with bugs. The women went to a designated place to wash, and she discovered black ticks all over her body. She pulled at them in horror, but some of them would not let go or, if they did, left their stingers in her flesh. "Mother, Mother!" she screamed, "I can't get them off. "

One of the Savannah women was summoned. She saw the problem and took a stick, placed it in the fire, and touched the ticks with the hot end. They turned loose and fell to the ground. The Salzburger women could not understand her words, but they quickly learned how to remove ticks.

Barbara had made a pillow of the gray moss, and her body was covered with itchy, red whelps, particularly around her waist. She soon learned that the tiny red bugs on the moss would get under your skin and cause these bites.

Everyone was covered with bites, and they had trouble not scratching constantly. They did not yet know the names of their tormentors, but they had met them intimately.

A breakfast of tasty soup was prepared for them by an early Savannah settler, a Jew from Germany, Mr. Benjamin Sheftal. Boltzius was so impressed by the generosity of this man that he promised himself that he would try to convert him to Christianity. He felt sure that he must be close to being a Christian now, to do such a charitable act.

Von Reck awoke on his first morning in Georgia, excited about the day's planned adventures. He was to be taken to the Indian camp near Savannah to meet their king, Tomochichi. Restlessly, he sat through Boltzius' long exhortation on Genesis 31, letting his eyes feast on the new surroundings that were in sight. Restrained energy coursing through him made it hard to stay seated on the hard bench that had been provided for the gentlemen.

Finally, the service was over. Von Reck met his guide, one of the Englishmen, and, filling a pack with raisins as a gift to the Indians, they set out to walk the one hundred paces to the collection of huts where some of the Uchee tribe lived.

The sandy trail, though well worn, was narrow in places and stickered vines ripped across his pants legs, causing small tears in the cloth. Even in the morning, gnats and mosquitoes swarmed around his face. He learned to keep a hand free for waving them off.

He had many questions he wanted to ask his guide but was hampered by his limited knowledge of English. The man was jabbering away, but von Reck could catch only a few phrases here and there. He had to rely on his eyes for information.

The village was a collection of what appeared to be hastily constructed shelters, with a center pole to which smaller poles were connected. These smaller poles were covered sometimes with slabs of cypress bark and sometimes with deerskins. In the larger huts, the opening at the top was closed; but in others, no such effort had been made. The front and back had no covering.

Hanging from the various poles were cooking pots, gourds for holding water, ladles made from buffalo horns, baskets, and leather pouches filled with dried or smoked items for eating.

If he could have understood his guide, he would have

learned that these Indians did not live in permanent houses, believing that life was too short to spend it building sturdy dwellings that they would soon leave.

The people who greeted them were short and stocky, the men wearing loincloths in the front and back. Many also had on deerskin leggings held up by a strap from the loincloth string. Their necks and breasts were tattooed, and their faces were streaked with yellow, black, and red paint.

Von Reck noticed a woman with arrows tattooed all the way up her arm, sitting at work on a deerskin. She wore a short skirt of deerskin, but no other clothing. She sat near a fire, for the day was not very warm. His artist's eye longed to sketch these quaint-looking savages, but that could come later.

King Tomochichi was unmistakable, for he had donned gifts from the Englishmen to greet this European visitor. He wore a woolen blanket, a loincloth, leggings, a coral necklace, and a top hat. If his bearing had not been so regal, he would have appeared comical.

The Yamacraw King greeted the young nobleman with what appeared to von Reck as courtesy and gestured for him to sit on a woven grass mat. Other men sat with them, and a pipe was passed around. Each person drew in the smoke and passed it to the next one. Von Reck had heard about this ritual and was prepared to participate.

His gift of raisins was given to King Tomochichi, who indicated his pleasure by eating a handful and passing them around. All the Indians ate the raisins with loud noises that von Reck interpreted to mean they liked his gift.

The visit was short, since little real communication could take place, but von Reck came away feeling that the Indians were friendly and would not bring harm to the Salzburgers. During the walk back to Savannah, he marveled that he had actually visited with a savage tribe in this wilderness. What stories he would have to tell when he got back to Europe. He congratulated himself for being adventurous and signing on for this dangerous mission.

Miss Sophie, the niece of Mr. Causton, the keeper of the storehouse and Mayor of Savannah, came with her aunt to greet the Salzburger women. Lonely for friends her own age, Miss Sophie made a point to speak to Catherine and Gertrude. She was appalled at how awful they smelled, although she knew they had had no water for bathing on the ship.

"Aunty, let's offer the young girls a bath in our bathtub. Otherwise, I'm not sure I'll be able to stand to be around them," she said, holding her handkerchief, with sweet shrub tied in the corner, to her nose.

Mrs. Causton spoke to Barbara through an interpreter and made the arrangements. Catherine, Gertrude, and Maria followed the English women to the Causton house, where they gratefully took turns washing in the big tub. Barbara and Mamma Anna were too busy preparing food for everyone and caring for the sick to join them.

Catherine luxuriated in the tub of clean warm water. She rubbed the harsh soap into her wet oily hair and over her body, washing away the accumulated grime of the long voyage. Bedbugs and lice floated to the top of the water.

Maria held Catherine's clothes while she and Gertrude waited their turns. "Won't it be nice when we have our own house? I'm so tired of being filthy and smelling like stale vomit," Maria said. "Johann has been looking at how the houses in Savannah are built, and he thinks he can construct one like them. Won't it be wonderful to have our own place again?"

"There's not much point in bathing when we haven't had time to wash our clothes yet," Gertrude complained. She was not as eager for this enterprise as were her two sisters, who cared much more about their appearance.

"Remember that big tub we had in Saalfelden? I wish we could have brought it with us," Catherine said. "I'd like to spend a whole day just soaking in it. Maybe I could wash off all this dirt if I did."

"Oh, sure, Catherine. How on earth were we supposed to

carry that heavy thing all the way across Europe," Gertrude laughed.

"We should have put wheels on it, and you could have pushed me all the way," Catherine replied. The three sisters giggled at that ridiculous idea, letting their high spirits come to the surface.

"Hurry up, slow poke. The water's going to get cold."

"Hand me my linen," Catherine said, "so I can wash it."

"You'll have to wear it wet, Catherine, and then you'll get sick," Maria warned.

"It'll dry on me. I just have to wash it. I can't put that dirty linen back on. It stinks so bad it makes me sick."

Catherine shivered as she slipped on the damp linen and reached for the outer garments. Her blouse and wool skirt were still covered with the stains of vomit and diarrhea from two months on the ship. At least she was clean on the inside.

The three young women assisted each other, and all three felt refreshed. They thanked Mrs. Causton and Sophie for their hospitality and left.

"We should have been helping Barbara and Mamma Anna instead of taking care of ourselves," Maria said. "But it sure feels good to be clean. Come here, Trudi, and I'll comb your hair." Gertrude sat down in the sun, and Maria began pulling the comb through her long blond hair. "I've always admired your yellow hair, Trudi. I've noticed some other people admiring it, too," Maria said, teasing her about the attention she had received from Tobias Lackner before he became so sick.

"Well, Mamma would never let her marry Mr. Lackner anyway, so there's no use talking about it," Catherine said.

"You seem to have an admirer, too," Maria said to Catherine.

"I don't know what you mean," Catherine said, but the color that rose in her face belied her statement.

"I've been watching the eyes of a certain gentleman. They spend a lot of time looking at you," Maria said, "and I think Barbara would not mind that match at all."

"Who are you talking about?" Gertrude asked. "Why

would anyone want to look at Catherine?" The three women laughed, enjoying the sun and the confidences.

"Besides, he'd never marry a peasant girl like me," Catherine said, secretly pleased that Maria had mentioned Pastor Gronau's attentions. "I mustn't even think about it."

"Who else is he going to marry in this wilderness?" Maria responded.

"Would someone tell me who you are talking about? You can't mean Pastor Boltzius?" Gertrude asked again.

"No, silly. The young one," Maria replied.

"Do you mean Pastor Gronau or Baron von Reck?" Gertrude asked in a puzzled voice. "The nobleman always seems to be looking at you, Maria, not Catherine."

"Gertrude, shame on you. I'm a married woman. No gentleman would pay any attention at all to a married woman. You mustn't say such things."

"I'm sorry, Maria. I didn't mean it was your fault. So, it's Pastor Gronau, huh?" Gertrude said, turning to Catherine.

"Keep your voice down, Trudi. Someone might hear you," Catherine admonished her sister.

"So that's why you were so eager to get yourself all cleaned up. Pride is a sin, Catherine," Gertrude said, shaking her finger at Catherine jokingly.

"You've got to promise me you'll say nothing about this to anyone, both of you," Catherine pleaded.

"Not a word, Catherine, I promise. No one would believe me, anyway," Gertrude laughed.

"Only to Johann, Catherine. We've already discussed it. You can count on his never mentioning it to anyone. He doesn't talk that much, anyway. All he thinks about is clearing the land, building a house, and planting crops."

The young women walked back toward the tents, stopping momentarily to watch the sailors and some of the Salzburger men unload the ship, lifting the heavy containers up the bluff with a pulley.

50

Savannah, March 1734

Von Reck, a constable, and a guide departed at nine o'clock the next morning to find the assigned land on which the Salzburgers would build their community. Mr. Oglethorpe had left instructions and three horses for Baron von Reck to ride to the land on which the Salzburgers were to settle. Soon after starting out, they were in deep, tangled woods. Spring rains had made the land soggy, and black water swamps blocked the way they were expecting to go. They thrashed about in this murky wilderness all day, returning that night to Savannah without having penetrated far enough to reach the Salzburgers' land.

Von Reck felt relief at sighting the little town of Savannah again. He had been thoroughly frightened by his first adventure into the wilderness. It had not resembled the forests of Germany at all, but was strewn with squishy, sulfurous swamps and woods so thick that the vines and branches had to be constantly dodged or cut. Occasionally, snakes hung like vines from the trees. Wild beasts, such as bears and buffalo, were glimpsed, and once they happened up on several long alligators on a creek bank, looking like logs. He was ready to believe they were quiet, unaggressive creatures, but his companions laughed and told tales of unwary people and animals who had been killed or maimed by the giant reptiles.

Mr. Oglethorpe had returned to Savannah during the day, accompanied by Mr. Jenys, the Speaker of the Carolina Assembly. Oglethorpe had delayed his trip to England to be sure the Salzburgers were properly settled. Von Reck was very glad to see him, for he had begun to doubt that his guide would be able to lead them to the site. Oglethorpe laid out a plan for the next day. He would lead the party to the Salzburgers' land. They would travel by boat, Mr. Jenys accompanying them. Oglethorpe asked the Indian chief for two

Indians to hunt for the travel party. Chief Tomochichi sent his Chief War Captain, Tuskenovi, and others to assist the group.

At daybreak they set out in a ten-oared boat, paddling against the current up the Savannah River. Their first stop was six miles upstream, where Mr. Musgrove was building a house. His wife Mary was an Indian who served as an interpreter for Mr. Oglethorpe in his dealings with the Indians. They camped in tents that night on the riverbank. Early the next morning, Oglethorpe, von Reck, and the Indians set off on land, the two gentlemen riding horses. The others continued by boat.

"How do you know which way to go in the forest?" von Reck asked in German, since Oglethorpe could speak German quite well. Von Reck had been following along for many miles, dodging branches and feeling completely lost, the woods closing behind them.

"See those barkings on the trees? I've already marked where roads will be built in the future. The Indians have led me through this way before, and I marked the trail," Oglethorpe replied.

Von Reck watched diligently from then on but decided that the slashes in the bark of the trees were too far apart for him to find his way alone. The Indians and Oglethorpe seemed confident that they knew the way, however. Around noon, they found themselves in a soggy area covered with cane so dense that they had to cut their way through. It was exhausting. Soon after getting through the cane, they reached a river that was too deep to ford. The Indians swam the horses across while Oglethorpe and von Reck shimmied across on a tree that had been felled to serve as a bridge.

When darkness came, the group camped on a small hill, and the Indians brought them wild turkey for their supper.

"Wouldn't it be easier to reach this place by water?" von Reck asked.

"I hope that's true, but it may be necessary to clear the streams before a boat can get through," Oglethorpe answered.

"Maybe a site easier to reach would be preferable," von Reck suggested.

"Building a new town in the wilderness is always hard at first, but eventually roads and streams will make the place accessible," Oglethorpe replied. He did not mention his real reason for choosing this particular site--its location on the major Indian trail from Florida to Carolina. If he had settlers there, he would know if the Indians were leading the French down the trail to Savannah or Florida, or if the Spanish were coming north from Florida. Oglethorpe was trying to secure for the King of England the land south of Carolina and north of the Altamaha River in Florida.

They continued their journey at daybreak and arrived at the Salzburgers' land at nine o'clock in the morning. The area was bordered by two small rivers that eventually emptied into the Savannah. The town was to be built near the larger river, which they named Ebenezer.

Von Reck walked over the land, seeing cedar, walnut, pine, cypress, and oak trees. He noticed an abundance of myrtle trees from which candles could be made by boiling the berries and extracting the wax. The people in Savannah used these strange green candles made from myrtle berries.

The woods were not as thick here, and there were open places where cows could graze. He noted in his journal the game he saw--roebuck, turkeys, eagles, goats, stags, hares, partridges, and buffalo. He noted the presence of sassafras, indigo, and china root. Flaming orange and yellow azaleas were blooming, with colors that quite startled him by their brilliance, and the open areas were shimmering with purple-topped flowers.

Von Reck walked over to the river and marveled at the black water, so smooth that the huge cypress trees growing in the river were so perfectly reflected it was hard to see the water line on the trees. The land looked like a paradise to the young German nobleman, and he readily agreed for this to be the place for the Salzburgers' settlement. Not being a farmer, he did not think to assess the soil.

The men set a marker about one hundred yards from the river. With the burnt end of a stick, Oglethorpe wrote the word "Ebenezer" on it. The Salzburgers and their pastors had told him that they wished to name their new town Ebenezer. They had made that decision on the ocean crossing after they had survived a violent storm. Pastor Boltzius had read from First Samuel 7:12, "Hitherto hath the Lord helped us."

The party coming by boat never arrived at the site, so they retraced their steps and returned to Savannah the way they had come. Oglethorpe needed to proceed to Charlestown as soon as possible in order to board a ship to England.

As von Reck was excitedly reporting to the assembled Salzburgers in Savannah the virtues of the land given them, Mrs. Rott suddenly screamed. Maria Mosshamer and Mamma Anna both ran to her and helped the laboring woman back to the tent where the Salzburger women were staying. Mrs. Rott had been difficult to like on their journey, but since she was a woman in labor, all the women felt sympathy for her.

Mamma Anna took charge and began barking orders to the other women who had gathered around. "We'll need water boiled, Barbara, and someone get some candles in here. Where are your clean rags, Frau Rott?" The woman motioned toward a chest next to her pallet.

The women made Mrs. Rott as comfortable as possible on a pallet on the ground. Barbara went out, built up the fire, and placed a pot of water over it to boil. News spread and, soon, some of the English women came with green candles. They stood the candles up in the ground around Mrs. Rott but decided to light only one until her time was closer. Mr. Zwiffler brought a potion for her to drink but left the birthing to the women. Mamma Anna tasted it to see what it was and, finding it to be a brew of willow bark, gave it to Frau Rott. She knew it would help the pain and the later fever. Mr. Oglethorpe sent over some linen for the baby.

Maria and Barbara stood outside the tent as dawn began to streak the sky over the river. Mrs. Rott's baby had been born around four o'clock, and both mother and child were still alive. Barbara wiped her face with a damp cloth that she had just washed after cleaning up the mother and baby.

"I'm glad Mamma Anna was here," Maria said. "I don't know if I'll ever be able to be a midwife alone. Mamma Anna talks like I'll have to, though, and soon. I'm frightened that I don't know enough. I've never even had a baby myself."

"She is looking old, isn't she? This long journey seems to be carved in her wrinkled face, and she moves around so slowly now. Remember how quick she used to be, walking all over the valley and seldom sleeping a whole night? I think she's right; we'd better all know how to help each other," Barbara said wearily. "In the wilderness we'll have to rely on ourselves completely--and God, of course. I'm glad she's taught you."

Mamma Anna walked out, cradling the baby in her arms. "This baby is very weak. I can hardly get it to cry at all. I think it about starved to death on that ship in its mother's womb. She may not have enough milk to feed it. We'll need to feed the mother well. Barbara, go see the pastors, and see what they can get for her to eat. Ask for meat and vegetables." As Barbara turned to go on her errand, Mamma Anna added, "And, Barbara, ask Mr. Zwiffler for some more willow bark for the fever and pain. We might as well use his instead of mine." Barbara nodded and walked quickly toward the house where the pastors were staying.

"Here, Mamma Anna, give me the baby. You sit down and rest."

Mamma Anna gave Maria a weary smile but said, "I can't rest, child, when there's a sick baby. I need to watch her."

"What do you watch for?" Maria asked.

"You watch her breathing and her color. She still has phlegm in her throat that needs to be shaken out so she won't choke. She isn't strong enough to cough it up. Frau Rott is weak, too. You go back to her and make sure she's not bleeding too much. Also, keep damp cloths on her head for the fever."

It had been a restless night for all the women. Margaretta Gschwandl was already up with her little girl. Anna, her sister, strolled with her along the bluffs by the river. The ground was carpeted with purple violets, and the sky was streaked pink and orange as the sun rose over the river.

"Having a baby is so terrifying," Margaretta said, a shiver in her voice. "I can still remember how I suffered with my little Greta. I dread the thought of having a baby in the wilderness."

"At least there will be Mamma Anna and Maria to help," Anna said reassuringly.

"I know I should trust in God like Pastor Boltzius says," Margaretta said, "but watching Mrs. Rott go through it last night frightened me. I guess I'm not quite right with God, or I wouldn't be afraid to die."

"I don't care what Pastor Boltzius says," Anna replied. "I think everyone is afraid to die."

"These purple flowers remind me of the star-shaped ones on the mountains in Gastein," Margaretta murmured. She stooped, picked a few, and gave them to Greta, who immediately put them in her mouth. "Greta will never remember the beautiful mountains because she never saw them. I think I miss the mountains almost more than anything."

"Well, if we hadn't come here, we would never have seen these flowers or this river. It's a lovely morning, isn't it?"

"Ja, Anna. Thank you for listening to me. I feel better now. Oh, goodness, I'd better get Thomas's breakfast ready. He'll be waiting for me."

51

Savannah, March 1734

Life in the little town of Savannah resembled any frontier settlement, with rough behavior fueled by a mixture of rum and adventurous men without the constraints of family life. Although Oglethorpe had forbidden its sale, rum nevertheless flowed freely. African slaves had been brought to the Islands to produce it from the sugar cane that grew there.

Boltzius tried to protect his flock from all worldly temptations and longed for the time they would be isolated from such rough company in their own wilderness home. With these simple and pious Salzburgers, he was sure they would be able to live in perfect community with God, once they were away from the evil ways of the sailors on the ship and the wastrels in Savannah. He was very concerned, however, about some of their group who would be going to Ebenezer, particularly Mr. and Mrs. Rott and the wife of the schoolmaster, Mrs. Ortmann. They had not yet put worldly thoughts behind them and were a bad influence on the others. He had worried, also, about the woman they called Mamma Anna while they were on the ship. She had behaved disgracefully with that sailor, carousing all night with him on the deck, but they needed an experienced midwife, and the women trusted her.

The two pastors ministered to the sick and spent considerable time preparing the people for communion, which was a great comfort to the Salzburgers, who fervently believed the pastors represented God among them. They constantly expressed thanks to the two clerics for God's mercy in providing them with their own pastors. They held the divines in such high esteem that sometimes Boltzius and Gronau felt isolated from the people.

Thomas Gschwandl, Georg Schweiger, Johann Mosshamer, and the Gruber brothers, along with the other Salzburger men who were not too sick, spent their days in Savannah unloading the ships and clearing the forest, for which they received a small amount in wages.

"I'm surprised that so many of the Englishmen sit around and waste time when the forest needs clearing and the boats, unloading," Thomas said to Georg.

"Well, at least it gives us a chance to earn a little. We'll be able to buy more tools and household things from the storehouse," Georg replied.

"I don't know how we're going to get ourselves and what we have been given already to our settlement place. Von Reck says it's a hard and dangerous trip, just getting there," grumbled Thomas.

"I figure we're a lot tougher than that fancy gentleman, Thomas. We'll get there if we have to build a road all the way."

Thomas chuckled. "We're not afraid of work, that's for sure. Some are weakened by sickness, though. I'm worried about Tobias. He looks worse every day. He would be out here working with us if he had one ounce of strength. I know how it grieves him that he can't be useful, but he can hardly stand up."

"What's that crowd doing over at the courthouse?" Johann asked, heaving on a pulley that lifted crates up from the ship below. The courthouse was just a wooden hut, but in it Mayor Causton and the judges decided justice.

"There's a trial going on. Seems an Englishman got drunk and sodomized an Indian woman," Thomas replied.

"It's a wonder the Indians didn't kill him," Georg said, as they all stopped working to watch the scene.

"Three hundred lashes for the sodomizer," they heard someone yell out.

As the Salzburger men and almost everyone else in town walked over to watch, the Englishman was stripped of his shirt and tied to a tree. The whip lashed out and popped on his back, causing him to scream. It was an ugly sight, but everyone seemed to agree that the man deserved the punishment. The cracks of the whip created a rhythm, and the mob counted out each stroke.

Suddenly, an Indian who had been told about Christianity burst through the crowd and shouted for them to stop hitting the man. He stood against the man and received the blows on his own back. Mr. Causton, the Mayor and keeper of the storehouse, held up his hand to stop the lashing. He tried to explain to the Indian that the Englishman deserved to be punished, but the Indian insisted that the beating was not Christian. Unable to convince him, Mr. Causton finally decided the Englishman had been punished enough and dispersed the crowd.

Later that day, the town was interrupted again when the husband of the Indian woman involved in the incident came into town and began showing off the ears and hair of his wife. That was the punishment he had given her, and he wanted everyone to know.

As they stood mesmerized by the sight, Gertrude asked Catherine, "Can you believe anything so awful?" Catherine turned away from the bloody mess and fought to keep her lunch down.

"Girls, get away from there," Barbara yelled at them. They turned and ran back to the tent.

"That poor Indian woman," cried the Salzburger women, turning their backs on the crowd.

"You girls keep close to me and this tent. There's plenty of work to keep you busy, nursing the sick and feeding everybody. Stay away from those Englishmen. It might have been one of you," Barbara fussed in the voice of a worried mother. "Here, Catherine, wash this bloody linen in that pot of water. Gertrude, you build up the fire. Boiling's the only thing that will get these stains out." Gingerly, Catherine took the pieces of stinking linen that one of the sick people had soiled.

"Whose are these?" Gertrude asked, holding her breath in order not to smell.

"They're poor Mr. Lackner's. He has no family, and he's so sick someone has to take care of him," Barbara said.

"I thought you didn't like him," Gertrude said, remembering how upset Barbara had been at his attention to her on the ship.

"Liking has nothing to do with anything. The man is dying and needs help. Now get that linen washed and hung up to dry," Barbara said testily.

Maria spent most of her time tending to the Hubers and their children, while Mamma Anna took care of Mrs. Rott and her new baby. No one was really healthy, for they all suffered from various stages of scurvy due to the deficient diet on the ship. Their joints were swollen; pustules appeared on their skin; and they all had bleeding gums. The most devastating effect, though, was the bloody flux, which made it impossible to eat and regain strength. Mr. Huber had even become delirious at times.

The next day another trial was conducted. Captain Fry of the *Purysburg* was brought up on charges of mistreating the Salzburgers on their voyage by not giving them the food and drink that had been provided by the Trustees. When Baron von Reck presented the charges, Mayor Causton and the other judges were astonished at the cruelty the Captain had meted out to the Salzburgers. Mr. Causton prepared reports that would be sent to the Trustees in London.

On March twenty-fourth, von Reck, concerned with the slowness with which the Englishmen were preparing to get the Salzburgers settled, set out with the English surveyor, Noble Jones, and a few of the single men to try to clear Ebenezer River of trees and debris so that the people could take their belongings to the settlement by boat. To accompany him, he chose his servant, Christian Schweikert, and also Hans and Peter Gruber, Georg Schweiger, and Balthasar Fleiss.

They left in a small boat and headed for Abercorn, a tiny settlement being built on the Savannah River near the mouth of the Ebenezer. However, they only reached Musgrove's Landing the first day due to a violent thunderstorm. By noon the next day, they arrived in Abercorn, and about five in the afternoon, entered a small river they believed to be the Ebenezer.

They paddled westward into the strangest world von Reck and the Salzburgers had ever seen. The water became as black as polished ebony but reflected the trees and sky like a mirror. It was hard to tell up from down. The river sometimes spread out like a lake, with groves of cypress trees standing in the water. Their trunks were four or five feet across and towered above their heads. The men struggled to stay in the main current of the river but were soon unsure where that current was. Sometimes, the river narrowed to a few feet across, clogged with fallen trees. They dragged the sodden branches to the shore, hating to enter the dark water where water moccasins might lurk.

Huge white cranes flew ahead of them as they rounded a bend, as if leading them further into the maze. Great blue herons rose majestically as they passed.

About nine o'clock that night, with no light left and no solid shore visible, they realized that the river was lost among the cypress trees and marshes. They entered another channel, very large, with a good stream, and continued westward. The river was filled with night noises, and moss dripping from overhanging branches brushed their faces.

"This is the spookiest place I've ever seen," Noble Jones finally said. He and von Reck, the young leaders of this expedition, had been pretending bravery, but their situation was serious.

"I suppose if we can't get through here, we can at least get back to the Savannah River, can't we?" von Reck asked.

"All we'll have to do is follow the current," Jones replied.

They all knew that was no easy task.

"I think we should stop for the night. We might get lost trying to navigate this in the dark," Jones said.

Von Reck was not at all sure they were not already lost, but he did not want to appear too inexperienced in the eyes of Jones, so he simply agreed.

They finally found a bank with some dry land and prepared to spend the night. Trying to sleep in this strange, watery wilderness was difficult for von Reck. He was physically exhausted, so sleep came quickly, but he kept jerking awake during the night when insects screeched and crawled, animals crept, fish splashed, and owls hooted. Sometime during the night, a huge raccoon walked right up to him and began licking his face, which still had grease on it from the fried fish they had eaten for supper. He screamed and jumped up. Jones laughed and shooed away the raccoon, whose eyes shown like orange saucers in the woods.

"That'll teach you to wash your face before sleeping," Jones teased the frightened von Reck.

Peter Gruber, the eldest of the men along, built up the fire to discourage further visitors. He sat by the flickering light, thinking about all that had happened.

The next morning, they continued up the river, but their difficulties did not diminish. Often, they would take the wrong channel, and the stream would disappear into a shallow marsh, where the boat would get stuck. They then had to get out, push the boat back into deeper water, backtrack, and search for the stream again.

The river was very disorienting. It was hard to stay in the channel, and the reflective water made sky and water reversible. They struggled all morning, and after midday came out of the small river into the Savannah again. Von Reck recognized the reddish brown, muddy water of the Savannah and breathed a sigh of relief that they were safely out of the swamp, although he was disappointed that they had not been able to get to Ebenezer. The small boat floated easily with the swift current and, after about eight miles, passed the town of Purysburg, a settlement on the Carolina side of the Savannah. They knew then that they had totally lost the Ebenezer River in their meandering in the black water swamp. Moving rapidly on the Savannah, they reached Abercorn before nightfall.

Von Reck was totally frustrated that he did not know how to get the Salzburgers to their destination. He was their commissioner, and it was his responsibility to see them settled; but he had not counted on the wilderness being so confounding.

They rested a night in Abercorn, then began clearing a road to Ebenezer, following the route Oglethorpe and the Indians had led von Reck earlier. Noble Jones and von Reck guided the men, who worked diligently to clear a path. They felled trees across the marsh and creeks and clearly marked the trail with numerous barkings. On arriving at the site, von Reck showed the men the stone Oglethorpe had set as a marker. The rains had washed off the name, however.

Peter and Hans Gruber walked over the land, feeling their shoulders straightening, knowing that some of this would be theirs to own one day. They were big, strong men who would have spent their lives in the Gastein mines if not for the disruption of the expulsion.

"I'm amazed that trees can grow to such heights in this sandy soil," Peter said. He reached down, picked up a handful of dirt, and noticed the black topsoil was only a few inches deep, with sand underneath.

"It'll be a lot of work, Peter, but won't it feel good to have land of our own without having to give all we raise to the landlord?" his brother Hans said. "I just wish our whole family were here. Wouldn't the boys...." He stopped abruptly, realizing that the thought of his sons back in Salzburg would spoil the joy of this moment for Peter.

As he approached, Georg said, "It is a pretty place. Just look at the flowers. Anna will love the flowers."

"Ja, but you can't eat flowers," the practical Peter remarked.

They strolled to the apex where two rivers came together and looked out at the clogged waterway. "I guess we'll have to clear the river from here down to the Savannah. If we start here, at least we'll know we're clearing the right river," Peter continued. He threw a small stick into the current to follow its movement. The stick slowly drifted eastward before catching on a log.

"It's going to be hard to get this forest cleared and fields planted in time for a harvest this year, with a road to build and a river to clear at the same time. I hadn't counted on those jobs to do on top of the other," Hans mused, as the work ahead of them became apparent.

"Well, it can't be much harder than working the Gastein mines," Peter laughed. "And the land will be ours when it's done, and we can worship God in freedom."

"Ja," sounded a chorus of replies from the others.

Von Reck decided to leave the Salzburger men at Ebenezer to build a shelter for the women and children, while he returned to Savannah with Noble Jones to bring the others and their provisions.

After the two gentlemen had left, Peter, as the eldest, took charge of the shelter building. He had studied carefully how the Indian huts had been constructed. They had no boards but used whatever was available. He figured they had three or four days before the people would arrive.

In a clearing, they placed small, crutch-shaped trees in the ground, spaced to hold sapling branches laid across the top. They stripped bark from the cypress trees, having been told that it was waterproof. These overlapping strips of cypress bark became their roof.

They had salt pork to eat, but no one had the stomach for it after having to eat it on the ship for two months. They hesitated to drink the black river water, but they had no other choice.

"Peter, can we kill the deer and fish?" Georg asked. "Do they belong to King George?"

"I don't think King George is going to know or care if we kill one of his deer," chuckled Peter, "but hitting the deer with that musket is another matter. The deer's going to care."

None of the men knew much about shooting a musket, or hunting or fishing. It had been illegal to hunt or fish in Salzburg, for the fish and game all belonged to the Prince or the Church. Even though a forest teeming with food surrounded them, the men were ill equipped to take advantage of it.

Hans reached into his pocket and took out a length of cord and a fishing hook, which he had purchased at the storehouse. He tied the cord to the hook, clumsily pricking his fingers, placed a slice of salt pork on the hook, and tied the other end to a branch that extended out over the river. The hook and meat sank into the water.

"Maybe I can catch us one of those fish for supper," he said.

"That turkey they served us in Savannah was delicious," Georg said. "Peter, can I take some time and try to shoot one of those turkeys? I think I heard some gobbling over that way," he said, pointing towards a thicket to the west.

"Be careful not to get lost. We don't know our way in these woods yet," Peter warned. "I'll keep the fire built up to burn this trash we've cleared. Don't lose sight of the smoke."

The men bent to their task of clearing out centuries of undergrowth and building a shelter. By nightfall, Hans had caught five good-sized fish, but Georg had been unsuccessful in shooting a turkey or anything else.

"You'd better save that gun powder in case we need it for protection against the wild beasts in the forest," Peter told Georg when he returned. "None of us shoots straight enough yet to hunt for food. I saw some tracks in the mud by the river that looked like they might be from a bear. They were this big," he said, spreading out his huge, working man's hands. "The claw holes in the mud were as long as my small finger."

A shiver went through the group sitting around the fire. The noises of the night drowned out their talk for a while.

"I'm glad to be one of the first of our people to be here," Peter said quietly. He then started singing, in his heavy baritone voice, the *Song of the Exile*. All the men joined in singing as many of the verses as they could recall.

The talk then turned to remembering life in the Salzburg Province. "This is the time of year we would lead the cows to pasture in the mountains. I'll miss the spring festival and the summer in the Alps, keeping the cattle," Balthasar said.

"They don't do that in this land?" Hans inquired.

"There're no mountains. The English just let the cows wander in the forest. It looks like they'd lose them," Hans said.

"This is a strange land, but it is where God has brought us, and we've not lost a single person. Some are sick, that's true, but perhaps God will see fit to let them recover."

The men tied their cooking pan and provisions up in a tree before sleeping, as Noble Jones had warned them to do, so they would be safer from the animals. They slept without incident in this new homeland, having already become somewhat accustomed to the choruses of the tree frogs and crickets, and the sounds of the other night creatures.

The next day was more miserable. It began raining in mid-morning. They tried not to let the rain slow down their work, but their heavy woolen clothes became sodden. The men took off all but their linen and hung their clothes on the trees. With more biting space available, the mosquitoes took full advantage of the opportunity. Soon, everyone was covered in itchy bites.

52

Savannah, April 1734

Mr. Causton transferred to Baron von Reck three-months' provisions for the Salzburgers, which included food, muskets, powder, and tools needed for constructing houses and tilling the soil. The men loaded the provisions on a boat to take them as far as Abercorn. All the Salzburgers boarded to begin the last portion of their long journey. Barbara and her girls huddled together. Johann and Maria helped the Hubers, who were still very weak, and Thomas Gschwandl carried Tobias Lackner and laid him on the deck.

"I don't think I'll make it, Thomas," Tobias said.

"You have to, Tobias. You're my oldest and best friend. Hold on to me. I won't let you die."

"You're strong, old friend, but not stronger than God. I think I'm close to my heavenly reward. Many times I've longed for it. The pain in my bowels is beyond bearing."

The last ones on board were some African slaves, loaned by a benefactor in Carolina to help the Salzburgers in the construction of their houses. Boltzius was quite uneasy about accepting this offer, not being comfortable with black slaves, but von Reck and Mr. Causton had made the arrangements nevertheless.

Water lapped over the side of the boat once everyone was on board. It was obvious that it was seriously overloaded.

"Everyone off!" shouted the English captain. The people were herded back on shore.

After much discussion and confusion, Mr. Causton and von Reck decided that the boat would proceed to Abercorn with the single men, the slaves, and the provisions and baggage, but the rest of the people would wait until the boat returned.

"Mr. Gronau, you go with the boat, and I'll stay here," Boltzius said.

"Baron von Reck, what about our provisions and baggage

on the boat? How will we live without our things? They may get lost or mislaid," shouted Thomas Gschwandl, who had been told to stay behind with his wife and child.

"They'll be safe. Don't worry," von Reck assured him.

"But we have nothing to eat or cook with here. Everything is on the boat."

The usually uncomplaining Salzburgers raised such a clamor about their circumstances that Mr. Causton opened the storehouse and gave them provisions for fourteen days.

Barbara, Gertrude, and Catherine sat with Maria on pine straw under a tree, resting for a few minutes after the noon meal had been put away.

"It seems like we're always left behind," Catherine complained.

"Well, it's given Johann more time to earn some money," Maria said, trying to put a positive light on the frustrating delay. "I don't see how Lorentz Huber and Tobias Lackner will survive another boat trip and a walk across land to inadequate shelter in the wilderness. I can hardly see how those of us who are healthy will survive."

"My other concern is what happens to us when all the men get land and build houses, and we are left without anything," Barbara said, her voice shaking with anxiety and emotion.

"Maybe we should ask Pastor Boltzius," Gertrude suggested. "He always knows the answer to every question."

"I don't think the answer to this question is in the Bible. It's in English law," Barbara responded. "But maybe you're right, Trudi. He may not have thought of our plight. He could discuss it with Baron von Reck and Mayor Causton."

"Johann and Thomas have mentioned the point to von Reck, but he just repeated the English law to them," said Maria. "Of course, you know Johann will see that you are provided for."

"I don't want to be a burden on you and Johann." Barbara touched Maria's arm and then continued wistfully, "I've been thinking so much about Peter and the little ones at home in

Saalfelden. My baby is almost three years old by now, if she lived. Do you think Johann would help me send a letter to them, to let them know what's happened to us and that we are well?"

"That's something else you might want to discuss with Pastor Boltzius," Maria suggested.

"I don't know if I have the courage to take up Pastor Boltzius' time with my concerns," Barbara hedged.

"Mamma, you may not talk much, but when you do, people listen. If you can defy a priest in Saalfelden and leave your husband and children for the sake of God, surely you have the courage to talk to Pastor Boltzius, who loves us and is concerned for our welfare," Gertrude said with a determined exasperation that surprised everyone.

"Gertrude, where did that fire come from?" Maria asked.

"Well, I'm tired of just talking about what's to become of us. I say we do something."

"What do you think we should do?" Catherine asked.

"I don't know. We've all cooked and taken care of the single men and the sick, but I don't see anyone paying us for our work."

The other women laughed at the absurdity of a woman getting paid for cooking and tending the sick.

"Gertrude, I think you've said enough," Barbara sharply admonished her. "Someone will hear you, and we'll be disgraced. God will provide for us."

"Maybe we could be servants in the houses of the two pastors," Catherine said. "Mother, you're the best cook around. Perhaps you could keep house for Pastor Boltzius."

"I suppose you want to keep house for Pastor Gronau?" Gertrude asked, with a touch of sarcasm.

"Well, if he would ask me, I would," Catherine said, blushing.

"They are gentlemen and can afford to take us into their households, and we could trust that they would behave properly towards us, but I had hoped for something better for you girls than being servants," Barbara said quietly. "Still, we must be obedient to God's will."

"Well, if that's the plan, the first step is for you to talk to Pastor Boltzius, Mamma," Gertrude reminded her. "Now's as good a time as any."

Barbara stood up, brushed off her skirt, and nervously straightened her hair and apron.

"Do I look respectable?" she asked.

"You're the most respectable woman in Savannah," Maria laughed. "Take him some of your raisin bread."

Barbara walked to Reverend Quincy's hut, where Pastor Boltzius was staying, and knocked on the doorframe, since the door stood open.

"Pastor Boltzius, could I speak to you for a minute?" she called weakly.

Boltzius was sitting in the only chair, writing in his journal, which lay in front of him on a roughly-made little table.

"Come in, Frau Rohrmoser," he said, standing up. "What can I do for you?"

Barbara shyly came as far as the door and held out the raisin bread. "I brought you some raisin bread, and I wanted to ask you a question." She felt embarrassed to be addressing this fine gentleman alone.

"Thank you for the bread; please come in and sit down." Boltzius gestured toward the chair.

"Oh, no, sir, I couldn't."

"Well then, what is your question?"

"Sir, I've been wondering what will happen to my daughters and me, with no husbands to claim land in our new town. I'm an experienced housewife, having left my husband and young children in Saalfelden for the sake of God, and I've trained Catherine and Gertrude to be accomplished in running a household. Will it be possible for us to have a house?"

Boltzius listened carefully and responded cautiously to this good woman's question. "The English law requires that only men may own property, and I don't see any way to change that. Besides, you'd have no man to build a house or clear and till the land." He hesitated, seeing the concern on her face. "We will live communally at first, sharing shelter and food. Each person will be issued provisions, so you will not be destitute. It is my hope that all the single women will be taken in by the families, when houses are built. Don't worry, my dear lady; God will provide. A true Christian community will let no one suffer. I have admired the devotion to God that you and your daughters have shown-- attending every service, studying the Bible, and working for the good of everyone. God will show the way for those who love Him. 'Hitherto hath he brought us thus far.'"

"Ja, Pastor, God has provided much more than I ever imagined possible when we left home. I am truly grateful for all the care that has been taken for our benefit. I'm most especially thankful to you and Pastor Gronau for your spiritual guidance. Now I know my daughters and I can follow your teachings and live our lives in such a way that Jesus will welcome us into Heaven. I feel much relieved of my worry. There's one more thing I'd like to ask you, though. Will it be possible to send a letter to my husband and children, to let them know where we are?"

"Of course. Do you need someone to write it for you?"

"No, sir. Johann can write it."

After Barbara left, Boltzius sat down and began eating the bread, pondering the problem of the single women. He would discuss it with Gronau when they got to Ebenezer. The Commissioner should handle matters of this sort, but the people kept asking his assistance, since he had made a point to know and talk with them. He didn't think von Reck would appreciate the problems of these "peasant women," as he insisted on calling them. But Boltzius knew that Barbara Rohrmoser had left a respectable life for the sake of God. Umm, this bread is exceptionally good, he thought.

On April fifth, the boat returned to Savannah for the rest of the Salzburgers. For the second time, the Saalfelden women said goodbye to the friends they had made among the English women. Even Miss Sophie, Mr. Causton's niece, wished Catherine and Gertrude well with hugs and smiles. For many of them, it would be the last time they would see Savannah, although they would spend the rest of their lives just thirty miles away.

Again, the sick were carried on board, and the short voyage up the river to Abercorn began.

Gertrude sat looking ahead at the trees hanging gracefully over the edge of the water. The sun was hot, and she felt the fair skin of her face burning. She looked down at Tobias Lackner, who lay on the deck next to her. His eyes were closed, and he gasped for breath. She felt very sad that this strong, sturdy man with such a tender heart was so sick.

Impulsively, she reached down, took his hand, and held it in both of hers. His eyes fluttered open, and an attempt at a smile moved like a shadow over his face, before they closed again.

Pastor Boltzius knelt on the other side of Tobias and quietly prayed.

"Will he live?" Gertrude asked the Pastor.

"I don't see how, Gertrude," was the reply.

Tears slowly rolled down Gertrude's face as she wept for this kind man. Boltzius watched her sorrowful face, and tenderness filled his own saddened heart.

Mamma Anna sat on a crate and allowed a heavy sigh to escape her mouth. She had not been able to save the Rott baby, but at least the mother was recovering. She was anxious about the life ahead in the wilderness. She was too old for another great struggle and felt that she would be a burden on the others. She looked around her at the other passengers. They carried the marks of scurvy, with skin rashes, stiff joints, and bleeding gums. She had lost most of her teeth, which made her look even more like an old hag. She noticed Catherine biting down on her finger, trying to keep her front teeth from falling out. She was determined to keep them in, no matter how loose they became. Most of the people had lost some teeth, including Barbara, whose hair had also thinned, showing her scalp.

She was sorry to be leaving Deutsch behind. He had become a good friend, and she would miss him. He had not cared how ugly she was. He always said he was the ugliest man alive, so next to him, she was beautiful. She could never remember anyone saying she was beautiful before, not even when she was young. She scratched her stomach, which itched from insect bites. She knew it was not polite to scratch in public, but she figured she had lived long enough to scratch when she itched if she wanted to.

53

Abercorn, April 1734

Tobias died, unnoticed, on Good Friday night while everyone slept, crowded into the few huts at Abercorn where the people lingered, waiting for the road to Ebenezer to be completed. His death galvanized the Salzburgers as they contemplated the end of the earthly life of this kind and patient Christian man and their own vulnerability.

The Gastein women washed his body and redressed it in his worn and dirty peasant garb, after discovering that he had no extra clothes. Thomas tied the stiff body to a board.

Pastor Boltzius, in his funeral oration, compared Abraham and Tobias in four ways: "First, in obedience to divine call, the former left idolatrous Chaldaea and the latter left Popery; second, in willingness to accept much unrest and discomfort; third, in patience and contentment, even in his last terrible illness; and fourth, in his unusual longing for eternal salvation and his constant hope to obtain it."

After expounding on those four points, Pastor Boltzius asked others of the congregation to speak about this good man.

Thomas stood and, in a sorrowful voice, began, "I won't ever forget Tobias leading everyone into our Entrische Kirche in Gastein. For those of you who don't know, we had a cave in a mountain, where we Protestants had been meeting secretly for two hundred years. The chamber where we worshipped was about a twenty-minute walk back into the cave. Tobias always arrived first and, with a lantern, led the people back to the chamber. He was at ease underground."

"Ja," chorused the people from Gastein.

"And I must tell you about the Salzbund in Schwarzach. Tobias and I traveled together, giving each other courage, and took the salt oath which led us to this place. Others of you were there, too. Tobias faced death square in the face that day and never wavered from it." Thomas sat down, overcome with his grief.

"Ja, that was the first time I met Tobias, and you, too, Thomas," Johann said.

"I remember Tobias changing the words of the Popish hymns and singing them in the church choir in defiance of the priests," Peter Gruber said, and a ripple of laughter went through those who recalled those days that now seemed so long ago.

As the stories continued, Gertrude examined her own memory of Tobias on the boat, looking at the castles along the Rhine River, when he told her she was as beautiful as a princess in a fairy tale. What a strange thing for this rough man to have said to her, she thought.

When the service ended, the former miners from Gastein picked up the board, hoisted it to their shoulders, and led the congregation in a procession to the grave that had been dug. Thomas and Peter wrapped the body in a cloth and laid it in the sandy Georgia ground. Each person shoveled in a spade-full of dirt. The first of the Salzburgers in Georgia had died.

The next evening, Pastor Boltzius received the news that a man from the area had not returned from the forest. No one knew exactly where he had gone or why. The pastor led the people in prayer for him, and everyone hoped he would find his way back the next day. The group decided that no one was to venture into the forest alone, and that they would always tell someone where they were going. Stories of the dangers of the wilderness began to circulate through the people.

Before leaving Abercorn, Barbara, Catherine, Gertrude, and Mamma Anna stopped to say goodbye to Maria and Johann. They had agreed to stay and care for the Huber family, who were still too sick to walk to Ebenezer.

"How are they today?" Mamma Anna asked.

"Mr. Huber is better, but Mrs. Huber had a violent attack of the red dysentery late yesterday. She's very weak. Mamma Anna, I wish you were staying to help me. I don't know what to do," Maria whispered.

"You can do as well as I could, Maria. Anyway, I was told to go on to Ebenezer. You and Johann were chosen to stay."

Lorentz Huber sat holding his wife, Maria, in his lap, rocking her gently back and forth in rhythm with the hymn he was softly singing. Her head rested on his shoulder.

Barbara knelt down beside them and kissed Maria Huber's hand.

"You know," Lorentz remembered, "she didn't want to leave Salzburg. She wasn't sure about the new religion, and the priests tried to talk her into not coming with me. Then I got too sick to travel, and we decided that if I got well, it would be a sign from God that she would go into exile with me. God saw fit to heal me, and we both came. We didn't want to be separated."

"That's true," Maria Huber said. "I told the priest that my marriage vow was more important than swearing to believe in purgatory, and then Lorentz got well, so we left Salzburg. It's been a long journey. My only prayer is that we're ready to meet our Lord Jesus Christ in Heaven." The husband and wife looked at each other and smiled, while in the corner their youngest child whimpered.

"Johann and I will stay with them until they can travel," Maria said. "Pastor Boltzius also needs Johann to help him guard the provisions until they can be carried to Ebenezer. I wish I could see Ebenezer with all of you, but I feel that God has called me to nurse the sick, and I am happy in that call. Mr. Zwiffler is staying and has offered to teach me about plants in the forest. Johann is studying English and theology with Pastor Boltzius." She hugged the women, and they followed the others into the forest.

Gertrude was excited to be on the way again. Her feet were no longer so swollen from scurvy, and walking was not painful anymore for her. The walk through the wilderness fascinated her, just as marching through the city of Salzburg had. "Look at that bright green bird, Catherine, the one with the big hooked beak. Oh, and see that red one. It's called a cardinal." At a stand of azaleas, she exclaimed at the hummingbirds and the brilliant flowers.

"You'd better keep your eyes on the ground and watch where you're going, or you'll fall in another river," Catherine admonished her. "They say the snakes in these woods are deadly, and you're going to step on one if you're not careful." Catherine walked along, avoiding every branch and bramble she could, scanning the ground constantly to be sure each root or vine was not a snake. The wilderness closed in on her, and she longed to get somewhere more civilized.

"Oh, Catherine, you're such a scaredy cat that you can't enjoy God's beautiful world."

"There's both good and bad in the world, Trudi," Catherine said, tight-lipped.

"Girls, that's enough." Barbara knew well the different temperaments of her daughters and did not want this conversation to lead to an argument, especially when she was feeling such pain in her insides. "Wait right here. I have to stop," she said urgently, putting down her pack and running to squat behind the bushes.

When she returned, Mamma Anna whispered to Barbara, "Was it bloody?"

"No, thank God."

They hiked over the seven bridges the men had struggled to build across the creeks and marshy places before reaching Ebenezer. The wilderness was barely touched, although the men had worked like beasts to cut trees and build two shelters, one of which was forty-five feet long. Stumps of trees and piles of branches surrounded the little clearing on the mossy bank of the river.

Gertrude put her pack down under the shelter and walked over to the river. The black water that both grew and mirrored huge trees charmed her. A slow, curlicued wave came down the middle of the water. The snake lifted its head and looked at her before continuing down the meandering stream. She remembered Mamma Anna telling her once that seeing a swimming snake was a sign of good luck. She had the feeling that the snake was welcoming her to Ebenezer. A great white crane slowly rose from the opposite shore and soared into the blue sky. Gertrude's soul lifted with the bird, and she felt as if her life was just beginning.

The community settled in as best they could and began the long, arduous process of clearing the land, hauling provisions, building huts, and planting crops.

The cypress-bark shelters allowed little privacy. Barbara hung quilts from the overhead saplings, partitioning off a small area for her family but also diminishing any breeze that might penetrate this low land. The women cooked the fish and game provided by Indian hunters, who were allowed to share in it. Everyone worked from dawn to dark. The men felled the trees and hauled provisions from Abercorn. The slaves sawed the trees into boards for houses. The women prepared food, tended the sick and young children, and cleaned out the underbrush. The stench from smoldering stumps filled the still air but helped keep the insects at bay.

Barbara knelt at the edge of the river to wash the bloody, diarrhea-filled linen of Hans Gruber, who had collapsed under the burden he was hauling from Abercorn. The girls worked hard but did not have the stomach for this duty. After washing the diapers of six babies, Barbara considered their squeamishness silly, but she knew they would get over it when they had their own children. As land began to be parceled out and the men built huts for their families, Barbara retreated into herself, selecting the jobs no one else wanted to do. Her mind was often in prayer.

"God, thank you for humbling me in this way. You know I had to overcome the sin of pride in my husband, farm, and children. Now I am the lowliest of creatures. I was an unworthy wife and mother, leaving behind my husband and babies for this miserable life, but I did it for you, Lord. I long to join you in Heaven, when it is thy will."

The men, who had once been strong and sturdy, eager to take on the wilderness, were pushing themselves beyond their endurance, having been weakened by scurvy. They struggled to clear the land and haul provisions on their backs down the swampy road they had built, while still suffering from the bloody flux and fevers. Most would not stop until they collapsed. Mamma Anna wiped Hans Gruber's brow with a damp cloth stained from the tannic acid in the river. She gave him willow-bark tea for the fever and pain, and he drifted into a fitful sleep. Her remedies were not enough for the scourges these people were experiencing, and the treatments of Zwiffler, the apothecary, were no better.

"Here's another patient, Mamma Anna," Pastor Gronau said, as he and Georg carried in Balthasar Fleiss and laid him on an empty pallet.

"What's wrong with him?" she asked.

"The same as everyone else, I guess. He passed out while he was dragging a tree back from the field we're clearing," Georg said, wiping sweat from his forehead with his sleeve. "He's a good man and wouldn't stop working."

She nodded her head and knelt to feel the man's burning face. "Pastor Gronau, I think you'd better have a talk with Hans Gruber. He's worried about dying a sinful man."

Pastor Gronau found Hans, crying with fever and fear. "I'm a sinful man, Pastor. I'm too sinful to be welcomed into Heaven. Help me, Pastor."

Israel sat down beside him and talked quietly for a long time, assuring him of God's forgiveness if, in his heart, he was truly repentant. Hans became calm after confessing his sins to the pastor and hearing his comforting words.

Mamma Anna watched them while she bathed the face of her new patient, trying to rouse him. She liked Pastor Gronau. He was quiet and unassuming, doing as much work as the other men. She was glad he was the pastor left at Ebenezer while Boltzius accompanied Commissioner von Reck to Charlestown. Pastor Boltzius was kind, but she had noticed he had managed to get a hut built as a church and school that would also be his home, without doing any of the work himself. He had also hired Barbara to cook and clean for him when he was at Ebenezer and not riding off somewhere on the horse Oglethorpe had given him. Israel Gronau, on the other hand, had cleared his own land and built his own hut, just like the others. Now he had to do all the pastoring, too.

Morning and evening prayers were led by Pastor Gronau and by Pastor Boltzius, when he was at Ebenezer, but the daylight hours were spent clearing land, building huts, and preparing the dirt for planting. They were anxious to get seeds in the ground, or they would not have a harvest this year. The farmers among them could already be heard grumbling about the poor soil on the land that they had been given. The people were determined to try to plant crops this year, even though time was running out. After the men felled the trees, the women and children were put to work clearing out the underbrush and turning over the soil.

Mamma Anna stopped the Pastor as he was leaving the shelter. "Pastor, I can't get Balthasar to wake up. You'd better find Mr. Zwiffler."

"He's gone to try to kill a deer so the sick can have something to eat besides salt beef." Gronau leaned against a tree. He looked exhausted and pale.

"Sir, I know it's none of my business, but you're not looking very healthy yourself. You've been working too hard and not taking care of yourself. You need someone to do your housework and cook your meals for you."

"Do you want to do that?"

"Me? Oh, no, sir. I'm better at nursing than cooking. You need someone young, like Catherine Kroehr, Barbara Rohrmoser's oldest girl. She'd do a fine job for you."

"Catherine Kroehr? Do you think her mother would allow her to work for me?" His face blushed as he thought of her.

"Why don't you ask her?"

That afternoon, Gronau found himself walking out to the hut the men had constructed for the Mosshamers, who were still caring for the Huber family in Abercorn. Gertrude and Catherine were struggling to clear the limbs and underbrush from a plot that Thomas and some of the men had cleared of trees, since Johann was not here to clear it himself. They were hoping to get a garden started in time to raise some vegetables this year.

The air was steamy from a noontime shower, and he was soon sweating as he plodded through uncleared scrub. He saw the sisters before they knew he was there. As they worked in the hot afternoon, he had a moment to observe them. Catherine was stacking tree limbs to outline the garden, and Gertrude was raking undergrowth into piles. Both girls looked healthier now that they were eating better food and working in the sun.

Catherine looked up and jumped with surprise when she saw the Pastor walking toward them. She automatically wiped her hand across her face, leaving smudges of dirt.

"Good afternoon, Frauleins."

"Good afternoon, Pastor Gronau," they responded.

"You're making good progress on the Mosshamers' garden." He reached down, picked up a heavy limb, and put it in place.

"Thank you, sir," Catherine said. "They've been delayed so long in Abercorn, so we're trying to get at least a small garden ready before it's too late. Did you come to help us?"

"No, I'm afraid I don't have time today, although I'll try to help another time. I came to ask you a question, Fraulein Kroehr. I spoke with your mother about your keeping my house and cooking for me, and she said that she would allow you to do that. I can pay a small amount. I need help, especially with Pastor Boltzius gone. The slaves who are cutting the boards steal from my hut when I leave it, and I don't have time to cook for myself. Can you help me?"

Conflicting emotions swept through Catherine. She wanted to be near this man and work for him, but she did not want to be just his servant. She brushed the dirt from her hands and, without answering him, walked over toward a tree, where they had a jug of water.

Gertrude was dumbfounded at her sister's behavior and

stammered, "Would you like a drink of water, Pastor? We have some cool spring water that Catherine fetched this morning."

Catherine offered him the jug and waited for him to drink from it, while she planned her response. "Sir, if it will help you in your godly work, I'll work for you. It would also help to support my sister and me. We do not want to be a burden on the congregation. Do you need me now, or shall I come tomorrow?"

"Tomorrow will be fine, and thank you, Fraulein Kroehr." Gronau had thought he was doing her a favor by employing her, and, yet, she had made him feel like she was doing him the favor.

When he was out of hearing range, Gertrude said, "You acted like you didn't want to work for him, when that's all you've talked about."

"I thought I wanted to, Trudi, but when he asked me to be his hired girl, I knew that wasn't what I wanted from him. I want more," Catherine said, with a determination in her voice that was unusual for her.

"You want to be his wife?" Gertrude asked, astounded.

"And why not? I think he likes me."

"But he's an educated gentleman and a pastor. I can't believe he'd marry one of us."

"He'll want to marry someone. Who else is he going to marry but one of us? He and Pastor Boltzius are always talking about every person being equal in the sight of God. Don't you think they believe what they say?"

"Well, of course, I'm sure they must, but...."

"Come on; help me wash my clothes and get cleaned up for tomorrow. I'm going to look my best."

"But what about the garden?"

"Gertrude, you don't understand. I must do this right. It may be my only chance for happiness in this miserable place. Will you help me?"

"What do you want me to do?"

"Go back to the shelter and get some soap and my other

clothes. Meet me at that little cove where the women bathe. Now hurry. I'd go myself, but I wouldn't want Pastor Gronau to see me. Run."

Catherine gathered magnolia blossoms as she made her way through the woods to the bathing cove. After bathing, she would crush the blossoms and rub them on her skin. She waited on the mossy bank for what seemed like a long time before Gertrude appeared, carrying her things in a quilt.

"What took you so long? I've been practically eaten alive by mosquitoes while I waited. Did you bring the comb?"

"People kept asking me to do things. Balthasar Fleiss is very sick, and Mamma Anna needed help. I came as soon as I could."

"Hold up that quilt," Catherine ordered, taking off her clothes and entering the pool of water. She prayed no one would come by in a boat and see her.

"Catherine, someday you're going to die from so much bathing. Frau Schweighofer says that if you open your skin pores with bathing, you let in diseases."

"Well, I don't believe that," Catherine said, lathering her hair. "Sophie Causton bathes every week, and she's healthier than Frau Schweighofer, who's always sick with something." She washed her body and her clothes before leaving the pool, then dressed in her other set of clothes. After hanging her wet laundry to dry, she combed her hair in the sun.

The next morning, Catherine dressed before daylight in her clean clothes. She rubbed more crushed magnolia blossoms on her arms and neck and went to Pastor Gronau's hut. The night before, she had rehearsed with her mother exactly what she would cook for breakfast. Cooking had never interested her very much. She had always preferred to sew and let others do the cooking.

"Good morning, sir," she said, smiling sweetly at the young pastor as she built up the fire in the yard. None of the huts had fireplaces yet. He showed her where his provisions were stored and left the hut to tend to his horse. She found flour, corn meal, corn, rice, sweet potatoes, and butter. She also found salt beef, pork, and honey.

She sliced off some salt pork and placed it in the iron skillet, which sat on legs over hot coals. When that was sizzling, she took corn meal, added salt and water, and stirred the mixture. Unsure how much water to add, she made the batter too thick. When the pork had fried crisply, she removed it from the skillet and put the corn meal mixture in the hot grease, a spoonful at a time, to make corn fritters. Before the fritters were done, it had started raining. She grabbed a pewter plate and hastily removed the fritters before they got too wet. They stuck to the pan and fell apart. Catherine wiped rain and tears of humiliation from her face, embarrassed as she served Pastor Gronau his first breakfast.

"I'll be going to Abercorn today to check on the Hubers. I'll be back before dark," the young pastor said before leaving. He felt awkward and embarrassed to have a young woman in his hut.

"Sir, do you have any rags I can use for scrubbing?" Catherine asked shyly.

"Scrubbing?" Gronau looked around at his hut and realized, as if for the first time, that trash and dirt were everywhere. There were leaves and spider webs in every corner. He rummaged in a pack and handed her some old linen. "Is there anything else?"

"Well, yes, sir. What do you want me to prepare for your supper?"

"Whatever is in my provisions. Sometimes one of the men will bring by a fish. You can cook that, and I'll pay him later. Don't stray far from the hut. The poor Africans come in and steal my provisions when no one is nearby. I can't much blame them since they're treated so cruelly."

"Yes, sir," Catherine said, staring at the ground. Gronau left, not at all sure that his meals would improve with Catherine doing the cooking.

After he left, Catherine rushed to get water from the river and began scrubbing the dishes, then the whole hut, from top to bottom. She sprinkled water on the dirt floor to keep the dust down. Barbara stopped by midmorning to see how she was managing and said, "Well, this certainly looks better."

"Oh, Mother, breakfast was awful. It rained while I was cooking the corn fritters, and they stuck to the pan. What can I cook for supper? I don't know where to begin. He said to cook a fish if someone brought one by, but what if they don't?"

"Calm down, Catherine. You'll do just fine. You've been cooking all your life, although it is harder without a real kitchen or oven." After looking over Gronau's provisions, Barbara continued, "Why not cook some rice? You can make gravy from pork or beef drippings and flour. A tiny bit of honey will sweeten it. Then you could bake some sweet potatoes in the ground. Dig a hole near the fire and put the potatoes in the hole. Rake some hot coals over the hole, and by afternoon the potatoes should be done. Mix them with butter, and you can fry what's left over for breakfast."

"But what if it rains and puts out the fire?"

"Then wait until the shower is over and peel and boil them in water. If you can't do things one way, don't panic; just think of another way."

"Oh, Mother, I'm just so nervous. I've never cooked for a man before."

"You've always cooked for men. What are you talking about?"

"Yes, but you were always there, and, anyway, that was different."

"Oh, I see," Barbara said, and left without asking what was different.

At the evening prayer service, Catherine received the smiles and nods of the women of the community, since word had gone around about her new position at Pastor Gronau's. Even with all their hardships, they enjoyed a little gossip. Anna Hofer made a point to sit beside her on the bench. "What's it like to work for him?" she whispered.

"Working is working," Catherine replied discreetly. She felt uncomfortable knowing people were talking about her.

She was glad Mrs. Ortmann had not come. She would certainly make something bad out of her working for the pastor.

"I have some news. Can you keep a secret?" Anna whispered again.

"Of course, what is it?" Catherine asked.

"The marriage banns will be read for Georg and me at church on Sunday."

"Really?" Catherine hugged her friend.

"Yes. He's finished his hut, and we'll get married the next week."

Catherine took Anna's hand. She was truly happy for her friend.

The next week was filled with disturbing events. Balthasar Fleiss, one of Georg Schweiger's closest friends from Gastein, died after Mr. Zwiffler performed a cupping on him. Mamma Anna stood near, watching the pharmacist cut into the young man's arm and catch the blood in a cup. She had watched cuppings before, done by real surgeons, and she was appalled at what she saw Mr. Zwiffler doing. She was not surprised when the patient died soon after. Pastor Gronau had to conduct his first funeral and the first one at Ebenezer. Catherine saw how nervous he was, as he prepared himself for the service. They selected a rise near the smaller river to bury this simple man. They had started their cemetery.

54

Ebenezer, May 1734

When Pastor Gronau stopped by the shelter later in the day to pray with the sick Hans Gruber and Maria Reiter, Mamma Anna pulled him aside. "Pastor, I know I'm just a midwife, but I've seen surgeons do cuppings, and Mr. Zwiffler drew entirely too much blood. He didn't know how to pinch it off. He isn't trained as a surgeon and should not be doing surgery on these people. I know it's not my place to complain about this, but...." Mamma Anna stopped mid-sentence when Mr. Zwiffler walked in.

"Frau Burgsteiner, surely you know that it was God's will that Herr Fleiss join him in Heaven," the pastor replied, surprised that this dirty old woman was questioning the work of a trained apothecary.

The next day, the Africans found a beehive in the forest, to everyone's joy. With great effort, the men moved the hive near the shelter for the convenience of the whole community. Then, during the night, the Africans set it on fire. Had someone not seen the fire, the whole shelter would have burned, risking lives and provisions. The Salzburgers could not understand why the Africans would do such a terrible thing. The strange behavior of these slaves was a constant problem that no one knew how to solve. Boltzius and Gronau were embarrassed to have slaves at Ebenezer, but von Reck had accepted them as a loan from a benefactor. The pastors did not approve of beating them or tying them up, but, without these treatments, they ran away into the forest or stole from the people. Pastor Gronau tried to talk to them about Jesus and God's love, but they did not understand him.

Gertrude watched the strange, dark men from a distance. She noticed that four of them did more work than the other ten. She asked Mamma Anna, "Did the Africans get to eat any of the honey?"

"I don't know, Trudi."

"If they didn't get any, maybe that's why they burned it up."

"I remember Deutsch telling me about being on a slaver and how terribly the Africans were treated on the ship. They were chained on top of each other in the hold, where they had to lie in their own filth and starve. I don't understand why men are so cruel to other people. Deutsch said lots of the people went mad from the treatment. These men may still be mad. Deutsch also said many of them tried to kill themselves rather than be slaves."

"Mamma Anna, do you think these men were treated that cruelly?"

"I'm sure of it, Trudi. Just look at the scars on their wrists and ankles from the chains, and on their backs from the beatings."

"Mamma Anna, why don't the pastors set them free. Wouldn't that be the Christian thing to do?"

Still smarting from Pastor Gronau's rebuke after Balthasar's death, Mamma Anna replied, "Humph, they'd probably just say it was God's will that these men are slaves."

Paulus Schweighofer became dangerously ill. His wife Maria and their three children were distraught with worry but were much comforted when Pastor Boltzius returned safely from Charlestown.

The whole community stopped their work to attend church on June fourteenth, when Georg Schweiger and Anna Hofer were married. It was the first wedding at Ebenezer, and Boltzius wanted to be sure it was celebrated appropriately, even while they labored to survive. He did not want the people to become discouraged and tried to hold before them the vision of a truly Christian community.

He asked Barbara to prepare a wedding dinner at his hut for the bride and groom, Pastor Gronau, and the Gschwandls. Barbara, Catherine, and Gertrude worked hard to roast venison and prepare special foods for this occasion. The girls cleaned and decorated the hut with white magnolia blossoms, which provided a sweet, heavy perfume.

"A toast to the bride and groom," Pastor Boltzius said, raising his wineglass. "May your new home honor the Lord Jesus Christ, and may your happiness together flow from his perfect love."

The guests raised their glasses and drank the wine. Anna smiled at her sister Margaretta. She had never been happier. She was excited about establishing her own home and family with Georg in this new land.

* * *

Word reached the settlement that Lorentz Huber had died in Abercorn and that his wife would probably follow him quickly into eternity. Boltzius worried about how to care for the four orphans who would be left. Having run the famous orphanage in Halle, he wanted to establish one here in Georgia for the Ebenezer community, but they were not able to undertake such a plan yet. The people did not even have houses or cleared farmland, and they still had to haul provisions overland.

"Pastor Boltzius," Peter Gruber called one morning. "A man just arrived who said he brought his boat two English miles from here." The Salzburger men dropped their tools and followed the Abercorn man through the woods, back to his boat.

"This would be a much easier way to carry our provisions if we could clear the river the rest of the way," Boltzius said. After discussing the feasibility, they decided that every man who was not sick would stop his other work and, together, they would try to clear the river for those last two miles. They already knew that cypress trees, which did not decompose in the water, had been falling into the river since time began, catching the debris that came downstream. This clogging caused the water to spread out into shallow swamps which only canoes and alligators could navigate.

It was terrible work, and they struggled valiantly, but they were not successful. The river was just too shallow, and the debris too thick. The effort cost them valuable time, and they finally cleared the woods for those two miles in order to be able to use their sledge to haul from the boat. Ebenezer owned no boat, so they still did not have access to Abercorn. Maybe after the planting they could build a boat, they thought.

By late evening on July fourth, the community became aware that Mr. Zwiffler had not returned from the forest, where he had gone to kill a deer. They had made a rule that no one would venture into the forest alone, but would always travel in at least pairs. Mr. Zwiffler had not been able to find a companion, however, and had gone alone.

A search party, with careful signals established to keep from getting lost, set out the next day to search for him. Meanwhile, three people died that day: Maria Reiter, one of the single women at Ebenezer; Mrs. Huber in Abercorn; and one of the African slaves, who had killed himself with a knife after being left behind when the others were returned to their owner.

Barbara, Catherine, Gertrude, and Mamma Anna huddled around a low fire that night, unable to sleep. It was too hot to need a fire, but the smoke kept the mosquitoes at bay. Gertrude was crying, her head on her knees. Catherine stared at the moon rising above the treetops, while Barbara and Mamma Anna both stared into their pewter cups. "Drink some of this, Gertrude. It'll make you feel better," Mamma Anna said, handing a cup of her brew to Gertrude. She had mixed in some herbs that soothed and calmed.

Gertrude lifted her head, wiped her eyes and nose on her apron, and took the cup. She drank it and said, "I know that Frau Huber and Maria Reiter will be welcomed into Heaven, but what about that poor African? He didn't know about Jesus. Does that mean God will condemn him to eternal fire?" The insect noises pulsating the wilderness engulfed them like a physical cloak in the silence that followed her question.

"Trudi, only God knows the answer to that. We just have to remain faithful to God in this life of travail. As Pastor Boltzius says, this life is a vale of tears through which we must pass in order to reach life everlasting in Heaven. We should thank God for both the good and the bad that come our way," Barbara said.

"I know about us, but what about that African?" Gertrude persisted.

Mamma Anna said quietly, "Maybe the African had his own god, Trudi, who will take care of him in the hereafter."

"Mamma Anna, don't talk such gibberish to my girls," Barbara said, shocked. "There's only one God, and the Bible says that the only way to God is through Jesus. You must give up these blasphemous ideas of yours, or your own soul will be in danger."

"Humph," Mamma Anna replied.

Knowing she had offended her, Barbara said in a sweeter tone, "Mamma Anna, with death so close to us in this wilderness, I just fear that we might not all meet again in Heaven. I'm so grateful that we have the pastors with us to make sure we stay on the right path to God. Otherwise, we might all be lost."

"I used to think drowning in the sea would be the worst way to die, but now, being lost alone in the wilderness seems more terrible," Catherine said.

They all looked at her in surprise, and their minds drifted back to Mr. Zwiffler, wandering alone in that black forest on the other side of their small circle of light.

The next day, Barbara was startled when she looked up from Pastor Boltzius' cooking fire to find five Indian warriors staring at her. She had not become accustomed to the sudden appearance of savages. They seemed to creep up silently and catch her by surprise. This group was a search party sent by Mayor Causton to help look for Mr. Zwiffler. Pastor Boltzius joined them, and the search went on for a week, but Mr. Zwiffler was not found, and the men reluctantly abandoned the search.

At the evening prayer service, Pastor Boltzius said, "It is with great sadness that we abandon our search. Our dear friend and medico, who knew forest lore well, must have been attacked and eaten by a wild animal. We are grateful to God for all that he did to cure the sick while he was with us. We pray that his soul will be lifted up by God and welcomed into his heavenly home."

At the same prayer meeting, Boltzius welcomed Johann and Maria Mosshamer to Ebenezer. After Mrs. Huber's death, they had come bringing the Hubers' four orphans. "These godly people have tenderly nursed the sick and cared for these children as if they were their own. Also, Johann has guarded our provisions as they've arrived in Abercorn from Savannah. In appreciation for your sacrificial work, the people at Ebenezer have cleared some land for you and built you a hut, since you were not here to build your own. We are grateful for what you have done in the name of God."

"Thank you, Pastor Boltzius, and all of you who helped us," Johann said. "Ebenezer is truly a Christian community-- to take care of our needs in this way." Tears ran down Maria's face. She was overjoyed to see everyone again, and to have this work done for them touched her heart.

"Maria, it's so good to have you here," Barbara said, hugging her.

"Catherine and I started clearing a place for a garden, but we didn't finish," Gertrude said. "Too many things happened. Come on, I'll show you where your land is."

"Where's Mamma Anna?" Maria asked.

"She's taking care of the sick. She'll be glad you've come to help her."

"I'm afraid that I brought more sickness with me. The Huber children are ill, especially the oldest girl. On top of everything else," whispered Maria, "she has epilepsy, poor thing." Maria shepherded the sad, pale children toward the shelter to get them arranged for bed.

That night, when they were finally alone in their own little one-room hut, Maria said to Johann, "Everyone looks exhausted. They look worse than they did on the ship."

"I'm also concerned," Johann confided, "that so little land is cleared and planted. That means we won't have a harvest and will have to live on the provisions from the King. We'll starve if we don't find a better way to haul in those provisions. Thomas tells me the soil is sandy, and he doubts that their efforts to plant will yield much. I'm afraid this is a sorry location for our town and that the rumors I heard in Abercorn are true."

"What rumors?"

"That Oglethorpe chose this land for military purposes, not because it was a good place for our town."

"What military purposes? The Salzburger men don't even know how to shoot a musket. What good would they be to the military?"

"You see, Ebenezer is on the old Indian trail from the north to the south. We would be on the path if the French and Indians come from the west or the Spanish come from the south."

"You mean we could be caught in the middle of a war?"

"Probably not that. We will just be in position to notify Oglethorpe if the enemy is near."

"As if we didn't have enough to worry about with so many people dying and Mr. Zwiffler lost. It's going to be a hard struggle to survive here, isn't it?"

"Yes, but this is a strong community. We've suffered hardships before, and we can do it again, with God's help."

* * *

Georg and Anna's hut was the last one edging the forest. Anna awoke alone on their pallet at first light. She felt the rumbling of morning sickness in her stomach. She and Margaretta both would have babies this year. She was glad that her child would have a cousin the same age. Nauseous urgency caused her to dash outside, and she gagged into the woods.

"Georg, Georg, where are you?" she called. It frightened her for him to venture into the wilderness alone, which he was prone to do, especially in the mornings. He said he had a special place not far away where he liked to pray, and he usually brought back blackberries for breakfast. He said he had to pick them early, before the birds got them.

Anna was building up the cooking fire when she heard something crashing through the trees. "Anna, I've found Mr. Zwiffler," Georg yelled. "He's alive, but he's out of his mind and won't come back with me." He dashed past her and ran on toward the other huts to alert everyone.

Soon, most of the Salzburger men came running and followed Georg back into the forest.

"He was near the blackberry patch over this way," Georg said. They found the deranged Mr. Zwiffler, sitting against a tree. His face and hands were covered with scratches, and his clothes were hanging in tatters. Pastor Boltzius approached him and took hold of his arm, but Zwiffler yanked back and tried to run away. Peter Gruber dashed after him, and he and Thomas dragged him back to Pastor Boltzius' hut. Barbara made a willow-bark tea, which calmed him a little.

"Mr. Zwiffler, what happened to you? We've been looking for you for ten days. How did you survive?"

Mr. Zwiffler's speech was practically incoherent, but he kept insisting that he had never been lost.

"Pastor Boltzius, the man is probably starving to death," Barbara said. "Does anyone have any venison that I can use to make a soup for him?"

"Simon brought by a rabbit he caught in his traps. Will that do?"

"Yes, sir. Why don't you let Mr. Zwiffler get some rest? He's not ready to answer questions yet."

"I believe you're right, Frau Rohrmoser," Boltzius replied. Barbara had seldom spoken to the pastor except in response to his questions. He was surprised that she was giving suggestions, but he approved of her advice.

* * *

Catherine stirred a pot of stew with a long wooden spoon. The men had killed one of the oxen that had been sent to them. She had never made a stew from oxen, but she found herself doing things everyday that she had never done before. She had learned to dress and roast a wild turkey and fry the bass Pastor Gronau caught from the river. He was becoming skillful as a fisherman and looked for times to get away by himself on the riverbank to fish. She worked hard to improve her cooking, always asking the other women for recipes. They were all improvising with new plants and animals.

Maria walked by Gronau's hut on her way to the shelter to check on the Huber children. "Maria, taste this," Catherine said, holding out the wooden spoon. "Does it need something?"

"I think it needs more salt," Maria replied. "You're going to have to teach me how to cook these new things, Catherine. That fish you fried last night was so crisp. How did you get it that way?"

Catherine swelled with pride to have Maria complimenting her cooking. She had taken some food to the Mosshamers after Pastor Gronau had finished, knowing they were not organized for much cooking yet. "Well, you must have your grease just the right temperature," she said.

"Where did you get the onion for that stew?"

"I used wild onion that grows like a weed around here. Mamma Anna said it wouldn't hurt you, and it gives a better flavor to the stew, don't you think?"

"Yes, it certainly does. I'll have to try that. It's good to see some civilization in this wilderness. You've certainly made great progress. Does Pastor Gronau appreciate your efforts?" Maria asked with a smile.

"Sometimes I think he does, but he seems afraid to say much. I catch him looking at me when he thinks I can't see him. He also brags about my cooking to the other men."

"You love him, don't you, Catherine?"

"I can't help it, Maria. I know he may never love me, but I can't help it. He's so kind and gentle, not rough like some of the other men, and yet he works just as hard as they do."

55

Ebenezer, May 1734

The soupy clouds turned into a thunderstorm during the afternoon, and Catherine sat on the bench in Gronau's hut, mending his coat that had been torn by briers in the woods. She had unraveled a thread from the hem and, using tiny stitches, carefully repaired the three-cornered tear. The wind blew rain through the door, and she closed it, plunging herself into semi-darkness since there was no window in the hut. She shivered when lightning cracked nearby and a loud clap of thunder shook the ground.

Israel Gronau burst through the door, dripping with rain. "Oh, Fraulein Kroehr, you're here," he said, surprised to see her sitting inside his hut. She usually worked outside.

"Yes, sir. It's raining," she said. "Should I leave?"

"No, of course not." He shook the water from his hat and took off his wet coat. The hut was so small that the only place for him to sit was beside Catherine.

"I was mending this waistcoat, Pastor. It was torn," she said, handing it to him. He held it up to the crack of light around the closed door.

"I can't even see the tear. How did you do that?"

"I love to sew. Mother always said I could make the smallest stitches she ever saw. If you'll get some of that cotton material I saw in Savannah, I'll be happy to make you a shirt that will be cooler than linen."

"Fraulein Kroehr, I can't tell you what a comfort it is to have you helping me. Life at Ebenezer has been so hard this spring, but I know that when I come home, you'll have food prepared and my hut in order. What spare time I have can be spent in reading and preparing for my ministerial duties. You've been a blessing to me."

"Thank you, Pastor. All of us are so grateful that we have you and Pastor Boltzius to teach us the way of God and help us build a Christian community here. Anything I can do to make your life more comfortable is my way of serving God." She stood up from the bench. "Come, sit down and rest while you have a chance." As she stood up and he approached the bench, another streak of lightning struck nearby, followed by a thunderous resound. He instinctively reached to protect her and held her tightly. As the thunder subsided, he continued to hold her, feeling her softness. She did not pull back but laid her head on his shoulder.

"Oh, Fraulein Kroehr, I've wanted to do that for such a long time," he said into her hair. Even in this dirty wilderness, she smelled like flowers. He looked down at her face, and she smiled up at him, tears overflowing her liquid eyes. He leaned down and kissed her gently on the mouth. "I've grown to care for you, Fraulein Kroehr."

"And I care for you, my Pastor," Catherine replied, her voice shaking with emotion.

They sat down together on the bench, and he brought her hand to his lips. Israel Gronau's mind was whirling. His body craved this woman, but his mind kept telling him he should not. He would have to discuss this with Pastor Boltzius. He could not do anything that might jeopardize God's mission here in Georgia.

Catherine looked at his face and read the emotions that appeared there. Although she knew he loved her, she also saw his hesitation. She felt that turning to God for help was her only hope. "My Pastor," she said, using those innocent words as an intimate endearment, "would you pray with me?"

He smiled at her and relaxed into more familiar territory. "Of course, Fraulein," he replied, continuing to hold her hand. "Dear Heavenly Father, be in our hearts this day. Guide our every move so that we will remain faithful to thy holy will. Bless the sick among us, and may they find heavenly comfort in thy Spirit."

His prayer wandered off, asking God's blessing on everybody and everything, it seemed. Catherine tried to keep her mind on what he was saying, but all of her being was focused on his hand holding hers. As she gazed out from under her eyelids, watching his face, hope and excitement raced through her. Almost as if he felt her stare, he opened his eyes, and they both broke into spontaneous laughter, having caught each other peeking. He never finished the prayer, but hugged her again and then abruptly stood up and left the hut, forgetting to take his hat and coat.

Catherine sat still on the bench for a while, listening to the rain on the wooden shingles over her head. Happiness shadowed by fear swept over her. The thundershower was soon over, and she left to find Maria. She needed mature advice.

56

Augsburg, July 1734

Hans drove his peddler's cart through the gate at Augsburg. His search in Prussia had turned up many old friends, but not Maria. Undaunted, he slowly made his way back to Augsburg where, according to one of his contacts in Regensburg, Samuel Urlsperger was organizing a second transport of Salzburgers to the English colony of Georgia. In every town and village along the way, he had asked for his sister and her daughters as he sold needles and lengths of cloth to the housewives who gathered around his cart.

The cart rattled along the cobbled streets of Augsburg into the square of St. Anne's Church, where he tied his horse, tossed a coin to a street urchin to watch his cart, and pushed open the heavy, carved door. He limped into a formal court-yard, where Salzburger peasants were milling around, and approached a dignified man. "I'm looking for Pastor Url-sperger. Do you know where I can find him?"

"He'll be here in a few minutes. We're waiting for him to speak to us. Are you going to Georgia with us?"

"No, I'm just trying to find my family. We were separated at the time of the expulsion. I'm Hans Burgsteiner from Saalfelden," Hans said.

"Paulus Zittrauer from Flachau. We almost went on the first transport but decided to wait for my brother to get here. The reports sent back from Georgia by the pastors have been favorable, so we've decided to go this time."

"Do you know who went on the first transport?"

"No, I met only a few of the people, but Urlsperger's clerk wrote down all the names. He kept careful records."

Hans stood before the clerk's desk and leaned over to read the names on the carefully scripted list. He shouted for joy when he saw Barbara Rohrmoser and Catherine and Gertrude Kroehr. "My sister and her daughters are on the list!" he exclaimed to the startled clerk. "This is the list of the people who went on the first transport to Georgia?" he asked again.

"Yes. I wrote down all the names, where they were from, who they expected might follow them, and how much money they had," he answered, showing pride in his efficiency.

Hans looked over the list again. He had not seen Maria's name. He saw Johann Mosshamer, his old friend from Saalfelden, and Anna Burgsteiner, but no other names that he recognized. Looking up at the clerk he said, "I'm also looking for Barbara Rohrmoser's stepdaughter, Maria Kroehr. Her name's not on the list. Do you know what happened to her?"

"Maria Kroehr. That name sounds familiar." He pulled out another ledger where all the marriages at St. Anne's Church were recorded. "Ah, here it is. Yes, she married Johann Mosshamer here at St. Anne's before they left. She's listed as his wife." He pointed to Maria's name beside Johann's on the transport list.

Hans' face drained of all color. "She married Johann?"

"Yes," the man said happily, then looked up to see the stricken face of the questioner. "Is something wrong? Are you ill?"

Hans turned and stumbled from the room. He sat down in a corner of the courtyard and put his face in his hands. Despair flooded over him. He had known she might not wait for him, thinking he was dead, but the dream of finding her was all that had kept him alive for the past two years. Now that he knew she was married, what did he have to live for? His need to see her again did not diminish but swelled when he imagined her facing the dangers of the Georgia wilderness. What if Johann died? What if she needed him? And Barbara and the girls? What if they needed him?

"You did not find your family?" Paulus Zittrauer asked the dejected-looking Hans.

"Yes, I found them; but my betrothed, thinking I was dead, married my best friend," Hans said. "Now what do I do?" he asked, looking up into the friendly face of the older man.

"That must be quite a shock, but, after two years, hardly surprising. At least you found them alive. So many people died from the persecution."

"I was almost one of the dead. Maybe I should have been."

"God must still have plans for you. Come with me. Let's find my brother, Ruprecht, and have a beer. He always knows where to find some." Hans allowed himself to be hefted up and led out of the churchyard into the busy Augsburg street.

The next day, with his head still heavy from too much beer, Hans signed up to go to Georgia. Urlsperger was somewhat hesitant to send a one-legged man to the Georgia wilderness, but the Zittrauer brothers insisted that Hans was strong and able to work as well as any man. "Why, this man was a hero of the Protestant movement in Salzburg. He was imprisoned in the Hohensalzburg and gave his leg for his faith." Urlsperger's eyes filled with tears, thinking of the sacrifice Hans had made, and he welcomed him to the transport.

57

Ebenezer, July 1734

"Catherine, you make the dumplings, and I'll roast the venison," Barbara said. "Gertrude, go fetch some water from that spring Mr. Rauner found. Take someone with you, though. Don't go alone."

"I'll get Maria," Gertrude said, running off. The women were busily preparing a special meal for Mayor Causton, who was arriving today from Savannah.

"Trudi," Barbara called after the running girl, "pick some flowers for the table." Gertrude waved her hand.

Cooking for the two pastors had turned out to be important work. They were always having to prepare something for visitors to Ebenezer. Pastor Boltzius invited everyone who came by to eat with him, including the Indians. Since Ebenezer was situated near the ancient Indian trail, many Indians and Englishmen came their way. Barbara and Catherine often worked together, for Pastor Gronau always ate with the important visitors, too.

Gertrude could not find Maria and headed for the spring by herself, carrying two empty pails. Her stomach was cramping, but she had not mentioned it to anyone. No one had time to hear her complaints; besides, everyone had something wrong. As she passed the Gschwandl hut, she stopped to talk to Margaretta, who had been ill ever since she became pregnant. Margaretta was hoeing the weeds from her vegetable garden. Thomas had traded with the Indians for squash and watermelon plants, which were flourishing. He prudently thought that native vegetables might be more successful than seeds brought from Salzburg. Margaretta had planted geranium seeds brought from their farm in Gastein, however. Although they were doing poorly by Alpine standards, they were still a bright red among the vegetables.

"Oh, Margaretta, your geraniums are blooming!" Gertrude

exclaimed. "They remind me of home. We always had them in our window boxes in Saalfelden."

Margaretta leaned on her hoe and smiled. "Thomas says we can't eat flowers. I think they make him sad, because they remind him of the good farm we left. But they make me happy. I don't feel as if we lost everything as long as we have the flowers."

"You have the best garden I've seen," Gertrude said. "What are those yellow things?"

"The Indians call it squash. It's growing well and doesn't taste bad, although I'm not sure how to cook it. I wish I knew how the Indian women cook it, but Thomas didn't bother to find out about that."

"How are you feeling?"

"I feel worse this time than before. You'd think I'd feel better. Last time, we were living out of a wagon and then in a barn. Now we have our own hut, but it's worse this time. My feet are swollen, and I'm losing my teeth." She brushed away a tear and looked over the garden and hut. "And there is so much work to do. I mustn't feel sorry for myself. God will see me through it."

"Mamma Anna said for you to come by and let her look at you," Gertrude said. "You know, she has trouble walking now and can't get out here very often."

"Where are you going?"

"To get water from the spring Herr Rauner found."

"You mustn't go that far into the forest by yourself. I can't go now because little Margaretta is asleep. Wait here until she wakes up, and we'll go with you."

"I can't wait. Mother and Catherine are cooking the dinner for Mayor Causton. They need water right away. I'll hurry. I know the way."

"Stop by on your way back and take them some squash for the dinner," Margaretta said.

Gertrude carefully followed the path the men had hacked through the woods. She scraped her legs on the sharp spikes of palmetto that crowded the underbrush. Her shoes were falling apart, and she had worn through one leather sole. Although she had stuffed cloth in the bottom, sand kept getting in the hole. She was soon sweating in the July heat, which was like steam. She did not remember it ever being so hot in Saalfelden, and, here, insects buzzed constantly in her face, sticking to the sweat. By the time she reached the spring, she felt faint.

Gertrude drank greedily out of her cupped hands and lay down to rest, her head on a root. Eyes were watching her from the trees, but she did not see them. Soon, ants crawling over her forced her to stand and brush herself off. She filled the two pails with water and started back.

Her arms soon ached from the weight she was carrying, but she hurried along, wanting to get out of the forest and back into the settlement as soon as possible. She heard an animal scurrying through the brush, and a flock of sparrows suddenly took flight right in front of her. She felt the wilderness closing in on her, and she looked around in panic, unable to distinguish the path from the rest of the woods. She spun in a circle, looking for something familiar, and saw the painted face of an Indian warrior behind her. She crumpled to the ground in a faint.

The Indian poured some of the water on her face to revive her, but she did not regain consciousness. He gently picked her up and carried her through the woods, following his own path. He suddenly appeared in the settlement, holding Gertrude in his arms. Pastor Boltzius was the first person to see him. The Indian handed Gertrude to him and melted back into the forest. Boltzius just stood there, holding the inert girl, too surprised to act. Barbara hurried over, her face white with fear, and they carried Gertrude to the shelter.

She was soon revived but lay on a pallet to recover her strength. "You go on back to your dinner, Barbara. I'll take care of Trudi," Mamma Anna lisped through toothless gums. "Get out of those clothes, Gertrude. You've gotten overheated." Mamma Anna bathed her whole body with cool water from the river. "Thank God that Indian found you and brought you back. You had no business going into that wilderness alone. You know better than that," Mamma Anna fussed. "I hate to think what might have happened to you if he hadn't found you. And just think what he might have done to you if he'd wanted to. I don't think he was even a Uchee. His face was painted differently from the Uchees. No telling what tribe he was from. Oh, Lordy, Gertrude, as if we didn't have enough trouble. That Huber girl had an epileptic fit last night and scared us half to death. Then there are those three men, too sick to sit up, just lying there waiting to die. I don't know what to do for them, and neither does that butcher, Zwiffler. It's too much, Trudi, too much."

Gertrude bore the torrent of words patiently, knowing that Mamma Anna was just worried about her and that she was too exhausted to control her talking. She watched the wrinkled old woman hobbling about on swollen, bare feet, talking non-stop through her sunken mouth and still trying to take care of everyone. Gertrude realized for the first time how much Mamma Anna had changed since they left Saalfelden. No wonder people feared her. She looked like an old witch. Gertrude vowed to begin taking care of Mamma Anna as soon as she was well again.

"I'll be fine, Mamma Anna. You see, God takes care of me. I don't know why, but every time I'm in real trouble, I always get rescued. God needs me for something important. I don't know what, but something."

"Humph. Well, if you think you're so important, young lady, it looks like you'd be more careful."

58

Ebenezer, September 1734

"Our little school isn't much yet, but at least we've begun, and the children are no longer running wild. Ortmann's doing a fine job with the younger children, and I'm able to teach the older ones some figuring, along with reading the Scripture. We'll make faster progress in the winter when their parents can spare them more often and when we have a bigger place for the school," Boltzius said to Gronau. The two pastors were discussing their parish while they walked out to the fields to inspect the progress of the crops.

"The Huber orphans are the poorest students, with no parents to discipline them. The Mosshamers have taken in the oldest one, Magdalena, because she's so ill, but the others have been neglected, I'm afraid. I'm encouraged by the performance of Gertrude and Catherine Kroehr, though. They are both excellent students, and their mother insists that they attend every class."

"That's something I want to discuss with you, sir," Gronau interrupted.

"What, Israel?"

"Catherine Kroehr."

"Is the school taking her away from her duties too much?"

"Oh, no, sir. That's not the problem."

"Then what is the problem? She has become a good cook under her mother's supervision, hasn't she?"

"Yes, sir. She's a fine cook and housekeeper and seamstress. In fact, I admire her very much. She's most devoted to God and sets a good example for everyone."

"Then what's the problem, Israel?"

"Sir, I want to marry her."

Boltzius stopped and turned to look at the younger man. "Marry her! But, Israel, she's an uneducated peasant girl. What would your family in Germany think? I would have thought you'd want to marry someone from your own station in life."

"Ebenezer is my station in life. I expect to spend my whole life here. I've been considering this for some time. I think a marriage with someone who is a part of the community and shares my love of Jesus would be happier than a marriage with someone who might not be willing to suffer the deprivations of the wilderness."

"I can't imagine what our benefactors in Halle and Augsburg and England would think of such a marriage. Even a hint of scandal could cause people to distrust us and turn their backs on us."

"But surely, sir, our esteemed colleagues would agree that we are all equal in the sight of God. I think our parishioners would gain a better understanding of God's love for them if I demonstrated that love by marrying a woman from the community. We've been concerned that the Salzburgers hold us in too high esteem."

"I can see that you have prepared your argument well. In our remote circumstances, I feel it is my duty to act as a father would and consider this proposition carefully before advising you."

"Of course, sir. I would want that."

"Have you said anything to the girl?"

"Not about marriage, sir. I wanted your blessing first," Gronau said reassuringly. Boltzius nodded his head.

Gronau continued with another point he had forgotten to make. "I cherish the fact that Martin Luther opened up marriage to the clergy. I am a man who needs to marry, sir, and I love Fraulein Kroehr." His voice broke as he finished his sentence.

"Hmm. Yes, I see." The two men walked along in silence.

* * *

"I never saw so many sick folks in my life," Mamma Anna said, collapsing on the bench next to Maria. She had become a regular at the evening prayer meetings, always sitting on the back bench where she could see everybody. "I don't understand this fever that people keep getting. I never saw anything like that in Saalfelden. Zwiffler says they told him it's common here in Georgia, caused by exposure to the night air. And then, the hand of that new carpenter, Rheinlaender, is all swollen up. And Peter Gruber came by my hut with some awful rash that's blistered up and itches like crazy. He said Zwiffler's poultice didn't help him at all. I didn't know what to do for it."

Maria sighed wearily as she listened to Mamma Anna's recitation of the ills of the community. "I've just been trying to look after the Huber children, but there's so much to do. I need to be planting turnips and cabbages now, but I'm so tired being up all night with Magdalena." Tears came down her face, and she lamented, "I just don't know anything to do for her except try to love the poor thing like a mother."

"That's all anyone can do," Mamma Anna said. "At least I'm not living in that shelter anymore since Johann got your house built and gave me your hut. I'm feeling better already. It actually has walls, and I have a place to lie down alone. You know, most of the dried herbs I brought from home got ruined in that shelter. I couldn't keep anything dry." She paused to watch Margaretta struggling to walk beside Thomas as they came in. "I'm worried about Margaretta. Look at her, Maria. She's not carrying that baby right. She's bleeding and sick all the time. Something's wrong. She and Thomas about killed themselves getting that house built and the fields planted. She's not strong enough for that and a pregnancy, too. These men should have left their wives alone until they got their farms established. It's too much."

"Shhh," Maria said, when the pastor began reading the Scripture.

After the brief service, Boltzius announced, "I will be conducting instruction for communion each midday, when it is too hot to work in the fields. Communion will be served next Sunday to those who are prepared."

Barbara was dismayed that Pastor Boltzius was adding another duty to his schedule. While working as his housekeeper, she saw the demands on the pastor, and she also knew he was not as well as he wanted the people to believe. She was the only one who knew that he also suffered from the bloody flux and the mysterious fever that weakened the body. She watched him work tirelessly, not only fulfilling his religious duties for the community and trying to start a school, but also managing the fair distribution of the provisions and land. He constantly wrote letters to their benefactors and stayed up late at night writing a journal to send back to Pastor Urlsperger in Augsburg for publication. She decided to speak to him about resting more.

Barbara noticed a spider web in the corner of the ceiling and cringed, hoping the other women would not see it and say she was a poor housekeeper for the pastor. Mrs. Ortmann had already hinted to Mrs. Schweighofer that it was Barbara's cooking that made the pastor ill. That woman was an awful gossip, always looking for something bad to say about someone.

Working for the pastor had been a revelation to Barbara. People came to him day and night with every sort of problem. She admired his patience, trying to help each one. She also learned more about the people than anyone else and made a point never to repeat what she heard. She became even quieter as she absorbed, silently, the pains and sorrows of the Salzburgers, as they discussed their problems with the pastor. She had also admonished Catherine to keep any overheard confidences to herself, if she expected to continue to work for Pastor Gronau.

* * *

Gertrude lay on a pallet in the hut Boltzius had given to her mother after his house was built. She was weak, but the Essentia Dulci that Pastor Boltzius had sent to her had relieved the bloody flux. He had brought this medicine from Halle for his own use but had shared his limited supply with her when he heard of her condition. She felt much better now. The cooler days of fall were refreshing after the debilitating heat of the summer. She decided that tomorrow she would be well enough to go back to school. She enjoyed learning, and Pastor Boltzius was always so kind to her. She supposed that he took a special interest in her education because her mother was his housekeeper. She would have liked to have a man like him for a father, but, unfortunately, her mother could not marry him, still being married to Peter Rohrmoser.

She slowly rose, dressed herself, and walked out into the September light, filtered through sun-dappled leaves. A refreshing breeze touched her face as she walked toward the river to her secret place. She climbed out on a large moss-covered limb that extended over the water, and lay along it, staring into the liquid blackness below. While the sea had reflected the blue sky and had sparkled in the light of the sun, this black water seemed to be squeezed out of the tangled darkness of the wilderness and reflected the giant cypress trees that arched over the narrow stream.

Gertrude missed the clear light of the mountains and the fresh breezes of the highlands. She had once sat on a large stone in Saalfelden and surveyed the panorama of her world. Now, she dangled like a snake from a grotesquely-shaped live oak tree and thought about how the wilderness closed in on you, pushing you down to the soggy, spongy earth. The men had worked tirelessly to clear enough space to plant their crops. She sometimes visited the fields just to be able to breathe some moving air that had been dried out by the sun.

A doe and half-grown fawn silently drank from the water upriver on the other side. They stood on a sandy beach left behind by the meandering river that oozed through the thick growth of palmetto. An iridescent blue dragonfly hovered over her limb, and a great blue heron, its head cocked toward movement in the stream, stalked the water's edge. Lying still, Gertrude blended into the tree, and life on the river continued unaltered. In the branches far above, she failed to see a mother opossum hanging by her tail while she and her clinging young slept through the day.

Splashing water caught her attention, and she noticed a line tied to a branch bending low in the water, indicating that a fish was on the hook. She was about to investigate when she heard footsteps, and Pastor Gronau appeared. Unseen, she watched him pull the squirming bass from the water and flip it over on the ground.

"That's a big one," she heard a woman's voice say. Looking through the leaves, she saw that it was Catherine. "How would you like it cooked, my Pastor?" Catherine asked flirtatiously.

"How about fried, my Fraulein," Pastor Gronau said, smiling up at her. He knelt on the ground, cut the hook from the fish's mouth, and placed the wriggling fish in Catherine's basket. They struggled up the riverbank, stepping over roots and cypress knees to check his other lines. Gertrude continued to watch as they stopped in a small clearing, completely sheltered by tall palmettos and leafy vines intricately entwined, reaching upward for a taste of the sunlight high in the branches above. Pastor Gronau put his arm around Catherine and bent to kiss her. She relaxed into his arms for a moment but pulled away when they continued upstream, then out of sight.

When Gertrude was sure they could not see her, she slid down from the tree, followed her marked path back to the settlement, and ran toward Maria's house.

"Maria, are you alone?" she gasped, bursting through the door.

"Shhh, Magdalena's asleep," Maria whispered from the semi-darkness of the windowless room. "Come outside." They walked away from the house, which was really two huts nailed together.

"How is she?" Gertrude asked politely, even though she was anxious to tell her news.

"Not well at all. She won't live much longer. We're just watching her die and praying that her soul is ready to be with God." She wiped away tears with her sleeve.

"I'm sorry, Maria, and after you've worked so hard to cure

her."

"So, what did you come running in to tell me?"

"Oh, Maria, I just saw Pastor Gronau kissing Catherine down by the river," Gertrude said, her face lighting up with excitement.

"Shhh, not so loud," Maria cautioned. "Someone might hear you, and the secret will be out."

"You mean you already knew about Catherine and the pastor?" Gertrude asked, hurt at being excluded evident in her voice.

"She made me promise not to tell anyone, Gertrude. If gossip starts, it might ruin everything. I hope no one else saw them. Pastor Gronau has asked Pastor Boltzius if he will marry them, and they are waiting for his answer."

"Does Mother know?"

"Yes, but I don't think anyone else knows, except me and now you. Catherine asked my advice on what to do. I advised her to be quiet about everything and leave the future in God's hands."

"It's unbelievable. My sister may marry Pastor Gronau. I knew she wanted to, but I didn't really believe it would ever happen. What do you think Pastor Boltzius will do? What if he says no?"

"I don't know, Trudi. We'll have to wait and see. Marriage is for a long time. It's just as well to consider it for awhile before taking such a big step."

"What's it like being married, Maria?"

"Well, I've been blessed to be loved by two wonderful men, Trudi, and married to one of them. The more I live with Johann, the more I love him. He is a surprising man, kind, gentle, and sympathetic with the sick and the poor. He's also a learned and spiritual man. I'm always gaining new insights into the faith from him when he discusses the books and pamphlets that Pastor Boltzius has given him to read. The pastor even takes Johann with him to talk to the people who are dying. He says Johann has a way of talking about the faith that people understand and find comforting."

"What if you'd married Hans instead of Johann?"

"Well, Trudi, that wasn't meant to be, now was it?" Maria said, not willing to get into that comparison with Gertrude.

"I can't imagine marrying anyone," Gertrude said. "I'm not sure I want to take care of a man and have babies. Mother's always teaching me how to run a house for a husband when I don't think I ever want a husband. Is there something else I could do?"

"I don't know what, Trudi. But you can do more than just be a wife and mother. You can find something that you like doing and become the very best at that, like Catherine sews better than anyone else."

"What is your special thing, Maria?"

"Can't you guess? My talent is nursing the sick, Trudi. I want to be the very best nurse possible. That's why I'm trying to learn all that Mamma Anna and Mr. Zwiffler know about healing."

"What is my special gift, Maria?"

"I don't know, Trudi. You'll have to find that out for yourself. I expect you'll change your mind about getting married when you get older. You're turning into a beautiful girl, and the men are already looking you over."

"I don't like being looked over by the men. It scares me."

"That's because you're so young. I noticed you were pretty excited about Catherine kissing Pastor Gronau."

"But that's her, not me."

* * *

On Maria and Johann's first anniversary, Magdalena died. They each held one of her hands and watched life slip from her after a violent epileptic convulsion.

Johann prayed aloud, "Receive this precious lamb into your welcoming arms, Lord Jesus." The Mosshamers felt a relieving calm after the frothing contortions of the convulsion. Maria folded the pale girl's hands over her chest and closed her eyelids, then clung to Johann, weeping into his chest.

"I'm so blessed to have you, my dear Johann," she said

chokingly.

"Oh, no, my beautiful Maria, I'm the one who is blessed."

"I'm no longer beautiful, Johann. I'm snaggle-toothed, with swollen joints and sores on my mouth. I don't know how any man could love me now."

"Maria, you're beautiful in spirit. No one else would have cared for this sick child with such devotion, not even her own mother. The more I live with you, the more I know what God's love is like."

"Oh, Johann, you always say the right thing, but I'm a poor imitation of living the godly life. I was so frightened when she had those terrible fits that I feared the demonic spirits were more powerful than God's love. I know that my heart is not always pure."

"So do I, my love, but God forgives our sins. We can take comfort in that."

59

Savannah, November 1734

Boltzius made the difficult trip to Savannah to discuss the distribution of land with Mayor Causton. He was accompanied by several men coming along to haul provisions.

"Your Excellency, I've come to ask you when the fields will be surveyed and officially granted to the Salzburgers. They desire to know for sure which land is theirs. I believe they would work even harder, and certainly with more satisfaction, if they were sure whose land they were working. We are grateful for all that you've done for us, but we do request a surveyor as soon as possible."

"Yes, I see, Pastor Boltzius. The Salzburgers have worked diligently, though I'm afraid their harvest is disappointing this year. I understand your point about assigning the land, but Mr. Jones, the surveyor, is not in Savannah at this time, and I'm not sure when he will return. Please be patient. These things take time."

"The harvest would have been better if the men had not been required to spend so much time building a road and carrying their provisions overland. And the land is not as fertile as we had first hoped. They are the hardest workers I've ever seen, although they have suffered much weakness due to illness."

"We are impressed with their willingness to work and their good conduct, but progress has been slower than the Trustees had hoped. I'll try to ensure that there will be continued provisions for you until the next harvest. More provisions should be arriving with the next transport of Salzburgers, which I understand has already docked in Charlestown."

"They are in Charlestown?"

"Yes, I received word from Charlestown yesterday of their ship's arrival. Their commissioner is Mr. Vat. You'll need to prepare to take these newcomers in when they get to Ebenezer. Mr. Vat intends to live at Ebenezer and will take over the management of the town. You will no longer have to bear that burden along with your spiritual duties," Mayor Causton said.

"That will be a great relief," Boltzius replied, "although the Salzburgers have been so cooperative that distributing their provisions fairly has been made easy. When there are disputes, Mr. Gschwandl and Mr. Mosshamer can usually work out the differences among the men. And when big decisions must be made, I call all the men together, and we talk about different sides of the issue until we reach agreement. The men appreciate having an opportunity to work things out in a way that suits them. It was in one of these meetings that they requested that I ask you to send a surveyor immediately."

"Yes, well, when Mr. Oglethorpe returns from England, many of our difficulties will be overcome; but, in the meantime, we must prepare for the winter and for the arrival of more settlers."

"You can be sure, Mayor Causton, that the good people of Ebenezer will take the newcomers into their homes and care for them until they can build their own houses. It will be easier for this group than it was for those on the first transport, who had to do everything." Boltzius paused and then said cautiously, "Mayor Causton, you have been a great friend to the Salzburgers, and we are very grateful. I would like to ask your advice on a personal matter."

"Yes, what is it, Pastor?"

"Do you think that the Georgia Trustees or our benefactors in England would object if one of our pastors married a Salzburger girl?"

Mayor Causton laughed. "I don't think they would have a negative opinion about that, Pastor, as long as the woman is a God-fearing Christian. Are you planning to marry, sir?"

"No, not I. My young colleague, Gronau, asked my advice on the matter."

"Ah, I see. And which girl does he have his eye on? I'm sure my wife and niece will want to know."

"He is interested in marrying Catherine Kroehr from Saalfelden. She, her mother, and sister are very accomplished housekeepers and educated, pious women."

"Well then, take this length of cloth as a wedding gift to the new bride," Causton said, ripping off a portion of dark indigo cotton material from a bolt and handing it to Boltzius. "Please offer my congratulations to the couple."

"That's very generous of you, sir," Boltzius said, suddenly realizing that he would have to approve of the marriage now or risk offending the Mayor. "I'm sure Miss Kroehr will be pleased."

* * *

Israel Gronau and Catherine Kroehr stood before the congregation and pledged their marriage vows. The dark blue cotton dress that Catherine had made with Barbara's help was in the style of the colonial women in Savannah, with a floor-length skirt, a high neckline, and long sleeves. She had designed it so that she could let out the waistline later if the need arose. The dress was without adornment, but the seams were so evenly stitched that the appearance was simple elegance.

The special gift from Mayor Causton only heightened the importance of this alliance. The symbolism of Pastor Gronau becoming a true member of the Salzburger community and committing his life to their well-being by marrying one of their women was apparent to everyone present. Catherine had conducted herself well as Pastor Gronau's housekeeper, with modesty, hard work, and pious devotion to God. There was little resentment at her good fortune, even among the other young women. She would be a good wife for the pastor, and their friend as well.

The whole community, except those who were sick, squeezed onto the rough benches and sang the hymns with gusto. They enjoyed the relief of a happy occasion in the midst of their relentless hardships. During the long sermon, Barbara's mind drifted away from the voice of Pastor Boltzius, back to the pain she had felt on leaving Saalfelden and her precious little children. Baby Barbara would be three years old now, and little Peter, a big boy able to help his father on the farm. God had led her on a strange path, but she felt that Catherine's marriage to this pastor was surely a sign that her path had been God's will. She thanked God for this great blessing and wept for the two children who might never know God's forgiving love, but who forever must live with knowledge of God filtered through Roman priests. Tears dripped down her face.

"This blood was shed for you for the forgiveness of sins," Pastor Boltzius said, handing Catherine the communion cup. Her hands shook as she sipped the sour wine. She had wanted to marry Israel because she loved him, but, until the banns were read last week and everyone started giving her advice about how to be a pastor's wife, she had not realized what she was getting into. Even Pastor Boltzius had taken her aside and admonished her to behave properly at all times. What if she did not do everything right? Would she turn people away from God like he said? She had never even known a pastor's wife. How was she supposed to know what to do? The words from the service about forgiveness of sins fell on her ears, but she did not hear them.

The modesty and shyness she displayed at the wedding feast were genuine. The people had all brought what they could to add to the dinner, and boards had been set across stumps to hold the food. Catherine was embarrassed to be the center of so much attention and frightened about her new responsibilities. Her bashful demeanor endeared her to the simple Salzburgers, who disliked displays of self-importance.

Anna Schweiger and Margaretta Gschwandl each gave her a hand-painted cup and saucer, which they had managed to bring from Gastein. Catherine knew how precious these gifts were to them and wept as she handled the delicate pieces. She looked at the swollen bellies of these two dear friends, and another fear was added to her already-long list.

That evening, Israel, with pride, watched her organize the

contents of their tiny hut. She carefully found a place for the gifts people had given them, as well as her own meager belongings. Gertrude's sachets made from the flowers of sweet shrubs, carefully dried and stitched into scraps of the blue material, were scattered among her spare linen in the chest Barbara had given her. Mamma Anna's gift of dried herbs for teas was placed on a shelf, along with the precious cups. The mat which Frau Schweighofer had woven from palmetto fronds went on the floor. The goldenrod, filling the pewter vase from Mrs. Ortmann, sifted its pollen on the plank table and Israel's Bible.

Catherine hesitated when she picked up the last gift. It was a linen nightgown that Maria had given her. The linen was not new, but Maria had remade it, embroidering blue flowers on the front from threads pulled from Mayor Causton's material. Israel, seeing her embarrassment, stepped outside the door while she undressed. When he returned, she wore the loose-fitting gown and knelt on the prickly palmetto mat beside the narrow bunk bed. Her honey-colored hair, bent by the released plaits, waved down her back. He blew out the green candle, enveloping the room in darkness and smoky myrtle.

* * *

Barbara and Gertrude cleaned and scrubbed Pastor Boltzius' new house, which Rheinlaender had finally finished. The upstairs served as a school and the church meeting room. They still had no bricks or stones, which made building a fireplace impossible, but Mr. Rauner, while searching for lost cattle, had found pink clay on the bank of Big Ebenezer, not too far upstream from the settlement. The job of digging and transporting the clay was being accomplished. Then they would have to learn how to make bricks.

"At least we can build an oven with the clay so everyone can bake bread," Barbara said, as she washed down the rough boards of the walls, careful not to snag her hand on splinters. "I miss baked bread almost more than anything."

"I miss the mountains the most," Gertrude said.

"I try not to think about the mountains," Barbara said plaintively. "God wanted us to build a town in this wilderness, so that's what we'll do. You might as well forget about mountains and be thankful for what God has given us."

"Yoo-hoo! Anyone home?"

"We're up here, Mamma Anna," Barbara called back.

The old woman slowly struggled up the stairs.

When she reached the top, she sat down on the nearest bench and said, "Braunberger died, and two others are near."

"Were the pastors with him?" Barbara asked.

Mamma Anna nodded her head. "And Zwiffler, too."

"Our Lord Jesus took a long time to call him home. The poor man's been miserably sick for half a year," Barbara said, as she sat down beside Mamma Anna and patted her arm. "I pray I'll go quickly when it's my time."

"Maria and Johann have taken in poor Hans Gruber to nurse. Peter couldn't take care of him and work, too, and he's one of the best workers, strong as an ox when it comes to pulling out stumps." Mamma Anna sighed deeply. "Too much death. This life's too hard for me, Barbara. Sometimes I think I should have stayed in Memmingen or Savannah. Maybe I'm just getting near the end, and I don't suppose it matters much where you are when that happens."

"Are you sick, Mamma Anna?" Barbara asked, alarmed.

"Just old age and crankiness and what everyone else suffers," she replied. Mamma Anna sat massaging the swollen joints in her hands and then went on. "I had a strange dream last night, Barbara. You know how you feel when a dream seems sent to you as a message from somewhere, like your dream of the trees and their mossy gray hair?"

"Yes. What was your dream about?" Barbara asked. Gertrude stopped her scrubbing to listen.

"Well, I'd been out in that little clearing near the cemetery, digging up sassafras root, feeling lower than a drowned log, and missing the mountains and home. And without even realizing it, I started saying the Grandmother's chant and facing the four directions. It comforted me, and I decided to do it again when I got back to my hut last night. I went through the whole ritual, you know, sprinkling the water in a circle and all." Gertrude's mouth gaped open, and water dripped unnoticed from her wet rag, while she listened to Mamma Anna in fascination.

"Then, after the trance, I went to bed; and the Grandmother sent me this dream. I saw Hans on a ship sailing up the Ebenezer River."

"Hans? My brother, Hans?" Barbara gasped, her eyes wide with astonishment.

"Yes."

"What do you think it means?" Barbara asked in a trembling voice, and Gertrude knew her mother took the dream very seriously.

"I don't know, but there is another transport of Salzburgers on the way. Of course, no ship will be sailing up the Ebenezer. You can't even float a log down it."

"Maybe it's just his spirit visiting us," Barbara said, logic taking over her thinking.

"Could be," Mamma Anna replied.

"You haven't told Maria, have you?" Barbara asked in an accusatory tone.

"No, I didn't think I needed to stir up any trouble with Maria," Mamma Anna answered quietly, "but I thought you might want to know, being his sister and all." Mamma Anna stood up slowly and started toward the stairs. "Come here, Trudi," she said. "Help me down these steps before I fall."

From the upstairs window, Barbara watched Mamma Anna, leaning on Gertrude's arm, slowly walk down the road, deep in conversation. She feared that Gertrude's inquiring mind would question Mamma Anna until she found out all about the Grandmother. She had hoped to protect her girls from the old superstitions, so that their hearts would be pure in God's sight.

"Who is the grandmother who sent you the dream, Mamma Anna?" Gertrude asked the old woman.

Mamma Anna hesitated. She had promised Barbara not

to tell her girls about these things. "Well, Trudi, your mother and I share the same grandmother. She was a great healer, who taught me about the plants and how to midwife. She was trained by her grandmother and so on back into time that's lost. Along with the healing knowledge, the grandmothers passed along some old chants and rituals that your mother doesn't want you and Catherine to be bothered with. She made me promise not to talk about it with you girls. She wants to keep your hearts pure for the God of the Bible. Maybe she's right."

"But, Mamma Anna, you don't have a grandchild to tell it to. Who'll know about it when you and Mother die?"

"Maria's heard some of it while learning the plants, but she's rejected it like your mother. All you need to know, Gertrude, is that, whenever you need her, the Grandmother is always there to hear you."

"That's what Pastor Boltzius says about God."

"Yes," Mamma Anna said simply.

"Is the Grandmother part of God?"

"You might say that."

They walked in silence back to Mamma Anna's hut. Then Gertrude broke the silence. "Something's been worrying me, Mamma Anna."

"What's that, child?"

"I can't figure out what my special talent is. Maria says that, even when you marry someone and have children, you can still have something that you are better at than anyone else, like Catherine's special talent is sewing, and Maria's is taking care of sick people. I can't think of anything special about me. Do you think the Grandmother would tell me what my special talent is if you did the chants?"

"Why don't you pray to God for the answer?"

"But I have, and I still don't know."

"I expect the answer will come in time. Now run along. I need to rest." Mamma Anna waved Gertrude away with an impatient hand, irritated that her promise to Barbara kept her from sharing her wisdom with Gertrude.

60

Ebenezer, November 1734

Peter Gruber, Thomas Gschwandl, Georg Schweiger, and Johann Mosshamer held the four ends of two poles supporting the planks that bore the lifeless body of Hans Gruber. The pastors led the way, and the schoolchildren walked behind the bearers, the congregation following, silently winding down the cemetery path cut through the forest. Mamma Anna stood with Maria while the body was lowered into the sandy earth and covered with a mound of dirt. Hans had stubbornly refused Zwiffler's medicines and welcomed death after his long illness.

Mamma Anna looked at the sad gathering. Of the twenty-five who had started out from Augsburg a year ago, seven had died and one had been lost in the forest. The only baby born had also died. Every soul standing there was either sick with something or other or just weak to the point of exhaustion, and some were lying in their huts close to death. With such a meager harvest, those left would still have to eat the provisions of salt beef, pork, and meal until the next harvest. They had no adequate shelter for the winter, no fireplaces in their houses, no heat. They were running out of everything, especially shoes. She looked down at her own swollen feet, wrapped in woolen strips because the leather of her shoes had worn through. She felt the dampness of the ground enter her feet and travel up her stiffening legs. She wondered if any of them would survive the next year.

The pastors might talk like death was to be welcomed with open arms, but she had spent a lifetime trying to keep people alive, and she always felt defeat when they died. Hobbling painfully back, leaning on Maria's arm, Mamma Anna remarked, "I couldn't help but wonder which ones of us will be underground this time next year. We've already lost so many; others are sick, and we have the winter to get through."

"I expect the winter will be mild since the summer was so hot," Johann said. "There is seldom any snow, I'm told."

They trudged along, pacing themselves to Mamma Anna's halting gait. Not wanting to discourage the women, Johann hid his own concerns. The winter gardens of cabbages and turnips had been flooded when heavy rains caused the rivers to swell their banks and drown the plants. They were still dependent on what their benefactors would provide, which was gratefully received but not reliable. "God will provide," he said stoically, putting his arm around Maria.

* * *

It was late November when the first hard freeze surprised the settlers at Ebenezer. Five Indian families had camped on their land, as if planning to spend the winter. The cattle entrusted to Rauner, who had been a herdsman in the old country, had turned wild, foraging in the forest, and Rauner could not find most of them. The nearby Ute Indians were useful in tracking lost cattle but helped themselves to whatever attracted their attention in the village, not having any concept of private property. Hiding anything of value was the most tactful deterrent to this problem, and the women became expert at this.

Mamma Anna huddled on a stump beside the yard fire in front of the Gschwandls' house and observed a hidden Indian woman's astonishment when she saw Margaretta bury her porcelain dishes among the cabbage plants. The puzzled look on the Indian's face caused Mamma Anna to chuckle. She probably imagined the crazy white woman thought she'd get more dishes if she planted some.

Boltzius and Gronau spent that cold morning together, splitting rails to use as fencing for their second attempt at a winter garden. What the flooding had not destroyed, the wild animals had eaten.

"I didn't expect a freeze last night," Boltzius said. "I wonder if that's unusual in this area. There was ice on the water bucket this morning."

Gronau paused and leaned on his ax. "Maybe there's little

point in attempting another garden, if the plants are going to freeze."

"I think we'd better persevere," Boltzius said grimly. "I'm concerned about our provisions for the winter. With forty-five newcomers to feed, we'll need everything we can manage to produce."

"They'll be allotted their own provisions, though, and won't have to eat from ours."

"Yes, but I think many people are sick partly because they haven't eaten enough fresh food. I find when I eat only the dried or salted food, I begin to have stomach problems. Their stores will not include fresh food, and there is still the problem of getting their provisions to Ebenezer from Savannah."

"You're more concerned about our welfare than I realized," Gronau said. "I share your anxiety. I hadn't wanted to mention it to you, but with a wife to think about, I'm naturally worried."

"I do believe that God will provide for us, one way or another. I take comfort in the fact that none of the Salzburgers has died unredeemed. What more could we ask of our Lord Jesus Christ?"

"I'm constantly renewed by your faith, Pastor Boltzius," the younger cleric said sincerely. "I too must place my complete trust in almighty God and put aside earthly worries." The two men shook hands in agreement and picked up their axes to continue their effort to shut out the foraging animals.

61

Savannah, January 1735

Hans used his powerful arms to climb the ladder hugging the bluff at Savannah harbor, trying to keep his wooden leg from tangling the rope. He stood swaying at the top, and the end of his peg leg sank into the sandy soil, throwing him more off balance. He pulled his leg out and righted himself. Walking in this land was going to be difficult, he realized. Even his good foot was swollen and painful from scurvy. He made his way to the most prominent wooden building, the storehouse, and sat down on the steps, leaning back against a post.

He was filled with apprehension as he came closer to Maria. He had known from the beginning of this journey that he would never be able to stay in Ebenezer, with Maria married to Johann, unless she needed him. He had arranged with Oglethorpe, while in London, to establish a trade route with the Indians and also to be an informant about their activities. His experience as a peddler in Europe and his reputation as a hero of the Protestant movement in Salzburg had caused Oglethorpe to place trust in him, even though he was not a gentleman. In fact, no one would suspect that a one-legged, itinerant, Salzburg peddler would be in the service of the King. With Oglethorpe, he had studied maps of the southern colonies and the Spanish territory and knew that Ebenezer had been strategically placed on the old Indian trail that ran north and south, making it possible for him to check on his family periodically. On the journey, he had studied English and as much of the language spoken by the Indians as he could find. The other Salzburgers on the transport knew nothing of his assignment. He was to present a letter from Oglethorpe to Mayor Causton on his arrival in Savannah.

Hans watched with interest as the townspeople greeted the new arrivals. Mayor Causton stood under a strangely contorted tree, talking with Commissioner Vat. The commissioner had been the cause of much deprivation on the voyage, not allowing the distribution of enough food to the Salzburgers. Hans watched to be sure that Vat did not steal any of the provisions for his own profit, although he would not call attention to himself by making a formal complaint to the mayor. He would leave that to others.

All of Savannah's inhabitants were mingling with the newcomers. He saw colonial ladies in long cotton dresses, Indians wearing breech cloths and war paint, roughnecks making drunken remarks about the new arrivals, English gentlemen in black leather boots, and bewildered Salzburger and English settlers staring in amazement at their new land.

In the late afternoon, while most people were preoccupied with preparing for the coming night, Hans presented himself to Mayor Causton in his office, a desk in the corner of the storehouse.

"Your Excellency, I have a private communication to give you from Mr. Oglethorpe," Hans said, attempting a bow.

Mayor Causton looked up in surprise at those words from one of the Salzburgers, but he reached out his hand to receive the document. Holding it in the light of a candle, he read its contents completely before looking back at Hans. "You're Hans Burgsteiner, I assume?" Causton asked, raising his bushy eyebrows in surprise when he encountered Hans' intense blue eyes staring deeply into his.

"Yes, sir. I bring you greetings from Mr. Oglethorpe. He was sorry that he could not return to Georgia on this voyage, but he had not completed his work in England."

"You come highly recommended, Mr. Burgsteiner. I will follow Mr. Oglethorpe's orders exactly, and you shall be outfitted with a horse to ride and an Indian guide. Should I also supply you with your peddling goods?"

"No, your Excellency. Those I brought with me, along with Bibles to distribute in both English and German, generously donated by missionary societies in England and Europe. I will need to store my goods here, with your permission."

"Yes, that's no problem. You are to report to me in Mr. Oglethorpe's absence," Causton said, referring to the document in his hand.

Hans nodded his head, his intense look never wavering. "Yes, sir. I can refill my peddler's pack at the same time."

"I recommend that you begin your mission by spending some time with Mary Musgrove, the Indian wife of a trader who lives up the Savannah River. She is our interpreter and the best person to teach you the Indian tongue. I warn you of the difficulty you will encounter with that language. It has not yet been written down and must be memorized from sound alone. My experience has been that every Indian says the same word differently. It's most confusing."

"I'm told I have a talent for learning languages. I assure you that I will work diligently. I may try to spend some time living with the Indians in order to improve my communications with them and establish a trade relationship."

"It will be a difficult life for someone who does not know the wilderness. Many have been lost who had years of experience. How well do you ride a horse and shoot a gun?"

"I'm comfortable with horses, but I have little experience with guns, sir."

"Then, before you leave, you'd better learn to shoot, or you'll be speaking bear or rattlesnake instead of Indian. I'll provide you with a musket and a skilled marksman to teach you, starting tomorrow. Report here by ten o'clock in the morning for your first lesson."

"Yes, your Excellency, and thank you for your assistance." Mayor Causton held out his hand and, when Hans shook it, the Mayor was surprised by the physical power of the grip, having thought of the man as a cripple. How strange for Oglethorpe to pick this Salzburger for a special assignment. Yet, there was something about the young man that inspired confidence, a self-assurance that most men did not possess.

* * *

Hans and his Indian guide had moved on to Musgrove's Landing before Pastor Boltzius, Johann, and Thomas arrived in Savannah to greet the newcomers. It took several days to make arrangements for boats to carry the large group and their belongings as far as Abercorn, from which they would travel overland.

Boltzius stood talking with Commissioner Vat and Mayor Causton, while Johann and Thomas helped the Salzburger men load the boats. "They don't look in very good health," Johann said to Thomas. "I haven't seen a single person, except the commissioner, who doesn't show some signs of scurvy."

"I'm afraid we'll lose some of them, and others will be too weak to work the fields," Thomas said, hefting a barrel of flour onto the deck of the small boat that the Salzburgers had built. He and Johann were still hauling some of the provisions of the first settlers. "If they make it through this winter, there should be time for them, arriving in January, to clear the fields and build their houses before the planting. Not like we faced, arriving in March and having roads to build and everything to do."

"With all these people, we'll begin to have a real town, not just a settlement. Commissioner Vat said that Pastor Urlsperger is already busy organizing a third transport. If the people keep coming, we'll be able to build a sawmill and raise cash crops," Johann replied.

"I don't think we'll ever get much cash out of crops grown at Ebenezer. That land is so sorry. I predict that next year's crops will be worse than this year's; whatever fertility it has will be used up in one year." Thomas complained, "I don't mind working the fields; in fact, I like it, but I don't like doing all that work on land that I know in advance won't produce much. I know it seems ungrateful to complain about what the Georgia Trustees have given us, but our land is sure a disappointment."

Paulus Zittrauer, one of the new arrivals, overheard Thomas's remarks and approached him. "Paulus Zittrauer, here.

You're Thomas Gschwandl, aren't you?   I met you in Augsburg."

"Yes, I remember.   Welcome to Georgia," Thomas said. "Do you remember Johann Mosshamer from Saalfelden?"

After greeting each other, Zittrauer said, "I couldn't help overhearing your remarks about the poor soil at Ebenezer. Did I hear you correctly?"

"I don't want to discourage you, Mr. Zittrauer, but I'm afraid that it's true. We have found some fertile land on the Savannah River that would be much easier to get to, but I don't know if the Trustees will allow us to move our town. In Mr. Oglethorpe's absence, nothing can be done to change our circumstances, it seems."

"Well, before we clear poor land and build houses, it would be more sensible for us to start out on good land, don't you think?"

"Yes, Mr. Zittrauer, I do. Perhaps you can ask Commissioner Vat to make that request," Thomas said.   "I believe Pastor Boltzius has already suggested the same to Mayor Causton."

* * *

The Saalfelden women stood together under the repaired shelter, watching the new Salzburgers walk into Ebenezer in a chilling rain. Barbara, Catherine, Maria, and Gertrude had worked all day preparing food for the new settlers.   Their cold, wet, weary travelers' faces brightened when they smelled the roasting deer and saw the settlement cut from the forest. The Ebenezer women opened their arms to the first women and children who approached the shelter, hugging the newcomers, who smiled with happy relief. Soon, the misery of the journey was forgotten in the warmth of the welcome they received. Many people were sick, and Mr. Zwiffler was kept busy doctoring them. Boltzius had stayed behind in Purysburg with a dying man, and several others were with Thomas, bringing up provisions. Pastor Gronau greeted Commissioner Vat enthusiastically and invited him to stay at Pastor Boltzius' house, as previously planned.

Barbara was assigned to help him get settled and prepare his meals. Gronau and Catherine organized the placement of the other people for the night. Many were taken into already crowded homes, while some stayed in the cold, wet shelter.

The deer was carved into small pieces and served with roasted sweet potatoes and soup made from corn and whatever else could be found to add flavor, such as dried onion and squash. Barbara hated that no oven had been built yet to bake bread, but they had made what the Englishmen who passed through called hushpuppies, a cornmeal dough fried in deep lard. The meal ended with pickled watermelon and pumpkin. The Ebenezer women served everyone else but ate little themselves. The newcomers were ravenous, not realizing that such a meal was a rare treat, and ate their fill.

The day ended with a prayer meeting held in the shelter, there being too many people to meet in Boltzius' house. Afterwards, as Barbara and the girls were washing up the plates and pots, sorting them out to return to their owners, Catherine said, "Well, I think they got a warm welcome, don't you?" She brushed escaped hair out of her face. "Pastor Gronau asked me to make sure they did."

"Pastor Boltzius asked me to do the same thing," Barbara said wearily. "We did the best we could. Whose pewter cups are these?" she asked.

"I believe those are Frau Schweighofer's," Gertrude said. "I'll take everything back tomorrow. I know this skillet is Margaretta's and that stack of plates belongs to Mrs. Rott. She's so stingy, I'm surprised she let anyone use her stuff."

"Gertrude, shame on you for speaking ill of someone," Barbara said. "Besides, she's trying to get on the pastor's good side because he's threatened to banish them after her fight with Mrs. Ortmann. Those two women are unbelievable." Barbara realized she was gossiping and said quickly, "Oh, God, forgive me. I didn't mean to say that. Gertrude, don't you repeat a word of this to anyone."

"I won't tell anyone, although they already know, except for the new people. I expect they'll find out soon enough.

Those two gossip on each other every chance they get." Gertrude looked up from the dishpan. "I didn't see Mamma Anna tonight, did you?"

"No, I don't remember seeing her, but I've been so busy I could have missed her," Barbara said. "Did you see her, Catherine?"

"No. It's not like her to miss meeting new people. Do you think we should check on her?"

"I expect Maria will, since her hut is on their place. It's too dark now. When you're returning things tomorrow, Gertrude, look in on her. We'll send her something to make soup. The poor old thing can't eat much else with no teeth."

62

Ebenezer, February 1735

Hans reined in his horse and sat quietly, looking over the Ebenezer settlement. The sun was already warming the day, and the air felt fresh. He recognized people from his journey, milling around in front of a shelter. He wondered which little house Maria lived in. He had heard from Musgrove that Catherine had married one of the pastors. He smiled, knowing how that must have pleased Barbara. He decided that the two-story house must be Pastor Boltzius'. He rode over to it and climbed down from his horse.

Barbara was stirring a pot over a fire in the front yard. She looked up as he approached, expecting to see another Englishman stopping by to visit the pastor or Commissioner Vat. He looked familiar, but she could not recall knowing anyone with a wooden leg. She squinted her eyes against the sun as he spoke.

"Good morning. I'm looking for my sister, Barbara Rohrmoser," he said, displaying a teasing smile. Recognition dawned on her when she heard his unchanged voice, and she dropped the spoon into the pot.

"Hans? Is it really you?" she stammered.

"It's really me," he answered. She walked toward him and reached out her hand to touch him, testing to see if he were an apparition instead of a solid creature.

He took her into his arms and hugged her until she could hardly breathe. "I can't believe my eyes," she gasped. "We thought you were dead. How did you ever find us?"

"I've searched for years," he said, overcome by emotion at finally being with family after all that time alone.

"Gertrude, come here," Barbara called into the house where Boltzius was conducting school.

Gertrude came to the door, her finger holding the place in the book she had been reading, and looked at her mother. "What do you want?" she asked.

"Look who's here," Barbara said. "It's Hans, your Uncle Hans."

Gertrude ran down the steps and looked up at the handsome man. Although his face had changed some, she still knew him. "It really is you," she said incredulously. "Mamma Anna had a dream that you were coming to Ebenezer. I never believed it could be true."

"So Mamma Anna's still consulting with the old ones, huh?" he asked, turning to Barbara. Looking back at Gertrude, he exclaimed, "I'm not sure I would have recognized you, young lady. You've changed from a scrawny little girl into a lovely young woman. My, my, my! Just look at you. You must be driving the young men crazy." He laughed, turning her around. Gertrude blushed and looked down at the ground.

"You're embarrassing her, Hans, and you'll make her vain," Barbara scolded mildly. "Trudi, run over and find Catherine," Barbara said. "She's married to Pastor Gronau," she added, a bit of pride in her voice.

"So I've heard. The marriage was the talk of Savannah," Hans said. "And who do you have in mind for Gertrude? I understand Mr. Oglethorpe is unattached."

"Now you quit teasing me," Barbara said. "I'm afraid there is something you need to know, Hans. Maria thought you were dead."

"And she married Johann Mosshamer," Hans said, finishing her sentence.

"You know?"

"Yes, I heard about the marriage," he said sadly. "How is she? Is she well and happy with Johann?"

"She's well enough. We've all suffered from scurvy and a hundred other ailments, but she's better than most. Johann is a good husband."

"Yes, he's a good man. I treasured him as a friend. I might even have died in prison if not for him." Hans looked up at the treetops. "Barbara, I didn't come here to cause trouble between Maria and Johann. I won't be staying, but I just had to see all of you and make sure you were well."

"You're not staying? But where will you go? All of the Salzburgers are here. We need you," Barbara said, all in a rush. "I need you," she added. "It hasn't been easy managing, with two daughters and no husband. If Pastor Boltzius hadn't hired me as his housekeeper, I don't know what we would have done. I'm grateful for what God has given us, of course."

"I don't think I could bear to live in the same community with Maria under the circumstances. Surely you understand. I'm not sure I should have come here at all, but I was so lonely in the world without any family."

"Where will you go?" Barbara asked.

"Mr. Causton has given me permission to be a trader with the Indians. I'd have a hard time farming with this wooden leg anyway, but I'll come this way now and then."

"When did you leave Salzburg, Hans?" Barbara asked, hungry to hear his story. He sat down on a bench near the cooking fire and began telling his tale.

"After I left the monastery in Salzburg, I rode with the peddler to Saalfelden, looking for all of you. This was in the summer of 1733."

"Did you see Peter and the children?" Barbara asked excitedly.

"Yes, they were well. Little Barbara was shyly peeping around the door, and Hans was a strong boy, leading the cows up to pasture."

"And Peter?"

"He looked older. His sister was keeping house for them."

Barbara wiped away tears, thinking about her lost family. Her little girl would never know her, and she and little Hans would live their lives as Catholics.

People began to gather around—Pastor Boltzius, Mr. Vat, and some of the new arrivals who knew Hans. Catherine came running up with Pastor Gronau, looking like a young housewife, and more introductions were made. "I'm keeping you all from your work," Hans finally said. "I'll open my peddler's pack later for any who have need of cookware, needles and thread, or other items of household use," Hans said with a flourish.

"We'll ring a bell to attract the people before the usual time for prayers. Will that be sufficient?" Pastor Boltzius asked.

"Of course," Hans replied. As people began to drift away, he turned to Barbara and whispered, "Which house is hers?"

Barbara pointed out the Mosshamers' hut. "She's probably nursing a sick child she's taken in. God has given her a great gift for healing. Johann is most likely in the fields."

Hans swung himself up on his horse and headed down the lane toward the Mosshamers' house. He had come this far; he had to see her.

While he was riding the half-mile, Maria was checking on her little patient. Finding him asleep, she closed the door, picked up her straw broom, and began sweeping the accumulated black sand from the splintery wooden floor. The long rectangle of sunlight on the floor suddenly disappeared, and she looked up to see who had blocked the sun. Brightness behind the man darkened his features, and she did not recognize him, but that was not surprising, with all of the new people in town. Noticing his wooden leg, she assumed he was sick and asked, "Are you in need of something?"

Hans looked at her, letting his eyes adjust to the dimmer light, and then said in a cracked voice, "Yes, my darling Maria."

Maria was so surprised at his response that she stood in stunned silence, sensing danger from this stranger. He shifted slightly, and, when the sun glazed the side of his face, recognition crept into her consciousness. "Hans?" she whispered, and crumpled to the floor. Hans knelt and took her in his arms. Tears flowed freely down his face, unnoticed, and he finally clasped to his chest the woman he had yearned for and loved for so many years. He kissed her forehead and brushed the graying hair back from her face. Maria opened her eyes and stared at him. Hans kissed her on the mouth.

Maria felt herself responding to him, but her mind screamed to be heard. She abruptly pulled away and scrambled up from the floor. "No, I'm married."

Hans sat on the floor, staring up at her. "Yes, I know."

"I thought you were dead. Johann thought you were dead. I did everything I knew to find you. Where have you been? How did you survive?"

Using the table, Hans pulled himself up and sat on a bench. "I woke up in a monastery hospital in Salzburg without my leg. I don't know how I got there, but apparently I had been unconscious for weeks. The nuns took care of me. When I was well enough, I began looking for you, but you had already left Salzburg. It's taken me until now to find you."

"You were in a monastery in Salzburg when we passed through there? I can't believe this. I had a feeling I shouldn't leave Salzburg without looking further, but the soldiers gave us no choice, and Gertrude had almost drowned."

"Gertrude almost drowned?"

"Yes. She fell in the Salzach River, and Thomas Gschwandl saved her." Maria sat down opposite him, keeping the table between. He reached across and took her hands in his, caressing them and bringing them to his lips.

"Your face has been before my eyes ever since I was arrested that day in Saalfelden. It's what kept me alive when I was near death. It's like God wanted me to see you again."

Maria could not take her eyes off him. Her mind was buzzing in every direction like a swarm of mosquitoes. She wanted to hold him and never let go. She could not betray Johann, though. Passion was sweeping her body. God would never forgive her. She had to get control of herself. With enormous effort, she began talking.

"I thought I'd die when they took you away. I wanted to. Then, later, when Johann came back from prison without you, I wanted to die again. I didn't marry Johann until we were coming to Georgia. It had been two years, and I didn't expect to ever see anyone I'd known before in this wilderness, especially you. Hans, we've built a life together." She stopped talking abruptly, seeing the pain on his face. Shifting her voice to that of a nurse, she asked, "What happened to your leg? Is it painful?"

"I'm used to it. Whoever cut it off probably saved my life."

Tears began to roll down her face, which she covered with her hands. "Oh, Hans." The deep anguish in her voice touched his soul, for he shared it.

"I shouldn't have come here. I've caused you more pain. I just had to see you again. God forgive me for disrupting your life like this. I'll go now." He stood up, and she rushed to him with desperation. He bent and kissed her again, then walked toward the door. Turning back, he said with infinite sadness, "If you had to marry someone else, I'm glad it was Johann."

Maria watched him swing his wooden leg over his horse and gallop away. She sat down on the bench where his warmth was still lingering, cradled her head on her arms on the table, and sobbed. All the pain of a lifetime filled those tears flowing from her body.

Barbara saw Hans riding toward Abercorn at full speed, not even stopping to say goodbye. She stirred her pot of stew for a while before calling Gertrude. "Stir this, Trudi. Don't let it stick." She handed her the wooden spoon and headed to Maria's. When she arrived, she sat down beside the weeping girl, rubbing her back to comfort her, but helpless to say the words that would end the torrent of tears. After a long time, Maria looked up and wailed, "It's too much, Barbara. I can't stand it. God is too cruel."

"Yes, you can stand it, Maria," Barbara said firmly. "You survived his death, and now you can survive his being alive." She held the limp woman, willing the strength from her body into Maria's.

Catherine looked in the door, and Barbara motioned for her not to come in. She mouthed behind Maria's back, "Go get Mamma Anna." Catherine nodded her head and ran toward the small hut.

As they approached Maria's cottage, Mamma Anna leaned on Catherine's arm. Without going inside, Mamma Anna kicked up the fire in the yard with her foot, poured water into a kettle, and hung it over the fire. She fished in her apron pocket, then sprinkled something in the kettle, and put the top on. When the water was boiling, she poured the mixture into a tin cup hanging on a nail and entered the house.

"Here, child, drink this," she said, blowing into the cup to cool the liquid. Catherine stood in the doorway and soon Gertrude joined her. Maria eventually raised her head and sipped from the extended cup. Her eyes scanned the room, seeing their anxious faces. "I guess I've made a royal fool of myself," she said, attempting a laugh, which turned into a sob.

"Well, that's only natural, given the crazy world we live in," Mamma Anna said, and, inexplicably, they all laughed spontaneously, breaking the tension in the room. Catherine and Gertrude joined Barbara and Mamma Anna, crowding around Maria, and the five women hugged each other.

"Gertrude, what about my stew?" Barbara, asked, suddenly remembering she'd given her orders to stir it.

"I kicked the log out from under it. Pastor Boltzius will just have to wait awhile for his dinner." Her sassiness set off another roar of healing laughter.

"And so will Pastor Gronau," Catherine said, causing them all to laugh so hard that they doubled up, panting for breath.

"I can't breathe in here. Let's go for a walk," Mamma Anna said. The five women walked with their arms around each other's waists, ignoring the stares of the townspeople, following a path that led to a sandy beach on the river. As soon as they were secluded on the beach, they all started laughing again. When the laughter had died down, Maria asked plaintively, "What am I going to do?"

"You're going to pull yourself together and get on with

living," Mamma Anna said.

"Maria," Barbara began, "you and Johann have a good marriage. You'll get beyond this shock. That's what marriage is. It's living on through the hard spots."

Mamma Anna said, "Remember that storm on the ship, how it blew so hard from one direction and then it died down and started blowing from the other direction just as hard? I remember remarking to Deutsch at the time that that's how life is." Four heads nodded in remembrance.

"As Pastor Boltzius says, this life is a trial. You can't control what happens to you, only how you live with what happens," Barbara said.

Maria looked up suddenly, "Has anyone told Johann that Hans has come back?"

"I doubt it," Catherine said. "The men haven't come in from the fields. Would you like for me to send Pastor Gronau to break the news to him?"

"Yes, he needs to hear it from someone other than me," Maria said. "And, please, don't tell anyone I pitched a crying fit. Poor, sweet Johann doesn't need to know that. And don't tell anyone in Ebenezer about Hans and me. Johann doesn't need to put up with that kind of talk. I can just imagine what Frau Rott and Frau Ortmann would do with that story."

Catherine left to perform her errand.

"How was he?" Mamma Anna asked. "I didn't get to see him."

"He looked fairly healthy for someone who has just crossed the ocean, but he has a wooden leg," Barbara said. "He was joking and teasing me like he used to, before he went up to Maria's. He shouldn't have just walked in on her like that. It was too much of a shock. I thought I was seeing a ghost when he first rode up."

"Where'd he go?"

"Headed back to Abercorn, I guess. That's the only road out of here. He said he was a peddler and would ride through here from time to time. He'd talked of staying overnight, but I doubt he'll come back today."

"Mamma Anna, your dream came true, just like Mother's," Gertrude said.

"What dream?" Maria asked.

"I didn't tell you about it, Maria, 'cause I thought it was just a crazy dream. Looks like it wasn't."

"You mean you dreamed he was coming?" Maria asked.

Mamma Anna nodded her head. "But sailing up the Ebenezer River on a ship," she chuckled, waving her hand dramatically toward the shallow creek.

* * *

Thomas's heart skipped a beat when he saw Israel Gronau approaching. He and Johann had been trying to dig up a stubborn stump. "Margaretta's baby must be coming," Thomas said, and began gathering up his tools.

"Is it the baby?" Thomas asked when Gronau stopped his horse.

"No, it's not for you, Thomas." He looked at Johann, "Catherine asked me to bring some news to you, Johann. She said to tell you her Uncle Hans was here. Seems everyone thought he died in prison, but he came on the transport."

"Hans Burgsteiner?"

"Yes, that's his name. I met him briefly. Has a wooden leg."

"Hans is here?" Johann asked again.

"Well, he was here, but he left rather abruptly. Catherine insisted that I come out and tell you anyway."

"Maria! How is Maria?" he asked haltingly, sitting down on a stump.

"Well, I don't know. I didn't see her. Are you ill?" Gronau asked, watching Johann's face drain of color.

"No, it's just the shock. We thought he was dead. We were in prison together."

"No wonder you're surprised at his showing up here. He said he'd been trying to find his sister for years and finally followed her to Ebenezer. It's a miracle he found her."

"Yes, a miracle," Johann said flatly.

"Do you want to ride back with me?" Gronau asked.

"You don't look well at all."

"No, thank you, Pastor. I'll finish here," Johann said. He was not ready to see Maria, yet. He needed time to think this through. He expected she did, too.

When Johann entered his house late that afternoon, Maria was rocking the little Huber boy back and forth, holding the whimpering child in her lap. Her face was splotchy, and her eyes were red from crying. She looked up at him and said, "I don't think he'll live much longer, Johann. Would you say a prayer for him?"

Johann knelt down beside them and bowed his head. "Lord, let your mercy pour down on this little boy. He's suffered so, Lord. Lead him out of his misery into your merciful salvation." He prayed on and on for a long time and finally closed by saying, "In the name of Jesus, who forgives all sins, we pray. Amen."

"Your supper is in the stew pot," Maria said, "but I can't serve you while I hold this child." They passed the evening without either one mentioning the return of Hans, but his presence was like an apparition between them. Maria sat by the child's bedside all night, and, towards morning, he died, the last of the Huber orphans.

63

Ebenezer, February 1735

Margaretta felt labor pains worsening during the night. "Thomas," she called out, when she could stand it no longer, "get Mamma Anna and Anna."

Margaretta lay on the pine straw mattress and endured the pains somehow, thinking that she would feel better when Mamma Anna and Anna arrived. That was not true, however, for the labor was difficult, and her own body was so weak from illness that she had little strength to assist in the birthing process.

"Push down, Margaretta," Mamma Anna said. "It won't come without some help. You can do it, child, like last time." Later that night, Mamma Anna took Thomas outside where the wind was blowing and turning colder so that she could talk to him. "She's not responding to me. I can't get her to push. She's getting weaker and weaker. Go get Maria. Maybe she can talk her through this."

Thomas ran off, pulling his coat tighter around himself for protection from both the cold and the fear. He could tell from looking at Margaretta that she was in trouble. Last time, she had flailed and screamed at the pain, but this time, she was too weak to do more than whimper. "God, what will I do without her?"

Toward morning, Anna and Maria watched Mamma Anna pull the baby from Margaretta's womb. The baby boy was blue and gasping for breath. Mamma Anna turned to Anna and whispered, "Tell Thomas to get the pastor to baptize this baby immediately." They all knew what this meant. When Anna left, Mamma Anna worked frantically with the tiny infant, trying to get him to breathe properly, but clearing his passages was insufficient. She said to Maria, who was massaging Margaretta to help her pass the afterbirth, "Maria, smell that birth fluid?"

Maria nodded her head in response. They both knew the

rotten smell that foretold the childbed fever that killed many new mothers. "Use that boiled water to clean her up."

Pastor Boltzius stood in the cold, dark room, holding the baby wrapped in a woolen blanket, and dipped his hand into the bucket of water. He made the sign of the cross on the little forehead and said the words that they believed would open the doors of Heaven to this new soul. "I baptize thee in the name of the Father, and of the Son, and of the Holy Spirit."

Anna watched the ritual and felt her own baby stirring inside. She wept at the sight of this little wrinkled child, probably already dead but whom everyone was pretending was still alive.

Mamma Anna stayed with Margaretta, who had fainted. She made no effort to revive her yet; instead, she tried to clean out as much of the smelly material as she could. She was not God, but she predicted from her experience that Margaretta would not live much longer. There was too much rot inside her.

Anna brought the bundle back to the bedroom and laid it in Margaretta's crooked arm. As Maria bathed her face, Margaretta opened her eyes and turned toward the baby. She saw the blue face. "Is he baptized?" she asked weakly.

"Yes, sister," Anna said.

"Thank God for that. Maybe I'll see him in Heaven soon."

Anna broke down and cried, sobbing more at the thought of losing her sister than at the loss of the baby. "No, Margaretta, don't say that. You're going to live."

Mamma Anna motioned Anna out of the room with an impatient gesture and said, "Get Thomas." When he came in, the women left him alone with his dying wife and son.

They buried the baby the next evening and waited for Margaretta to die. Many times during the following weeks she was ready for that blessed event and spent hours praying and talking with the pastors, confessing her sins and begging God for forgiveness. The pastors and the people gathered around her, reading aloud from the Bible and from Arndt's *True Christianity*, and singing hymns, preparing her for death. Still, she lingered, in miserable pain, longing to die before she drifted away from God again.

In late March, Mamma Anna was called after midnight to come tend to Anna, who had gone into early labor. She routed Maria on the way, and they found Anna doubled over in pain at Margaretta's bedside. Thomas and Georg placed her on a bed and carried her to the Schweigers' house. The premature baby died, and the midwives smelled the dreaded infection again, helpless to cure it.

The two sisters lay dying in separate houses. Catherine and Maria took turns caring for Anna, while Barbara and Mamma Anna looked after Margaretta and her little girl. Thomas was sure that, with the warmer weather of April, Margaretta would recover. On a beautiful day when the sun was shining brightly and purple flowers bloomed from a pitcher on the table, Margaretta told Pastor Boltzius, "Our Lord means well for me. It will change if it is his will; more I do not want." Before the pastor left, she died. Six days later, Anna followed her.

Catherine placed flowers on their graves and the graves of their babies several weeks later. She wept bitterly, hiding among the trees to keep anyone from seeing. She missed these companions she had expected to have as friends her whole life, to raise their children side by side. They had left her after traveling such a long way together. They had both died in childbirth. The thought chilled her soul with fear.

A season of death had begun, just as new life was returning to the land. People of the second transport began succumbing to the illnesses of the wilderness against which their bodies had no defenses. The first to go were the weakest-- Mrs. Eischberger's twin babies, followed by Mr. Schoppacher, whose child had died in the winter. Mr. Madreiter, swollen double from the waist down, was nursed by the Mosshamers but soon died. Despite their best efforts, Mrs. Steiner's baby, Agatha, died. Both Mr. and Mrs. Schweighofer were dangerously ill.

Catherine, who attended all the funerals as the wife of Pastor Gronau, began to feel that they had planted people as often as they had planted corn. She stared up at the live oak tree above her head, the limbs spread out like the arms of a monstrous octopus draped in ghostly gray moss. Her bleeding was late, and she imagined the great tree snatching her up and devouring her to become part of the wilderness. She cringed in fear, huddled against the tree that frightened her. She remembered how scared she had been on the ocean voyage. When they had finally landed in Savannah, she thought she could survive anything after that, but now death by drowning seemed clean and purifying, compared to death from childbed fever like she had witnessed with Margaretta and Anna.

"O God, help me," she moaned, as she doubled up and rolled on the ground.

"Is someone there?" a man asked. Catherine recognized Thomas Gschwandl, who must be visiting the graves, also.

Catherine sat up and began straightening her clothes and hair. She stood up. "Hello, Mr. Gschwandl," she said. "I brought some flowers for their graves, and I was just resting a minute under this tree." She forgot her own troubles when she looked at the poor widower's stricken face. Dry, sunken eyes, almost like a madman's, stared out of his gaunt face. He stood before the mound of dirt that covered Margaretta's grave, his shoulders slumped as if he would never experience joy again.

"I loved her, Frau Gronau. She was so full of life and sweetness when I married her back in Gastein. I don't know why she had to suffer such a miserable death. God's will is hard to understand at times like this. What sin did she ever commit to be punished with such pain? Why is God so cruel to gentle creatures like Margaretta and Anna and their little babies?" He looked up at her as if expecting her to have an answer to his questions.

"I don't know, Mr. Gschwandl. Maybe you should ask the

pastors those questions."

"I did, but I still don't understand. Pastor Boltzius said that she stood her trial with such devotion to God that she surely would be rewarded in Heaven. Do you believe that?" he asked her abruptly.

Catherine had no idea how to respond to this grieving man. She often asked the same questions in her own mind and also knew the answers that the pastors gave, but she did not know what she believed. She just tried to believe what they told her to believe. They certainly knew more about God than she did. Not knowing what to say, she changed the subject. "Have you made the headboards yet?" she asked. She had noticed that Peter Gruber had seemed to find some comfort in carving a headboard for his brother Hans.

"I've done the baby's, but not Margaretta's."

"Let's go back and have some supper, Mr. Gschwandl. You look like you haven't been eating enough. You have little Greta to think about. You must take care of yourself," Catherine said, realizing she was repeating words she had heard her mother use to comfort the bereaved. She took his arm and led him back to her house, where she served him a gourd of soup.

64

Ebenezer, May 1735

One evening late in May, Thomas and Georg accompanied Ruprecht Zittrauer in the Salzburgers' boat to Purysburg, a Swiss settlement on the Carolina side of the Savannah River, where Ruprecht promised they would find solace from their sorrows. The three men got roaring drunk from the rum available there. When they returned to Ebenezer three days later, reports of their behavior had already reached Pastor Boltzius. He called them to his house, admonished them to beg for forgiveness for their transgression, and banned them from communion until they repented their behavior in front of the congregation on Sunday morning.

Barbara had heard this stern talk from Pastor Boltzius before as he tried to keep his flock faithful to God. The most trouble had been with the Rotts and the Ortmanns, but, with so many new people, life at Ebenezer was getting more complicated. She knew how it must have broken his heart that two of his most faithful Salzburger men had fallen into evil ways.

Martin Boltzius sat at his table, the smoke from the myrtle candle blowing in his face from the slight breeze blowing through the open door. He coughed and waved his hand to clear the air. He was deeply troubled. He seemed to be losing control of his congregation. Thomas and Georg's behavior was an added blow. He was not surprised at their companion, who had shown a weakness for alcoholic spirits ever since he had arrived, but he was especially disappointed in Thomas. Thomas had been one of the leaders of the congregation. He had not been himself since his wife and child died. He somehow could not accept their deaths as the will of God.

And then there was the problem of Mr. Vat. What was he going to do about that situation? The man was impossible. He handed out provisions and land unfairly, favoring the people who came on the second transport, and failing to provide for the original settlers, who had suffered the most. He had even given all the chickens sent by a benefactor to the new people, ignoring the first settlers completely. Today, Boltzius had heard him cursing Mr. Hertzog when he complained about the unfair treatment. Boltzius knew he would have to speak to Mr. Vat the next day, but he also knew his suggestions would not be welcomed. The man seemed to be ruder to him every day.

Boltzius' dream of an ideal Christian community, free from worldly temptations, was slipping away. He'd have to try harder. Perhaps he was not doing all that he could to create a perfect community. He wished he could talk these things over with Gronau, but he had a wife, and Boltzius hated to disturb them at night. Tonight, burdened with problems, he felt lonely and longed for a companion to share his life. Ever since Gronau had married, he had realized his own need for a family. If he ever wanted children, he should marry soon. He was already thirty-six. Should he marry someone from back home or someone from Ebenezer? He could not think of any suitable women from Halle. None of them could stand the difficult life at Ebenezer. Zwiffler's new wife, who had come over from Europe, complained constantly and continually tried to convince him to return.

Gronau had made the best choice, a girl from among the Salzburgers. Boltzius stood up, stretched, and, feeling restless, strolled out into the night. Mosquitoes buzzed around him, but the night was pleasant outside. The stars were bright through the clearing of the trees over the river, and the moon shimmered in the water. The chorus of insects and tree frogs pulsed rhythmically, like the heartbeat of the land. Boltzius leaned against a great tree, and let his mind rest, absorbing the vibrations of the night.

He found himself silently listing the single women at Ebenezer, dismissing some for their lack of devotion or their foolishness, some for their dullness or lack of education, some because they talked too much or too little, and some who were too young or too old. He needed someone who could run his house, entertain visitors, and be a good mother to his children, an example of pious devotion, and a companion in conversation. He yearned for someone to bring a small measure of contentment and happiness to his difficult life.

Mrs. Rohrmoser was certainly the most accomplished housekeeper, and he would hate to lose her services by marrying, but she was out of the question, already being married. How would the good woman earn her keep without her job in his household? He would have to consider her welfare, and Gertrude's, too. Gertrude would probably soon marry some young man, however. She was lively and lovely, his best student of the Scriptures. She had an inquisitive mind that sought out the meaning of each passage. He would hate to see her turn into the tired, haggard wife of one of the Salzburger farmers.

Of course, if he married Gertrude, he could keep her mother as a housekeeper and protect Gertrude at the same time. It was a new idea for him. He had thought of her as a father thinks of a child. But she was almost grown. He remembered how dull the schoolroom was when she was absent. It was as if the sun had not come out that day. But would she want to marry him? He was old enough to be her father. She seemed to take little interest in the young men, but that might just be her modesty and Christian upbringing. Marrying Gertrude would make him a brother-in-law to Gronau. He liked that idea.

By a process of elimination and logical reasoning, Boltzius had solved his problem of whom to marry, but he had no idea how to go about winning the girl's heart, being ignorant in the nuances of romance. He decided he should speak to her mother first.

As he lay on his feather bed later that night, his mind drifting between consciousness and sleep, he thought about how it would feel to caress Gertrude's yellow hair and pale body. He had held her once, when she had fainted, and he remembered how surprised he had been at her substance, for she had always seemed so filled with light.

After she had served him breakfast the next morning, Boltzius said to Barbara, "Mrs. Rohrmoser, would you close the door and have a seat. There's something I wish to discuss with you before the students begin arriving."

Barbara did as she was instructed and sat down facing the pastor, wondering what he wanted her advice about. Occasionally he sought her counsel on how to handle some problem with the Salzburger women.

"Mrs. Rohrmoser, have you thought about Miss Kroehr's future?"

Barbara was surprised at this question, but replied, "Yes, many times, sir. I've been teaching her to cook and keep a man's house, preparing her for marriage."

"Did you have a prospect in mind for her?"

"No, sir. She's still young. I've been so grateful that she's had the opportunity for schooling with you, sir. But if you think she's learned enough...." Barbara hesitated, not knowing where this conversation was going.

"Mrs. Rohrmoser, would you consider me as a suitor for your daughter?"

Barbara was so surprised that she just stared at the Pastor in amazement. "You, sir?" she finally asked, not sure she had heard correctly.

Boltzius, surprised at her response, had a moment of fear that she might turn down his request. "Yes. I realize I'm older than she is, but I believe I could offer her a better life than she would have as a farmer's wife. I do have a salary that will continue even after the benefactors cease supporting the community. I have given this matter considerable thought, and I believe she is the most suitable girl for me to marry."

"Oh, Pastor Boltzius, God has truly blessed my girls," Barbara said, a smile transforming her countenance to joyful ecstasy. "I would be honored for you to be Gertrude's suitor. I'll speak to her immediately."

Boltzius stood and held out his hand to Barbara. "Thank you, Mrs. Rohrmoser." She stood, also, and took his outstretched hand, giving it a firm shake. She looked into the pastor's eyes and held his gaze, knowing that she would have liked to marry such a man. At least Gertrude would have what she had been denied.

Barbara could hardly contain her excitement as she ran across the settlement to the hut she shared with Gertrude.

She found her feeding scraps from her breakfast to a stray dog left behind by the Indians. Barbara did not bother to scold her for wasting food on the mangy creature. Instead, she grabbed her arm, saying excitedly, "Gertrude, come inside. I have some wonderful news for you."

"What is it?"

"Pastor Boltzius has just asked me if he can be your suitor. Isn't that wonderful? I can't believe how God has blessed us. Two daughters married to men of God."

"Pastor Boltzius and me?" Gertrude asked incredulously.

"Yes, isn't it exciting? I can't wait to tell Catherine and Maria. We'll have to do everything properly. After all, he is the senior pastor and must conduct himself with the utmost decorum."

"But, Mother, he's so old," Gertrude cried, filled with distress.

"Don't be silly, Trudi. Older men make the best husbands. They're steadier, and, as he pointed out to me, his salary will continue even after the provisions from the benefactors cease. He'll be able to provide for you better than any of the farmers would. And, Trudi, you'd be the senior pastor's wife," Barbara said, clapping her hands with happiness. "You'll be the most important woman at Ebenezer."

"But I don't want to be the most important woman at Ebenezer. I just want to be me," Trudi wailed. "Besides, he hasn't asked me yet."

"He will if we conduct ourselves properly," Barbara said, feeling very irritated with Gertrude's reaction. "He told me he's considered the matter for some time, and you are the most suitable girl for him to marry."

"But, Mother, I thought I'd marry someone I loved, like Catherine did."

"You'll learn to love him, Trudi," Barbara said, realizing she had rushed things. After all, her young daughter was only sixteen. "Hasn't he always been kind to you? Don't you care for him at all?"

"Of course I care for him, but I thought his kindness to me was like a father's. I never thought of him as a husband."

"Gertrude, now sit down and listen to me. I've had two husbands, one of whom beat me, and I've seen my children taken from me and my world turned upside down. I've always believed there was some great purpose that God had in mind for us. Don't you see? That purpose must be for you and Catherine to help these two pastors establish the faith in this new country. Pastor Boltzius needs you to help him."

"You mean, you think it's what God has planned for me?"

"I'm sure of it."

"But I don't know how to be Pastor Boltzius' wife."

"If it's God's will, you'll find the way."

"Oh, Mother, I'm scared. I've been praying that God would reveal his purpose for my life, but I never expected this."

"God's purpose is often frightening. You know what Hans has experienced for the sake of the faith. What you're being asked to do is much easier."

"I hope so, Mother, but I'll need your help," Gertrude said.

"Of course, darling. You can count on that."

* * *

The next evening, following prayer meeting, Pastor Boltzius asked Barbara for permission to walk Gertrude home. Only the Saalfelden women knew of Boltzius' intentions toward Gertrude until the others saw the two walking out together. As Boltzius took Gertrude's arm to lead her down the lane in the direction of her hut, the congregation became abuzz with whispers and stares. When the two stopped to talk under a large live oak tree, in full view of the townspeople, their new relationship was evident.

"We've caused quite a stir, I'm afraid, Miss Kroehr.   I hope you're not offended."

"Oh, no, sir," she responded, looking down at the ground. She had never felt so ill at ease in her life.

"Unfortunately, I have little experience talking with young ladies, Miss Kroehr, except as their pastor, but I want you to know that I have admired you for some time."

"You have?"

"Why, yes.   You sound surprised.   Haven't I often said you were my quickest pupil?"

"Well, yes, sir. I didn't know that's what you meant."

"I've admired other things, too."

"You have?" she asked, not knowing what else to say.

"Uh, yes." Boltzius was suddenly on unfamiliar ground, but he steeled his nerve and plowed on. "I've admired your devotion to God and your understanding of the Scripture." Gertrude looked down again, disappointed. "And I've admired your yellow hair when the sun shines on it," the sweating pastor said, dropping his voice almost to a whisper.

Gertrude looked up at the man who was a head taller than she and smiled. Her smile relaxed him, and he took her hand. She felt his hand trembling and realized that the always confident Pastor Boltzius was as terrified as she was. Feeling a surge of energy, she became aware that, somehow, she had the power to make this distinguished gentleman tremble. That kind of power must come from God, she thought, and I must use it reverently. "And I admire you, too, sir," she said softly.

"You do, Miss Kroehr?" It was Boltzius' turn to be surprised.

"Yes. I admire your kindness to everyone, sir, and your devotion to God," she said, gaining courage as she spoke. "And I admire your eyes, sir, for God's love seems to flow from them."

Boltzius looked at this fragile young girl and felt his insides melting and jumping about. He wanted to hold her close but knew that many eyes were watching. He took the hand he held, placed it around his arm, and they began slowly strolling toward her hut. "Miss Kroehr, may I call on you tomorrow afternoon? The blackberries are ripening. Perhaps your sister and Israel Gronau can join us in picking some before the birds and animals eat them all. Would you like that?"

"Yes, Pastor Boltzius. I'd like that very much."

"Good. I'll make the arrangements."

"Good night, sir," Gertrude said when they reached her door, relieved that this first encounter was over.

65

Ebenezer, July 1735

Gertrude, who had always moved with ease and grace, comfortable with the Salzburgers and free to think her own thoughts, felt her throat constricted by her role as Pastor Boltzius' companion. It seemed that every word she said was examined and judged for its appropriateness. Her mother and Catherine were always telling her how to behave, what to do and not to do, what to say and not to say. She was so confused that she could not keep their advice straight or trust her own instincts. People treated her more formally and with a respect that felt isolating. Depression pushed down on her natural buoyancy, causing her to walk stiffly, talk hesitantly, and avoid people.

One afternoon when she should have been sewing the long seams on a dress Barbara had insisted they make for her, she lay on her special limb over the river. She did not want to wear a long skirt like the Savannah ladies. She preferred the length of her Alpine attire. She could walk better. It had been so hot that her sweaty hands could not hold the needle, which kept slipping. Finally, in frustration, she had thrown it on the table and run to the river. Her tears salted the green moss on the limb under her cheek. As her mind calmed down and the living creatures around her forgot she was there, Gertrude began to feel a part of her surroundings and tried to sort out her feelings.

Because everyone told her she should be happy about what was happening to her, she had started pretending that she was happy. Why wasn't the happiness real? She liked Pastor Boltzius well enough, and wouldn't mind thinking about someone like him as a husband someday, but not yet. She didn't want to grow up and be a woman like Barbara was pushing her to do. For practical reasons, though, she knew she should not turn down this opportunity. It would make life easier for her and for her mother, who certainly deserved better than she had. And if it was God's will for her to marry Pastor Boltzius, then she must be obedient to that will. But how could she be sure?

Then she prayed, remembering the words Jesus had used when facing arrest by the Romans. "O God, take this cup from me, if it be thy will; nevertheless, not my will, but thine."

She heard someone coming down the path, and she lay very still, hoping they wouldn't see her. "Gertrude, is that you?" Maria asked.

"Oh, it's you, Maria. I'm up here."

Maria climbed up the tree and sat on the same limb, leaning against the trunk. "It's very peaceful here," she said. "No wonder this is your special place." Maria looked at Gertrude, still stretched out on the huge limb, and wondered what to say to help her. Barbara had sent her to try to talk some sense into her rebellious daughter before she wrecked everything with her youthful willfulness.

"Mother sent you, didn't she?" Gertrude said with irritation. "She watches me all the time now. Everyone watches me. I feel like I can't breathe."

"Oh, that won't last. Soon, something else will take everyone's attention," Maria laughed. "Remember how I was the talk of the town when Hans came back, and Herr Zittrauer innocently told everyone about my being Hans' fiancée? I couldn't stand to go to prayer meeting for getting stared at, and I couldn't stay at home and be talked about. Nobody even thinks about that anymore."

"You mean, if I marry Pastor Boltzius, things will go back to normal?"

"Well, your life will change, that's for sure, but people will soon find someone else to stare at and talk about. You don't need to be afraid of them, Trudi. They've suffered the same persecution we have, and they find hope in this difficult new land when they see you and Catherine make good marriages. They begin to believe that we are all equal in God's sight. After being scorned for so long for their faith and poverty, they find it hard to feel worthy. But here at Ebenezer, people are trying to build the kind of town they've always dreamed about, where faith is central to life and everyone is equal in that faith. Pastor Boltzius and Pastor Gronau believe in that dream, and the people are counting on them to make it happen. For the distinguished Pastor Boltzius to marry one of the persecuted Salzburgers demonstrates that belief." Maria paused after her long speech, then added, "And I think he loves you."

"You do? He's never said he does. He says he admires this or that about me, but I'm not sure he loves me. He may just think marrying me will help the town or something."

"Oh, there were a lot of other women he could have married if that's all it was, or he could have remained single. No, I think he loves you. I've seen him watching you over the years, as if waiting for you to grow up. He'd move in beside you when he saw some young man near, or his face would light up when you walked by. He often remarked about your devotion to God or your serious study of the Scripture. I think he's been waiting for you."

Gertrude pondered these words as she rested in the arms of the giant tree, watching a caterpillar munch away at the tender leaves on a twig.

* * *

Staring down at her hands, Gertrude nervously twisted her apron into a ball, while Pastor Boltzius asked her mother for permission to marry her. The three of them sat around the roughly-hewn, pine table in the little hut he had provided for them when his own house was completed. He discussed business matters with Barbara that Gertrude could not follow in her agitated state, but he avoided looking at his intended bride. Without asking her opinion, the two contemporaries decided that the banns would be published next Sunday and the wedding would be on August fifth.

When he rose to leave, a smile appeared on his solemn face. He bowed to Gertrude and Barbara, donned his hat, and walked out into the evening air. Gertrude watched him walk away, slapping at mosquitoes that descended on his un-covered face. Although she had seen him daily for almost two years, Gertrude still felt like she was marrying a stranger. She did not understand his world, filled with adult responsibilities.

"Mamma, I don't know how to be his wife. I don't under-stand half of what he talks about."

"You'll learn, my child. Working as his servant has taught me many things about him. He is kind, even to the worst kind of people, always sure he can win them over to godly ways. I've heard him discuss with Pastor Gronau their mission here. He dreams of a town based on Christian love and obedience to God. I've learned that he is respected by important people in Savannah, London, Halle, and Augsburg. He corresponds regularly with Pastor Urlsperger in Augsburg, Chaplain Zeigenhofer in London, and Professor Francke in Halle.

"But the most amazing thing about him is his absolute dedication to the Scripture and to Christ's teaching that all are as one in the sight of God. That's why this distinguished gentleman can willingly lower himself to marry the poor daughter of a Salzburger peasant." Tears ran down Barbara's face as she marveled at the miracle of a man like Pastor Boltzius. "He is truly a holy man, Gertrude. God has blessed you in a most remarkable way." She put her arm around Gertrude's shoulders. "Would you ever have thought back in Saalfelden that you and Catherine would marry Prot-estant pastors?" she laughed.

"Never in a million years. I didn't even know they ex-isted."

"We'd better get to work. We have only three weeks to plan the most important wedding Ebenezer has had. Since everyone is so busy with their summer gardens and the new babies, we'll have to do most things ourselves. It wouldn't look right to expect people to leave their work to prepare for a wedding. But it is also important that everything be re-spectable." She lit a candle, took out the dress they were making, and ripped out a seam that was crooked, causing the material to pucker. Gertrude winced, remembering how long it had taken her to put in that seam, but she said nothing. Tomorrow she would ask Catherine for help in making the dress.

"I wonder if we could get word to Hans. He should be here for the wedding, and we could use some thread from his peddler's pack. I'll ask Pastor Boltzius to send word to Mayor Causton in case he returns to Savannah."

66

Florida, August 1735

Hans Burgsteiner dodged a low limb and spit moss that had slavered over his face from his mouth. He saw no sign of a path, but his Indian guide was riding rapidly ahead, as if the way were clearly marked. Hans knew they were probably in Spanish territory by now, for they had been riding south for four days after leaving Frederica Island. His mission was to establish trade with the Indians in the Spanish territory, and in the process, find out if they were planning a drive north with the Spaniards.

The months since his arrival in Savannah had been difficult and uncomfortable, for he had spent few nights in a real bed under reliable shelter. Remarkably, however, his body had toughened, and he had enjoyed the adventure of exploring a strange, new land. His communication with his Yamacraw Indian guide Geechee, given him by Mayor Causton, had improved somewhat. Geechee was one of Chief Tomochichi's band. He was at the mercy of the Indian's knowledge of the wilderness and its inhabitants and dependent on his good will. Sometimes, Hans suspected that the Indian knew more German and English than Hans had learned of the Indian language. Mutual respect and trust had developed between them as they traveled together, however, and Hans had begun to recognize differences between his guide and other Indians that they encountered. Geechee was careful to avoid the Yamassee Indians in the south, who had fought with the Spanish against the English.

The Indian held up his hand, stopping his horse abruptly. Hans pulled in his own reins, wondering if they had come upon marshy water again. This land was so hard to traverse because you never knew when it would suddenly turn to soggy mud, crawling with fiddler crabs. Geechee motioned silence when Hans pulled up beside him. Together, they listened as the clamorous noise of insects and birds yielded to the sound of horses' hooves and the clatter of metal on metal, mixed with human voices.

The Indian pointed to the left, where the sound emanated. As Geechee dismounted, Hans took the reins of his horse, motioning him to see who was nearby. Geechee crept silently through the dense, sharp spears of palmetto and cabbage palms, disappearing in the tangle of semi-tropical vegetation. Insects located Hans as he sat still, and he wondered how many flying or crawling pests he had killed since coming to Georgia. He had never before imagined that this many species existed. What could God have been thinking when he created so many?

Hans shifted in his saddle after a while. He no longer heard human sounds in the forest, and he wished the Indian would come back, so they could move on. The bugs were not so bad when you were moving. He took off his hat and wiped away the sweat that had accumulated under the brim. Not a breeze stirred the hot, humid air. He was not sure how long he had been waiting there, but it must have been at least a half-hour.

He swung down from his horse, tied the two animals to a tree, and lay down nearby in the shade, noting the position of the sun in the sky. It was beginning to curve toward the west. He closed his eyes and soon drifted off into a fretful slumber, hugging his musket.

He awoke in the dark to whinnying, stamping horses and the smell of sour breath, staring into the face of a brown bear. Fear caused Hans to grab his musket and swing it wildly to scare off the beast. The startled bear grabbed his upper arm in his huge mouth, puncturing the skin with his teeth. The scream that escaped his mouth startled the bear, which let go of his arm and reared up on its hind legs. Hans grabbed for the knife sheathed on his belt and slashed away at the belly of the towering bear. The wounded animal scraped his claws across Hans' face, plowing even rows into his right cheek. When the bear dropped down on all four feet, Hans sliced open its throat. Blood poured from the bear's neck into his face, mingling with his own. The huge, furry beast collapsed on top of Hans in dying agony.

Struggling to breathe with the weight of the bear on his chest, he rolled as far as he could, shifting the weight enough to free his right arm. With enormous effort, he pushed the bleeding creature to the left, finally squeezing out from under him. Hans lay in the dark panting, then forced himself to sit up and examine his injuries as best he could in the hazy moonlight. His fingers gingerly touched the wounds on his arm and face. His arm was bleeding badly from four puncture wounds. He ripped his sleeve with his teeth and knife and clumsily tied a tourniquet. He then lay back, exhausted from the fight; while his blood seeped into the sand, darkness engulfed him.

* * *

Maria awoke suddenly from a deep sleep and bolted upright in her bed. "Johann, wake up! Something's happened."

"What is it?" he asked groggily.

"I don't know, but I feel like something terrible has happened to someone."

"Who?"

"I don't know." Maria realized how foolish she must appear to Johann. "I'm sorry I woke you. Go back to sleep. I just had a bad dream."

Maria forced herself to lie back down, but sleep never returned, and she longed for the grayish cast of morning, when the day's activities would blot out her uneasiness. There were only four more days until Gertrude's wedding to Pastor Boltzius, and she had not yet finished making the cotton muslin gown she was giving her.

Midmorning, she sat on a bench she had dragged outside and squinted in the sunlight, embroidering flowers around the neck of the gown. She had never worked on cotton before and found it more difficult to embroider than linen, which was stiffer and held its shape better. But cotton was cheaper in Savannah and cooler to wear in the summer heat.

They had been unsuccessful in growing flax for linen, but Savannah farmers had learned to grow cotton.

"Good morning, Frau Mosshamer," Frau Schweighofer called from the lane. "Frau Eischberger and I are going berry picking. I'm going to show her where the best blackberries grow. We want to make preserves for a wedding gift. Would you like to join us?"

"No, thank you," Maria called. "I'm trying to finish my own gift for Gertrude. Be sure to mark your trail carefully. It's easy to get turned around out there," she said, gesturing toward the surrounding woods.

The two women waved their hands and continued down the sandy lane, swinging their buckets.

That evening, while Barbara was washing the supper dishes, Mr. Schweighofer came up. He ignored Barbara, who was working outside, and stomped through the open front door, finding the pastor at the table, writing in his journal.

"Pastor," he said, "I'm getting worried. Maria and Eischberger's wife haven't come back from berry picking in the woods. It'll be dark soon, and they should have been home by now."

"When did they leave?" Boltzius asked.

"Midmorning. My wife knows better than to stay out there after dark. She'd never do that unless something was wrong. I should have gone with them, I guess, but she knows her way to the berries and back. She's done it many times before, but I'm worried. Maybe they were attacked by a bear or lost their way or...."

Boltzius looked up at the waning daylight. "We'd better organize a search party." A gathering of people had assembled as news of the missing women moved through the community. Soon, a party of men had volunteered for the search. The most experienced woodsmen were selected, and they planned their strategy.

"The most important rule is to never move off alone. Always stay near someone. Leave a trail you can follow back.

We'll leave at first light. There's no point in risking more lives trying to search in the dark." Thomas Gschwandl was directing the effort, again assuming his accustomed leadership role among the men, which he had set aside after Margaretta's death and the Purysburg caper.

Schweighofer responded, "Thomas, you may not be going out tonight, but I am. What if a wild beast has wounded them? They'll need help now, not tomorrow. They can't be too far away."

"I agree," said Eischberger.

"I'll go tonight," Resch said. "We'd better not waste any more time."

"Then it's decided," Thomas responded, and the party of ten men set out to search the darkening forest.

The remaining neighbors built a bonfire, sang hymns, and banged on pans all during the night to guide the missing women home and help the searchers keep their bearings.

Gertrude sat between Maria and Mamma Anna on the outskirts of the fire. The night was hot, and the fire only increased the temperature, but the smoke kept the mosquitoes at a distance. The Saalfelden women, along with everyone else, had discussed every possible thing that might have happened to the two women, some blaming Frau Schweighofer for her foolishness in getting lost, and others describing attacks by Indians or wild animals, and still others imagining critical illness or snake bite. Those of the first transport told about others who had been lost and never found, and about Mr. Zwiffler, lost ten days and found deranged.

"Mamma Anna, how do you keep from getting lost when you search for your herbs and roots?" Gertrude asked.

The old woman was slow to speak, savoring her secret. "You see, Trudi, I always leave at dawn and mark my direction by the sun. When entering a new section of the forest, I stop and sit quietly for a spell, watching where the birds and animals are going. I notice the location of their nests and burrows in relation to the sun, and then I mark in my mind where the herbs and roots are in relation to the nests or an oddly-shaped tree limb. I braid the scrub vines, too, always pointing back to the settlement. They grow that way and become markers to use for years. Once I've learned a section, it's as familiar to me as my own hand," she said, holding her gnarled old hand up to the fire. "I go slowly and study the section until I know everything about it. Then it is always home, and I'm not afraid. It's when you go too fast to learn your surroundings that you panic and get lost, because nothing feels familiar."

Gertrude pondered Mamma Anna's words and then sighed quietly. "Sometimes I feel like my life is going too fast into unfamiliar territory, and I'll get lost."

Mamma Anna patted Gertrude's arm and cackled, "Just study each day at a time until it's familiar and feels like home, child. But don't forget to braid the vines that point back to the original Gertrude. That way she won't get lost to you in this new life."

"How do I do that, Mamma Anna? What are the vines of a life?"

"Oh, well, I guess they're memories and dreams and the shape of your own soul before it gets poured into someone else's mold."

Gertrude thought about these ideas, resting her head on her knees. Her marriage to Pastor Boltzius on Sunday would make her whole life different, she felt. At least, with this latest disaster, no one was paying any attention to her. Everyone's attention was focused on the lost women.

Around noon the next day, three gunshots alerted the settlement that the women had been found. Within an hour, they returned, accompanied by all the searchers except Mr. Resch. In the excitement of welcoming the lost women back, no one realized that one man was missing.

"Where's my husband, Mr. Gschwandl?" Frau Resch asked.

Thomas looked around before asking Peter Gruber, "Did you see Resch?"

"No, didn't he come back?"

"No. Who was he with?"

"I don't know. Seems like he was on the right end of the search party."

"Rauner, when was the last time you saw Resch?" Thomas asked.

"It was hard to keep track in the dark. I expect he'll come in soon. I never saw him after daylight, though, come to think of it," Rauner replied.

"We'll wait awhile before searching for him. Peter, fire another three shots. Maybe he didn't hear the first ones."

After an hour's wait, another search party of eight men set out, two by two, and the community settled in for another vigil of waiting.

Barbara served soup to the two women, and Maria bathed their hands and faces with soap and water to clean the scratches. They were both still shaking from their ordeal.

"It was my fault," lamented Frau Schweighofer. "I wasn't careful enough. I followed some honeybees, hoping to find a beehive full of honey, and I didn't mark the trail enough. When we gave up that chase and started back, I was hopelessly lost. Every tree looked alike, and I couldn't find anything familiar. When it got dark, I knew we should stop before we wandered further away from home."

"You need to go home and rest," Barbara said, and the two women, leaning on their husbands, went to their houses.

At dark, the searchers returned without Mr. Resch. "We'll start again at dawn," Peter Gruber said. "He can protect himself against wild animals. He has a musket and a knife. It was foolhardy to search the forest last night. We mustn't make that mistake again." Everyone agreed.

They resumed the search on the following morning, and, although they searched for days, they never found Mr. Resch. His wife was inconsolable, weeping at Pastor Boltzius' house until she was ill from crying. Barbara summoned Mamma Anna who, with Maria's help, led the distraught woman home, gave her a calming tea, and stayed with her until she slept.

67

Ebenezer, August 1735

The marriage of Pastor Boltzius and Gertrude Kroehr on Sunday, August 5, 1735, was simple and dignified. Pastor Gronau conducted the ceremony at the close of the regular service. The vision of Mr. Resch wandering lost in the wilderness was never far from anyone's mind, but the whole community joined in the celebration of the wedding of their pastor and Gertrude.

Gertrude stood between her sister Catherine and Pastor Boltzius. She felt small and insignificant beside this distinguished gentleman, and her hand shook when she took his. When she looked up at him, he seemed far away, and she supposed he was communing with God in a way that she was probably incapable of. Why would a great man like Pastor Boltzius want to marry me? she asked herself for the thousandth time.

After the vows were exchanged, they knelt, and Pastor Gronau served the bread and wine. Pastor Boltzius then rose and left her side, joining Gronau in serving the congregation, thus establishing a pattern that would define their long marriage. She returned to the front bench to sit beside the women in her family.

A great outpouring of love and congratulations greeted the couple at the wedding feast prepared by the whole settlement. Gertrude was caught up in the excitement, as friends called her Frau Boltzius and presented her with their gifts, most of which were handmade or precious mementos carefully transported from Salzburg. Food was laid out on boards stretched across stumps, and beer brewed in the yards of Ebenezer was passed around to everyone.

Barbara and Catherine arranged the many dishes they had prepared for the feast. Barbara's fresh raisin bread, which she knew was Pastor Boltzius' favorite, was cut into slices. Large containers of sweet potatoes, squash, and corn were set out. Johann was busy carving a wild turkey that he had trapped and Maria had roasted. Mr. Vat had contributed a deer obtained through trade with an Indian.

The Saalfelden women had decided early in the planning to include everyone in the dinner and the celebration. Pastor Boltzius had preferred that plan to a more exclusive dinner, so each family had brought what they could to the feast.

Martin Boltzius was surprised at the outpouring of so much love and respect showered on him and his bride. All of the settlers had suffered so many trials together, and he had so often been the target of their complaints, that he had forgotten that, through all their difficulties and irritations, they nevertheless loved him.

Thomas Gschwandl spoke for the congregation when he toasted the couple from a stump. "God has truly blessed us. We started out on this long, trying journey, poor and persecuted, with only God as a beacon before our eyes. I will never forget my first introduction to Fraulein Kroehr, swirling down the Salzach River in Salzburg."

"You saved her life that day," Barbara interjected. "It was God's will that you appeared as you did to rescue her from the river. It was for this day." Tears ran down Barbara's face, as she looked from the man on the stump to her Gertrude, standing beside Pastor Boltzius.

"Perhaps it was providential that those of us from Gastein met the Saalfelden people that day," Thomas continued, ducking his head in humility. "And God's hand guided us all to Augsburg and Pastor Urlsperger." Here, all of the heads nodded in agreement. "And then in Rotterdam, we first met our pastors. We were so afraid that we would not be worthy of these two educated men. We saw only their fine clothes and heard their strange accents. We didn't know, then, the love of God that dwelt in their hearts. By marrying the Kroehr girls, we can be sure they have cast their lot with us to build a community faithful to God. I make a toast to the future happiness and prosperity of Pastor Boltzius and his bride," he said, raising a tin cup of homemade beer to his lips.

"And I want to raise another toast to Ebenezer, 'Hither God hast brought us thus far.'"

The crowd now looked to Pastor Boltzius, anticipating another speech. He acquiesced and mounted the stump Thomas had vacated.

"My dear Salzburgers, this outpouring of your love for us has touched our hearts. It is truly through God's love that we are here together today, just as it is God's will that some of our dear loved ones are not present but have joined our blessed Savior in Heaven."

With fascination, Gertrude watched the setting sun filter through the trees, silhouetting Pastor Boltzius in a ring of light, as he spoke from the stump. She blinked as the same rays struck her eyes, illuminating her face in an unnatural glow. As Martin Boltzius glanced over, he saw her shining in the sun and sucked in his breath mid-sentence. He clumsily ended his speech and stepped down, visibly overcome with emotion. The people busily began to dismantle the feast and drift off to their homes, leaving Martin and Gertrude to face each other across his kitchen table, piled high with wedding gifts.

Gertrude's hands fluttered over an article made of cotton, and she picked it up blindly, her eyes locking on his face. He was staring at her as if he had to memorize each feature for a test. Abruptly, he turned, closed the outside door, and slid the wooden latch into place. He strode around the table and enveloped her in his arms. Pleasure mixed with fear shivered through her, and she relaxed into his embrace. He ushered her into his bedroom to begin their intimate life together.

Later that first night together, they began to talk to each other as they lay with hands entwined on the bed. The moon slowly rolled its way across the sky and still they talked, each pouring out secret thoughts to the other in a most remarkable way. Each received the other's words as a precious gift. He told her about his life in Germany before he met her, and she described the Saalfelden valley and its people. That first night, with inhibitions broken down by physical intimacy and feelings of being loved, they began the conversations that would continue throughout their shared life. Neither had ever before known such amazing friendship.

* * *

Hans woke up to a loud clap of thunder and a deluge of rain beating down on his body. He was almost floating in water, but the force of the wind knocked him down whenever he attempted to stand. The roar of the storm was furious, and uprooted trees and other debris flew crazily through the air.

He gasped for breath, wiped water from his eyes, and discovered piercing pain in his left arm. He recalled the attack in the night as if it were a dream, but there was no mistaking the great hulk of the brown bear, lying beside him. An instinctive urge to survive yet another disaster welled up in him, and he managed to prop his head on the cold, stiff carcass to keep his face above the rising water. Panic-stricken, he looked around for the horses, but did not see them.

The rain whipped horizontally with apocalyptic fury from what he thought was an easterly direction. "O God, if it be your will, I accept your marvelous grace and willingly give my life to you. I do not know why you have led me into such a desperate situation. I know I have sinned. I have lusted after another man's wife. I've failed to discover your will and do it. I've been arrogant, believing in my own strength. Forgive me, Lord. O Jesus, help me. I beg your forgiveness and long to leave this world of pain and join you in Paradise."

Though he prayed to die, he did not. Hours of trapped misery exhausted him. He could not stand because his wooden leg sank into the mud and water. Slowly, the realization came over him that God was not yet ready to welcome him into Heaven, but was giving him another chance to find the divine will and follow it. He had to live again. It was God's will.

As the rain lost its power and settled into a steady downpour, Hans reluctantly began to plan his survival. The rain had cleansed his wounds and clotted them. That was a blessing. His dried meat and hardtack were on the horses, and they were either dead or lost. He had lost his musket, and his guide through this wilderness was gone. He would not be able to walk until the earth absorbed some of this water. All he had was the bear. He found his knife still lodged in the animal's throat and pulled it out with his good right hand. He sliced open the bear, cut off a strip of meat, and began sucking it. The bear, which had almost killed him, would now save him.

68

Ebenezer, September 1735

Rain pelted the soaked wooden houses in Ebenezer for the fifth day in a row. The carefully tended fields and gardens were under a foot of water, the creeks overflowing their banks and flooding the land. The late summer crops were destroyed, the settlers' hard labor washed away. Martin Boltzius lay beside Gertrude, listening to the steady dripping of the water leaking through the shingles and walls, and the rain pounding the roof. He had slept poorly, being visited again by the violent, shaking fever. It would be another dismal dawn.

O God, why is thy will so hard? Couldn't you have shown us some mercy? Another winter without fresh food. What have we done to displease you so? What are we doing wrong? We've worked hard. We've established a church and school. We've built a community based on your love. Why are you punishing us so? He pleaded his case before God in silence, not wanting to disturb Gertrude. It was rare that Boltzius questioned God, but despair overwhelmed him. He rose from the bed, pulled on his damp pants, and went into the kitchen. There he lit a candle, sat at the table, and opened his Bible. If he studied hard enough, surely the answers would be revealed to him, he thought.

Barbara and Gertrude joined him at first light and began preparing breakfast. Barbara continued her duties as housekeeper. She looked pale and weak, for she had been suffering from the dysentery that was sweeping through the community again. Their spirits were low. Each one knew without discussing it that, without a good crop, they faced another fall and winter of hunger and sickness. Boltzius also knew that he would again be forced to beg the Trustees for provisions while, in London, their rotted crops might be interpreted as indolence and laziness.

A knock came at the door. It was Mamma Anna, soaked to the skin.

"Mamma Anna, what are you doing out in this rain?" Barbara exclaimed, as the old woman entered the room dripping.

Mamma Anna, in her deliberate way, first accepted a cloth to wipe her face, then slowly sat down on a bench before answering. "It's the Mosshamers," she said, "Johann, Maria, and the orphan. I can't remember this one's name. Anyway, they're all sick with the bloody flux and fever. Maria managed to hang a white rag from the back window, which I saw from my hut. That's the signal we have that something's wrong. I went up there, and they're all terribly sick. Johann was half out of his mind, but he was asking for you, Pastor. His fever's as hot as I've ever seen. Maria's not much better. I think you'd better come."

Boltzius had already begun preparations to leave before she had finished speaking. He began issuing orders to the other two women. "Gertrude, you come, too. Plan to stay; they're going to need help." He stuffed his Bible into a canvas bag to protect it from the rain. "I'll need wine for communion," he said to Barbara, who was already packing a basket with what food was available, some baked sweet potatoes and leftover rice. Gertrude grabbed the basket her mother had fixed and the square of canvas she used to protect herself from the rain.

They all looked at Mamma Anna, who was totally spent. "You stay here and dry out," Boltzius said firmly to her. Mamma Anna nodded her head in agreement, welcoming the respite.

The situation at the Mosshamers' was desperate. Maria was too weak to attend to Johann and the sick child. Frau Bacher came by and took the child home with her to nurse. Pastor Boltzius restrained the arms of the delirious Johann, while Gertrude bathed his face with rainwater. "How long has his fever been this high?" Pastor Boltzius asked Maria, who had collapsed beside Johann on the straw mattress.

"He's been having the shaking fever for several days now. Usually it doesn't last more than a week and is gone. During the night, he was so hot he was out of his mind. I haven't been able to make any tea for him because of the rain. I can't build a fire outside, and with no inside fireplace...."

Boltzius nodded in understanding.

"Pray for us, Pastor. Only God can save him now, if it's meant to be." Maria began sobbing quietly. She had nursed enough dying people to know what she was seeing in Johann. She was exhausted and weak from fever and dysentery herself.

Gertrude naturally assumed the role of nurse and caretaker, as if she had always done so, although she and Catherine had usually watched while Maria, Mamma Anna, and her mother had taken care of everyone. She wiped Maria's face gently, cooing softly, "Just relax, Maria; I'll take care of you and Johann now. You just rest and get your strength back."

Maria closed her eyes and began breathing deeply. Pastor Boltzius knelt beside the bed and prayed silently, while Gertrude rummaged in the basket that she had brought to see what her mother had packed. She found a cloth sack of willow bark, good for fever, but how could she boil water for the tea they always made from it? Why am I the one here? she thought, panicking. Why didn't Mother and Mamma Anna come? Then she remembered that her mother wasn't well, and Mamma Anna was wet and spent. Pastor Boltzius had assumed that she was able to care for the sick like any other wife. What should I do first? she thought, looking frantically around the small house.

She took a dipper of water from a bucket on the floor and put in a piece of the willow bark. It just floated on top. She took it out and, using a knife, sliced the pieces as small as she could and put them back in the dipper. She carefully carried the mixture to the bed. Boltzius held Johann's head, while she tried to get him to drink the water. The poor man could not focus on swallowing and, in his raving, knocked the gourd from her hand.

Pastor Boltzius said, "I'll go get Mr. Zwiffler. You stay here with them."

"But I don't know what to do," Gertrude cried, tears running down her face. "What if Johann dies?"

"Whatever happens is God's will," the Pastor said piously, although he was obviously shaken at the thought of losing his friend. Johann, although he lacked education and training, was the one Salzburger that he considered his intellectual and spiritual equal.

Maria rose up weakly. "Please, not Mr. Zwiffler. I don't trust him. Get Barbara and Mamma Anna."

"But he has medicines that might help you and your husband," Boltzius said.

"Not Zwiffler," Maria said, before collapsing back on the bed.

Gertrude went to the door with Boltzius. She placed her hand on his arm and whispered, "Maria has told me before that Mr. Zwiffler has run out of the medicines that he brought from Europe and has begun experimenting with plants here. She thinks his medicines are causing people to die because he doesn't know what to give or how much."

Martin Boltzius' face registered shock. "Why hasn't anyone told me about this?" he asked.

"I'm telling you now," Gertrude replied meekly, looking down at the floor. "Maria trusts Mamma Anna's knowledge of the plants."

"I can't believe she'd put more faith in that ignorant old woman than in a trained apothecary. There are some who even call her a witch."

"That's because she was an herbalist in Saalfelden. The Catholics accused all herbalists of being witches. I was there with the other Protestant women in our valley the night she was arrested, and we feared that she would be put to death along with other herbalist women. But Mamma Anna convinced them that she was only guilty of being a Protestant, and they exiled her instead." Gertrude gazed over at Maria, remembering those events that seemed so long ago now. She continued plaintively, "Mamma Anna nursed me back to health from pneumonia in Memmingen. Maria knows that Mamma Anna would never give a person a medicine that she was not sure of. She hasn't known what to do for the shaking fever or the bloody flux, though. No one in Saalfelden ever had those sicknesses. Mr. Zwiffler doesn't seem to know, either."

Boltzius looked down at the earnest Gertrude with a puzzled look on his face. He realized there must be many things he did not know about this young wife of his. When he opened the door, they both noticed that the rain had diminished and the sky had lightened to a ghostly white.

Gertrude returned to the bed and bathed the faces of the Mosshamers. In a few minutes, Peter Gruber's large head appeared around the open door. "How are they, Frau Boltzius? I met Pastor Boltzius, who told me they were bad off."

"Not well at all, Mr. Gruber. Come in."

"They took care of my brother Hans when he took sick. I want to do what I can for them. I've brought some dry wood. I'll see if I can rig up a way to cover a space to make a cook fire."

"Oh, thank you, Mr. Gruber. That will be a great help." Gertrude knew that Mr. Gruber was one of the handiest and hardest working men at Ebenezer.

By the time Mamma Anna returned about midday, rested and dry, Gertrude and Mr. Gruber had brewed and administered the willow bark tea, and both patients were resting quietly. Mr. Gruber had taken care of the Mosshamers' animals, fetched clean water, and left a supply of dry wood. "Oh, Mamma Anna, I was so scared. I was afraid Johann would die. If Mr. Gruber hadn't helped me, I don't know what I'd have done. Thank goodness you're here now."

"You're doing fine, Trudi. Thought I'd make some ginger tea to soothe Maria's stomach. Here's a chicken your mother sent. Boil it, and we'll feed them the soup. Here, put a pinch of this in the pot," Mamma Anna said, handing Gertrude a small cloth bag.

"What is it?" Gertrude asked.

"That's some dried garlic from home. Sometimes that helps calm the mind. I want to give some to Johann."

"Mamma Anna, how did you learn all about plants?"

"My grandmother taught me mostly, but she never saw anything like this shaking fever that keeps coming back on people. I don't know what to do for it except try my old fever remedies. They help, but they don't cure."

Pastor Gronau stopped by later in the day. He prayed with the Mosshamers and told Gertrude that Catherine would come and spend the night, so that she could go home and rest.

"That child needs to take care of herself. She doesn't need to be here right now. You tell her Mamma Anna said to stay away from sick folks until that baby comes. I'm rested. I'll stay up with them." Mamma Anna rummaged in her basket and handed a root to the young pastor. "Here, tell her to make a tea out of this to settle her stomach. She was in a bad way when I saw her this morning."

Pastor Gronau handled the knobby ginger root with revulsion, but he put it in his pocket without arguing with the old woman. He motioned for Gertrude to follow him outside. The air, newly washed by the rain, smelled fresh and clean to them after being in the sick room all day. Gertrude felt steam rising as the afternoon sun sucked up the accumulated water.

"Pastor Boltzius wanted me to tell you that, although he intended to get back today, another situation demanded his attention after school let out."

"What happened?" Gertrude asked, fearing another death in the community. "Did someone die?"

"No, nothing like that. It's Mr. Vat. Pastor Boltzius tried again to reason with him about equal distribution of the provisions, and I'm afraid they had quite an argument. Then Mr.

Zwiffler came by and cursed Pastor Boltzius when he questioned his use of unknown plants to treat the sick. It was a most unholy way to behave. Pastor Boltzius had no choice but to refuse him communion until he repents before the congregation. Well, what Mr. Zwiffler said after that was... well, unkind in the extreme."

"Poor Pastor Boltzius. He must be so disappointed that he can't get them to see the love of God."

"Yes, and he had hoped to get Mr. Vat's help in asking Mr. Oglethorpe for better land before we all starve here. Some of the men have found an ideal spot on Red Bluff. It's right on the Savannah River and would make hauling our provisions so much easier. The land is fertile, too, and high enough to drain off excess water."

"Do you think Mr. Vat will cooperate?"

"He is so obstinate that sometimes I wonder. He seems to care less about the welfare of the Salzburgers and more about pleasing the Georgia Trustees, who want us here, to watch the Indian trail."

"Where is Pastor Boltzius now?"

"He's visiting Mr. Kalcher, who is also sick. He'll stop by here as soon as he can."

"Pastor Gronau, thank you for telling me these things. Pastor Boltzius seems to want to spare me, and I don't always know what trials he is contending with. And Mamma Anna's right. Catherine ought not to come tonight. It's more important that she keep her strength for the baby."

"She really wanted to help out, especially since it's the Mosshamers."

"I know, but we've lost so many babies since coming here; we don't want that to happen to hers."

Pastor Gronau nodded his head and walked toward home.

69

Ebenezer, September 1735

Despite all they could do, Johann Mosshamer died on September second. Maria was still dangerously ill and unable to attend the service for her husband. Standing beside the grave, Pastor Boltzius said, "Johann Mosshamer always said the right things to people, with humility and simplicity. All of us in the congregation lost something most precious with him."

People continued to stop by to sit with Maria. A great sadness pervaded the community. Johann had been the one that others had looked to for spiritual guidance and example. They watched Maria anxiously, for she shared with him that sweetness of spirit that had led them to take in the orphans and the desperately ill.

The Saalfelden women took turns caring for Maria and greeting the visitors who came to share the vigil. Even in her grief and physical weakness, Maria was able to provide a spiritual gift to each person who came. They seemed to believe that she was closer to God than an ordinary person, and they brought their problems and confessions to her, sometimes exhausting her with their worries rather than offering her comfort. Frau Schweighofer spent an hour crying about her guilt at being the cause of Mr. Resch's being lost in the forest. Mamma Anna finally took her arm, led her outside, and instructed her not to upset Maria again like that.

A large group gathered at the Mosshamers' house late one evening when Pastor Boltzius came to give her communion, which she had requested. The bloody flux had weakened her to the point that she could not eat, and her fever had returned. Mamma Anna looked at the crowd, both inside and outside the little room, and grumbled to Barbara, "She doesn't need all these people hanging on every breath. She needs some rest. She might get well if we could get everybody to leave her alone."

"You know she won't have it any other way. She thinks she's going to die anyway and might as well spend her last days giving comfort. She confessed to me that her past sins are so great that she must do all that she can to please God before she dies."

"Humph, with that attitude, she will die. She needs something to make her want to live again."

After the communion, Maria rallied, saying, "You know, Pastor, God acts like a mother who imposes upon her child only a small and light burden, while carrying the heaviest portion herself."

"Yes, Maria," Pastor Boltzius agreed.

Peter Gruber came by every day to do the heavy chores before leaving to work in his fields. He had the most successful harvest of Indian corn in the community, partly due to having higher ground than some, but mostly from hauling ash from the fires and plowing it into the sandy soil. He had observed the Indians following this practice in their fields on the northern side of the Ebenezer River. His ash-enriched land had produced healthier crops. He had also planted native seeds this year, like pumpkin, watermelon, squash, and beans, along with the corn. They seemed to grow best in this land. He seldom came into the Mosshamers' house without bringing something, silently taking care of Maria in his own way, asking for nothing in return.

Thomas Gschwandl fell in beside Pastor Boltzius as he left Maria's house one evening. "How is Frau Mosshamer today?" Thomas asked politely.

"Her soul is pure and sweet and ready to meet her God," the pastor replied.

"Life is short and should be lived well," Thomas said. "Maria's lived well like my Margaretta did. But life goes on for those left behind." Thomas looked up at the sky, gauging the weather. "Sir," he continued stiffly, "my life has been hard and lonely since Margaretta died. I think it's time I married again. My little girl needs a mother, and I need a wife. Mr. Vat has already told Frau Resch that she will have to give up claim to her husband's land, since he has not been found and is presumed dead. I would like to ask her to marry me and move into my house. Will you marry us, Pastor Boltzius?"

Martin Boltzius walked along silently, his head bowed in concentration. Finally, he shook his head back and forth. "I'm sorry, Thomas, but there is still no proof that Resch is dead. I cannot marry you until there is proof or until more time has passed. We can discuss this again next year if he still hasn't turned up," he said abruptly, as if the logic were obvious.

Inwardly, Boltzius had become so angry when he heard of the way Mr. Vat was treating poor Frau Resch that he had little sensitivity to the pain his reply had caused Thomas. He knew that he would not be successful if he tried to intervene on Frau Resch's behalf. It dawned on him that the dear, sweet Maria Mosshamer would suffer the same fate and be dispossessed soon, now that her husband was dead.

The men walked along in stony silence, Thomas harboring his pain and Boltzius, his fury. Neither wanted the other to know the depth of his emotions. They parted paths with only a nod of the head.

Mamma Anna had watched the two men as she walked behind them. She had hoped for an opportunity to speak to Thomas, but not in the presence of the pastor. She had a plan, but she needed Thomas's help to carry it out.

She waited until Thomas turned into the lane to his house before cutting through the trees to catch up with him.

"Mr. Gschwandl, Mr. Gschwandl," she called after him, puffing from the fast walking. "Wait a minute, please. I need to talk to you."

Thomas stopped, a scowl on his face, still upset with the pastor. "What is it, Mamma Anna?" he asked shortly.

Mamma Anna realized she had picked a bad time to approach him for a favor, but there was nothing left but to go ahead with the request. "Sir, I heard that you were going to Savannah to bring up the next load of provisions."

"That's right. We leave at dawn. Do you need for me to get something for you in Savannah?" he asked.

"Not exactly, sir. I need for you to take me with you."

"I can't do that. The women aren't allowed to make that trip. It's too hard, and there isn't room for passengers who can't help with hauling the provisions across land. Besides, we'll be stopping in Purysburg, and that's too rough a town for our Salzburger women. Pastor Boltzius would never allow it."

"I know he wouldn't allow it. I wasn't planning to tell him. He'll never know I'm gone. He doesn't keep track of my whereabouts."

"Why do you need to go to Savannah, anyway?"

"I need to get some medicine to save Maria," she replied in a reverent tone of voice.

"I can bring back whatever is needed. Just tell me what you want."

"I don't know what I want until I've seen it. I can't tell you what it is, but I'll know it when I see it." There was a stern defiance in her voice that commanded authority. "I'll be ready at dawn," she said, as if he had already agreed.

"Now, wait a minute. The other men won't let you go. You won't be able to keep up."

"Oh, I'll keep up, and you can convince the other men if you want to. Just tell them it's for Maria." She turned and walked away with something of her old bounce and energy. The adventure ahead had given her a new purpose in life.

Mamma Anna whispered her plan to Barbara that night as they changed Maria's linen. She knew that the Saalfelden women needed to know where she was; otherwise, they would sound the alarm when they discovered her missing.

"But Mamma Anna, Pastor Boltzius would never approve of a Salzburger woman making that trip with the men."

"Then don't tell him. Somebody needs to go, or we're going to lose Maria. If I can find Hans and bring him here, Maria will have something to live for again. Mayor Causton will know where he is and how to reach him."

"But wouldn't it be better for one of the men to look for him?"

"The men will have to come back as soon as they get the provisions. I may need more time than that. No! I've thought this through from every side. Nobody pays much attention to my comings and goings. I won't be missed for awhile, if you don't tell anyone. I'm the best one to go. Besides, I don't want to risk any hint of scandal concerning Maria and Hans. Involving someone else might lead to talk."

"Mamma Anna, do you have the strength for a trip like this?"

The old woman laughed, and her eyes sparkled. "I haven't felt this strong since I talked my way out of a hanging in Saalfelden. Don't worry. I can do it. You just keep Maria alive until I get back."

* * *

The provisions party included several men from Gastein who had come on the first transport. Thomas Gschwandl, the leader, and his former brother-in-law, Georg Schweiger, who was courting a woman in Purysburg, were the first to arrive at the edge of Ebenezer Creek. Soon, Ruprecht Zittrauer joined them. He had volunteered to come, hoping to partake of the rum available in Purysburg when the party stopped there. As soon as the six men assigned by Mr. Vat to make the trip had assembled, Mamma Anna stepped out from behind the trees with a pack on her back and fell in behind the party as they began the two-mile hike down the creek to the spot where the water was deep enough to keep their boat.

The men eyed Thomas to discern his reaction to Mamma Anna's following them, but he ignored them and her. He did not know what the Saalfelden women were up to, but Barbara Rohrmoser had stopped by his house before dawn with a parcel of food for him to take along, making a special point to tell him to have a safe journey. She had never done that before, so he knew she must be in on this, too. Well, if the women needed his help and did not want the pastors or Mr.

Vat to know about it, he did not mind. There were some things he didn't want them to know about, too. Vat wasn't being fair about the provisions, and Boltzius would not let him marry. Sometimes he got tired of not being allowed to make his own decisions. He figured there was more to Mamma Anna's mission than medicine, but he also decided that, if Barbara Rohrmoser and Mamma Anna needed his help, it must be important.

The men objected when Mamma Anna climbed into the boat.

"She can't go with us," Ruprecht said. "It's not allowed for women to make this trip."

"She can come. She has to get medicine for Maria Mosshamer in Savannah," Thomas said brusquely, as if he had been given this unpleasant order by Vat.

"Why can't Zwiffler get the medicine? He's the apothecary," Ruprecht insisted.

Thomas chose not to reply, but simply cast off from the shore and settled down to paddling the boat, leaving Ruprecht's question hanging in the air. Georg glanced at Thomas with a puzzled look on his face, said nothing, and dipped his paddle in the water, picking up the rhythm of the others.

As the boat moved smoothly down the black stream, the only sounds were the swish of the wooden paddles and the chorus of birds, frogs, and insects, which paused abruptly as they rounded each curve. Mamma Anna noticed slashes in the cypress trees that the men had cut to mark the proper channel. The confusing swamp, spread out in all directions, reflecting itself, dazed her. She remembered how long it had taken them to learn their way through this watery wilderness. She marveled that they had ever found a path. Some first-transport men always came along to lead the later settlers through, even though Mr. Vat might not let the first settlers share in the provisions.

The trip downriver to Savannah was hard but uneventful. Mamma Anna spoke little, and Thomas chose not to stop off in Purysburg. He would save that for the trip home, when a rest from fighting the current upriver with a loaded boat would be badly needed. The men pointed out Red Bluff when they emerged from Ebenezer Creek into the Savannah. It stood high and imposing, overlooking the swiftly flowing river.

"Now that's where we should have settled," Georg said. "I spent some time walking that area, and the land is fertile, unlike ours. We could get to Savannah without so much trouble, and it wouldn't flood everytime it rains."

"How did we wind up with such poor land?" one of the newcomers asked.

Georg and Thomas looked at each other. "Oglethorpe talked von Reck into our location because he wanted settlers to guard the Indian path. Then von Reck went home, Oglethorpe went to England, and we're stuck until the Georgia Trustees agree for us to move. I have my doubts they ever will," Georg said cynically.

Thomas added quickly, "When Oglethorpe returns I believe we can convince him of the need to relocate. He struck me as a Christian gentleman, truly concerned about our welfare. The problem is that no one in Georgia can make a decision until he returns from England. God only knows when that will be."

As they pulled into the dock in Savannah, Mamma Anna noticed a tall sailing ship anchored in the river. With her poor eyesight, she could not make out its name.

Thomas issued orders. "We'll get the boat loaded today and leave at first light." The men followed him up the hill towards Mayor Causton's office and storehouse, where their provisions were stored.

Mamma Anna hung back. She needed to talk to Mayor Causton, too, but not with the other Salzburgers around. She walked along the waterfront, noticing the changes that had occurred since she was here two years ago. Some sailors from the ship were lolling about, waiting to take on the timber and cotton stacked up on the dock. She turned and walked toward the first square, seeing that more houses had been built, though they were still crudely finished, with oiled-paper windows. At least the forest had receded, allowing more light in the town. Ebenezer, by comparison, still seemed to be tangled in the shadows of the trees.

She inhaled deeply and felt her lungs fill with a sense of freedom. She was on her own again, not afraid to do and say what she pleased. She had not realized until now how buried she had felt at Ebenezer for the last two years, hemmed in by forests, hard work, sickness, and pious people. It was as if she had suddenly come alive after a long illness. Her mind flicked back to Maria, lying so weak and lifeless, and her resolve to complete her mission toughened.

She had not learned much English, and, since this town spoke English, she would need an interpreter. Turning back toward the river, she approached a group of sailors and asked in German, "Do any of you speak German?" They looked at her with cockeyed smiles, surprised that a local woman would speak to them but not understanding what she said.

"Is that German you're speaking?" one man asked.

Recognizing the word German, she nodded her head enthusiastically.

"Somebody wake up Deutsch over there," he said, pointing toward a drunken-looking sailor, face down in the grass.

"Deutsch? Did you say Deutsch?" she squealed in surprise.

Hearing his name, the sailor raised his head and turned his scarred face toward her. There was no doubt in her mind that he was the same man who had saved her life on the ship coming over. The man sat up slowly, rubbing his eyes, trying to focus them on the woman standing over him.

"I don't believe it. It's Mamma Anna. I figured you'd been eaten by a 'gator after such a long time in the wilderness." He tried to stand up but could not quite make it.

She assumed he was drunk, but, looking again, she saw the yellow cast to his skin and the shaking limbs, and recognized too readily the signs of an advanced case of shaking fever.

"Deutsch, it is you, right when I needed a friend. You always seem to show up at the right time. But you look sick. How long have you had this fever?" she asked, feeling his forehead with her practiced hand.

"Long enough, I guess. We shipped in three weeks ago, and, if we don't ship out soon, the foul air in this place will kill me. I'd hate to die on land."

"Where are you staying? I'll take care of you. I owe you that much after you saved me from a watery grave."

"I'm staying right here. The Captain doesn't want me back on board until the fever's gone. He's afraid of contaminating the whole ship."

"But you need to be in bed. I'll see if I can find a room where you can get well."

"You can try, but nobody wants a sick sailor under their roof. What are you doing in Savannah, anyway? I thought you went with the saints to some outpost in the wilderness."

"I did. We've built a town called Ebenezer, where half the people have died and the other half are sick. I'm here trying to save Maria Mosshamer. Do you remember her?" Deutsch nodded his head. "Well, her husband died, and she's real sick. She's just about given up on living. I've come to look for some medicine and for a friend who might make her want to live again. Actually, I need your help, since you speak both English and German. I need to talk to Mayor Causton, and I don't want the other Salzburgers to know about it. But you don't look like you have the strength to stand up, much less be an interpreter."

"Get me a cold drink of water, put some of it on this hot head, and I'll feel better," Deutsch replied.

He lay back down under the tree to wait, while Mamma Anna bustled off to get water from the public well. Using a gourd from her pack, she filled it with cool water and returned to kneel beside the sick man. He drank the water thirstily, and she fetched more to bathe his face and hands.

As she watched the loading of the Salzburgers' provisions, she saw Mayor Causton walk back to his office in the storehouse. "How are you feeling?" she asked Deutsch. "Do you think you could help me now?"

The sick man opened his eyes and sat up. "I believe I can." She helped him up and supported him as they walked the fifty yards to the crude building where Savannah's business was conducted. She felt the eyes of the Salzburgers watch her progress, but she ignored their stares. They would just have to wonder what she was doing.

"Mayor Causton?" she asked hesitantly, not knowing if he would talk to a stranger who was a woman. He looked up from his work and eyed her disheveled appearance. He recognized the Salzburger attire, but he did not remember the woman. He also looked at the bizarrely scarred face of Deutsch, whom he had noticed with the other sailors. That face was hard to forget.

"Yes?" he asked in a business-like tone.

Deutsch stepped forward and said haltingly in English, "I'm Deutsch from the ship out there, and this is Anna Burgsteiner from the town of Ebenezer. She don't speak no English and asked me to talk for her."

Puzzled, Mayor Causton nodded his head to proceed. Mamma Anna began pouring out her story in rapid Saalfelden German until Deutsch held up his hand and stopped her. "Just ask him where Hans Burgsteiner is. He's a relative of mine, and I need to get in touch with him."

"Hans Burgsteiner?" Mayor Causton seemed not to know the name.

"Tell him he came on the second Salzburger transport and went off peddling. Ask if he's heard from him. He's a one-legged, blond fellow with blue eyes."

The Mayor's eyes signaled recognition and then, remembering that Hans Burgsteiner was on a secret mission for Oglethorpe, suspicion came over his face.

"Why do you need to reach him?" he asked.

Mamma Anna was not sure how to answer that question to her best advantage, so she asked her own. "Do you know where he is?"

"Why do you need to know?" he repeated, becoming more wary of the odd couple.

Mamma Anna decided that she might be more successful by just telling the truth. She hoped that she could trust him not to tell the other Salzburgers, but she was not at all sure about that.

"Sir, do you remember Johann and Maria Mosshamer who took care of the sick people in Abercorn and then in Ebenezer?"

"Yes, Pastor Boltzius has talked very highly of them."

"Well, sir, Johann Mosshamer died recently of the fever, and Maria is close to death. We don't have any medicine that helps the fever."

Mayor Causton shook his head in agreement for, indeed, Savannah had no successful treatment for the dreaded fever, either.

She continued, "Well, ever since her husband died, Maria just hasn't wanted to live." Tears ran down her wrinkled face. "I think she has the strength to survive the fever, but she doesn't seem to want to."

"Please, what does this have to do with Hans Burgsteiner?"

"Well, sir, Maria Mosshamer was once engaged to marry Hans Burgsteiner back in Saalfelden and then we thought he was dead because he never came back from prison. So, she married Johann Mosshamer and was a faithful wife." Mamma Anna paused to let that sink in and then went on. "It occurred to me that she might want to go on living again if Hans could visit her."

"Burgsteiner may have already married someone else," the Mayor replied, irritated with himself that he had wasted his time with a foolish matchmaker.

"Have you heard that news, sir?" Mamma Anna asked, as if the thought had never occurred to her.

"No, but I haven't heard from him in quite a while now. The last I knew of him, he spent a week at our fortification on Frederica Island down to the south. I don't know where he is. He could be lost in the swamps of Florida or peddling in the mountains to the north. He could be dead, for all I know. He wasn't well equipped to survive the dangers of the wilderness. I warned him against it."

"But you haven't heard that he's dead, have you?"

"No. If he shows up here, I'll tell him about Frau Mosshamer, but I wouldn't count on that possibility to save the good lady."

"Yes, sir. Thank you for your time."

He dismissed them with a wave of his hand, and the two petitioners backed out of his presence, as if from royalty. "Thank you, Deutsch, for all the good it did. At least if Hans does show up here, he'll get the news. That's all he'll need to hear to come galloping back to Ebenezer." She looked at the sagging Deutsch. "Why don't you sit down here on the porch out of the sun and let me see what I can do for you." Deutsch sank down on the wooden floor, leaning back against the wall of the building gratefully.

She walked down to the boat where the Salzburgers were still adjusting their load, looking for the best balance.

"Mr. Gschwandl," she called to Thomas.

He walked over to her. "What is it, Mamma Anna? Did you get any new medicine?"

"Not yet, sir. The Mayor didn't know of anything that helps the fever. I did find that sailor who saved my life on the *Purysburg*. Do you remember Deutsch?"

"Is he the one who's as ugly as the Devil?"

"Yes, sir, that's him. Well, he's got the fever and is in a bad way. He needs a bed to rest in and a roof over his head. Do you suppose you could help me find one?"

Thomas shook his head. Spare rooms were rare, and sailors were expected to stay aboard ship. "Why doesn't he go back to his ship?"

"The Captain won't let anyone with the fever on board. He's afraid everyone else will get it. Once they finish loading that ship, they'll leave, and Deutsch is afraid if he doesn't get better, they'll leave him behind. I feel like I owe it to him to try to help him. After all, he saved my life once."

Thomas was sorry he had ever gotten involved with Mamma Anna. He did not need complications on this trip. He was already beginning to worry about how he would explain to Mr. Vat and Pastor Boltzius about her coming along in the first place. It was unlikely that no one would tell them. It was one thing to get away undetected. It was another to get back that way. If he had not been so disappointed by the pastor's rejection of his marriage, he would never have let himself get into this fix. It seemed like his emotions were making decisions lately instead of his good sense.

"I'll ask about a room for you, you being a woman and all, but that sailor isn't my concern." With that, he trudged off, his shoulders slumped, as if carrying a heavy load.

Mamma Anna went back to the porch and sat near Deutsch, doing what she could with water and a cloth to lower his fever. He was shaking so hard she could almost hear his teeth rattle in his head.

As the shadows began to lengthen, Thomas returned and said he had found an old shack. It was not much, but the occupant had been gone for some time and was not expected back tonight. There was nothing in the hut but a rope bed with no straw tick, but at least it was more respectable than a woman sleeping on the ground in the open.

Mamma Anna thanked him and waited until he had disappeared around the corner before she helped Deutsch up and led him to the hut Thomas had pointed out. After she had Deutsch laid out on the ropes with what padding she could manage from the extra clothes in her pack, she went back to find Thomas.

He groaned inwardly when he saw her coming. He did not want to know what she was doing with Deutsch. She motioned him away from the others. "Thomas," she began sternly, using his first name like a mother would, "I'm not leaving with you tomorrow. I'm staying here to nurse Deutsch."

"Now wait a minute, Mamma Anna. That wasn't part of this. I'm responsible for you. No, you're coming back with us if I have to tie you up."

"Just tell them I came to get medicine for Maria, and I haven't gotten it yet. You had to get the provisions back to Ebenezer so that the people wouldn't be hungry. I have a place to stay and a little money. I'll get by."

"No, you're getting on that boat tomorrow if I have to drag you on board."

"Thomas, if it were you sick and dying, I'd stay to take care of you."

"Well, what about Maria? Don't you need to get back to nurse her?"

"Barbara and Gertrude can care for her as well as I can. You know that. I want to find out what the Indians use when they get the fever. Their village is near Savannah."

"Humph. They seem to die from the fever as fast as anyone else. You're talking foolishness and heresy. Most of their medicine seems to be conjuring up the Devil. No, you're coming back with me and that's the end of that." Thomas stomped back to the other men.

Mamma Anna was sorry she'd mentioned the Indians to Thomas. She'd forgotten that he shared the prejudices of most of the European settlers about the savages and their heathen ways. He still planted the wheat from Salzburg, which did so poorly here, and would not try the Indian ways of farming. She figured that the Indians had lived in this climate for a long time and had probably learned what plants were helpful with the diseases here.

She hurried back to the hut, mumbling to herself. After making a fire and boiling water for tea and gruel, she mixed in her best remedies for fever and held the gourd while Deutsch sipped the bitter brew. All the time she was planning how to hide from Thomas. She knew he really would force her to go back. As Deutsch drifted off into a fitful sleep, she said quietly to him, "I can't stay tonight, but I'll be back soon to care for you. I'll leave some gruel and tea. Drink it in the morning. Now rest good and don't worry."

A light rain chilled her when she left the hut. She had carefully plotted the number of steps from the side wall to the path that led to the Indian village outside of town. When she could feel the foliage on each side, she walked in a westerly direction, checking constantly that she was still on the path. After walking about thirty minutes, she spotted a red glow from a banked fire and knew she was close. She skirted the camp, trying to keep near the smell of the smoke, a difficult task in the rain. Afraid of going too far, she stopped when she felt the oily leaves of a huge magnolia tree. The big limbs came all the way to the ground, and she climbed the tree until she found a fork of branches where she could sit comfortably. She tied herself to the trunk with her apron sashes to keep from falling if she fell asleep. When she realized that she could no longer smell the Indian camp, she hoped she was not lost in the dark wilderness.

70

Ebenezer, September 1735

When the provisions party returned to Ebenezer two days later than expected without Mamma Anna, Barbara was alarmed. She whispered to Thomas anxiously, "What happened to Mamma Anna?"

Thomas replied with his own furious whispering, "I don't know. She ran away from Savannah. We searched everywhere. She told me the night before that she wasn't coming back with us because she'd happened up on Deutsch, that ugly sailor from the *Purysburg*, and he was sick and dying with the fever. She wanted to stay and nurse him. I told her that she couldn't stay, but when I went to get her the next morning, she was gone. Nobody saw her leave."

"Do you think she could have been kidnapped by the Indians?"

"What would the Indians want with that crazy old woman? No, I think she went off in the wilderness and hid, if you want my opinion."

"What are you going to tell Pastor Boltzius? All of the men in the party knew she went with you."

"Don't you think I know that? I can't believe I let myself get into this mess."

"We'll just have to tell him the truth. Let's do it now, before someone else talks to him."

"You don't have to be involved. I'm the one who did wrong. It might go bad for you and Gertrude if he knows you deceived him."

"No, I knew she was going and why, and kept it a secret. My heart will never rest easy unless I tell the whole truth. We live too close to death to have deceitful hearts."

The two walked grimly to the Boltzius house and found the pastor writing in his journal. Gertrude was staying with Maria that night.

"Pastor Boltzius," Barbara began, "we have something unpleasant to tell you. We have been deceitful, hoping to do good, but it has turned out badly."

Boltzius was surprised to hear these words from the good and pious Barbara Rohrmoser and looked at Thomas with suspicion, assuming he had led her astray. He listened first to Barbara's explanation and then to the details of the story from Thomas, sitting back in his chair as if stunned. He massaged his forehead, feeling the beginnings of a headache triggered by this added problem.

"We'll have to tell Mr. Vat," he said wearily, dreading that confrontation. "But, before we do, kneel with me in prayer for the soul of that foolish woman, who may at this moment be lost in the forest." As they knelt to pray, Barbara sobbed inconsolably. She could not bear the thought of losing Mamma Anna, who, even with her eccentric ways, had been like a mother to her.

Mr. Vat greeted Thomas, Barbara, and Boltzius haughtily. He took his role as secular head of the community with great seriousness and resented the Salzburgers' respect and love for the two pastors, especially Boltzius, who had run the community after von Reck left and before Mr. Vat brought the second transport. Boltzius had often challenged as unfair Mr. Vat's distribution of provisions to the people on the first transport, much to his irritation.

Thomas Gschwandl took the lead in the conversation. He was well aware of the animosity between Mr. Vat and Pastor Boltzius. "Mr. Vat, I have to confess that, without permission, I allowed Anna Burgsteiner to go with the provisions party to Savannah. After she refused to come back with us, we searched for her for two days and finally came back without her. I believe she was hiding from us in order to stay in Savannah to nurse a sick friend. I ask your forgiveness and God's forgiveness for my foolishness in allowing her to go, but she convinced me that she needed to find medicine for Maria Mosshamer. It is true that nothing Mr.

Zwiffler or the women have done has helped poor Frau Mosshamer."

"Mr. Zwiffler tells me that Frau Mosshamer refuses his help," Mr. Vat said sternly. "Mr. Gschwandl, you have committed a grave error in judgment and will no longer be allowed to lead a provisions party. I'll consider further punishment for you later. As for Frau Burgsteiner, she will not be welcomed back at Ebenezer. Her conduct is beyond repair with this community. I think we are well rid of her. I've had my suspicions about her for some time. I'll notify the Trustees that her provisions will be stopped."

Barbara was most distressed to hear this harsh judgment against Mamma Anna and decided she had to speak on her behalf. "Mr. Vat, may I say something, please?" Mr. Vat was not accustomed to communicating with the Salzburger women.

"I don't see what you can offer to this situation," he replied.

"But, sir, Mamma Anna is an old woman. Without her provisions, she will have no way to live. Besides, we need her as a midwife."

The man did not bother to respond to Barbara's supplication, but turned and walked back into his house. Before closing the door he said, "Boltzius, I'm sure you will demand Gschwandl's public repentance of his sin."

"Of course, sir," Boltzius replied in a tight voice. He did not like receiving orders from Mr. Vat on spiritual matters, since they were strictly his domain, as Mr. Vat had pointed out often enough.

* * *

Mamma Anna discovered that she was sharing her hideout with a noisy mockingbird that was not pleased to have his territory invaded by such a big creature. They soon became accustomed to each other, though, neither willing to give up such a comfortable tree. Mamma Anna left the protection of the sprawling limbs only to look for water. She braided vines, following the direction she had seen the bird fly first thing in the morning. She found roots that she knew were safe to eat if taste was not considered. During the day, she could occasionally hear voices and other noises of the Indian village, but no one approached her tree. She spent her idle hours weaving a bit of a shelter with the large magnolia leaves and twigs.

Early in the morning, after the second secluded night, she crept from her bower and stiffly walked back toward Savannah, carefully avoiding the Indians. She stayed in the forest until she could get a glimpse of the river. She figured that Thomas would not look for her more than two days before he started back, and sure enough, she saw the Salzburgers' loaded boat struggling up the river. When the sun was high and they were too far away to hear shouting, she left the forest and went to check on Deutsch. Her arrival caused an uproar, since half the town had been searching for her. She decided to pretend that she had gotten lost and had miraculously found her way back.

Mayor Causton's wife fluttered over her, offering help until another group from Ebenezer came to Savannah. Mamma Anna said she could earn her keep by midwifing and nursing the sick. She said she would start with the sick sailor, who was willing to pay her a little. Heads nodded at her willingness to work, and Savannah returned to its own affairs, soon ignoring the old nurse and her patient.

Deutsch's fevered delirium caused the Captain of his ship to leave him behind when he sailed. Mamma Anna bathed his scarred, emaciated body and scrounged bits of food for the two of them. She found his meager sailor's pay in the pocket of his pants, but that was soon gone. She foraged in the forest, collecting familiar roots, such as sassafras, which she sold in the market. She knew that she would need some kind of work if they were going to survive the fall and winter, so she asked Mrs. Causton for a job as a servant in her house.

Mrs. Causton already had two indentured English servants and could not take on anyone else, but she arranged for

Mamma Anna to be a servant to the new, young Anglican pastor, John Wesley, while he was in Savannah. Some of the time, he traveled with his brother Charles to the islands in the south, where fortifications against a Spanish invasion were being erected. The young cleric had been impressed with the German-speaking Moravians, who had sailed with him from England and settled in Carolina, and he was glad to have one of the pious Salzburgers as a servant. His father, Samuel Wesley, also an Anglican priest, had been sympathetic to the plight of the Salzburgers and had, in fact, worked with Oglethorpe and other Georgia Trustees to gain the support of the missionary society that had sponsored their settlement in Georgia.

The arrangement was beneficial to Mamma Anna because, as his cook, she had access to food for herself and Deutsch. She worked hard to please the young man and used the language barrier to prevent a full explanation of why she was in Savannah and not with the other Salzburgers in Ebenezer.

One morning in late September, Deutsch opened his eyes and looked around. He was soaked from having sweated during the night when his fever had broken. Mamma Anna was already up from her straw bed on the floor when she heard him say, "Where the Devil am I?"

"Deutsch, is that you?" she asked, and felt his forehead. A smile spread across her face. "Looks like you've survived the fever."

He tried to jump out of bed, but weakness stopped him. "I have to get back to my ship. How long have I been here?"

"Lie back down now. You're not strong enough to go anywhere."

"But they might leave without me."

Mamma Anna did not reply, not wanting to upset him with bad news until he was stronger. She began spooning a thin gruel into his mouth.

Deutsch slowly recovered and, when he learned that his ship had left without him, sank into a deep silence, waiting for the next ship to come to Savannah.

When Wesley was on his travels to the various Georgia outposts, Mamma Anna began visiting the Indian camp and watching what native plants the people used for various ailments. One older Uchee woman welcomed her to her fire if Mamma Anna brought something to contribute to the pot. They communicated mostly through grunts and sign language. One day, while they were sitting in each other's presence, comfortably sipping sassafras tea, a man stumbled into the village, causing great excitement. Mamma Anna assumed that he had returned after a long journey. Then she learned who he was--Hans Burgsteiner's guide who had come with him to Ebenezer.

She wanted to ask him a hundred questions, but she did not know how. She sat on the outskirts of the circle and watched while he told his story to the men of the village. She understood when he acted out a great storm, but she could not tell what had happened to Hans. Breaking the ritual of the storytelling, she went up to the man and asked, "What happened to Hans Burgsteiner, the man you were with?" Frowns from the men did not phase her in her excitement.

"Hans Burgsteiner," the man repeated. He made the sign for lost, but she did not understand it. When the assembled people made a groaning sign, she assumed he might have died, but she thought she knew the sign for that, and this was different.

"What's...," she asked, repeating his sign.

The man searched his mind for the word, first saying it in his own language and finally saying "lost," in English. She then searched her limited English vocabulary for its meaning.

Mamma Anna walked back to Savannah and, collecting Deutsch, went to Mayor Causton's office. "The Indian guide

Geechee, who went with Hans Burgsteiner, is back without him. Can you find out what happened to Hans?"

Mary Musgrove, the mayor's Indian interpreter, was sent for, and the story was told to Mamma Anna through two interpreters. Hans and the guide were separated during a great storm. He had spent many moons searching for him, but had not found him. It had taken a long time to walk back without a horse.

"Then he might still be alive?" Mayor Causton asked.

"I did not find him dead," the man replied. "However, it was a marshy wilderness filled with alligators and snakes. He had not learned enough to make his way alone. Unless the Creeks in the area found him, he is probably dead."

"Will you send a search party to the Creek village?" Mamma Anna had Deutsch ask the Mayor.

"No, that's Spanish territory. I can't authorize such a party. If they came into conflict with the Spaniards, it could lead to war. My orders are to avoid the possibility of such situations until Oglethorpe returns with further instructions."

71

Ebenezer, October 1735

Maria sat on her front steps, absorbing the warmth of the sun. Laughing children skittered down the lane toward Pastor Boltzius' house and the school. Their happy faces reminded her that she had lost the joy of living in the last few months. She had been buried under mountains of sickness and death and had forgotten about life and laughter.

She lifted her eyes out of childhood habit to the mountains, but, of course, there were none. The low air surrounded by wilderness seemed heavy and oppressive, even with the coolness of October. Homesickness teared her eyes, and she longed for the pure Alpine vista of her special mountain rock in Saalfelden. Memories of the last time she and Hans had watched the sun setting from that perch drifted through her mind, but her weakened body and spirit failed to respond to that long-ago passion. She had known happiness then, but that life was irretrievably gone, and she would live out her days in this jungle of a forest.

She wept for her dead Johann and for her guilt at never quite loving him fully, always holding back a part of herself for Hans. She wept for the children they never had and wondered if God had made her barren because of her indiscretion with Hans. She wept for Hans, lost in the Florida wilds. When she thought of him, guilt overwhelmed her, and she sobbed until her body was shaking with dry heaves.

This is how Barbara found her when she arrived to bring food. Gertrude was helping Catherine and Pastor Gronau move into their newly finished house. Both girls would be in houses with a fireplace for this next winter. For that she was grateful. She was worried about Catherine, though, and hoped the new house would distract her from those anxious spells she had about her pregnancy. That girl had always been afraid of whatever was ahead. All the talking in the world failed to convince her that she could trust in God. She always came back with "Yes, but what if...."

Barbara's mind was also heavy because she had overheard Pastor Boltzius and Pastor Gronau discussing their problems with Mr. Vat. She had heard them say that he wanted the widows to leave their homes because the land had belonged to their husbands, unless they had a grown son. English law forbade women to own property. Boltzius had argued that all property at Ebenezer was still communally owned, since no survey had been done to assign property to individuals, another problem that Mr. Vat should bring to Mayor Causton's attention. Barbara was afraid Maria might have to move from her house, and she wanted to warn her and offer to share with her the hut Mr. Boltzius had let her use. Eventually, Pastor Boltzius wanted to start a home for the orphans. His plan was that the widows would take care of the orphans, but there was not yet money to build an orphanage.

Barbara sat down beside Maria, put her arm around her, and said gently, "Cry it out, Maria darling. It's good to just cry out your grief and sorrow. You know in your heart that Johann is with Jesus in Heaven. There was never a more Christian man alive."

"Why didn't I die with him, Barbara? I was ready. I wanted to."

"Only God knows the answer to that."

Maria pulled herself together while Barbara made tea.

"When is Mamma Anna coming back?" Maria asked. "Why did she go to Savannah, anyway?"

"Maria, Mamma Anna went to Savannah to find out about Hans. She thought if he came back you might care about living again."

"Why, that interfering old woman," Maria said, and they both laughed. "I can't believe she'd do such a thing." Maria paused to take in this startling information. "Didn't you tell me that, when Pastor Gronau went to check on her, he found out that Hans was lost in Spanish territory?"

"Yes, that's right. His Indian guide returned without him."

"Well, why didn't Mamma Anna come back with Pastor Gronau?"

"You see, Maria, Mr. Vat has said that she's not welcome back at Ebenezer. She found Deutsch, that sailor who saved her life on the *Purysburg*, sick with the fever in Savannah, and she stayed to nurse him. Because her behavior was so unseemly for a woman, Mr. Vat says she can't come back."

"Nursing a sick man is unseemly? I can't believe that. What's unseemly about nursing a sick man?"

"Well, according to him, she left without permission. She wouldn't come back with the provisions party, and she was living alone with Deutsch in a one-room hut in Savannah."

"How was she going to nurse him without staying with him? Why, I've done the same thing."

"But you had Johann with you."

"Ruprecht Zittrauer leaves without permission all the time to get drunk in Purysburg, and they don't expel him," Maria said indignantly.

"He's a man," Barbara replied simply. "There's one good side to this, though."

"What's that?"

"Pastor Gronau said that she didn't seem to be too upset about staying in Savannah. She's working for the Anglican priest, and Deutsch is recovering, although his ship has sailed without him. She was concerned about you, but he assured her you were doing better. She did ask, when you were able, if you could pack up her things and send them with the next person coming to Savannah. I'll help you do that when we move your things."

"My things? Where am I going?"

Barbara looked down at the ground and watched busy ants carrying off the crumbs from their meal. "Maria, your house and land was Johann's, Mr. Vat says...." A catch in her voice prevented her from finishing the sentence. "I want you to move in with me if Pastor Boltzius will agree. I'll ask him tonight."

Maria's face grayed as the reality of her situation sank in. "When would he want me to move out?" she said with a deep sadness.

"I don't know. He was waiting to see if you would die."

"Like a vulture."

"Now, Maria, we've all been through too much to succumb to bitterness. Remember when you said that God is like a mother who takes the heaviest burden on herself? This burden is not as heavy as God's."

"That's true, but how am I going to take care of the sick orphans without my house? No, I'm not moving."

* * *

The events of October 1735, drifted in and out of the blurred consciousness of Martin Boltzius, as he shook and sweated through a bout of fever. As Maria and Barbara joined Gertrude in attending to him, he overheard their animated conversations about how Peter Gruber and Thomas Gschwandl had confronted Mr. Vat about the widows' keeping their houses and how Mr. Vat had backed down, after the men had agreed to take responsibility for helping them out.

Mr. Zwiffler called daily to offer his advice, but none of them had a cure for the awful fever, and the Saalfelden women relied on warm teas to soothe the internal fires. Maria soon disappeared from his bedside, and the women reported to him that she had been called away to care for Frau Rottenberger, who delivered sickly twins. Although God spared the mother, both babies died, a day apart. He heard Barbara and Gertrude discussing Catherine's increased fears as she counted up the number of dead babies buried in the cemetery at Ebenezer. Her anxiety was relieved somewhat when Frau Kalcher had a daughter who looked healthy enough to have a chance at life.

While nursing the sick pastor, Gertrude and Barbara struggled to keep the busy household running, with constant visitors and with schoolchildren running up and down the steps to the schoolroom on the second floor. Pastor Gronau taught his colleague's classes at the school and then ministered to the sick and dying late into the evening. He also took over the Sunday service, but held evening Bible study only once a week.

More flooding was followed by more sickness, and the men struggled to salvage their crops. Their hard work had produced a dismal harvest. Church services always ended with the men standing around discussing what they could do to get better land before they all starved. They knew that the Trustees would not support them with provisions indefinitely. The people on the first transport were already expected to be self-sufficient. If only Oglethorpe would return to Georgia. They trusted that he would be sympathetic to their plight.

Pastor Boltzius struggled out of bed to marry Georg Schweiger to the woman from Purysburg, as he had earlier agreed to do, but the effort was too much for him, and he returned immediately to bed. Barbara and Gertrude would not allow Ruprecht Zittrauer to bother him with his request to marry the bride's mother, and Pastor Gronau refused to decide the matter.

Through his daily discussions with Gronau, Boltzius knew that Mr. Vat was insisting that the Salzburger men take turns on guard duty every night to watch for who might be passing by on the Indian trail. Then he refused to let the men on guard build a fire on cold nights. This added hardship was difficult, and the cold contributed to more sickness. Pastor Gronau's pleading with Mr. Vat was to no avail. Gronau also told Boltzius that the ill-tempered Frau Ortmann, the schoolmaster's wife, was forced by Mr. Vat to send her English servant girl back to Savannah, after she had beaten her unmercifully.

As Boltzius' health slowly improved, he began to pick up his duties again. This had been the most serious illness he had ever experienced, but he had survived. "It's those warm teas that you served me, Frau Rohrmoser," he said one

morning after he had begun to recover. "I'm going to recommend that everyone take warm drinks when they're sick."

"It's God's will," Barbara replied. "This community still
needs you," she said, but smiled at the compliment.

* * *

Peter Gruber brought a load of cut firewood and stacked it
against the front wall of Maria's house. Maria had taken the
sick orphan child back to nurse. The boy was so weak with
the bloody flux that she did not expect him to live much
longer. She saw Mr. Gruber, came out, and asked him to
join her for a warm drink. The two sat on the front stoop,
cradling bent pewter cups in their hands and letting the steam
warm their faces. The November air was crisp, and Maria
noticed frost on the grass.

"You don't have to keep bringing me wood, Mr. Gruber,"
Maria said. She had become embarrassed by how much Mr.
Gruber had done for her while she was sick. "I'm strong
enough to chop my own wood now."

"It's easier for me to chop wood than for you," he said
matter-of-factly.

Maria looked at his huge, muscled arms and shoulders,
hardened by backbreaking work. Although he was not tall,
no fat padded his frame, and his presence felt massive when
he entered a closed space. He seemed more at ease outdoors.

"I don't know if I've thanked you for all that you did when
I was sick," Maria said hesitantly. "I'd like to give you
something for your trouble." She walked around to the crude
enclosure where she kept her few chickens and picked up a
hen. She tried to hand the squawking bird to Peter, but he
refused to take it.

"You don't owe me anything. You and your husband
nursed my brother when he was sick. I was just taking my
turn at doing for you." He looked at the tiny house and said,
"A woman like you shouldn't have to live alone and with no
fireplace. You're going to need someone to do the heavy
work and raise the crops." The diffident man looked down at
his worn boots patched together with cloth and uneven sew-

ing. "I'd start building a house on my land this winter if I thought there was any chance you might be willing to...." He did not finish the sentence when he saw the shocked alarm on her face.

Maria stroked the hen, which she had never put down. She did not know what to say to this good man. "Mr. Gruber," she began and then choked, tears running down her face. She set the hen on the ground, and he watched it run off as she wiped her eyes with her apron.

"I can see I've spoken too soon. I just didn't want anyone to get ahead of me. You let me know if you're interested." He stood up and started to walk away.

"Wait, sir. I've come to admire your helpful ways and hard work. Your kindness surprised me, that's all, but I do need more time."

Peter nodded his head. "I can see that. You just let me know. I'll be by later to build you a chicken coop before it gets too cold for the hens." He walked away with a lightness of step, relieved that she had not turned down his offer, just asked for time. He was proud that he had mustered the courage to speak to her at all. He had never proposed to a woman before, but he had never loved one the way he loved her. Some people thought she was too good for him, but, since he had brought in the best crop of anyone at Ebenezer, he figured that ought to count for something.

72

Ebenezer, November 1735

"What's wrong, Mother?" Gertrude asked, seeing Barbara grab her abdomen and double over groaning, dropping into the fire the wooden spoon she had been holding.

Barbara gasped for breath, as Gertrude rushed over and eased her onto the bench against the wall. "What happened?"

"I don't know. I have an awful pain in my side. It's like something broke." The blood drained from her face, giving her skin a ghostly hue. "Get something, quick," she said, putting her hand over her mouth. Gertrude grabbed a bucket and held her mother's head while she vomited.

"Pastor Boltzius!" Gertrude called toward the schoolroom overhead. "Help! It's Mother."

Martin Boltzius came clattering down the stairs, followed by the children, who wanted to see what was happening. He shooed them out the door with his hand and rushed to Barbara and Gertrude. "Let's put her on our bed," he said. "Do you think you can walk?" he asked.

Barbara nodded her head, assuming she still had the power to walk across the room, but when she tried to stand up, the pain was too overwhelming, and she started falling. Boltzius caught her and carried her into the bedroom.

"You watch her, and I'll go get help," he said, rushing out the door and running toward Mr. Zwiffler's house. Pastor Gronau saw him and asked what was wrong. "It's Frau Rohrmoser. She's collapsed," he shouted. Gronau ran to his own house to get Catherine, and they both hurried to the Boltzius house as fast as Catherine could run in her advanced stage of pregnancy.

Gertrude rushed to her older sister and threw herself into her arms, weeping hysterically. Catherine looked at Barbara over Gertrude's shoulder and shook her loose. "Stop it, Trudi," she said sharply, and pushed her aside. Catherine was accustomed to receiving sympathy, not giving it. Gertrude, embarrassed at her show of emotion, wiped her face with her apron, as Catherine and Pastor Gronau bent over the bed to talk with Barbara.

"Since you're here, I'll go find Maria," Gertrude said, knowing she needed some fresh air to compose herself. When she went outside, Maria was already running toward the house, the children having spread the news throughout the community. Maria saw Gertrude's terrified face and enfolded her in her arms. She asked quietly, "What happened?"

Gertrude said, with catches in her voice, "She just doubled over with pain and said something broke inside. She's been vomiting and can't stand up. Oh, Maria, what will I do if she dies?"

"You'll do just fine, Trudi. Besides, you have a good husband."

Gertrude blushed with shame, since she had a husband and Maria did not. "But Mother did everything. I don't know how," she said in a small, stiff, little girl's voice.

"Then you'll learn. Let's go, Trudi. We have work to do, or she will die." Following what she had learned from watching Mamma Anna deal with anxious family members, she knew Trudi needed to get busy doing something in order to calm her mind. As they walked into the house, she said, "Trudi, go boil some fresh water and make some ginger tea to settle her stomach."

Maria asked Pastor Gronau to leave, and she and the girls loosened Barbara's clothes. Maria felt her abdomen, and Barbara screamed with pain when she touched the right side. She and Barbara both had known people with severe pain in that spot. Usually they died a very painful death. Her eyes met Barbara's, and she knew that Barbara understood what to expect.

Gertrude brought in the ginger tea, which was steaming in a cup. "Blow on it, Trudi, until it cools some," Maria said. The spicy smell of ginger filled the room, causing Barbara to vomit again. "We'd better wait for the tea, Trudi. She's not ready yet. Take it back into the other room."

Catherine's own stomach was churning, and she left also. Barbara looked up at Maria after the girls had gone. "I pray God takes me quickly before this pain drives Heaven from my mind." Maria held her hand and nodded. "I may need the nightshade. You know where it is."

"I could never do that, Barbara," Maria said. "Don't ask it of me. Trust in God."

"Yes, you're right. It's the pain talking. I haven't gotten used to it yet. Pray for me."

Maria breathed deeply until she tapped calmness inside. Gently massaging Barbara's forehead, she began singing familiar hymns, beginning with the *Song of the Exile*. Slowly Barbara's body relaxed, enabling her to bear the pain.

In the other room, the two sisters looked at each other awkwardly. Gertrude was still holding the cup of ginger tea, which she held out to Catherine. "Here, you might as well drink this. We shouldn't let the ginger go to waste." Catherine sat down at the table and took the offered tea.

"Sit with me, Trudi. I'm sorry I pushed you away. I'm frightened, too. I'd been counting on Mother to help me with my baby and now...."

"I understand. I just panicked. At least you know how to run a house. I don't. I've depended on Mother, and now she won't be able...."

Their eyes met across the table, and they both looked away. "Here we are, selfishly worrying about ourselves and forgetting about poor Mother and her suffering," Catherine said.

"I don't think we've forgotten; I think we just can't bear to think about it."

Catherine nodded her agreement. Gertrude looked in on her mother and saw that she was resting calmly while Maria sang. Maria motioned her out. Gertrude closed the door and sat back down with Catherine. Pastor Gronau was outside, talking to the townspeople who had gathered when they heard that Barbara had taken sick.

"At least Maria didn't die. We can be grateful for that, particularly with Mamma Anna gone," Gertrude said in a shaky voice.

"We keep expecting the worst. She may get well. Maybe God will cure her," Catherine said.

Pastor Boltzius and Mr. Zwiffler hurried into the room and headed for the bedroom door. Gertrude jumped up and blocked the way. She noticed the shock on their faces and looked across to Catherine for help.

"Perhaps you gentlemen would like a cup of tea. Mother seems to be resting quietly right now." She began pouring tea from the teapot that was steeping on the table.

Mr. Zwiffler's face became indignant at being blocked from a patient to whom he had been summoned. "I think I should examine her at once. I was told it was an emergency," he said, looking sternly at Boltzius.

"You look exhausted from running over here. Drink some tea, and I'll make sure mother is ready to see you," Gertrude said as diplomatically as possible. She opened the bedroom door and closed it behind her.

"Who is it?" Barbara asked, as Gertrude approached the bed.

"It's Mr. Zwiffler, Mother. Do you want him to see you?"

"Yes, let him come in."

Maria stood up and whispered to Gertrude, "Let's make sure we prepare any potions he recommends. That way we can avoid what we aren't sure of. I don't think she'll be able to keep anything down, anyway. The nausea hasn't stopped."

Barbara groaned, shifting her body away from Maria and toward the door. Gertrude opened the door and ushered in the waiting apothecary.

Barbara held up her hand and said graciously, "Oh, Mr. Zwiffler, how good of you to come."

Mr. Zwiffler's feelings were somewhat assuaged by Frau Rohrmoser's greeting, and he chose not to acknowledge the presence of Maria Mosshamer, who had refused his services for herself and her husband. He also ignored Gertrude Boltzius, whose rude behavior had surprised him. That girl had a lot to learn about how to act in the presence of gentlemen. He felt sure that Pastor Boltzius would take care of that situation, however. He had obviously been shocked at his wife's behavior.

After his examination, he discussed with Pastor Boltzius his opinion of what should be done. "She needs surgery. Although I've never performed this operation, I've seen it done, and I'll be willing to do it. Otherwise, she'll die a painful death."

"I'll have her daughters discuss that with her," Boltzius said. Even he was leery of allowing an untrained surgeon to operate on Barbara, but he was anxious not to offend the man who had become the confidant of Mr. Vat.

"In the meantime, I'll prepare a medicine for her."

Gertrude said as sweetly as she could, "Oh, just give it to Catherine and me, and we'll be glad to follow your instructions, sir. We're so grateful for anything that will help Mother."

The man opened his black leather bag and took out some bottles of dried plants. He mixed several together into a folded paper. As he opened one bottle and shook some of the crushed, dried leaves into the mixture, Catherine and Gertrude looked at each other in alarm, both recognizing the leaf as nightshade. He handed the completed concoction to Catherine, whom he was more willing to trust to follow his instructions than Gertrude. "Steep this in boiling water and give it to her every hour. It should relieve the pain and help her rest."

"Thank you, Mr. Zwiffler," Catherine said. She began immediately to empty the teapot and fill it with more boiling water. "I almost forgot," she said, as he watched her pour the mixture into the teapot, "Mrs. Schweighofer sent word that her husband is worse and needs you."

The arrogant man bustled around importantly, closing up his satchel, and left. When he was gone, Catherine dumped the contents of the teapot into the slop bucket.

"Why did you do that?" Boltzius asked in horror, while Gertrude sighed with relief.

Catherine was not sure what to say to the pastor, and this time it was she who looked to Gertrude for help.

Gertrude put her hand on her husband's arm. "Sir, we noticed that one of the plants in the mixture was nightshade. That can be a poison if too much is given. Forgive me, but I agree with my sister that we should not give that to Mother."

"How do you know more about plants than Mr. Zwiffler? He was trained in Europe."

"Sir, I'm sure he knows much more than I do, but Mamma Anna often pointed out that particular plant for us to avoid because it can be poisonous. Catherine just didn't want to take a chance with Mother's life."

"Pastor Boltzius," Maria called from the door, "would you come pray with Frau Rohrmoser? She fears more for her soul than for her body."

"Of course," the pastor said, picking up his Bible as he entered the bedchamber.

* * *

Barbara's Ebenezer family gathered around her bed. She had taken no nourishment for eight days and was close to death. Pastor Boltzius had tried to administer communion, but she could not swallow the wine. She took the pastor's hand and said to him, "How blessed I have been to have you as my pastor. You have taught us all the way to life eternal. My only wish is that my little children left behind in Saalfelden could be here to be taught in your school. I hope God will forgive me for leaving them and my husband. At least my daughters and my grandchildren here at Ebenezer will benefit from your knowledge of God. For that reason alone, I do not regret coming."

Martin Boltzius knelt beside her. He had witnessed many deaths at Ebenezer, but none affected him like this one, for she had served his personal needs graciously and efficiently, without complaint. She had become a quiet support for him to lean on, one who never doubted his good intent. She had truly been a servant of God, at great sacrifice to her own happiness. He knew in his heart that he had probably learned more about the Christian life from her than she had from all his preaching. He tried to say these thoughts to her, but tears prevented his speaking.

Barbara looked up at Gertrude, who was standing beside her husband. "Trudi, take care of him. He has a great work to lead all the people to God. He will need your help."

"I'll do my best, Mother, but...."

"God will show you the way, darling."

"Pastor Gronau," Barbara said, "I've watched you quietly work among the people and have marveled at your gentleness and love, which must come from God. You have provided for me and all of us exiles an example of a Christ-like life."

"Thank you, Frau Rohrmoser. You've been like a mother to me."

"Catherine, be brave," Barbara said, patting her daughter's hand. "My one regret about leaving this life is not seeing your baby. With God's grace, I'll be watching you from Heaven.

"Maria, you've been more like a sister than a stepdaughter. Take care of my girls."

"Yes, Barbara. You've been my best friend for so long. Life will be hard without your presence."

"I'll always be with you in spirit," Barbara replied. Pain contorted her face. "Do you remember that dream I had at Mamma Anna's house in Saalfelden?" Maria nodded. "I believe God led us to this land. Imagine God giving someone like me such a message. I've often thought about that." She gasped for breath. "I'm grateful to God for a quick death and that I was spared the long suffering that some have endured. I long to be with God entirely." She lifted her hands toward Heaven and let them fall on the bed as her wish was granted.

All work ceased, and everyone who was able to walk gathered at the Ebenezer cemetery to lay Barbara Rohrmoser to rest. People had trouble articulating why she was so important to them, for she had led a quiet, unobtrusive life as a servant among them. Frau Schweighofer remembered how Barbara had comforted her with a cup of tea after she had wept with Pastor Boltzius over her guilt when Mr. Resch was lost. Georg Schweiger remembered her caring for Anna and their baby until they both died and how she kept bringing him food during his time of grief. He remembered, too, how she had welcomed with open arms his new bride from Purysburg, although some people had not wanted him to marry outside the community.

The people on the first transport had come so far with her, and she had mothered them all. Even the new arrivals had felt an especially warm reception from this woman. She had made them feel welcome when they came to Pastor Boltzius' house, usually offering them food or drink and words of encouragement while they waited to see the busy pastor. They often sought her advice on practical matters related to living in the Georgia wilderness. She freely showed the women how to cook the new foods and shared her experience with them. She had known most of their secrets but offered them only sensible advice and comfort, never criticism. She could be trusted to be discreet, hardworking, and unselfish.

Pastor Boltzius stood beside the grave, with her body, wrapped by her daughters in rough linen, lying in the hole dug by Thomas Gschwandl, who had insisted on providing that last service for her. Thomas realized for the first time how mysteriously linked his life had been with this woman. Their accidental meeting in Salzburg when he saved Gertrude from the river had led eventually to the joining of the people from Saalfelden, for whom she had been the leader, and the people from Gastein, who had followed his decision to come to Georgia. The linking together of these two groups of exiles had resulted in a strong center for this community. She was like the founding mother.

Pastor Boltzius' words intruded on Thomas's thoughts. "She was one of the silent of the land who keep treasures in their hearts rather than let others see them. She lived quietly before God and tended her affairs faithfully, guided by prayer."

The three daughters did not follow the others when they left the cemetery, but stood with arms entwined, staring at the mound of sandy dirt covering the grave.

"It's just us now," Gertrude said sadly. "Mamma Anna's gone and now Mother."

Maria was the next to speak. "It feels so lonely to be alive when Johann and Barbara are dead. It's like I've been left behind."

"That's how Mother always felt about leaving behind her children and husband in Saalfelden. Now it's our turn to be left," Catherine added.

They shared the noisy silence of the November forest, with its stark, leafless tree limbs caressed by gray moss, a breeze playing through the branches. A large white crane swooped down, shoulders hunched, and dived into the river, then awkwardly rose, flapping its great, white wings, and flew away with a squirming bass in its mouth.

"Gertrude, the people will be waiting for us at the house. We have to greet them," Catherine said.

Gertrude took a deep breath, squared her shoulders, and shivered in the chill air. The three young women from Saalfelden walked back to Ebenezer. God had brought them thus far.

* * *

The old Grandmother visited Mamma Anna as she slept in Savannah, and flew with her over the treetops, where she looked down at a fresh grave in Ebenezer. Gray moss brushed her face, and she felt the knowing. It must be Barbara. She awoke with a soft sense of peaceful loss and waited patiently for the news to reach her.

73

Savannah, Winter 1736

The thunderous firing of guns startled Mamma Anna one afternoon, and she hurried with everyone else to the river to watch a tall sailing ship make its graceful way slowly up the muddy Savannah. Everyone was excited at the appearance of the ship, because the long-awaited Oglethorpe was returning from England. Mamma Anna, however, knew that Deutsch would sign on with this ship if he could and leave her. Oglethorpe arrived with great dignity, along with the majestic Indian chief, Tomochichi, who had traveled with him, creating a sensation at King George's Court. The attention that the Indian stimulated helped the Georgia Trustees keep their project before the King, who continued to offer support, but after much delay.

The excitement of Oglethorpe's return spread throughout the colony. The firing of guns as the news traveled from settlement to settlement was finally heard in Ebenezer. Rejoicing followed, with prayers of thanksgiving for his safe arrival, led by the pastors. Hopes for an improvement of their situation soared, enlivening every man, woman, and child in Ebenezer. Martin Boltzius was sure that permission would now be granted to move the Salzburgers to Red Bluff, where their community could prosper.

Hans heard the guns as he rode his horse along the Indian trail toward Ebenezer. No one noticed the bearded man, who quietly approached the settlement amidst the dancing and celebration. Someone handed him a cup of homemade beer, and he drank it down in one thirsty gulp. Paulus Zittrauer was the first to recognize him. "Hey, weren't you on the ship with us?" he asked, his face flushed from the alcohol. "I remember the wooden leg, but what happened to your face?"

"Ja. Hans Burgsteiner. You're Zittrauer, right?" Hans automatically reached up to touch the scars on his face, only partially covered by his wild beard. "A bear decided to plow my face," he joked.

"We heard you were lost in a storm in Spanish territory."

"You heard right. But I found my way back." Hans looked over the crowd. "Where might I find my sister, Barbara Rohrmoser, in this mob?"

Paulus looked down, then back up. "In the cemetery, I'm afraid. She took sick awhile back and never recovered. She was spared a long illness, thank God."

"Which way is the cemetery?"

"Follow that lane, and when you get to a fork, turn right and keep going. The path is well worn."

Hans tipped his broad-brimmed leather hat and kneed his horse into a slow walk. He had lived alone in the wilderness for so long now that he felt uneasy in a large company of people. He stayed mounted on his horse, which had become an extension of himself ever since the mare found him huddled against the stinking bear after the storm.

He gazed down at the wooden headboard that had Barbara's name carved on it. He was still and silent as he paid his respects to his beloved sister.

"Hello, Hans," he heard behind him, and looked up, flinching. "Mr. Zittrauer told us you were here. We thought you were dead, but you keep coming back."

"Maria. You look changed." Her dark hair was streaked with gray, and her face had a drawn, sagging appearance, lacking the rosy color of past memories.

"So do you." Maria might not have recognized Hans at all if she had not been told. His beard was mostly gray and matched the color of his face, except for the purplish scars the bear had left. The high cheekbones that had enhanced his appearance in his youth now protruded sharply, outlining his squinting eyes sunk into his skull. He had the startled look of a wild animal.

"I guess I am." Hans paused and looked at the woman standing there for what seemed a long time before he continued. "One reason I came back was to make my peace with

Johann. When I almost died in the storm, I felt like God spared me so that I could do that."

"He's right over there," Maria said, a melancholy sadness in her voice as she pointed to her husband's grave.

She walked to his mound and brushed aside the dead holly she had left on another visit.

"When did he die?"

"In the early fall. We both had the fever. I almost went with him. Often wish I had."

Hans painfully dismounted and steadied himself against his tired horse before trying to walk toward Maria. She watched him struggle to reach her, then took his arm, led him to a stump, and helped him ease down.

"I'm sorry about Johann, Maria. He was my good friend."

"Yes, he was, Hans." Their voices were stiff with awkwardness. "If it hadn't been for me, you would have stayed friends. I came between you." She paused for a deep breath. "And you came between Johann and me. That's the guilt I can't get rid of."

Hans watched her with narrowed eyes, trying to put her in focus. "Guilt? Why do you feel guilt, Maria?"

"Because I never loved him as much as I should have, until he died. Then it was too late."

Hans continued his silent scrutiny of her, trying to read her soul.

"Why did you need to make peace with Johann before you died, Hans?" she asked.

"Because I loved his wife and forced her to be unfaithful to him."

"He never knew what happened when you came to Ebenezer that day, but he knew something did. He never asked, and I never told him. We didn't speak of you again, but it was like an unacknowledged mountain between us."

"Do you still love me, Maria?"

Maria hesitated a long while before answering. She wanted to be entirely honest. "I don't know," she said, shaking her head. "I don't know who you are anymore, and I'm certainly not the girl you knew in Saalfelden."

Hans looked down at his half-crippled arm and wooden leg, whose stump was infected and paining him. He had not seen himself in a mirror since the bear scraped his face, but the image that gazed back at him when he drank from the dark creek water wasn't familiar. No wonder she did not love him. What woman could? He was only half a man.

He nodded his head and tried to stand up. "I guess I'll be going."

"Where are you going?"

"To Savannah. Oglethorpe's back. I have to make a report to him."

"You don't look to me like you can make it to your horse, much less Savannah," Maria said. "Stay here for a few days, and let me take care of you." She noticed blood seeping from the infected stump. "My house is the closest thing Ebenezer has to a hospital. I already have one patient, a sick orphan girl. I think I can handle one more."

"You sound just like Mamma Anna, ordering folks around," he chuckled. "Is she in this burying ground, too?"

"No, she's in Savannah taking care of a sick sailor," Maria said, filling Hans in on the people and activities of the town. She half-carried him to his horse and led him back to her house. After getting him settled comfortably in her bed, she brought soup and spooned it into his mouth.

"Now sleep," she said firmly.

"No," he replied drowsily. "This may be just another dream. Keep talking to me. I want to know everything that has happened to you since we parted on that meadow in Saalfelden, when Johann and I were arrested."

"And I want to know your story."

"You go first."

Maria took his hand and began.

Epilogue

New Ebenezer, Georgia, 1741

Gertrude, Catherine, and their children took up a whole pew in the church. The wiggling youngsters had already received a stare of rebuke from Pastor Boltzius. Gertrude reached out to place a hand on the knee of five-year-old Samuel, sitting beside his cousin Christian, who was six. The younger of her two boys, Gotthilf, slept in her lap, which was growing large with the next baby. Maybe it would be a girl. Gertrude's eyes drifted out the open window, as a breeze floated up from the mist on the reddish-brown Savannah River, disturbing the smoke from the chimneys, swaying the gray moss in the live oak trees, and turning the tin swan of Martin Luther, which was perched on the steeple. A sudden chill caused goosebumps to pop out on her arms, and she felt the presence of her mother, hovering outside. She wanted to run out and find her, but she could not disturb the service.

Gertrude looked over at Catherine, who was pulling her cloak tighter and shifting the restless Hannah, who at three could outrun her quieter, more sedate brother, Christian. She glanced back at Maria, who had her newest orphans on each side of her. There never seemed to be a shortage of orphans, and Boltzius had insisted that an orphanage be built before the church. Maria rubbed her arms, trying to warm them, but continued to look straight ahead.

Gertrude thought about all that had happened since Barbara's death, almost five years ago now. Oglethorpe had finally allowed them to move to Red Bluff. In return, they had promised to keep the same name for their town and to leave all buildings in place at the old site for his soldiers to use. Forced to start over, they had cleared new land and built their houses, again without adequate provisions and with a third transport of Salzburgers which arrived in the spring of '36. That first summer, they were further hindered by a fever epidemic that swept the area, including Ebenezer. The first to succumb were the new arrivals, already weak from scurvy and not yet seasoned to the Georgia climate, but even the seasoned people suffered the ravages of the fever, which left them weak and unable to do the hard work required to establish a new town.

The following winter had been unusually cold, and no one had indoor fireplaces built yet. Inadequate shelter, insufficient food, especially for the first transport people, who no longer received provisions from the King, resulted in the death of about half the people at New Ebenezer. Those who survived were tough and courageous. When spring came, they began anew the unending struggle to build a community of faith that could prosper in the wilderness.

Mr. Vat went back to Europe, and the Zwifflers moved to Philadelphia. The Rotts moved to Savannah after behaving outrageously. Baron von Reck returned to Ebenezer with the third transport, primarily to make sketches of the area, and stayed for a time before returning to Europe with his drawings. Boltzius had been relieved to see him go since, in a drunken rage, he had struck a Salzburger woman, knocking her down.

Gertrude's adventurous Uncle Hans had ridden off again into the wilderness, not comfortable with the constraints of town living and unable to convince Maria to leave Ebenezer. Maria finally married Peter Gruber, who happily accepted the orphans she mothered and never complained when she was away midwifing or brought patients home to nurse. He just planted more crops and built on additional rooms as they were needed, becoming one of the most prosperous farmers at Ebenezer. He and the others were happy when the surveyor finally divided up their land, and each man drew a lot to farm. He was finally a landowner. Thomas Gschwandl married the widow Resch and settled down to become a leader in the church and town. He worked hard, building and operating the sawmill.

Mamma Anna came back to Ebenezer after Mr. Vat left and Mayor Causton ran her Savannah employer, the Reverend Mr. Wesley, out of town. The cleric had refused to give communion to the mayor's niece, Sophie. Mamma Anna thought the Anglican pastor had fallen in love with Miss Sophie and was angry when she married someone else. Peter Gruber arranged for Mamma Anna to live in her own little cottage on his place. She was Ebenezer's oldest citizen. Although her mind wandered sometimes, the women often came to her for advice about their various ailments, and she would make a tea or poultice for them. She would show them how to cure an earache with warm onion juice and a hot rock, or whatever else was needed. Maria consulted her regularly when she brought food from her own well-stocked pantry. Gertrude and Catherine's children liked to sit and listen to the old woman tell stories about Salzburg and Saalfelden, and about coming to Georgia. Their own parents were too busy to spend an afternoon telling tales, but Mamma Anna always had the time.

Gertrude smiled to herself, fingering her cotton dress, which was not as fine as the silk she had learned to make. Necessity had forced her to find something she could do better than anyone else. King George had given Ebenezer mulberry trees to grow the worms that wove tiny threads of silk. She had become most expert at tending the worms and extracting the silk. She liked being outside, watching the tiny worms grow and spin their cocoons. At night, while Pastor Boltzius wrote in his journal, she studied the books he had ordered about raising silkworms, then kept careful notes of each stage of the process until she understood what the worms needed in order to produce the best silk. People even came from Savannah to consult with her, for Ebenezer was developing the most successful silk production in Georgia.

Pastor Boltzius' journals continued to be published in Augsburg by Pastor Urlsperger. The journals were widely read, and Ebenezer was famous in Europe. Boltzius often fretted over the fact that Urlsperger edited out accounts of most of the hardships they endured, believing he could attract more people to come to Ebenezer and raise more money if the people thought the community was prosperous. Another transport of people had arrived this week, making nine transports in six years. She knew from experience that probably half the new people would die the first year, and, though she never told anybody, she would mentally try to guess who would live and who would die from the new diseases they encountered.

She had noticed a Johann Scherraus in the new group of settlers. Remembering the Scherraus family in Memmingen who had taken them in years ago, she invited this Scherraus family to stay with them until their house was built.

Outside, the spirited breeze diminished as the sun shafted through a cloud and shone on the town, lighting up the neat rows of houses, with their barns and vegetable gardens, the orphanage and school, the sawmill, the mulberry trees with their silky cocoons, the weaving house, the outlying plantations planted with corn, beans, cotton, and rice. The sun struck the silver chalice on the altar, given to Pastor Boltzius in Dover, England, just before they sailed to Savannah. Gertrude had polished it last night, and she noticed how it sparkled beside the Protestant cross and Maria's golden loaf of bread, resting on the white altar cloth delicately embroidered by Catherine.

The congregation of Salzburgers stood to sing Luther's hymn, *A Mighty Fortress Is Our God, a Bulwark Never Failing*.

"Hitherto hath God brought us," Gertrude thought, as she set Gotthilf on the floor to stand beside her.

THE END

Historical Notes

All the main characters in *The Grandmother Trees* are actual people with three exceptions--Mamma Anna Burgsteiner, Hans Burgsteiner, and Deutsch, who are fictional. I have tried to be true to the available factual information about the historical characters and events depicted, using my own imagination to fill in the gaps.

The historical sources are sometimes contradictory, and I was frequently required to make choices. For example, Maria Kroehr is sometimes listed as Barbara Rohrmoser's stepdaughter and sometimes as her sister-in-law. I chose stepdaughter. The published rumors about Prince Archbishop Firmian and the mistress at Schloss Klessheim may have been true or may only have been Protestant propaganda.

The following historical events have been compressed or shifted in order to enrich the story: Two meetings took place at Schwarzach in July 1731. There is no evidence that any of the Georgia Salzburgers attended these meetings. However, if they did not, others like them did. Hans Mosegger preached his famous sermon in a field near Wagrain, not at Schwarzach. There is no evidence that Johann Mosshamer was arrested and imprisoned in the Hohensalzburg, although other Protestants were. Most of the Gastein miners probably emigrated in 1733 rather than earlier. John Wesley did not actually come to Georgia until the winter of 1736, although I have placed him in Savannah in the fall of 1735.

About the Author

Rose Shearouse Thomason was born and reared in Georgia. She lived and worked there, in Florida, and in Virginia. During her career in education, she taught students from the elementary through the graduate level. She earned degrees in English and Education from Emory University and an Ed.D. from the University of Florida, with a specialty in reading. She is the author of professional and other articles, poetry, including a volume entitled *Warmth Against the Chill*, and a memoir, *Shoring Up My Soul: A Year with Cancer* (2001, Infinity Publishing.com). She was married for forty-two years and, with her husband Robert, had two sons and seven grandchildren. The seeds for *The Grandmother Trees* were planted early by her father as he shared tales of his Salzburger ancestors and encouraged her interest in their amazing story.